MR GUM

and the
Secret Hideout

Shabba me whiskers! Andy Stanton's **MR GUM** is winner of the Roald Dahl Funny Prize, the Red House Children's Book Award AND the Blue Peter Book Award for The Most Fun Story With Pictures. AND he's been shortlisted for LOADS of other prizes too! It's barking bonkers!

PRAISE FOR **MR GUM**:

'Do not even think about buying another book – This is gut-spillingly funty.' Alex, aged 13

'It's hilarious, it's brilliant... Stanton's the Guv'nor, The Boss.' Danny Baker, BBC London Radio

'Funniest book I have ever and will ever read... When I read this to my mum she burst out laughing and nearly wet herself ... When I had finished the book I wanted to read it all over again it was so good.' Bryony, aged 8

'Funny? You bet.' Guardian

'Andy Stanton accumulates silliness and jokes in an irresistible, laughter-inducing romp.' Sunday Times

'Raucous, revoltingly rambunctious and nose-snortingly funny.' Daily Mail

'David Tazzyman's illustrations match the irreverent sparks of word wizardry with slapdash delight.' Junior Education

'This is weird, wacky and one in a million.' Primary Times

'It provoked long and painful belly laughs from my daughter, who is eight.' Daily Telegraph

'As always, Stanton has a ball with dialogue, detail and devilish plot twists.' Scotsman

'We laughed so much it hurt.' Sophie, aged 9

'You will laugh so much you'll ache in places you didn't know you had.' First News

'A riotous read.' Sunday Express

'It's utterly bonkers and then a bit more – you'll love every madcap moment.' TBK Magazine

'Chaotically crazy.' Jewish Chronicle

'Designed to tickle young funny bones.' Glasgow Herald

'A complete joy to read whatever your age.' This is Kids' Stuff

'The truth is a lemon meringue!' Friday O'Leary

'They are brilliant.' Zoe Ball, Radio 2

'Smooky palooki! This book is well brilliant.' Jeremy Strong

'They're the funniest books . . . I can't recommend them enough.' Stephen Mangan

For Leah Thaxton, Katie Bennett
and the amazing David Tazzyman

DEAN

Mr Gum and the Secret Hideout
This edition published 2019 by Dean, an imprint of Egmont UK Limited,
The Yellow Building, 1 Nicholas Road
London W11 4AN

Text copyright © 2010 Andy Stanton
Illustration copyright © 2010 David Tazzyman

The moral rights of the author and illustrator have been asserted

mrgum.co.uk
www.egmont.co.uk

A CIP catalogue record for this title is available from the British Library
Printed and bound in Great Britain by the CPI Group

70881/001

MR GUM

and the
Secret Hideout

ANDY
STANTON

Illustrated by David Tazzyman

DEAN

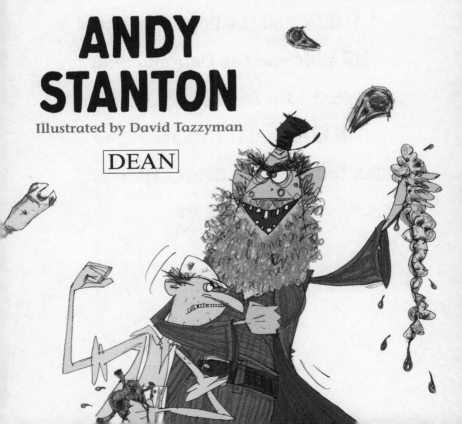

Read all of Andy Stanton's books!

You're a Bad Man, **MR GUM!**

MR GUM and the Biscuit Billionaire

MR GUM and the Goblins

MR GUM and the Power Crystals

MR GUM and the Dancing Bear

What's for Dinner, **MR GUM?**

MR GUM and the Cherry Tree

MR GUM and the Secret Hideout

Natboff!

THE PANINIS OF POMPEII

Contents

1 The Secret Hideout   1

2 The Department of Clouds and Yogurts   13

3 The Badsters Yick it Up   32

4 'Vestigations and Birdseed   41

5 Down by the Riverside   58

6 The Midnight Meating   73

7 Prisoners!   94

8 Ship's Biscuit   107

9 The Captain and Elizabeth   126

10 Old Granny on the Hoof   143

11 Mr Gum Gets a Surprise   168

12 Clouds of Sorrow, Clouds of Joy   198

Epilogue

Contents

1. Introduction

2. Public Debates, Private Doubts

3. Henry, Nellie, H. Crane

7. Pleasure

9. New Bearings and Old Myth

11. An Essay in Europe

12. On the Subject of Opinion

Epilogue

Some of the crazy old townsfolk from Lamonic Bibber

Mrs Lovely

Friday O'Leary

Billy William the Third

Old Granny

Mr Gum

Martin Launderette

Alan Taylor

Polly

Chapter 1

The Secret Hideout

Mr Gum was a fierce old blister with a face as angry as a thousand walnuts and a big red beard which smelt of menace and beer. He hated children, animals, fun, comics, pop music, birthday parties, books, Christmas, the seaside, computer games, people called 'Colin', Mondays, Tuesdays, Wednesdays, Thursdays, Fri– Actually, it would probably be quicker to tell you what he liked instead. What he liked was snoozing in bed all day, being a horror and secret hideouts. And the secret hideout he was in right now was the best secret hideout he'd ever seen.

'This secret hideout's flippin' brilliant!' shouted Mr Gum as he paced up and down in his hobnail boots. 'It's got everythin'! Rats! Cockroaches! Pipes what keep drippin' slime everywhere! An' it stinks! It's like what I always imagined Heaven would be! An' best of all, no one's ever gonna find us here!'

'Yeah,' agreed Mr Gum's dreadful accomplice, a scrawny butcher by the name of Billy William the Third. Billy was standing by a great iron furnace, shovelling old bits of meat on to the flames. And not just any old old bits of meat, but the stalest, grubbiest, most appalling specimens imaginable. Strings of ancient entrails, withered old horse legs, rubbery turkey necks . . .

On they all went, on to the flames. Billy was covered in soot and he was dripping with gobs of hot fat, but he hardly noticed. And why? I don't know, I'm not him. He just didn't.

'Faster!' commanded Mr Gum, hopping from one foot to the other like an unstoppable quail. 'Shovel them entrails, Billy me boy! Chuck it on, chuck it on! An' stoke it all up with coal or I'll bash ya!'

'Right you are, Gummy me old rattler!'

laughed Billy, chucking on a piece of coal that was twice the size of a piece of coal that was half the size of the piece of coal I'm talking about.

ROAR! bellowed the furnace. A great long lick of flame flicked out and singed off Billy's eyebrows, cruel as a scarlet donkey.

'Ha ha ha!' cackled Billy, who loved to see people getting hurt. 'Someone jus' got their eyebrows burned off!' Then he realised who that someone was, and he let out a bloodcurdling howl.

'OOW!' yelled Billy, hopping up and down in agony. 'How come I gotta do all the shovellin' 'round here anyway? How come you ain't doin' none?'

'Shut up!' roared Mr Gum, whacking Billy over the head with a silk handkerchief. He didn't have a silk handkerchief, so he used a cricket bat instead. 'We gotta keep gettin' that power up! We can't afford to rest for a moment. Now, you carry on shovellin'. I gotta rest for a moment.'

Mr Gum threw himself down on a filthy old sofa he'd found on a rubbish tip, all covered with stains and moss. The cushions were cold and soggy, and a big rusty spring poked uncomfortably into his back, but Mr Gum was such a lazer he didn't really care.

'I tell ya, I love this secret hideout,' yawned Mr Gum as he lay there staring up at the ceiling, his hands behind his head and his head behind whatever was in front of his head, probably just a bit of air or something. 'This is the life, eh, Billy?'

'Yeah, this is the life,' said Billy.

'Yeah, this is the life,' said another voice.

'Who the blimmin' flip said that?' shouted Mr Gum.

'It was I!' cried a man, jumping out from behind the sofa.

'I'm Surprising Ben! I pop up here, I pop up there! Surprise! Surprise! I'm everywhere!'

And off he ran, giggling like a packed lunch.

'Well, that was surprisin',' scowled Mr Gum.

'It certainly was,' said Billy, chewing a piece of coal to see if he could turn it into a diamond but actually just hurting his teeth. 'Anyway,' he continued, spitting it into the fire. 'Soon we'll have a blaze so powerful it'll be the most powerful in history! Even more powerful than itself, even though that's impossible!'

'Yeah,' grinned Mr Gum, rubbing his hands

with glee. Then he rubbed his hands with brie, which is sort of the same but a lot smellier. 'An' the more powerful that blaze gets, the closer we gets to winnin' once an' for all!'

'Ha ha ha!' said Billy William. 'It's funty!'

And the rats they scuttled and the pipes dripped slime and the vats they bubbled and Billy he shovelled in the secret hideout where the two men hid, cos they were low-down villains and that's what they did.

Chapter 2

The Department of Clouds and Yogurts

*L*ater that day, a nine-year-old girl and an oldish fellow in a nice friendly hat were sitting in the town square watching something very peculiar. It was the clouds. Every now and then

one would just fall out of the sky – **FLOOOOOOP!** – and land on the ground – **BUFFSH!**. See? Very peculiar indeed.

Now, the nine-year-old girl was Polly and the oldish fellow was Friday O'Leary. And if you're thinking, 'Who even cares about them, not me, I like stories with heroes in, not stories with some idiotic little girl and a bloke who's named after a day of the week,' then I'm afraid you've just made an astonishing fool of yourself. Because

Polly and Friday *were* heroes. They were two of the best heroes the town of Lamonic Bibber had ever seen. They were as brave as bees, as true as trees, as cheerful as cheese and as knowledgeable as knees. Not so clever now, are you?

FLOOOOOB!
BUFFSH!

Another cloud flopped out of the sky and landed on a hen, startling it so much that it accidentally laid an egg out of its mouth.

'Hmm,' said Polly. She had a worried expression on her face and Friday had a bit of strawberry yogurt on his. Friday loved yogurts.

'Frides,' said Polly at length. 'Do you know what I'm a-thinkin'?'

'Maybe,' said Friday hopefully. 'Are you thinking, "I ought to go and buy Friday an enormous yogurt, he deserves it?"'

'No,' replied Polly. 'I'm a-thinkin' there's somethin' well strange goin' on with them clouds up there. I never done seen 'em fallin' out the sky before. It can't be no good, that's what I says.'

'Yes,' said Friday thoughtfully. 'Well, that was interesting,' he continued. 'Now let's go and get some delicious yogurts and not think about it ever again.'

'But, Frides, if we jus' ignore them clouds who knows what might happen?' frowned Polly. 'Jus' imagine. Without no clouds, there won't be no rain. Without no rain, the grass won't grow.

Without no grass, the cows'll die. Without no cows there won't be no milk. An' without no milk –'

'There won't be any yogurts!' cried Friday in alarm as another cloud fell down with a soft furry bang somewhere in the distance. 'We've got to do something, Polly! We've got to! We've got to! We've simply GOT to!'

''Xactly,' said Polly. 'So I was thinkin', why don't we starts up an office an' do some 'vestigations?'

'THE TRUTH IS A LEMON MERINGUE!' yelled Friday, as he sometimes liked to do. 'I've always wanted to work in an office!'

It was true.
Friday O'Leary had
done all sorts of jobs in
his time. He had been
an inventor, a travelling
musician, a sailor,
another sailor, an American
footballer, a fashion model,
a Lego model, the King
of Sweden, the Queen
of Sweden, the first
man never to have walked on the moon,

a jet pilot, a detective, a mountaineer who explored mountains, a fountaineer who explored fountains, a ninja, a stunt-car racer, a film star, an earthworm-tamer, a famous French chef called Monsieur Canard, a TV presenter and a professional apple.

'But all those jobs were completely boring!' said Friday, jumping up so high he almost hit the sun with his face, narrowly missing it by only 149.599 million kilometres. 'What I've always wanted is to work in an office. That's the life for me!'

So Friday went home and got some planks and nails, and after a few hours of hammering and saying, 'Ouch, I just hit my thumb with a hammer,' there they were, sitting in their brand-new office in the town square. It was so cool. There was a big desk with some pens and a stapler on it. And there was a clock on the wall so you could see what time it was and a broken clock next to it so you could see what time it wasn't. And there were some chairs to spin around on and a photocopier so you could copy words and a photocopier so you could copy words and a photocopier so you could copy words and a photocopier so you could copy words and a photocopier so you could copy words and a photocopier so you could copy words and a photocopier so you could copy words and a photocopier so you could copy words –

'Stop playin' with that photocopier, Frides,' said Polly, 'an' help me think up a brilliant name for our new office. Then we can get started on our 'vestigations.'

'OK,' said Friday. 'How about *"THE DEPARTMENT OF CLOUDS AND YOGURTS"*?'

It was a brilliant name, apart from the yogurt bit. But Friday would not give in, so that's what they called it.

Polly went home and got some paint, and together she and Friday made a wonderful sign to hang above the office door:

THE DEPARTMENT OF
CLOUDS AND YOGURTS
Established: 15 minutes ago

After it was painted, Polly added some glitter and stickers of hearts and ponies around the words and Friday hung some broccoli from it 'for good luck'. It looked excellent. And if you looked at it twice, it looked twice as excellent. But if you looked at it three times, it still only looked twice as excellent, which just goes to show, things can get a bit boring if you look at them too much.

Then Friday went and bought suits and ties for them both. And then they sat at the desk with their hands folded in front of them, looking extremely serious.

'Now, Mr Friday,' said Polly. 'I done some 'vestigations in my head an' I reckons all the clouds are probbly bein' mucked up cos of bad pollutions in the air.'

'Exactly, Mr Polly,' said Friday, who was busy sharpening his tie in the electric pencil-sharpener.

'So we gots to work out where all them pollutions is comin' from,' said Polly. 'That's our first job.'

'Yes,' agreed Friday. 'That's our first job.'

'Yes,' said a voice in the corner. 'That's our first job.'

'Who said that?' said Polly.

'It was I!' cried a man, jumping out of the wastepaper basket. *I'm Surprising Ben! I pop up here, I pop up there! Surprise! Surprise! I'm everywhere!'*

And away he ran, giggling like a tortoise.

'That was quite surprising,' said Friday. 'But now it's time to get to work. I have here a map of Lamonic Bibber,' he said, unrolling a huge map from his sock. 'Now, look carefully, Mr Polly. I drew this map myself, many years ago. See, there's my signature in the corner.'

DRAWN BY FRIDAY 'LEONARDO' O'LEARY, NOVEMBER 14TH 1973

'I don't want to sound boastful or anything,' said Friday modestly, 'but this is probably the most incredible map anyone's ever drawn in the history of all human existence. Look, every street, every house, every hill in Lamonic Bibber – it's all there.

'Now,' he continued. 'We will go looking for the pollution. We will investigate a little of the town each day. Then we will come back and colour in bits of the map to show we've investigated them.

And also because we like colouring things in.'

'Hurrah!' laughed Polly, clapping her hands.

FLOOOOOB!
BUFFFSH-SH-SHII

A big wheezy cloud flopped out of the sky and landed right outside the office.

'There's no time to wastes, Mr Friday,' said Polly as the poor bit of weather was licked up by a stray baby. 'We better start doin' our 'vestigations.'

Chapter 3

The Badsters Yick it Up

BOING!
BOING!
BOING!

'That's it, Billy me old demonic melon!' laughed Mr Gum as he **BOING!**ed up and down on his grimsters old sofa. 'Chuck that meat on the heat!'

'Right you are!' cackled Billy, shovelling a pile of horse bladders on to the fire where they exploded in a dirty shower known as 'Butcher's Fireworks'. 'But why we doin' all this again, Mr Gum, me old Spanish woodworm?'

'Cos it's our flippin' masterplan, Billy me boy,' growled Mr Gum, **BOING!**ing higher than ever. 'The more we heat up them stale meats, the more poison gases goes up that massive chimney an' in the air. An' the more poison gases goes in the air, the hotter an' nastier it gets in Lamonic Bibber. It's called "Townal Warmin"'.'

'Oh, yeah,' laughed Billy. '"Townal Warmin".' Now I remember. An' once that stupid town gets hot enough, then –'

'SPLASH!' finished Mr Gum, grinning so nastily that a nearby mouse dissolved with fright. 'The weather goes crazy, Lamonic Bibber falls in the sea an' then we rule over it forever!'

'How we gonna rule over it if it's fallen in

the sea?' asked Billy through a mouthful of coal dust.

'Oh, yeah,' said Mr Gum. 'I never thought of that. Well, forget it. We'll just stick to destroyin' Lamonic Bibber by makin' it fall in the sea. That's evil enough for now. OI!' he shouted. 'Why ain't you shovellin' that meat? Get back to work, you lazy old trumpet!'

'But there ain't no more meat *to* shovel,' whined Billy. 'Them horse bladders was the last of it. We run out, see?'

'Well, take yer stupid cap off an' chuck it on the blaze!' yelled Mr Gum. So Billy took off his butcher's cap and threw it on the furnace, where it quickly burnt to a crisp.

'Now burn yer apron!' yelled Mr Gum. 'Now burn yer shirt! Now burn yer trousers! Now burn yer boots! Now burn yer socks! Now burn yer pant – nah, on second thoughts keep yer pants on, you disgustin' lettuce.'

'Well, that's it then,' said Billy as he stood there in his grubby grey boxer shorts. 'We burnt all the meat. We burnt me clothes. There's nothin' left to burn.'

'What we gonna do now?' scowled Mr Gum, stroking his beard into the shape of a gigantic red question mark.

'There's only one thing for it,' said Billy. 'We gotta go an' get more meat off that strange little bloke what helped us out last time.'

'It's true,' growled Mr Gum. 'But we gotta be crafty, Billy der Willy der Wills. We gotta be so crafty 'bout it that even we hardly know what we're up to ourselves. What's that thing called when it's all dark an' there's that stupid thing in the sky what's not the sun but the other one what's not so big?'

'Night time?' suggested Billy.

'Yeah, that's it,' grinned Mr Gum. 'That's the time to do our evils, Billy me boy – "Night time". When no one can see us, when no one can catch us an' when no one can stinkin' well stop us!'

Chapter 4

'Vestigations and Birdseed

Old Granny sat out on the high street, creaking back and forth in her ancient rocking chair from before the War.

FLOOOB!
BUUFFFFSH!

'Terrible days!' she cried, as a cloud plummeted from the sky and landed on her hat. The air was hot and sticky, and so thick that Old Granny's raspy lungs could hardly breathe it down. But in all her life she'd never missed a single day of sitting outside in her chair, 'And I'm not going to let a bit of weather stop me now!' said she.

SLUUUUUUUUUURRRRRRP!

Old Granny took a thoughtful suck at a six-mile long drinking-straw that led directly to her secret sherry supply. And she shook her head so hard that you could hear the sherry swishing around inside her skull.

'Terrrible days! Terrible days!' she cried. 'Terrible days indeed!'

Old Granny's drunken words followed Polly and Friday as they walked along the high street, kicking up clouds of dust from the cracked, dried pavement.

'Right, Mr Friday,' said Polly, wiping a single bead of sweat from her brow and a whole necklace of sweat from her neck. 'We gots to find out who's doin' all them pollutions. It's time for THE DEPARTMENT OF CLOUDS AN' YOGURTS to gets to work!'

'Are you the one who's doing all the pollution?' they asked a little girl called Peter.

'No,' she said. 'I'm just playing with my doll.'

'Are you the one who's doing all the pollution?' they asked David Casserole, the town mayor.

'No,' he said. 'I'm just playing with *my* doll.'

'Are you the one who's doing all the pollution?' they asked William Shakespeare.

'Probably not,' he said. 'You see, I've been dead for about five hundred years. Now leave me alone, I'm trying to write *Hamlet II – Yorick's Revenge.*'

'FRUSTRATERS!' exclaimed Polly at the end of a long morning's work. 'We done millions of 'vestigations an' no one knows nothin', an' it's all boilin' hot an' itchy an' I had ENOUGHS!'

'Let's go back to the office,' suggested Friday.

But just then, they came upon a forlorn-looking fellow sitting in a silver birdcage at the side of the road. It was Crazy Barry Fungus.

'Tweet tweet?' he said hopefully. 'Tweet tweet?'

Now, Crazy Barry Fungus suffered from a rare medical condition called 'Stupidity'. Or in other words, he thought he was a chaffinch. Most people just passed him by as if he wasn't there. But Polly was far too kind-hearted for that.

'Here you goes, little birdy,' she said, fishing a handful of birdseed from her skirt pocket.

'Tweet tweet,' said Crazy Barry, licking it

gratefully from her palm. It was the kindest thing anyone had done for him in years.

'I don't expect he can help us,' said Friday. 'He's only a chaffinch. He knows nothing of the danger our town is in.'

But as Crazy Barry Fungus watched his visitors go, a gleam of light came into his eyes. 'Tweet tweet,' he said thoughtfully. 'Tweet tweet tweet tweet tweet.'

Back at the office, Polly and Friday coloured in all the places they'd visited on the map. It was quite fun. Polly did her bits in pink and Friday did his bits in 'bunch-paraka', which was a new colour he had invented that morning.

'Well, Mr Polly,' said Friday. 'We covered quite a lot of the town today – but there are still a few places left to investigate. Now, how about a nice cup of tea?'

So Polly put the kettle on, Polly put the kettle

on, Polly put the kettle on –

'Hey, are you playin' with the photocopier again, Mr Friday?' said Polly.

'Sorry,' said Friday. 'Hey, let's have a rubber-band fight!'

But just then, the office door flew open – and there stood Crazy Barry Fungus, flapping away in his birdcage, his face full of excitement and his mouth full of birdseed.

'Tweet!' he cried as he struggled through the

doorway. 'Tweet tweet!'

'I think he wants to tell us somethin'!' said Polly. 'Come in, Mr Crazy! Come in!'

Very carefully, Crazy Barry Fungus bent his head and began spitting out a message on the floor. A message written in birdseed.

'I'm sorry I have to spell out messages in birdseed,' he spelt, 'but I cannot talk as I am only a chaffinch. But you were kind to me earlier, and now I want to help you in return. For I see –'

Then he ran out of birdseed and had to lick it all up off the floor and start spitting it out again to carry on with his message.

'I see a lot of strange things on my travels,' wrote Barry Fungus, 'and lately I have seen something very peculiar. Something very –'

Then he ran out of birdseed and had to lick it all up again.

'This is really, really disgusting,' said Friday – but Polly hushed him.

'Something very peculiar indeed,' spat Barry Fungus. 'I have seen mysterious comings and goings down by the river. Yes, down by the river, when it's late and only us chaffinches are awake!'

'Comin's an' goin's down by the river?' said Polly. 'But what's that gots to do with them pollutions?'

Crazy Barry Fungus ran out of birdseed and licked it up again.

'I do not know,' he spat. 'Maybe something. Maybe nothing at all. Maybe I am just a silly old featherbrain who doesn't know what he's on about. But –'

Lick lick lick. Spit spit spit.

'I think you should go down to the river tonight and investigate. That is all. Good day to you both.'

And – GULP-IT-DOWN-CHAFFINCH-BOY-YOU-GOTTA-GULP-IT-DOWN! – he swallowed all the birdseed in a single almighty gulp.

'Thank you,' said Polly as the helpful creature hopped out of the office.

'You're welcome, don't mention it,' replied Crazy Barry Fungus in a deep booming voice. 'I mean – tweet tweet tweet, I can't talk. I'm only a chaffinch!'

And off he hopped in his silver cage, chirping all the way.

'What a lunatic,' marvelled Friday, who was

busy measuring the desk to see if it had secretly shrunk since they'd last seen it. Friday had a theory that desks were always trying to shrink, in order to fool people.

'Well, lunatic or not, he's the only one what done helped us so far,' said Polly. 'I says we go down to the river tonight to sees what's whats!'

Chapter 5

Down by the Riverside

Night time, and two mysterious figures were creeping through the darkness in their hobnail boots. Actually they weren't all that mysterious. They were Mr Gum and Billy, obviously. Although Billy had burned all his clothes back in Chapter Three, he was wearing a brand new uniform of butcher's apron, cap and trousers. And why? Because butchers are like lizards and can grow their skins back at any time.

'Feel how hot it's gettin', Billy, me old funnel?' said Mr Gum as they walked along.

'Yeah,' laughed Billy William. 'The air's as thick as muck. An' look,' he remarked, snatching up a gigantic fly with bright blue wings and about eight million legs and poison dripping from its jaws. 'Dirty tropical weirdies everywhere!'

'Yeah,' agreed Mr Gum, kicking a nearby tarantula in the face. 'An' it's all down to the miracles of poisonous gases an' pollution!'

Laughing softly, Mr Gum and Billy William crept through the night, and all around them strange insects and animals buzzed and flapped and hooted. But after quite a bit of creeping, Mr Gum realised something was wrong.

'Billy,' whispered Mr Gum. 'Here we are, creepin' along, an' all this time we forgot about the First Rule of Evil.'

'Oh, yeah,' said Billy, slapping himself on the forehead. 'What is it again, I forgot.'

Mr Gum regarded him with a frown. 'You really are an idiot, Billy. The First Rule of Evil is:

*Whenever you are goin' creepin'
through the darkness,
Sing an evil song as you go by!*

'Oh, yeah,' laughed Billy. 'Now I remember.'

And with that, the two villains started up with their evil song, and though they sung it soft on the wind, all over town children suddenly started having nightmares, and all the milk turned bad, and a horse in a nearby field went mad and started frothing at the mouth, and then a moth flew by and the horse started frothing at the moth. For the song was indeed a terrible evil affair, and it went a little bit sort of something like this:

THE TEN RULES OF EVIL

CHORUS:

It's the Ten Rules of Evil
It's the Ten Rules of Evil
An' you jus' will not believe all
Of them tricks we like to play!

Rule One, whenever you are
goin' creepin' through the darkness
Sing an evil song as you go by!
Rule Two, if you see happy children
watchin' cartoons
Turn the channel over so they cry!

Rule Three, if you see insects,
pick 'em up in a bag
An' chuck 'em in people's food!
Rule Four, if there's a knock
at your front door
Open it an' shout out
somethin' rude!

CHORUS:

It's the Ten Rules of Evil
It's the Ten Rules of Evil
Oh, you jus' will not believe all
Of them tricks we like to play!

Rule Five, if there's a great big
circus comin' to town
Beat up all the clowns an' all their friends!
Rule Six, if you see somebody readin' a book
Rip the last page out so they
can't find out how it ends!

Rule Seven, if you ever meet
the Devil in the moonlight
Kick him in the tail an' run away!
Rule Eight, if he tries to come after you
Run away a little bit more!

CHORUS:

It's the Ten Rules of Evil
It's the Ten Rules of Evil
Oh, you jus' will not believe all
Of them tricks we like to play!

Rule Nine, if you should ever
get invited to a party
Puke on all the guests an' make a fuss!
An' as for Rule Ten, well, we ain't gonna tell ya
Cos we don't want you to end up
Quite as evil as us!

(Two hour drum solo played on Billy's head

with a 'silk handkerchief')

FIN

'What a brilliant song that was,' said Mr Gum.

'Yeah,' said Billy William. 'What a brilliant song that was.'

'Yeah,' said a voice in the darkness. 'What a brilliant song that was.'

'Who's there?' shouted Mr Gum, turning this way and that, his bashing fists at the ready. 'I'll – oh, it's you.'

'That's right! It is I!' said Surprising Ben, jumping out from a bush.

'I pop up here, I pop up there! Surprise! Surprise! I'm everywhere!'

And off he ran, giggling like a moonbeam.

'I'm gettin' sick of Surprisin' Ben,' growled Mr Gum. 'Anyway, who cares – here we are at last.'

Yes, folks, Mr Gum and Billy had come to the Lamonic River, which is like the rest of Lamonic Bibber, only wetter and with more crisp packets floating around on it.

Swisheroo. Swisheroo. Swisheroo.

☾ ☾ ☾

The soft waters lapped against the riverbank. The insects buzzed overhead. Somewhere in the distance a dog barked. Or maybe the dog was actually much closer than that, and just barking quietly to pretend it was further away than it seemed. Dogs can be crafty like that.

'Whadda we do now?' whispered Billy as they stood there on the hot, steaming riverbank, toads and vagabonds dribbling on their boots.

'Now we give the signal,' grinned Mr Gum, and he looked so awful in the smog and the fog that even Billy felt afraid and fell back a step. Still grinning, Mr Gum removed his hat to reveal an enormous candle made of sheep fat stuck on his pointy head.

'Light me up, Billy me boy,' whispered Mr Gum, so Billy lit a match by just looking at a match and hoping it would somehow light. Then he lit the candle on Mr Gum's head and all at once it blazed up with a horrible green and orange glow, like a Halloween pumpkin who simply will not behave. The ghastly light spilled over the scene, cutting through the smog and making Billy see all sorts of shapes and phantoms in the mist.

'Ha ha,' said the shapes and phantoms in the mist. 'We are shapes and phantoms in the mist.'

And then there was a whisper from downriver – 'That's it, lads! There's the signal!'

And something came gliding through the murky waters to meet them.

Chapter 6

The Midnight Meating

Swisheroo. Swisheroo. Swisheroo.

The waters lapped gently in the hot tropical night.

Chug. Chug.

The dark shape came slowly down the river.

Bzzzz. Bzzzzzzzz.

Swarms of mosquitoes, drawn to the candlelight, circled lazily around Mr Gum's head.

Phwick! Snark! Slurrrrp!

Billy flicked out his tongue and scoffed one down.

And lying hidden beneath a pebble, watching the whole horrid scene unfold, were Polly and Friday. Their eyes widened as the candle spat out the last of its grisly light.

'So Crazy Barry Fungus was right,' whispered Polly. 'There's well mysterious goin's on goin' on! An' it looks like Mr Gum's behind it all!'

Chug chug chug.

Slowly the thing on the river came into sight. It was an old-fashioned steamboat, its battered, patched-up sides lurching drunkenly in the moonlight. A paddlewheel on the side turned as it chugged along, and a huge funnel bloated out clouds of greyish-black smoke into the night sky. A ragged flag hung from the prow, showing a pig's skull with two pork chops crossed beneath.

'Shudder!' whispered Friday. 'They're flying the "Jolly Rasher"! They're I.M.P.s!'

'Imps?' said Polly. 'Like them little spiky things what runs round kitchens ruinin' the pancakes?'

'No, not imps,' said Friday. *'I.M.P.s! International Meat Pirates!'*

And then, all of a sudden a voice boomed out, a voice that chilled the blood in Polly's veins and froze the marrow in her vegetable patch.

'Fifty degrees starboard! Pump

the pedals! Throw the ropes! Stoke the engine! Starbuck – make me a cup of coffee, semi-skimmed milk, two sugars! Look lively, lads! All hands on deck!'

And now Polly could see him, a puffed-up little dandelion of a fellow standing at the helm, his grey hair teetering on his head and his right arm thrust forward, pointing the way. He looked a lot scruffier than when she'd last met him, and his nose hadn't been polished for quite some time. But there could be no mistaking who it was.

'It's George Washington!' trembled Polly. 'I mean – it's Captain Brazil!'

And Polly was right to tremble, because Captain Brazil was an absolute **CRAZER**. He was the terror of the high seas and his adventures were legendary. For instance, he had once killed a sailor just by looking at him for ten minutes. And then shooting him through the heart with a pistol. And you know the Lost City of Atlantis that lies beneath the ocean waves? Well, it was Captain

Brazil who had lost it. It had fallen out of his pocket when he was playing marbles. Once he had commanded the *Nantucket Tickler*, a fine sailing ship indeed, but lately he had fallen upon hard times and was reduced to this, a grotty little steamer called the *Sirloin* which stank of sweat and rum.

'What on earth's he doin' here?' whispered Polly. 'He's as mad as a bulldozer's cousin!'

STOP
THE
BOAT!

'Stop the boat!' commanded Captain Brazil, so loudly that his hair automatically stuffed itself into his ears to stop him from going deaf.

'Aye aye, sir!' said Starbuck, the Second Mate.

'Now quickly start the boat again and then stop it so everyone falls over!' commanded Captain Brazil.

'Aye aye, sir!' said Starbuck, quickly starting the boat and then stopping it so everyone fell over.

'Now say, "That was completely pointless!"' commanded Captain Brazil.

'That was completely pointless!' said the crew.

'Good work, men. Right. Lower the gangway – and look lively about it!'

'Aye aye, sir,' laughed one of the sailors, an enormous hulking nit by the name of Brendan Jawsnapper. His muscular arms bulged as he turned the handle, and down creaked the gangway on to the riverbank.

'Make way, make way!' cried Captain Brazil, disappearing from sight. 'I am coming ashore!'

For a couple of minutes nothing happened. The *Sirloin* sat bobbing gently in the water, its engine purring quietly and its funnel miaowing loudly.

'What's takin' him so long?' snarled Mr Gum. A couple more minutes passed. Then a couple more. Then there was a long flushing sound and finally Captain Brazil stepped ashore, wiping his hands on Nimpy Windowmash, the First Mate.

'Sorry about that, I was doing a poo,' said Captain Brazil with a graceful bow. 'Now, Mr Gum. What brings you back so soon?'

But then he spotted Billy William and a look of astonished wonder came over his weather-beaten face.

'Elizabeth!' cried Captain Brazil, throwing his arms wildly about the startled butcher.

'My dear Elizabeth! What mean you, turning up like this after all these years? You broke my heart once – must you come back now to break it all over again?'

And kissing Billy passionately on the lips, the little captain threw himself down into the long grass and began weeping uncontrollably.

'Why must love be so painful?' he protested. 'Why, Elizabeth, why? Why, Elizabeth, why? Why, Elizabeth, w–'

'Um, 'scuse me, you complete weirdo,' said Mr Gum, after about half an hour of this. 'But that ain't no beautiful lady, it's jus' Billy.'

'So it is,' said Captain Brazil, standing up and brushing himself off. 'Sorry about that. Now, gentlemen. What can I do for you on this fine night? Surely ye haven't run out of meat already?'

'Well, we have,' snarled Mr Gum. 'So give us some more – or I'll wallop you up!'

'Yeah,' grinned Billy. 'An' the rottener

the better!'

'So be it,' said Captain Brazil grandly. 'Men – unleash the cargo!'

'Aye aye, sir,' said Brendan Jawsnapper. There was a mighty snap as he bit through a rope, and then

BUMP!
JOSTLE!
BASH!

A great heap of barrels came rolling down the

gangway like an avalanche made of wood. One hundred barrels! Two hundred barrels! Three hundred barrels! Yes, if you like barrels, this is definitely the scene for you!

Mr Gum opened the first barrel by telling Billy to open the first barrel. Then the two villains hunched eagerly over it, their eyes agleam in the moonlight.

'Meat,' drawled Mr Gum, reaching in and scooping up a sloppy green and red mess as if it were a heap of fine emeralds and rubies.

'Rotted to perfection!' said Billy, taking a long admiring sniff.

'I don't understand,' said Captain Brazil. 'We have many fine meats aboard my vessel. But each time you come, you take only the poorest and dirtiest meats. Why, gentlemen, why?'

'Cos they burn the best,' said Billy proudly. 'An' they make the most poisonous-est gases what mucks up the weather. See, me an' Mr Gum here is hidin' out in a secret hideout –'

'Shut up, you muncher!' hissed Mr Gum, boxing Billy's ears with a cardboard box. 'You never know who might be listenin'!'

'Well, I always knows who might be listenin'!' announced Polly as she and Friday sprang up from under their pebble. 'THE DEPARTMENT OF CLOUDS AN' YOGURTS, that's who! Freeze, you naughties – you're all under arrests!'

Chapter 7

Prisoners!

'Who be these two whippersnaps?' roared Captain Brazil as Friday and Polly emerged from the darkness.

'I'll tell you who they be,' snarled Mr Gum so furiously that the *Official Mr Gum Fury-O-Meter* strapped to his chin went all the way up to 1000 and then exploded in a spray of glass and mercury. 'They be MEDDLERS! Always gettin' in the way of me business!'

'Well, you hasn't gots no business doin' that sorts of business,' said Polly. 'It's a nasty business, an' it's our business to stop it. You're all under arrests for so many reasons I can't even be bothered to count them all, you flibs!'

'Exactly,' said Friday, taking out his notebook. 'Now, tell us your names so we can send you to the prisons where you truly belong.'

'Me name's Little Carlos,' pleaded Mr Gum, dropping to his knees and clutching pitifully at Friday's ankle. 'I am only a poor shepherd boy from Portugal and I ain't got no idea what's goin' on. Please don't arrest me – for then who will look after me faithful sheep, Splinters?'

'That's me,' said Billy William the Third, dropping to all fours and nibbling at Friday's other ankle. 'Baaa! I'm Splinters the sheep. Baaaa!

Baaaaa! Hello.'

'Oh, dear,' said Friday in confusion. 'I think we've arrested the wrong people, Mr Polly.'

'Frides, they're not no innocent shepherds an' sheep, they're lyin'!' said Polly. But in all the confusion, no one noticed that big beefy whaler of a sailor, Brendan Jawsnapper. He had one more barrel left, the biggest of the lot. And now he was creeping along the deck of the *Sirloin*. His tattooed muscles rippled as he hoisted that barrel over his head . . . And then . . .

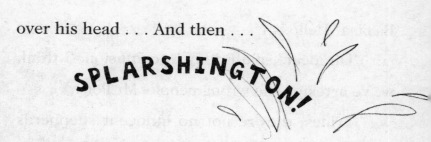

SPLARSHINGTON!

A slew of pig intestines, horse livers and albatross hearts rained down on the heroes.

'URGH!' said Polly.

'URGH!' said Friday.

Everyone waited, in case Surprising Ben was about to pop up and say 'URGH!' as well.

But he didn't. You see, that was actually the most surprising thing about Surprising Ben – just when you expected him to surprise you he surprised you by not surprising you at all.

'Yaar-har-har!' laughed Captain Brazil, who had recently been listening to a CD called **Teach Yourself to Laugh Like a Pirate in Ten Easy Lessons**. 'Get 'em, mateys! We'll take 'em prisoner an' steam off to China an' sell 'em to the circus, yaar-har-har!'

'Oh, no!' said Friday, as the crew of the *Sirloin* came smashing down the gangway to get them. 'Whatever's going to become of us?'

'He jus' said,' replied Polly, as she was hoisted off her feet. 'He's gonna take us prisoner an' steam off to China an' sell us to the circus.'

'Oh, right,' said Friday, who was dangling over Starbuck's shoulder. 'I couldn't hear. I had some sheep's lungs in my ear.'

'HA HA! So much for the *DEPARTMENT OF CLOUDS AN' YOGURTS!*' laughed Mr Gum, as he watched the heroes being bundled aboard. 'Looks like we're free to do our evils after all!'

'Yeah!' said Billy William the Third.

And the last thing Polly saw as the boat pulled away was Mr Gum and Billy tap-dancing on the barrels of meat, singing 'The Ten Rules of Evil' and slapping their thighs with bits of bone and gristle.

Captain Brazil stood on deck, looking down with contempt on the prisoners as they struggled in the sailors' brawny arms. Then he realised he wasn't tall enough to look down with contempt on the prisoners as they struggled in the sailors' brawny arms, so he stood on a little stool and looked down with contempt on the prisoners as they struggled in the sailors' brawny arms.

'Throw 'em in the brig!' he exclaimed.

'NO!' protested Friday. 'Not the brig! Anything but the brig! Please, I beg you – not the brig! If you've an ounce of mercy in you, please – do not throw us in the brig! Also, what is a "brig", by the way?'

'It be the ship's prison, where the rats'll pick at yer toenails to get at the tasty cheese, an' the weevils'll make their homes in yer nostrils,' said Captain Brazil.

And even as he spoke, Brendan Jawsnapper threw open a heavy iron door and tossed the heroes inside as easily as if they were a couple of bags of flour.

KLANK! went the door.

CLICK! went the lock.

'OH, THE CAMPTOWN LADIES SING THIS SONG, DOO DAH!

DOO DAH!' went the ringtone on Captain Brazil's mobile phone.

And they were prisoners!

Chapter 8

Ship's Biscuit

And now began an ordeal so awful that Friday and Polly would remember it for the rest of their lives, apart from Friday, who instantly forgot it as soon as it was over. For hour upon hour the two friends sat in the cold damp gloom of the brig, with only a thin crack of light coming

from under the door by which to see.

From time to time a small metal hatch would open and a sailor would throw in some food. It was always but a single crumb of bread, except for one time when the hatch opened and in came eight roast chickens, gravy, garden peas, buttered parsnips, a choice of side salad or spicy Cajun potato wedges and a 'Smiley Meal' plastic toy.

'Oops,' said the sailor from the other side of the hatch. 'I accidentally threw the prisoners our supper instead.'

But apart from this stroke of good fortune, it was a miserable time. The two friends hardly talked, but sat in silence, Polly wondering what was to become of her beloved hometown of Lamonic Bibber, and Friday thinking of new flavours for yogurts. Slowly, slowly the night passed as the *Sirloin* chugged its way upriver, heading for the open sea and then China. The engine thrummed and the big wheel on the side of the boat turned and splashed, turned and splashed, turned and splashed again.

Captain Brazil's cabin must have been directly above the brig, for sometimes Polly could hear him stamping around and moaning, 'Oh, Elizabeth! Elizabeth! Come back to me, Elizabeth!' And then it seemed she could hear him weeping, and soon after – 'More rum! Starbuck! Bring me more rum!' Then all would be silent for a while until the stamping began once more, and the moaning. 'Oh, Elizabeth! Elizabeth! How I love thee, sweet Elizabeth!'

And so the long night passed, in wails and moans and splashes and groans and sighs. Did Polly fall asleep? She did not know, for in that near-darkness, what was real and what was not became blurred and mixed together, like when you're on a 'plane with your mum and dad and you pour all the pepper and salt and little pots of milk and things into your orange juice in that plastic cup they give you and you even put in that little face-wipe that smells of lemons, and then you stir it around and it looks like puke and then you dare your sister to drink it and then your mum says, 'Stop that, act your age!' and then the stewardess comes round to collect everyone's stuff and your mum hands her your disgusting cup and says, 'Sorry about my children, they're very immature.'

Yes, in that near-darkness, what was real and what was not became blurred and mixed together.

So did Polly fall asleep? She thought she did. For surely it must have been a dream, the way she felt. As if every part of her body was as light as a cloud, as light as a fluffy little cloud . . . And then suddenly, standing before her, she seemed to see a boy whose honest face she knew well.

'Hello, child,' said the boy, though he was no older than she. 'I like your suit and tie. But tell me – what are they feeding you in this place?'

'Mostly jus' some crumbs,' exclaimed Polly glumly.

'I see,' said the lad. 'And do they not feed you Ship's Biscuit?'

'No,' said Polly. 'We never gets no Ship's Biscuit.'

'Well,' laughed the boy kindly. 'Perhaps you don't need any. Perhaps you already have all the biscuit you need.'

And then the moment was gone – if it had ever really happened. But as Polly sat shivering and blinking in the gloom, she replayed the strange dream over and over in her mind.

'"*Perhaps you already gots all the biscuit what you need*",' she murmured. 'What did that 'mazin' spirit mean?' For she felt sure she had just been visited by the Spirit of the Rainbow, who was a force for good and could do mysterious things like get into your dreams and give you clues.

'But I hasn't got no biscuits,' she said. 'Unless . . .'

Polly patted the jacket of her suit – and there was a small lump in the top pocket!

'Could it be?' she wondered . . . She reached into the pocket and her hand closed on something rough and crunchy. It was Alan Taylor, her tiny gingerbread friend!

'So you're the "ship's biscuit"!' marvelled Polly. Alan Taylor was fast asleep and there was a sign around his neck which said 'HIBERNATING

– *DO NOT DISTURB UNTIL SPRING*'. He looked ever so peaceful and his electric muscles whirred gently in time with his delightful sugary snores.

'Sorry, A.T., but we needs you now,' whispered Polly, tickling him softly under the chin with a weevil.

'Zzzz,' snored Alan Taylor. 'Zzz – hee hee! Ooh, that tickles! Zzzz – hee hee!'

And then he was awake and standing in the palm of her hand, his electric muscles glowing feebly in the gloom.

'Polly!' he blinked. 'Is it spring yet?'

'No,' whispered Polly, 'but I'm ever so glads to see you, cos me an' Frides is in the biggest trouble of our lives.'

And then Friday awoke and the three friends hugged each other in the darkness and Friday asked Alan Taylor what he was doing in Polly's pocket in the first place.

'Simple,' replied Alan Taylor. 'Every year, we

gingerbread men like to find a nice warm pocket in which to curl up and hibernate. It is the way of my people. Always has been and always will be.'

'Well, I'm jus' glad you picked my pocket to sleep in, you glorious little nibbly,' said Polly. 'By the way, do you thinks you can get out that little crack under the door?'

'For enormous overweight giants like you two it would be impossible,' said Alan Taylor proudly. 'But my tiny size means I can pass through even the smallest cracks! It is the way of my people.' And he slid under the door like a thing sliding under another thing and he was gone.

A few minutes later they heard a scrabbling noise outside the door and then the sound of a key turning in the lock.

'Can you open the door?' Alan Taylor whispered. 'It's too heavy for me.'

'Oh, so now you want the help of us "enormous overweight giants", do you?' said

Friday. But Polly pushed the door open and the exhausted biscuit tumbled back in, clutching a big brass key almost as large as himself.

'The key was hanging around the First Mate's neck,' he explained. 'I managed to hop up on to his fat stomach and remove it without waking him. It is the way of my people.'

'Well, what are we waiting for?' said Friday. 'THE TRUTH IS A LEMON MERINGUE! Let's get out of here!'

'I don't think that would be a good idea,' said Alan Taylor. 'We could make it up to the deck but there's nowhere to run. And we can't jump overboard, because I noticed the sea was full of massive sharks and krakens and that guy out of *Pirates of the Caribbean* who's got tentacles all over his face.'

'Hmm,' said Polly, who was examining some ropes and old sacks in one corner of the brig.

'Elizabeth, oh, my sweet Elizabeth!' moaned Captain Brazil from his cabin.

'Hmm,' said Polly again. 'Listen up, gang, not with jus' one or two of your ears but with ev'ry

single last one of 'em. Cos I think I gots a
'genious plan.'

Chapter 9

The Captain and Elizabeth

'Twas the wee hours of the morn and the *Sirloin* chugged slowly through the mist and the fog. 'Twas the wee hours of the morn when things get strange and ghostly, and Captain Brazil could not sleep. 'Twas the wee hours of the morn and he was stumbling around his cramped wooden cabin, a-frighted by the spectres of the past.

'*Remember meeeeeee?*' he seemed to hear a papery voice whisper. '*I am the ghost of that cabin boy who you dressed up as a cake and threw to the sharks.*'

'Leave me alone!' sobbed Captain Brazil, tearing a chart from the wall and shredding it to bits.

'*Remember meeeee?*' said another voice. '*I am the ghost of Captain Barnaby Weed! You sank my ship just because I didn't invite you to my party! But now I'll sink YOU!*'

'Get out of my head, you horrors!' begged Captain Brazil. He picked up a decanter of rum and hurled it at the wall. 'Leave me aloooooone!'

But of all the faces from the past, one was even more painful than the rest. 'Oh, Elizabeth,

Elizabeth!' cried Captain Brazil in anguish and also in English. 'Why did you leave me, Elizabeth? Oh, what I would give to hear you knock-knock-knocking at my cabin door this moment! Oh, how I would –'

KNOCK KNOCK KNOCK!

'What?!' cried the captain, turning on his heel, his tailcoat flying out behind him. His drunken eyes rolled madly in his head. 'Who goes there? Who dare troubles me at such an hour? Yargh!'

Squinting through the smoked glass he could just make out a tall figure, a figure with long flowing hair . . .

'Is it possible?' whispered Captain Brazil. Trembling like an oyster-butler, he staggered to the door and threw it wide open to the cold grey of the early sea dawn and the figure standing before him.

'Hello,' said the figure in a high-pitched voice. 'You know that beautiful woman you're always going on about? What's her name again, I've forgotten?'

''Tis E-Elizabeth,' stammered Captain Brazil.

'Oh, yeah,' replied the strange visitor. 'Well, that's me. I'm Elizabeth.'

And with that, Elizabeth stepped into the light. Her hair was long and ropey, her dress looked a bit like an old sack with flowers drawn on in biro, and her lipstick looked like it might have been done with an orange crayon. But Captain Brazil would have recognised her

anywhere, especially as he was unbelievably drunk on rum.

'By the shilly-shally fish of the Sea of Procrastination!' he cried. ''Tis you, 'tis really you! Oh, Elizabeth! I ought to shower you in kisses and spicy fruits! But tell me – why did you leave me, all those years ago? Why did you turn your back on me and walk out of my life like an unfeeling potato?'

'Um . . . I had to sew a button on to my dress,'

replied Elizabeth.

'What, you've been sewing on a button for the last forty years?' said Captain Brazil in astonishment.

'It was a very big button,' replied Elizabeth solemnly. 'But now I have returned to be by your side.'

'Oh, Elizabeth,' said Captain Brazil, dropping to his knee and accidentally squishing a weevil. 'Won't you say those sweet words you used to say to me? Those sweet words of love that always took the trouble from my brow and made me feel like a happy little baby in a bucket of seahorses?'

'Um . . . OK,' said Elizabeth. 'What were they again?'

'Fie! Fie! Fie!' cried Captain Brazil. He leapt to his feet and drew his cutlass. 'Can thou not remember those sweet words? Perhaps thou art not Elizabeth after all!'

'THE TRUTH IS A LEMON MERINGUE!' cried

Elizabeth in fright. 'No, I'm definitely Elizabeth, I'm sure of it!'

'Stop stalling for time and say those words!' bellowed Captain Brazil, pressing the tip of the cutlass against Elizabeth's neck.

'OK,' gasped Elizabeth. And screwing her eyes shut in concentration, she bent down and whispered into the captain's ear.

'Captain Brazil,' she whispered,

'From the sun-coasts of Jamaica
to the icy shores of Sweden
From the tip of Argentina
to the springs of Manderley
I will always love you, Captain,
for you guide me through the oceans
La la la la
La la la la
La la la la
Something else.'

'These are not the words you used to say!' cried Captain Brazil. 'You used to say, "Hey, Captain Brazil, buy me a pair of new shoes or I'll knock your block off." But I like these new words even better,' he said, wiping a tear from his cheek. 'They are beautiful. Now, you have proved you are probably Elizabeth after all and I will do anything for you.'

'Hmm,' said Elizabeth, flinging herself into Captain Brazil's lap and tenderly stroking his earlobe. 'Actually, there is something I would like you to do, my love.'

'Anything for you, my darling,' breathed Captain Brazil, gently caressing Elizabeth's shoe. 'Anything at all.'

'Well, then,' said Elizabeth. 'I would like you to turn this steamship around and head back to Lamonic Bibber right now. And then I'd like you to release the prisoners and bid them farewell. Oh, and you know Friday O'Leary?' she added.

'You should definitely give him some yogurts. He likes yogurts.'

'It is done, m'lady, it is done!' cried Captain Brazil. 'CREW!' he thundered, and at once his men came running. 'TURN AROUND! EIGHT MILLION DEGREES STARBOARD! CHECK THE RUDDER! FLY THE FLAG! MAN THE THINGS! DO THE STUFF!'

'Thank you, my darling,' said Elizabeth. 'Now, I must away and prepare for our wedding in the morning.'

'Oh, Elizabeth,' cried Captain Brazil as the *Sirloin* started to turn. 'You have made me the happiest man alive. Come on, crew! Shake a leg! We're heading back to Lamonic Bibber! And I'm getting married in the mo-oor-ning!'

Chapter 10

Old Granny on the Hoof

The sun was rising when they reached Lamonic Bibber, but it was not a nice sun. It was fierce and red and bloody and it gazed down like a terrifying football that had gone insane with its own power to score goals. The yellow clouds swarmed sulkily overhead. Strangely-coloured worms and mosquitoes roamed freely in the sweltering heat. A seagull tried desperately to open a bottle of suntan oil with its beak. It was a tropical paradise. OF DOOM.

'By the second-hand tutu of old Captain Ballerina!' exclaimed Captain Brazil as the *Sirloin* swayed drunkenly towards shore. 'The river has burst its banks and 'tis flooding the land! Yaar, yaar, yaar! It be terrible! Heave ho, mateys! We are here – though were it not for Elizabeth, I would never have returned to this accursed place! Nimpy! Release the prisoners!'

'Aye aye, Cap'n,' said the First Mate, Nimpy Windowmash. He unlocked the brig and Polly and Friday stumbled out, coughing and gasping in the thick, crowded air.

'Prisoners,' announced Captain Brazil grandly. 'You are free to go. Now, be off with you and trouble me no more. Oh, I just remembered,' he added, turning towards Friday. 'Elizabeth asked me to give you these.' And he pressed a few pots of yogurt into Friday's hand.

'Excellent!' exclaimed Friday, putting them into his secret Yogurt-Storing Compartment, otherwise known as his mouth. 'I love yogurts.'

'An' so 'tis farewell,' said Captain Brazil, standing to attention and saluting until Polly and Friday were out of sight. 'And now to marry Elizabeth!'

But sadly for Captain Brazil, Elizabeth never

did show up that morning or even the next. And eventually he gave up waiting and headed back to sea.

'For the sea she never does let ye down,' he told his crew. 'An' there's adventures out there for the takin', me boys! With a heave an' a ho an' a bucket of wine, there's adventures out there for the takin'!'

'Come on!' cried Polly as she and Friday raced into town. 'There's no time to lose! We gots to get THE DEPARTMENT OF CLOUDS AN' YOGURTS rollin' again. We gots to 'vestigate every last buildin' and find them villainers!'

Overhead, the ugly clouds roiled and broiled and groiled. The rising waters snaked along after them and with every step, the air grew thicker and sludgier with the stench of rotten meat.

'Oh, no!' exclaimed Alan Taylor from Polly's pocket. 'I can't breathe this, I'm a vegetarian!'

Soon they were on the high street – but Polly barely recognised it. There was hardly anyone around, just a few people sitting quietly in shop doorways or stretched out hopelessly on the cracked and dusty ground.

'It's – so hot,' croaked the little girl called Peter. 'We can't – breathe!'

'And there's a – beached whale by the town hall!' gasped Martin Launderette, who ran the launderette.

'I'm not – a – beached whale!' replied Jonathan Ripples, the fattest man in town.

'Yes – you are,' croaked Martin Launderette unkindly.

FLOOOOB!
BUFFFFFFSSSH!

Clouds fell from the sky.

The sun beat down mercilessly.

Cactuses had started to grow through the pavements.

'Terrible days!' cawed flocks of brightly coloured parrots from the rooftops. 'Terrible days! Terrible days! Awk!'

Old Granny sat out in the middle of the street, rocking back and forth in her chair. 'Terrible days! Terrible days!' she muttered, taking a suck on her six-mile long straw. 'Temperatures rising! Rivers bursting their banks! A cactus growing under my feet! The world's turned upside-down!'

But THE DEPARTMENT OF CLOUDS AND YOGURTS had no time to spend listening to Old Granny's ramblings.

'Billy said they was hidin' out in a secret hideout,' said Polly. 'We gots to search everywhere we can think of an' even some places we can't!'

'We must leave no stone unturned!' said Friday, turning over a stone in case the secret hideout was underneath. 'Let's go!'

So Polly and Friday got the map from their office and all that morning they searched beneath the sweltering sun, colouring in bits of the map as they went.

And all that morning Old Granny rocked back and forth in her chair and shook her head. And all that morning the cactus grew higher and higher between her legs until she and her chair were ten feet off the ground. The heat was almost unbearable but Old Granny was a tough old macaroon and she would not be moved, not even when the first muddy waters from the river began flooding the high street.

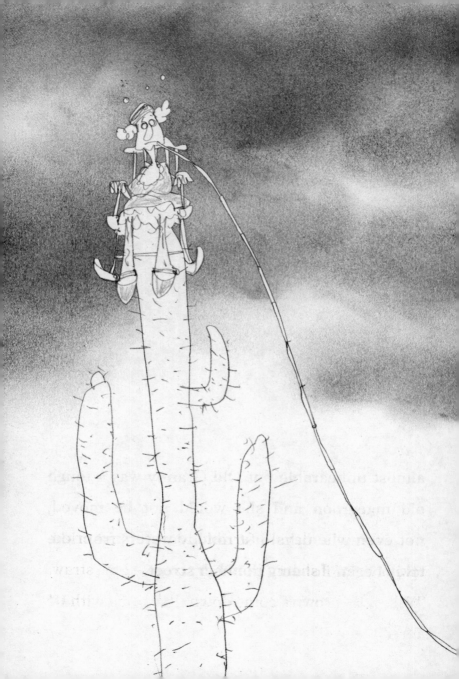

'Terrible days! Terrible days!' she cried, taking a sip of sherry from her six-mile long straw. 'Well, if this town's going down, I'm going with it! Terrible days!'

'Where ARE they?' said Friday, running past Old Granny's dangling feet. 'Those villains must be hiding SOMEWHERE!'

'Terrible days,' nodded Old Granny. 'Terrible days indeed.'

'We must of missed a bit,' said Polly, scanning the map from top to bottom. 'We must of, Mr Friday, we must!'

'No,' said Friday sadly. 'I told you – that map

shows the entire town. Every house, every street, every hill, every –'

But just then they heard a horrible noise. 'EEEEEUUUURRRRGGGH!' cried Old Granny from above.

'What is it, O.G.?' cried Polly, whipping round so fast that Alan Taylor flew out of her pocket, did a spectacular triple somersault, and landed in a palm tree.

'The – the sherry,' gasped Old Granny, gobbing out massive bits of phlegm to rid herself of the taste. 'I was just – I was just having a little sip, you know, to calm my nerves. Anyway, I was sucking on my straw and then – there was something stuck in there! So I sucked harder and – oh, it was shocking! A hoof! I swallowed a hoof!'

'What's a hoof doin' in your sherry?' said Polly. She picked up Old Granny's straw and placed the end to her lips. 'Mr Friday, is it OK if I try a little bit of sherry? I'm only nine.'

'Yes, Mr Polly,' said Friday. 'You may. It could be an important clue.' So Polly took a little sip and –

'EEEURGGGH! It tastes all meaty!' she exclaimed. 'Old Granny, where does this straw lead?'

'Why, to Finnegan's Sherry Factory on the edge of town,' said Old Granny.

'Finnegan's Sherry Factory?' said Polly. 'But that isn't on Mr Friday's map. Hang on a minute . . . O.G., do you knowed when they done opened that fact'ry?'

'Yes,' said Old Granny with a dreamy look upon her wrinkled old face. 'They opened it on the fifteenth of November, back in 1973. I shall never forget it, because it was the happiest day of my life.'

'JUMPIN' RHINOCERERS! Mr Friday, that's IT!' said Polly. 'You done drewed your map THE DAY BEFORE they opened up that fact'ry! That's why it's not on there! An' I'll bet you that's where them villains is hidin' out – an' that's why Old Granny's sherry's gone all meaty!'

'THE HOOF IS A LEMON MERINGUE!' shouted Friday. 'You're right, little miss! Let's go!'

So Friday jumped on to his motorbike, which by a lucky coincidence just happened to be standing right next to him, and Polly jumped into the sidecar with Alan Taylor clinging to her hair. And they tied Old Granny's cactus-and-rocking-chair tower to the back with a rope because as she said, 'If there's sherry in trouble, I'd better come along!'

And then – **WAAAAAOOOO!**

– Friday squealed up the engine, the enormous

cactus flew out of the ground with Old Granny hanging off the end, and with a cry of 'I'VE SAID NOTHING FOR ABSOLUTELY AGES!' from Alan Taylor, they flamed it up the high street like a monstra, the rising waters lapping at their heels.

Chapter 11

Mr Gum Gets a Surprise

'It's the Ten Rules of Evil, them amazin' Rules of Evil!' sang Mr Gum and Billy as they unloaded another barrel of meat on to the furnace. 'An' you jus' will not believe all of them tricks we like to plaaaaaaaaay!'

'What a laugh it all is, Billy me old air-polluter!' grinned Mr Gum. He was covered in grease and bits of bones, and his beard was singed and blackened but none of that mattered to him now. All his thoughts were on the destruction of Lamonic Bibber, and he had never wanted anything so badly in his bad life.

'I never wanted anythin' so badly in me bad life,' roared Mr Gum as he sloshed a heap of tripe on to the flames. 'I can hardly even breathe but who even cares?'

'An' who'd've thought we was hidin' out in Finnegan's Sherry Factory what's on the edge of town miles away from anyone?' laughed Billy William the Third through a mouthful of entrails. 'No one'll ever find us here!'

'Well, that's jus' where you're wrong again!' said a voice behind them. And wheeling around, Mr Gum and Billy were confronted with the sight they hated most of all – heroes coming to save the day. Because perched on the rim of a massive vat of bubbling hot sherry were Polly, Friday, Alan Taylor, Old Granny AND a special bonus of Jake the dog, who they'd picked up along the way.

'DEPARTMENT OF CLOUDS AND YOGURTS!' chorused the heroes.

'WOOF!' chorused Jake, even though you can't really chorus on your own.

And then they did this really cool thing of

standing on each other's shoulders in an amazing human-and-dog pyramid, which was an idea Friday had come up with on the ride over.

'You're under arrests!' cried Polly from the top. 'This time you gone too far, Mr Gum, you unpleasant vine! An' I'm not very impressed with you neither, Billy William the Thirds.'

'MEDDLERS!' screamed Mr Gum. 'How the blibbin' blib did you find us, you blibbin' blibberers?'

'Cos you done carelessnesses, that's what,' said Polly, pointing to where a few hooves and entrails floated in the vat of hot, bubbling sherry.

'You MUNCHER!' roared Mr Gum, turning towards Billy. 'You been droppin' meat in the sherry an' now you've ruined everything!'

'I never,' protested Billy as he dodged a kick from Mr Gum's hobnail boot. 'I never!'

'Shabba me whiskers!' scowled Mr Gum, turning away in disgust. 'Well, come on then!'

he shouted to Polly and her friends. 'Come down here, I dares ya!'

Well, true heroes like the brave men, women, dogs and biscuits of THE DEPARTMENT OF CLOUDS AND YOGURTS do not hesitate in the face of fear. For as their motto goes:

Doo-doo-doo! Doo-doo-doo!
Doo-doo-doo!
Yeah!

And now Polly jumped down off the vat and her brave colleagues jumped down behind her, and soon the air was full of punches and smoke and heat and bacon as the final battle began.

'SNARP!' yelled Mr Gum, getting Friday
in the ribs with some spare ribs.

'YISK!'

shouted Billy, as Polly
stamped on his foot.

'WOOF!'

said Jake, as he
licked up a bit of
chicken liver.

'I DO NOT CARE FOR THE WAY
YOU HAVE ABUSED THIS SHERRY
FACTORY; AND FURTHERMORE I
FIND YOUR LACK OF CONCERN

FOR THE ENVIRONMENT GREATLY DISTURBING!' exclaimed Old Granny as she swung her enormous black handbag from before the War into Mr Gum's nose.

'YAAAAA! You stupid old woman!' he cried, teetering back towards the furnace. His grotty arms pin-wheeled for balance as he regained his footing. And suddenly – FLISSSSH! – his great red beard and his stovepipe hat were aflame, and as he emerged from the furnace he uttered a yell from the very depths of his soul.

'YOU MESSED UP ME PLANS FOR THE LAST TIME!' roared Mr Gum. And now it was as if he were possessed of a strength much greater than his own, for in his fiery fury the last of any goodness that might have been inside Mr Gum was burnt up, and he was more of a monster than a man. Or a 'manster' for short.

'NAAAAAAARRGH!!' he wailed.

'FRRRRRRRRRRRRRRR-RRRRRB!'

Roaring like a chimney, Mr Gum picked up Polly and hoisted her into a corner as if she weighed but an ounce.

'SBUNVV!'

He whacked Friday across the room like a Brown Davy, the smallest species of insect known to man, which is smaller than one thousandth of an atom.

'URGO-NASURN-GRUK!'

He grimaced at Old Granny and she fell over

and everyone saw the weird old veins in her legs.

'STTTRRIIINGGG!'

He kicked Alan Taylor the entire length of the factory floor.

'NUUUURG!'

He whacked Billy in the face with a shovel.

'OW!' shouted Billy. 'Whaddya do that for?'

'Oh, yeah,' said Mr Gum, helping the poor butcher to his feet by spitting on him. 'Sorry, I gone out of me mind with uncontrollable rage there for a moment. Now come ON,' he growled.

'Let's get shovellin' again! One last barrel o'meat an' that ought to do it! One last barrel an' Lamonic Bibber slides into the sea like the idiot it is!'

The villains resumed their dark work, furiously stoking the furnace until from where she lay, limp on the floor, all Polly could see was smoke and all she could smell was meat, and all she could see was smoke. But I already told you that, pay attention.

'He . . . He . . . can'ts get away with this,'

Polly wept. Desperately she pulled herself across the factory floor. She was so tired she could hardly move – but she had to try, for she wasn't just anyone, she was Mr Polly of THE DEPARTMENT OF CLOUDS AND YOGURTS!

'Hooray,' said Polly weakly as she inched towards the villains. 'Hooray for all what's good an' lovely in the world. Hooray for snowmen. Hooray for when you wakes up an' you thinks it's school but then you remembers it's a Saturday an' there's millions of cartoons on TV. Hooray for that time I done went to that restaurant an' you was allowed to make your own desserts an' do as much ice cream as you wanted an' you could put brilliant sprinkles on top. Hooray for friends who's always stickin' up for you, even if you accident'lly break their fav'rite doll cos you was tryin' to make it fly in their back garden. Hooray for all that an' much much more! Hooray, I says, hooray!'

Mr Gum barely heard her. He was holding

a huge gristly cow heart, already aflame from the heat.

'This is it, Billy me boy!' grinned Mr Gum. 'One last bit of meat! One last bit what's gonna tip Lamonic Bibber into the sea once an' for all!'

'Yeah,' cackled Billy William, who was so excited that he'd accidentally eaten his shovel.

Mr Gum hoisted the cow heart above his head.

He brought it towards the furnace.

The sunlight blazed through the window like dragon's breath.

Billy did a burp which tasted of shovel.

'Chuck it on! Chuck it on!' he chanted.

And then –

'OH-NO-YOU-DON'TS!' cried Polly. With one last effort, she launched herself from the floor and wrestled the flaming cow heart from Mr Gum's grasp. 'You isn't never gonna beat the Forces of Good, you unbearable, unbelievable ROO-DE-LALLY!'

'Give that BACK!' yelled Mr Gum, yanking at the burning piece of meat.

'NEVER!' cried Polly, yanking back twice as hard.

The cow heart stretched as it was pulled first one way, then the other. Great orange flames spurted from its rubbery tubes.

'IT'S MINE!' yelled Mr Gum through gritted teeth.

'IT'S MINE!' yelled Polly, digging her heels in.

'IT'S MINE!' said a third voice, bursting out of nowhere. 'Yes, it is I! *Surprising Ben! I pop up here, I pop up there! Surprise! Surprise! I'm everywhere!*'

And before anyone knew what was happening, Surprising Ben grabbed the flaming cow heart for himself and off he ran, giggling like a tangerine.

'Hee hee!' he giggled. 'Hee – whooooooooooa!'

And then it was Surprising Ben's turn to get a surprise. He skidded on a scrap of tripe and the cow heart went flying from his grasp, trailing a great long streamer of fire behind it.

In the middle of the factory the vat of sherry bubbled and sloshed.

'WOOF! WOOF!'

Jake's doggy eyes tracked the cow heart as it span through the air.

'It's going to land in the sherry!' cried Old Granny. 'The factory's going to blow!'

The heroes of *THE DEPARTMENT OF CLOUDS AND YOGURTS* raced for the door. But Mr Gum and Billy weren't listening.

'You idiot, Billy! If you never led them meddlers here, none of this would've happened! It's all your fault!'

'MY fault? That's a laugh, Mr Gum me old gobbler!'

The flaming cow heart flew through the air . . . – 'Mr Gum! Billy! Stop your squabblin's, we gots to get out of here!'

– 'Shut up, you meddler! We're busy!'

– 'Come on, Mr Polly! Leave them to it!'

– 'I can't! I gots to save 'em, Mr Friday!'

The heart tumbled down towards the vat . . .

– 'Come *on,* Mr Polly!' shouted Friday.

– 'WOOF! WOOF!'

– 'OW! Let go of me nose, Billy me boy!'

– 'OW! No! You let go of MY nose!'

– 'No, you let go of MY –'

With a sickening splash, the flaming cow heart hit the bubbling sherry.

– 'SHABBA ME WHIS–'

plop.

Chapter 12

Clouds of Sorrow, Clouds of Joy

SHHHWWUFFF!

Friday was hurled to the ground as the factory exploded behind him. Something whizzed past his head. It was Old Granny, riding her cactus through the sky like a Mexican rocket. Alan Taylor and Jake came somersaulting along after her in a rain of broken bricks and rubble. And behind them came Surprising Ben, covered in soot and coal dust.

'Surprise! Surprise! I'm – COUGH! – *everywhere!'* he managed. And off he stumbled, wheezing like a flannel.

'Wh-what happened?' said Old Granny as she lay there on the stony ground. 'Wha–' But then she remembered, and looking back she saw one of the saddest sights of her long and drunken life. A sherry factory that would never make a single drop of sherry again.

'No,' she whispered, clutching at her heart. 'It's not fair! Why? Why? WHY?'

But Friday and Alan Taylor were scanning the wreckage with horrified expressions on their faces.

'Where is she?' breathed Alan Taylor.

'I – I don't know if she made it,' said Friday, turning his head from the flames. 'The truth is a lemon meringue,' he said softly.

And there, on the scorched grass, Friday O'Leary closed his eyes and wept hot bitter tears. And Alan Taylor staggered on to his back and hugged a couple of his vertebrae, which is as much as he was able to get his little arms around. And Old Granny forgot about the sherry and joined them and Jake lay down and whimpered softly.

And there they sat, weeping and whimpering, even as the flames grew higher and higher. Higher and higher and –

'Hiya,' said Polly. 'What you all cryin' 'bout?'

'Oh, you know,' sniffed Friday. 'Because you died in that explosion.'

'Oh,' said Polly. 'That's well sad. Mind if I joins you?'

'No, no,' said Old Granny. 'Be our guest.'

So Polly sat down on the grass and together

they all sat there crying and hugging and holding one another in their grief.

And Friday said, 'What's it like being dead, Polly?' and Polly said, 'Well, to be honest, Frides, it don't feel all that diff'rent from bein' alive really, 'cept everyone's cryin' more than usual.'

And then Alan Taylor said, 'Well, maybe you're not dead after all.'

'Well, maybe I'm not,' said Polly in astonishment.

And then everyone realised at once, and their tears of grief turned to tears of joy and their sobs turned to laughter and Jake's whimpers turned to barks of fun, and Friday turned to Polly and said, 'Look, Mr Polly. The clouds are coming back!'

And it was true, for the flames from Finnegan's Factory had reached high into the sky, licking the poisonous gases away with their soft orange tongues. And the first bits of blue were beginning to creep back overhead. And yes, the clouds were coming back, and with a sigh of relief they uncurled and began to make themselves into the fluffle-y little darlings they loved to be.

And somewhere on a high-flung branch a bluebird gave a joyful chirp and all the mosquitoes and tarantulas died because it wasn't tropical any more, but the parrots stayed alive because everyone loves parrots. And the world could breathe again.

'But hold on,' said Friday suddenly. 'What

about Mr Gum and Billy?'

Everyone turned to look at the charred remains of the factory. The villains were nowhere to be seen.

'Nothing could have survived that,' said Old Granny.

'So that's that then,' said Polly quietly. 'Mr Gum an' Billy – gone forever. They were the worst crimers what I ever saw in my life, an' they never meant no good for no one. But you knows what, Frides? It don't make me feel no happiness, it don't make me feel no happiness at all. No one deserves that, not even them two Johnny-Come-Latelys.'

Friday nodded wisely. 'Little miss, I am proud of you and your kindness towards rotters,' said he. 'But what's done is done and what's not done is not done and what's yet to be done is yet to be done and what can't be done will never be done and look at my shoelace, it's come undone.'

And as Alan Taylor said, 'We did what was right, Polly. It is the way of my people.' And as Old Granny said, 'I still can't believe the sherry factory's gone. Oh, well. Never mind.' And she took a sip of sherry from the emergency bottle she always kept hidden in Jake's fur, and it didn't taste of meat at all.

THE DEPARTMENT OF CLOUDS AND YOGURTS walked back into town and as they did so, the heavens opened and the clouds roared their approval with a torrent of lovely fresh rain to wash everyone's worries clean away. Soon the heroes were splashing and skipping merrily through the puddles like a gang of carefree bellybuttons, and Friday took out his harmonica and blew a funky little number called '**Butterscotch Betty on the Two Thirty-Nine**', and Alan Taylor rode on his hat and turned somersaults and once he fell off and Jake caught him on his tail and flipped him halfway into space for a giggle.

'Hooray for THE DEPARTMENT OF CLOUDS AND YOGURTS!' said Mayor Casserole as the heroes entered the town square. 'You've saved us all from sinking into the sea!'

'Hooray!' said the little girl called Peter. 'You've saved me and my doll!'

Then Jake ate her doll.

'Never mind,' said Peter. 'I didn't like that stupid doll anyway. She had a boy's name.'

'Hooray!' said Jonathan Ripples. 'I'm in such a good mood that I'm not even going to sit on Martin Launderette for calling me a beached whale!'

'Hooray!' said Martin Launderette.

'But *I'm* going to,' said a voice. And spinning around Martin Launderette saw a sight that made him quiver like a washing machine.

'Hello,' said the voice. 'I'm Jessica. Have you been making fun of my little brother?'

'Oh, no!' trembled Martin Launderette. 'You're even fatter than Jonath–'

But the rest of his words were lost as he was squashed under the tremendous weight of Jessica Ripples, the fattest woman in town.

And after that the lovely fresh rain stopped, and the sun came out in a blaze of triumph and a magnificent rainbow arched over the entire town, and it even had an extra stripe of 'bunch-paraka', the new colour that Friday had invented. And gazing up at that rainbow, Polly thought she heard a voice whispering, whispering to her alone.

Well done, child, the voice seemed to say, though it was no older than she. *Once again you have made the world glow with happy colours. See you around, tingler!*

And when she looked down there was a fruit chew lying at her feet, and it was a strawberry one, the best flavour of all, or at least equal with blackcurrant. And *way* better than the green ones.

'Well!' cried Mayor Casserole. 'What are we waiting for? Let's have a feast!' And soon the townsfolk were yibbing it up with the biggest and best feast of their lives. Roast ox and smoked salmon and strawberry jam, sausage rolls, Dover sole and green eggs and ham, and trifles as big as your head, my boy! Trifles as big as your head!

And Crazy Barry Fungus hopped up in his silver birdcage and everyone patted him and fed him birdseed and said what a remarkable creature he was, and they gave him the title *Birdus Magnificus* and presented him with the Order of the Golden Feather, which is the highest honour a chaffinch may be awarded.

And Old Granny announced that she was going to marry her cactus, because she had grown very fond of it, and everyone cheered and threw confetti in the air and the dancing went on all day and night, and you never did see such a thing in your life and the dish ran away with the piper's son, hickory dickory dock.

It was late in the evening, and Polly was sitting on Boaster's Hill with her friends. Jake was being Jake and Alan Taylor was being Alan Taylor, which was the way of his people. Old Granny was sipping from the bottle of sherry she always kept hidden in her cactus. And Friday – well, Friday was having a bit of a snuggle with Mrs Lovely, who had returned from an adventure of her own, battling robots in another dimension.

'You knows,' said Polly as she sat there gazing up at the soft night sky. 'Before all this, I never really thought much 'bout them clouds up there in the heavens, but now I understands how important they truly are.'

'Well said, little miss,' said Friday, strumming a lonesome chord on his blue guitar. 'You see, clouds are like people. They appear for no reason anyone can understand, they hang around for a while, and then they move on. And sometimes you don't really appreciate them until after they're gone.'

'Oh, Friday,' sighed Mrs Lovely affectionately. 'You do talk an awful lot of nonsense sometimes.'

Well, everyone nodded at that, even Friday,

and there they all sat, gazing up at the evening sky as if seeing it for the very first time. And there we shall leave them – Polly and Friday, and Mrs Lovely and Alan Taylor and Old Granny and Jake the dog and all the rest of them, gazing up at the great wide yonder and wondering at the shapes and the sights they see there. And there we shall leave them, happy in their dreams.

THE END

EPILOGUE

Portugal, one month later

*L*ittle Carlos the shepherd and his faithful sheep Splinters stumbled along the windswept hilltop.

'Come on, Splinters, you idiot,' growled Little Carlos, kicking the sheep in the rear to hurry him up. 'I gotta find a telly an' quick –

"Saco de Varas" is about to start.'

'Saco de Varas' was the Portuguese version of 'Bag of Sticks'. It was a picture of a bag of sticks for half an hour, but with Portuguese subtitles. (Little Carlos was the only person in the country who ever watched 'Saco de Varas'. Everyone else turned over to watch 'Tempo de Diversão com Crispy'.)

'Baaa! Baaaa!' said Splinters as they reached the top of the hill. Spread out below them was the friendly-looking little town of Santa del Wisp.

'Urrgh,' said Little Carlos, his big ragged beard flapping in the wind. 'What a friendly-lookin' little town. I hate it.'

But then his eyes lit up.

'Know what, Splinters, me old faithful sheep?' grinned Little Carlos. 'It looks like just the kind of place for us to get up to our evils.'

'Baaa! Baaaa! Hello,' agreed Splinters.

The two of them started down the hillside towards Santa del Wisp. The sun was going down and a chill was creeping into the evening air. And though they whispered it soft on the wind, if you listened carefully you could just make out the words they sang:

'Oh, you jus' will not believe all of them tricks we like to plaaaaaay . . .'

FIN

Hello again, you adorable little chestnuts. You are, aren't you? Yes, you are! You cheeky little conkers! Look at you all with your shiny little chestnut faces! Look at you all, tumbling down the hillside and rolling through the park like you haven't got a care in the world! You're simply ADORABLE! Aren't you? Aren't you? You happy little chestnuts. Yes, you are! Yes, you –

Sorry about that. I don't know what came

over me. Anyway, forget it – here's a bonus story instead. Just for you. Oh, you adorable little chestnuts. You are, aren't you? Yes, you are! You really, really are! Oh, you're just SO adora–

Sorry, everyone. Seriously, I'll shut up now. Here's the story. Sorry.

Contents

1 The Crossword Emerges   1
Before the crossword, The earliest crosswords, Definition-type
puzzles, Quiz and general knowledge puzzles, Tutorial puzzles

2 The Basic Crossword Grid   20
Checked and unchecked squares, Opening up the grid

3 Beyond the Simple Definition   26
Double definitions, Cryptic definitions, Tutorial puzzle

4 The Anagram   30
From 'anag.' to anagram indicator, First steps in clue analysis,
Tutorial puzzles

5 More Basic Clue Types: Charades, Container and   35
contents, Reversals
Charades, Container and contents, Reversals, Tutorial puzzle

6 Yet More Basic Clue Types: Hidden words,   40
Vocal clues, Subtractive clues
Hidden words, Vocal clues, Subtractive clues, Tutorial puzzle

7 Non-word Elements in Subsidiary Indications: 45
Abbreviations and symbols, Numbers, Bits and pieces
Abbreviations and symbols, Numbers, Bits and pieces, Tutorial
puzzle

8 The Orchestration of Subsidiary Parts: 52
Complex clues, Linking clues together
Complex clues, Linking clues together, Tutorial puzzle

9 The & Lit. Clue   58
What is an 'and lit.'?, The 'semi & lit.', Some 'non & lits.', Tutorial puzzle

10 Crossword Lingo   62
Definitions, Anagrams and other indicators, Some give-away words
for short subsidiary components, Tutorial puzzle

11 Basic Principles of Crossword Grammar   66
Fair Play, Fair and unfair clues, Challenges to Ximenean standards,
Why does Crossword Grammar matter?, Tutorial puzzle

As far as D. F. M.'s prowess as a solver is concerned, let me mention a recent incident. He and I were travelling by train together to record a crossword programme, in which we were asked to comment on clues which had appeared in some of the previous week's dailies. At Oxford station, Don bought four of them: *Times, Independent, Guardian, Telegraph*; and without any assistance from me he had completed them all just before we reached Reading. Twenty-three minutes.

The programme in question was *Crosstalk*, and its aim was to reach some of those potential solvers who bemoan the fact that they aren't clever enough to do the cryptics. Well, it is precisely to such an audience that Manley is talking here. Is it any real joy to complete the clue 'A well known movie: Gone ___ the Wind (4)'? Yet what a delight it is to solve a clue that is grammatically fair, is reasonably challenging, is happily penny-dropping! Delight? Oh yes—because solving crosswords is the most civilized and enjoyable way of wasting one's time that has yet been devised. And in this manual Manley puts things simply and clearly: 'Ultimately crosswords should be fun rather than inquisitorial.'

Jump in then for a delightful time—and a delightful pastime. 'Isn't the swimming-pool so much more enjoyable once you can swim?' These are Don Manley's words—and with *Chambers Crossword Manual* you'll very soon find yourself swimming.

Colin Dexter
Oxford 2001

Foreword

Dons—and rightly so—are held in high esteem in Oxford (the city from which I write) perched happily as they are on the topmost twigs of the groves of academe. Indeed, meeting even a single one of them can be quite something. And here, in *Chambers Crossword Manual* (revised edition), we are privileged to meet *three* of them: Don Quixote, Don Giovanni, and Don Pasquale. But no, not three—just the one: the man (he has other sobriquets) who for so many years has been setting crosswords for virtually all the prestigious broadsheets and magazines with such enviable distinction.

He is D. F.M.—Don Manley.

The new edition, just as the earlier ones, guides the would-be beginner, tyro, novice (it is useful in this business to have your synonyms ready) *gradatim* through a series of gentle training-sessions, each with its civilized 'donnish' tutorial, until our greenhorn, apprentice, neophyte has completed the ascent from the foot-hills of the dreary definition to the pleasing peaks of the cryptic.

Those familiar with some of the (few) works available in this field cannot fail to be impressed by the innovative notation system used here to explain the anagrams, charades, contents and containers, hiddens, reversals, and the other less common clue-types. Such structural analysis is lucidly set out, and in Manley's hands is far more comprehensible—and far more interesting—than any instruction manual on stripping a Jaguar down to its gaskets. Indeed, the incisiveness of the author's mind is matched by the clarity, the gentle wit, and the lightness of touch which characterizes his writing.

This revised edition is comprehensive in its range, since anything and everything to do with crosswords is to be found within its covers. Particularly enjoyable (for me) are several authoritative addenda to the earlier editions: 'Challenges to Ximenean Standards', 'Ten Clues to Edit', 'Ten Tips for Editors', etc., together with fascinatingly controversial comments on those grey areas in the realm of fair and unfair cluemanship.

With the advent of Azed in *The Observer*, following the death of Ximenes in 1971, D.F. Manley's star rose to the zenith of the firmament. And since that time he has been the most successful of all those distinguished clue-writers participating in that most prestigious of all crossword competitions. Some few of his prize-winning clues will be found in the text here. But apart from such brilliancies, there are so many other gems which litter the grids of his regular puzzles. Particularly memorable for me over these past few months: 'Company car (3-6)'; 'Who you'd expect to find at gay weddings in the Isles?!(8)'; 'I'm one who had lit snout—genus nonsensical (3,4,4,1,8,4)'. I could go on and on…

In loving memory of my father
Chave Manley
1904-1978

and of my mother
Alma Manley
1906-1992

This new edition is also dedicated to my wife Susan

Published by CHAMBERS
An imprint of Chambers Harrap Publishers Ltd
7 Hopetoun Crescent
Edinburgh EH7 4AY

www.chambers.co.uk

Third edition
© Don Manley 2001

First edition 1986
Second edition 1992
Third edition 2001; reprinted 2004

A CIP catalogue record for this book is available from the British Library.

ISBN 0550 12006 8

Designed and typeset by Chambers Harrap Publishers Ltd
Printed and bound in Great Britain by Cox & Wyman Ltd, Reading, Berkshire

CHAMBERS

CROSSWORD MANUAL

Third edition

A guide for the novice
and the enthusiast

by

DON MANLEY

with a foreword by
Colin Dexter

CHAMBERS

CHAMBERS

CROSSWORD
MANUAL

THOUGHT **MR GUM** WAS WEIRD?
WELL, JUST WAIT TIL YOU MEET . . .

THE

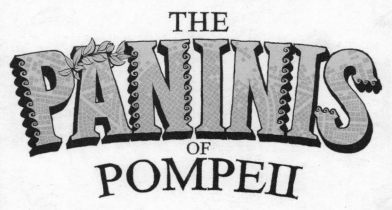

OF

POMPEII

VESUVIUS →

CAECILIUS

DON'T ASK

SLAVIUS

A FROG

BARKUS WOOFERINICUM

FELIUS

ANOTHER FROG

More mind-bending craziness from

ANDY STANTON

Illustrated by Sholto Walker

IT'S TOGA-LLY TERRIFIC!

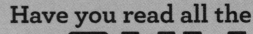

Have you read all the MR **GUM** books?

They're WELL BRILLIANT!

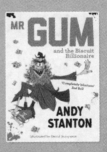

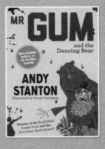

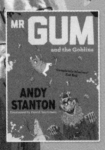

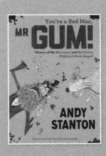

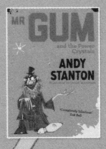

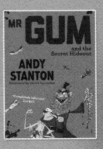

About the Illustrator

David Tazzyman lives in South London with his girlfriend, Melanie, and their son, Stanley. He grew up in Leicester, studied illustration at Manchester Metropolitan University and then travelled around Asia for three years before moving to London in 1997. He likes football, cricket, biscuits, music and drawing. He still dislikes celery.

About the Author

Andy Stanton lives in North London. He studied English at Oxford but they kicked him out. He has been a film script reader, a cartoonist, an NHS lackey and lots of other things. He has many interests, but best of all he likes cartoons, books and music (even jazz). One day he'd like to live in New York or Berlin or one of those places because he's got fantasies of bohemia. His favourite expression is 'Rumble it up, Uncle Charlie!' and his favourite word is 'platypus'. This is his eighth book.

agreeing with things much more than he liked disagreeing with things.

'Oh, look,' said Polly. 'It's a lovely bright autumn morning.'

It was a lovely bright autumn morning, the sort of lovely bright autumn morning that makes you say, 'Oh, look, it's a lovely bright autumn morning.'

A Backwards Sort Of A Day

'Backwards?' suggested Friday.

'It's almost like everythin's goin'...' said Polly.

'It's true,' said Friday. 'But what is it? I can't quite put my finger on it.'

'Hold on a minute,' frowned Polly. 'Somethin's not quite right.'

Friday found disagreeing with things quite disagreeable.

'It is indeed,' agreed Friday, who liked

visit our good friend Alan Taylor up at his school on Boaster's Hill because he might have an idea what's going on and anyway it's a nice day for walking up hills and I could do with the exercise because Mrs Lovely says I'm getting a little bit portly around the belly area, which is the part of the body between your legs and your face.'

'Yeah, that's it!' exclaimed Polly as a golden-brown leaf flew up from the ground and attached itself to a tree. 'Frides, what's a-goin' on?'

what's a-goin' on?' she asked.

'That was a well long sentence what Friday just said,' thought Polly.

'Well, little miss,' said Friday, scratching his nose thoughtfully with an electronic nose-scratcher made from the leg of Hercules. 'I know all about the mysteries of time and space but I've never seen anything like this before, not in all my years, and to be honest I'm rather confused and a little bit worried, so perhaps we should go and

After a while they were quite near the top.

They weren't anywhere near the top.

It was a long walk to the top.

So off they started, up Boaster's Hill.

'Oh, I expect so,' said Friday. 'He is a headmaster after all. And headmasters know everything, like the names of famous blackcurrants and how many grains of rice there are in the sky. Come on, Polly – let's start walking.'

'Frides, do you think Alan Taylor will know

coming out to meet them. 'I'm glad you're here. What on earth's going on?'

'!PEEHC' said a bird, flying backwards through the air.

'I does hope Alan Taylor knows what's a-goin' on,' said Polly as they saw 𝕾𝖆𝖎𝖓𝖙 𝕻𝖙𝖊𝖗𝖔𝖉𝖆𝖈𝖙𝖞𝖑'𝖘 𝕾𝖈𝖍𝖔𝖔𝖑 𝖋𝖔𝖗 𝖙𝖍𝖊 𝕻𝖔𝖔𝖗 gleaming in the sunshine on the top of the hill.

And eventually they were at the top.

Then they were very near the top.

'I said it's really rather interesting, isn't it?'

'What?' said Friday, who hadn't really been listening.

'Yes,' said Polly.

'No, absolutely no idea, I'm afraid,' said Alan Taylor, his electric muscles whirring cheerfully. 'But it's really rather interesting, isn't it?'

'Oh,' said Polly. 'We was a-hopin' you could tell us.'

'Polly! Friday!' cried little Alan Taylor,

'BARK!' said Jake and everyone laughed to see that Polly had been right.

'I bet Jakey's gonna bark in a second,' said Polly.

'Oh, look, here comes Jake!' cried Polly, who loved Jake the dog more than any other dog in the world, even that one on TV who can talk.

'Forget it,' said Alan Taylor.

'What?' said Friday. 'Sorry, I didn't hear you that time either.'

'A old silver pocket-watch from the Victorian days what was ruled over by Queen Victorian!' she exclaimed.

Alan Taylor jumped out of Jake's mouth and handed the spit-covered object to Polly.

'What a lovely dog he is!' said Alan Taylor, climbing inside Jake's mouth and stroking his tongue affectionately. 'Hey, what's this I've found in here?'

'Oh, no!' said Polly. 'Frides, you was meant to wind it *forwards*! But you jus' gone an' wound it backwards even faster, you silly!'

So Friday took out a little key and wound up the silver pocket-watch and everyone waited to see what would happen.

'Could it somehow be controllin' Time itself?' said Polly in excitement.

'And look,' said Friday. 'It's running backwards! The hands are moving the wrong way!'

THE END

'We'll fix it in a minute,' laughed Alan Taylor as a nearby sparrow turned into a dinosaur. 'But not just yet – this is the coolest thing I've ever seen in my life!'

'Oops,' said Friday as they sat there watching the trees turning into seeds, the passers-by turning into ancient Romans and the sun setting and rising over and over again.

12 More on Grids   80
    Tutorial puzzles

13 The Basic Advanced Cryptic Crossword   91
    Barred grids in advanced crosswords, Tutorial puzzles

14 Advanced Clues   99
    The moving letter(s), The substituted letter(s), Alternate letters,
    The missing-words charade, The subtractive container-and-
    contents, The composite anagram, Tutorial puzzles

15 Special Crosswords   108
    Printer's Devilry, Misprints, Playfair, Letters latent, The Common
    Theme, Theme and Variations, Carte Blanche, Right and Left,
    Definition and Letter-Mixture, Wrong Number, Other Specials,
    Tutorial puzzles

16 Crossword Competitions   132
    Ximenes, Azed

17 Crossword Setting: a Case Study   140
    Filling the Grid, The Across Clues, The Down Clues, The Complete
    Puzzle, Postscript on Computers, Tutorial puzzle

18 The Complete Cruciverbalist: Solver, Setter, Editor   148
    The Complete Solver, Ten Tips for Solvers, The Complete Setter,
    Ten Tips for Setters, The Crossword Editor, Ten Tips for Editors,
    The Social Dimension

19 The Use of Computers   157
    The computer revolution, Using the computer to set puzzles,
    Computer solving, The Internet, Are computers a threat?

20 A Crossword Romp   160
    Tutorial puzzles [Puzzles No. 37–90 plus introduction]

Solutions, Notes and Commentary   277
Appendix 1   317
    Some common indicators for one, two and three letters

Appendix 2   325
    Books on Crossword Theory and History, Dictionaries, Thesauruses
    and Crossword Dictionaries, Other information books, Crossword
    Cribs, Periodicals

Introduction to First Edition

This book is dedicated to the memory of my father, who must take much of the blame for my obsession with crossword puzzles. Chave Manley solved six puzzles a day (two each in the *Daily Mail*, the *Daily Express* and the *Daily Telegraph*) and one a week – usually on a Sunday afternoon – in the *Radio Times*. Until, that is, his son (with elder sister Jean's help) began filling the odd word in the 'small puzzle' of the *Express* and the 'quick crossword' of the *Telegraph*. By my teens I was hooked and was pestering my father to explain how the cryptic puzzles worked. Soon the back page of the school common-room *Times* was being inked in, and not long after I left school I made my crossword setting debut with the *London Evening News*, followed within 18 months by *Radio Times*. Then a few years later a whole new world opened up with the discovery of the *Observer's* Ximenes and *The Listener*.

Not everyone has a father – or even a close friend – to explain the mysteries of the cryptic crossword, but I know that there are many in the ranks of the would-be solvers. 'You need a twisted mind for crosswords,' they say wryly – or else they denounce crosswords as a 'waste of time' without sounding convincing about it. The fact is that you *do* need to twist your mind to solve any problem, but why not? 'Problem solving' is very much the fashion at the moment in the school curriculum. And there are, I believe, some real benefits in struggling with a good crossword: mental discipline and an increased vocabulary are two. But the benefits must not be overstated. Crosswords are primarily for fun, but isn't the swimming pool more enjoyable once you can swim?

Curiously, there have been very few books actually *about* crosswords; those that I know of are listed in the bibliography at the back. There is of course an insatiable demand for actual puzzles, and those who want a good selection should not be disappointed by the offerings in this book. My priority, though, has been to tutor the reader in the basic essentials *and* the essentials at the more advanced level. *Chambers 20th Century Dictionary* [now *The Chambers Dictionary*] has long been the basic 'word bible' for the advanced crossword solver, but there has been little written to explain the puzzles for which it is so necessary. I hope I am putting this right.

In this work I deal with the background to the crossword, followed by the basic cryptic puzzle (such as you would find in your daily newspaper), and finally the more advanced puzzle. The ways in which clues are constructed have been described in detail and so too has 'crossword language'; but this is in no sense a complete 'crib' for the lazy solver. My method, with its small tutorial puzzles, is essentially heuristic, and I want to encourage solvers to learn for themselves.

Dr Johnson may not have 'read books through' but my intention is that the complete novice should treat this particular book as a sequential course. Try the tutorial puzzles, and if you cannot finish them look up the answers and learn from the notes before moving on. Then by the time you get to Chapter 12 you should be ready to enjoy a cryptic each day in your daily paper. Many readers reach that stage and settle there quite happily. To them I say 'Buy a Chambers and try to stretch yourself a little further. There are further joys for you in store!'

I must thank all those who have made this book possible. Many fellow-setters and their crossword editors have been most generous in allowing me to reproduce their puzzles, and a list appears [now] on pp. xvii-xviii. My family allowed me to escape to the study for hours when domestic duties beckoned. Jonathan Crowther, Les May, Michael Holroyd and Alec Robins have all lent me interesting material; the Bodleian Library enabled me to track down some crosswords of yesteryear. Richard Palmer and Derek Arthur spotted numerous errors in the original script and made many useful suggestions for improvements. Micro Initiatives used the wonders of modern technology to computerise the diagrams and to word-process the MS. Catherine Schwarz of Chambers has been an encouraging and supportive editor. Making crosswords look good is no easy task when so many things can go wrong; I am grateful for the patient expertise shown by Jack Osborne, Production Director of Chambers. I can only hope that our efforts are not in vain. Whatever your current level of attainment I hope you will find something of benefit within these pages.

Don Manley
Oxford 1986

Introduction to Second Edition

A lot has happened to me and a lot has happened to crosswords since I wrote the first edition six years ago, so I am delighted to have the opportunity for an update. When I wrote before, I had many years of experience behind me but no regular work as a crossword setter. Since then I have written puzzles for *Today* (a brief spell writing clues only), *The Independent* (from there I moved to *The Independent on Sunday* every week), *The Times*, and *The Guardian* (where I have taken on the new pseudonym Pasquale). I also edit puzzles for the *Church Times* every week and continue with solving whenever possible. All this with a family and full-time job!

The advent of *The Independent* has increased the range of good daily puzzles and the Saturday Magazine puzzle has plugged a gap between the dailies and the so-called 'advanced' puzzles. Never has there been so much variety before. Solvers are spoilt for choice.

In the press and on radio and TV the profile of crosswords and cross-worders has been raised quite distinctly. That great Ximenes and Azed clue-writer Colin Dexter named his two principal characters Inspector Morse and Sergeant Lewis after C.J. Morse and 'Mrs B. Lewis', two fellow clue-writers. The Inspector likes nothing better than listening to Wagner and solving a difficult crossword, so I wonder whether the successful TV series has led to as many people tackling crosswords as taking up an interest in classical music. In one episode, Morse clutched a *Listener* while visiting a lady of ill repute, and in that same episode one Edward Manley perpetrated two murders. *The Listener*, alas, is no more, but we can be thankful that *The Listener*'s crossword has been resurrected in *The Times* every Saturday.

With so many new puzzles appearing, I have sought to change several of the puzzles in the first edition. Of the original 80, I have removed some old ones and added several new ones, giving a net gain of four puzzles. As before, I have worked on the principle that I should contribute half of the puzzles.

In reading through the first edition, I quickly became aware of how some of my attitudes have changed over six years and how much I missed out last time. I am still firmly a 'Ximenean' (you will get to know what this means) but realize, more than ever, that some issues regarding fair play are not so cut and dried. The successor to Ximenes, Azed, is still pondering over certain aspects of grammar in clues after 20 distinguished years with *The Observer*. I have given us lesser mortals a chance to see how he now views clues, especially in a new Chapter 17 with its 'further thoughts on fair play'.

The other major additions arise from my own day-to-day experience of crossword setting. Many people continue to ask me about how I set a cross-word, so I have followed the tradition of Ximenes and Alec Robins in their books of taking the reader through the process step by step. In my further experiences as a setter I have collected many extra resources, and these have been added to Appendix 2.

As before, I have so many people to thank. In addition to those mentioned in my earlier Introduction I want to mention Mrs Chris McHugh, who patiently interpreted the scribbled amendments to this edition and typed them on my Amstrad, Mrs Alfreda Blanchard who read the script for errors at manuscript stage, and Richard Jeffery who checked the proofs – and, of course, all those who have contributed the new puzzles. My wife (Susan) and children (Richard and Gilly) continue to give me an easy time with regard to domestic duties while the study is occupied evening after evening.

I hope this new paperback will open up a fascinating pastime to ever more folk than before.

Don Manley
Oxford 1992

Introduction to the Third Edition

When I had written the second edition I wondered whether there would ever be anything new to say in a third edition. In fact I have laid my script to rest this time feeling there is more to say than I shall ever manage.

The 1990s saw some interesting developments, among which was the increased use of the computer. I have made some attempt to cover this, but am aware that the Internet itself will offer the best prospects for explorers of that domain. But at least I have provided some starting-points.

Whatever the computer has brought—or may yet bring—crossword puzzling remains essentially a battle of wits between the setter and the solver centred on 'Crossword English' (as I have termed it in the *Chambers Crossword Dictionary*). Readers of previous editions will know that I am at heart a 'Ximenean', a crossword grammarian who likes to have particular rules in respect of how clues should be put together. Having said that, though, I have to admit that there are a number of grey areas and a number of rival views about what a proper 'Crossword Grammar' might be. I have tried to be fair to these views in this new edition.

In terms of crossword availability UK newspaper readers are more spoilt than ever, especially at the weekends. Since 1991 we have gained a Jumbo in *The Times* every Saturday and a special barred puzzle called 'Enigmatic Variations' in *The Sunday Telegraph* every week. Space does not allow us to include any of the Jumbos but I have included two 'EV' puzzles and several other new puzzles of the past decade besides. There is one worry, though—are enough of the up-and-coming generation catching on? Well, let's hope that this book will help them to.

Any author needs lots of helpers to turn a script into a handsome volume. My special thanks go to Elaine Higgleton and Una McGovern at Chambers Harrap who have encouraged me at each stage and Liz Bowler who (not content with deciphering my handwriting at work) has slaved over keying in many new pages of scribble at home. A particular acknowledgement is due to Ross Beresford who (as well as supplying me with his *Sympathy* software) pointed out that the Torquemada's surname was Mathers, not Mather, an error which I have perpetuated for far too long. And I have a belated thank you to offer my fellow Azed solver Professor Frank Palmer whose Penguin book *Grammar* I now see as the inspiration behind my structural analysis of cryptic clues.

As ever, I have a patient and long-suffering wife in Susan who continues to rescue me from spending too long in the study. It is to her that I dedicate this new edition.

Don Manley
Oxford 2001

Sources and Acknowledgements

The source of each puzzle is given below along with the copyright holder who gave permission (where appropriate). Every effort has been made to contact all copyright holders, but if there are any omissions we shall be glad to make amends at the earliest opportunity. Some puzzles have been slightly amended/corrected. My own puzzles are asterisked.

Crossword No.	Source	Permission given by
1	New York World	St. Louis Post-Dispatch
2	The Crossword Puzzle Book (First Series)	Simon & Schuster
3–5	London Evening News*	London Express News and Features
6	The Independent*	Newspaper Publishing plc
7	Crossword	Crossword Club/ Carroll Mayers
8	Sunday Telegraph	The Sunday Telegraph
9	Daily Telegraph	The Daily Telegraph
10–16	Specially set for this book*	—
17	Games and Puzzles*	—
18	The Independent*	Newspaper Publishing plc
19	Hamlyn Book of Crosswords No. 1*	—
20	The Independent on Sunday*	Newspaper Publishing plc
21	Hamlyn Book of Crosswords No. 4*	—
22	Oxford Times*	Oxford & County Newspapers
23	Church Times Crosswords*	The Canterbury Press Norwich
24–28	Specially set for this book*	—
29–30	Games and Puzzles*	—
31	Specially set for this book*	—
32	The Spectator*	The Spectator
33	Crossword*	Crossword Club
34–36	Observer	The Observer
37	The Word Square Puzzle Book	Hamlyn Publishing
38	Observer	The Observer
39	Sunday Companion	—

40	*Daily Telegraph*	The Daily Telegraph
41	*Radio Times**	Radio Times
42–43	*The Times (43*)*	The Times / Wm Collins
44	*Guardian*	The Guardian
45	*Observer*	The Observer
46	*The Independent**	Newspaper Publishing plc
47–48	*Financial Times*	*Financial Times*
49	*Guardian*	The Guardian
50	*Birmingham Evening Mail**	The Birmingham Post & Mail
51	*Sunday Express*	London Express News and Features Services
52–54	*Quiz Digest**	Quality Puzzle Magazine
55	*Tough Puzzles**	Quality Puzzle Magazine
56	*Armchair Crosswords*	Penguin Books
57	*Observer*	The Observer
58–59	*The Independent on Sunday*	Newspaper Publishing plc
60	*Sunday Times*	The Sunday Times
61	*Observer*	The Observer
62–63	*Sunday Telegraph (63*)*	The Sunday Telegraph
64–65	*Games and Puzzles**	—
66–67	*The Independent (67*)*	Newspaper Publishing plc
68	*New York Magazine*	New York Magazine / Stephen Sondheim
69	*Atlantic Monthly*	*Atlantic Monthly*
70	*Games and Puzzles*	Eric Chatterly
71	*New Statesman*	New Statesman
72–75	*The Listener*	BBC publishing
76*	*The Times* Listener	The Times
77–80	*The Listener*	BBC publishing
81–82	*The Times* Listener	The Times
83–85	*Observer*	The Observer
86	*Crossword**	Crossword Club
87–88	*Observer*	The Observer
89–90	*The Azed Book of Crosswords (89*)*	Jonathan Crowther

Thanks are also due to *The Guardian* for permission to reproduce the puzzle*
in chapter 17, *The Observer* and Colin Dexter for the poem about Ximenes,
and Jonathan Crowther for permission to quote from the Azed slips.

About the author

Don Manley has been setting crosswords since he was a teenager. He sets for a number of national newspapers under the pseudonyms Duck, Pasquale, Quixote, and Giovanni, and is also the crossword editor of *The Church Times*. He has made a specialist study of cryptic clues and won several national clue-writing competitions. Between crosswords he finds time for his family in Oxford and manages a day job in educational publishing.

The Crossword Emerges

Before the crossword

The Victorian age is commonly portrayed in terms of unmitigated gloom; and yet it was also an age of fun and invention, and certainly it was the age of the word puzzle. In 1892 you might have bought *Everybody's Illustrated Book of Puzzles* (selected by a certain Don Lemon) for 6d. That Don of yesteryear offered you 794 puzzles complete with answers, and if we look at a few we shall see hints of what was to come when the crossword emerged in the twentieth century:

No. 6.—Anagrams

For the benefit of very young readers we will explain that making an anagram consists in forming a new word or words from the letters of other words. An illustration is: Cheer sick lands—the anagram for Charles Dickens. We now invite you, with the permission of Good Housekeeping, to an anagrammatical Dickens party, the guests of which are prominent characters in Dickens' writing: Blame Crumple; We debtor to toys; Clever fop I did pad; Pair my ages; His by a linen clock; Toy lily blows; Canny Skyes; Mere Walls; O, feel my corn bed; We kill red vics; Over it wilts; Bug ran by dear.

No. 200.—Double Acrostic

Two words are here to be found out,
Both you have heard of, I've no doubt;
One is a thing that gives its aid
To ships engaged in peaceful trade.
The other thing is often found
The war's chief weapon closely bound.
These stars replace with letters true,
And both the things will look at you.
In the first letters, downwards read,
Is that by which the vessel's sped;
And in the last, if downwards spelt,
That which adorns the soldier's belt.

Ist line— What a bull does, if he can.
2nd line— What is the most beauteous span.
3d line— Hog in armor is my third.
4th line— Boy in barracks often heard.
5th line— What the street boys often run.
6th line— What gives light, not like the sun.
7th line— What makes doctors oft despair.
8th line— What is black, with curly hair.
9th line— What is very hard to bear.

```
    *       *       *       *
  *   *   *   *   *   *
  * * * * * * * * * *
  *   *   *   *   *   *
  *   *   *   *   *   *
    *       *       *       *
  * * * * * * * * * *
    *       *       *       *
    *       *       *       *
```

The word square was so well established that it evidently didn't need a diagram to explain it, but just in case you don't know what one looks like, here is the puzzle followed by its answer:

No. 420.—Easy Squares.

(a) I. Crippled. 2. Hot and dry. 3. A deposit of mineral. 4. Paradise.

(b) I. An article of food that appears early on the bill of fare. 2. To glance sideways. 3. A Turkish soldier. 4. The plural of an article used in writing.

(a) **LAME**   (b) **SOUP**
ARID   **OGLE**
MINE   **ULAN**
EDEN   **PENS**

Some of the puzzles are even given titles like the one below, but this is not yet the true crossword:

No. 541.—Cross Word Enigma.
My first is in cotton, but not in silk;
My second in coffee, but not in milk;

My third is in wet, but not in dry;
My fourth is in scream, but not in cry;
My fifth is in lark, but not in sparrow;
My sixth is in wide, but not in narrow;
My seventh in pain, but not in sting;
My whole is a flower that blooms in spring.

Anagrams, acrostics and word squares had in fact been going since the times of the Greeks, the Romans, the Hebrews, and the medieval monks. You may like to know, for example, that Psalm 119 was an acrostic based on the Hebrew alphabet. But the most remarkable word square from ancient times is the 'reversible' one found on a Roman site at Cirencester:

```
R O T A S
O P E R A
T E N E T
A R E P O
S A T O R
```

which is Latin for 'The sower Arepo controls the wheels with force' and which can be rearranged in 'crossword' form as:

```
            A
            P
            A
            T
            E
            R
A PATERNOSTER O
            O
            S
            T
            E
            R
            O
```

'Could this be an early Christian crossword with A for alpha and O for omega?' some have asked. But enough of ancient history, fascinating though it is. The fact remains that the Victorians (for all their ingenuity) remained 'stuck' at a certain level, and so it was that the crossword *per se* took longer to emerge than Einstein's theory of relativity!

The earliest crosswords

It was in 1913 that a certain Arthur Wynne produced the puzzle below for the *New York World*.

CROSSWORD No. 1

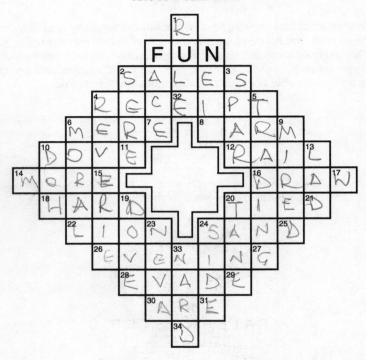

2-3	What bargain hunters enjoy
4-5	A written acknowledgement
6-7	Such and nothing more
10-11	A bird
14-15	Opposed to less
18-19	What this puzzle is
22-23	An animal of prey
26-27	The close of a day
28-29	To elude
30-31	The plural of is
8-9	To cultivate
12-13	A bar of wood or iron
16-17	What artists learn to do
20-21	Fastened
24-25	Found on the seashore
10-18	The fibre of the gomuti palm
6-22	What we all should be
4-26	A day dream
2-11	A talon
19-28	A pigeon
F-7	Part of your head
23-30	A river in Russia
1-32	To govern
33-34	An aromatic plant
N-8	A fist
24-31	To agree with
3-12	Part of a ship
20-29	One
5-27	Exchanging
9-25	To sink [Sunk?] in mud
13-21	A boy

Wynne, an immigrant from Liverpool, remained a leading crossword setter for about ten years, and then (sad to say) he faded into obscurity.

It wasn't until the 1920s that crosswords took off in a really big way. Messrs Simon and Schuster launched an amazingly successful publishing company in America and their *Cross Word Puzzle Book* was published in England by Hodder and Stoughton (a copy of which I purchased second-hand in the 1960s for 6d!). The book begins with a detailed account of how to do a crossword. For the benefit of my one reader who has never seen any crossword and the entertainment of the others here is how the book started:

THE CROSS WORD PUZZLE BOOK
FIRST SERIES

Cross word puzzles are a great deal simpler to explain than to solve. And as the quickest and clearest way to explain any game is by demonstration, let us do a typical, if rather easy, example together.

Here is the puzzle:

[CROSSWORD No. 2]

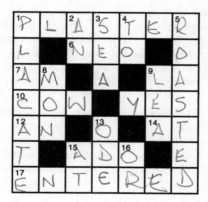

HORIZONTAL
1 A pasty composition
6 Prefix, meaning new
7 Exist
9 Sixth note of the musical scale
10 A domestic animal
11 Affirmative particle
12 Indefinite article
14 In
15 Fuss
17 Went into

VERTICAL
1 Pacify
2 Indefinite article
3 Large body of water
4 Toward
5 Cooked before a fire
8 Male human being
9 Meadow
13 Short poem
15 Near
16 Alternative

All the puzzles are not the same square shape as this, but all have one thing in common: the black squares among the white make a symmetrical pattern, so that the whole looks like a piece of cross-stitch needlework, as for instance an old-fashioned 'sampler'.

What have we to do?

Each white square represents a single letter. The puzzle is—to find out what letter belongs in each white square. And you determine this by working out the words from the definitions, which you will see beside the puzzle. When you have completed the puzzle correctly you will find that it consists of a number of words *which read both horizontally and vertically*, interlocking round the pattern made by the black squares.

You will notice numbers in many of the white squares, corresponding to numbers in the lists of 'horizontals' and 'verticals'. These show the starting-points of words, sometimes a horizontal word (e.g. 6), sometimes a vertical word (e.g. 2), sometimes both horizontal and vertical words (e.g. I). Each word starts in the first space to the *right* of a black square if it is a horizontal, and in the first space *below* a black square if it is a vertical. Some words of both kinds of course start on the outside squares, i.e., we imagine a ring of black squares all round the puzzle.

We now know where the words begin. How long are they to be? Each will consist of just as many letters, one letter to a square, as it will take to reach the next black square (or the edge of the puzzle where no black square intervenes) in whichever direction we are going. For example, 'I horizontal' will be 7 letters long, and so will 'I vertical'. But '6 horizontal' will have only 3 letters; '2 vertical' will have only 2 letters; '7 horizontal' will have only 2 letters; and '13 vertical' will have 3: and so on.

Sometimes a letter will come between two blacks in the pattern. In this case it will only be used in making one word, either a horizontal or a vertical one: for instance, the last letter of '3 vertical' or the first of '13 vertical'. But generally a letter has got to fit into two words—one horizontal and one vertical. For instance, the second letter of '6 horizontal' must also be right for the second letter of '3 vertical'.

And then the fun begins.

Now let us work out this puzzle. (It's a very simple one; you won't have such an easy time again, I warn you!). Start with 'I horizontal'.

'A pasty composition'. How many letters? Seven—since there is no black square right the way across the top line. 'A pasty composition' of seven letters? Let us try PLASTER. (Write it in lightly. You'll soon find you need india-rubber at this game.)

Now is this the right word? We can soon find out; for if it is the right word, it has given us some splendid clues for no less than five of our 'verticals' (I-5).

¹P	L	²A	³S	⁴T	E	⁵R
	■	6			■	
7	8	■			9	
10			■			
12		■	13	■	14	
	■	15		16	■	
17						

What about 'vertical I'? 'Pacify', seven letters beginning (apparently) with 'P'. How about PLACATE? Yes, it fits. Write it in lightly. One check is not enough. But we can soon get proof positive that we are on the right track. For it looks as if '2 vertical', which as you see has two letters only (and therefore ought to be easy to guess), ought to begin with 'A'.

What is '2 vertical'? 'Indefinite article'. Obviously AN. It fits, and it begins with 'A'. Write it in. But we can check again. For '3 vertical' presumably begins with 'S'. It has three letters. It is a 'large body of water'. Exultantly, we write in SEA.

And so it goes on. You may like to note incidentally that the practice of putting the number of letters in brackets after a clue had not yet been introduced.

Newspapers also latched on to crosswords in the 1920s, and by 1930 crosswords were commonplace. Indeed dictionaries were torn apart in libraries, worries were expressed about eyesight, and crosswords were increasingly regarded as an 'unsociable habit' (how little times have changed!). One of the developments in the twenties and thirties was the big-money puzzle with alternative answers. A clue might be offered as follows:

[I.I]   A yellow addition to your food (7)

with a corresponding answer in the diagram printed as:

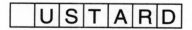

Solvers were invited to use their skill to choose between MUSTARD and CUSTARD and see if they could reach the same set of answers as the panel of experts. Lotteries like this thrived in *Titbits* and other magazines until well after the Second World War, but they have little appeal for the true aficionado, so we can forget them without further mention.

Definition-type puzzles

This book is mostly about *cryptic* crosswords, those puzzles that offer more than plain definitions for their clues. Before we get to these, however, we shall have look at some modern *definition-type* puzzles, starting with three of my own from London's *Evening News*. Contributors in the 1960s were exhorted to avoid proper nouns, foreign words, abbreviations, and two-letter words. Although the clues are largely plain definitions, there is a hint of the cryptic in the clues to 34 across of No. 3, 3 down of No. 4 and 10 across of No. 5. These are examples of the double definition clue which we shall be looking at in Chapter 3.

CROSSWORD No. 3

By D. F. Manley from the *London Evening News*

ACROSS
1 Wicket (5)
5 Fragrance (5)
9 Apartments (5)
10 Impel (4)
12 Fool (5)
13 Not total (7)
15 Quick look (4)
17 Retinue (4)
18 Den (4)
19 Machine (5)
22 Set (3)
23 Obliterate (5)
26 Love intensely (5)
28 Regulations (5)
31 Signify assent (3)
32 Mount (5)
34 Only a fish? (4)
35 Cask (4)
37 Warbled (4)
39 Settle (7)
41 Hair (5)
42 Detect (4)
43 Salute (5)
44 Music time? (5)
45 Tendency (5)

DOWN
1 Odd (8)
2 Fervidly hot (8)
3 Cringe (5)
4 Sharpener (4)
5 Snake (3)
6 Subdued grumbling (6)
7 Song (4)
8 Valley (4)
11 Wins (5)
14 Fitting (3)
16 Trudge (4)
20 Expiate (5)
21 Attention (4)
22 Hold out (4)
24 Annul (8)
25 Widened (8)
27 Poles (4)
29 Supplant (5)
30 Landed property (6)
33 Instigate (3)
34 Show contempt (5)
35 Sun-bathe (4)
36 Run (4)
38 Encourage (4)
40 Personality (3)

CROSSWORD No. 3

CROSSWORD No. 4

By D. F. Manley from the *London Evening News*

ACROSS

1 Prize vessels (4)
4 Posters (8)
10 Ratify (7)
11 Too (4)
12 Opening (8)
15 Spy on (4)
16 Tidier (6)
17 Image (4)
19 Unit of work (3)
20 Tended (6)
22 One of two (6)
26 Epoch (3)
27 Before (3)
28 Grease (6)
31 Traps (6)
33 Shed (3)
34 Speech impediment (4)
35 Fame (6)
38 Passage (4)
39 Temperature line on map (8)
41 Deserve (4)
42 Absconding (7)
43 Costs (8)
44 Cliques (4)

DOWN

1 Instrument (8)
2 Concerning shepherds (8)
3 Eating clubs? (6)
4 Blabbed (6)
5 Cut off (3)
6 Vindicate (7)
7 Cover with wax (4)
8 Disorderly flight (4)
9 Prophet (4)
13 Biting (4)
14 Venerates (7)
18 Clergymen (7)
21 Individuality (3)
23 Particle charged electrically (3)
24 Something transmitted from ancestors (8)
25 Answers (8)
29 Awkward boor (4)
30 Circular frames (6)
31 Tramples (6)
32 Foreigners (6)
35 Fully developed (4)
36 Ceremony (4)
37 Next (4)
40 Small deer (3)

CROSSWORD No. 4

CROSSWORD No. 5

By D. F. Manley from the *London Evening News*

ACROSS

1 Little scamps! (4)
3 Swellings (8)
10 A rope for the artist? (7)
11 Employer (4)
14 Came back (8)
15 Lowest point (5)
16 Stupid (5)
17 Apartments (4)
20 Estranged (9)
21 Dance (3)
23 Weights (4)
24 The truth (4)
25 Work unit (3)
26 Shopkeeper (9)
28 Arrive (4)
30 Performers (5)
33 Goods (5)
34 Lengthen (8)
36 Female (4)
37 Simpleton (7)
38 Sideboards (8)
39 Platform (4)

DOWN

1 Flood (8)
2 Depositing as security (8)
3 Room for a drink? (3)
4 Spoke falsely (4)
5 Pecuniary stakes (9)
6 Stupefy (4)
7 Smooth and concise (5)
8 Bird (4)
9 Flank (4)
12 Tars (7)
13 Ascents (5)
18 Grassland (9)
19 Flower-clusters (7)
21 Unbroken view (8)
22 Demands upon energy (8)
24 Pertaining to central point (5)
27 Extra payment (5)
29 Metal (4)
30 Cupola (4)
31 Incites (4)
32 Excitement (4)
35 Printer's measures (3)

CROSSWORD No. 5

All newspapers carry definition-type puzzles. The Quick Crossword in *The Daily Telegraph* is noted for its pun formed by the first two across answers, a pleasing gimmick picked up by *The Independent* as the next puzzle (also one of mine) shows.

CROSSWORD No. 6

Concise by Quixote from *The Independent*

ACROSS

1 Parrot's name (5)
4 OT book (6)
9 Towed vehicle (7)
10 Keepsake (5)
11 Require (4)
12 Confidential (7)
13 Insect (3)
14 Asterisk (4)
16 Conceal (4)
18 Drunkard (3)
20 Embankment (7)
21 Blemish (4)
24 Tree (5)
25 Salad plant (7)
26 Ridicule (6)
27 Spy (5)

DOWN

1 Obvious (6)
2 Depart (5)
3 US university (4)
5 Undiluted (8)
6 The Netherlands (7)
7 Projectile (6)
8 Rubbish (5)
13 Short rest (8)
15 Storm (7)
17 Investigates (6)
18 Manner (5)
19 Silver (6)
22 Lacking polish (5)
23 Covered walk (4)

CROSSWORD No. 6

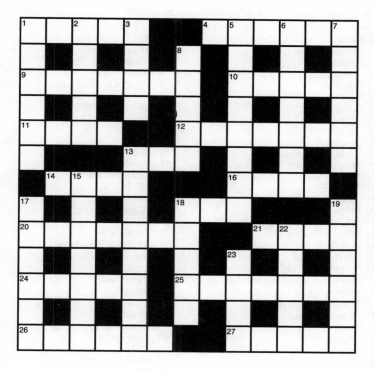

In America there are still many more definition-type puzzles than cryptics, and Puzzle 7 is a typical example. You will notice that *every* letter belongs to an across answer and a down answer so in theory you need only solve half the clues. However, you may well find that your lack of knowledge about such a thing as Indonesian coinage and Thomas Tryon's works forces you to look at nearly all the clues!

CROSSWORD No. 7

By Amigo from *Crossword*

ACROSS

1 Coarse Algae
5 Mistake
10 Pardon me!
14 Situs
15 Scene
16 Unaspirated
17 Columbus, e g
19 Ionian Sea gulf
20 Unsound
21 Indonesian coin
22 The abomasum
23 Vehemence
25 Oppose
26 Stud
30 Scion
31 Washington State port city
34 Gracefully delicate
36 Sea duck
38 Healthy
39 US Foreign Policy goals: F D Roosevelt congressional message, 1941 (phrase)
42 Chief Babylonian god
43 Film actor and director: _____ Davis
44 Peepshow
45 Stoat
47 Anchor tackle
49 Tableland
50 Hindu mantras
51 Matrons
53 Corrupt
55 Entangle
56 Bruits
61 Baltic Sea gulf
62 Criticize
64 Hebrew month
65 Impassive
66 Gottfried's sister
67 Confined
68 Import
69 Arabian tribesman

DOWN

1 Moslem judge
2 Emerald Isle
3 Minus
4 South American rodent
5 Jewish ceremonial vessels
6 Surface measure
7 Prosopopeia
8 Grimace
9 Merit
10 Visigoth king
11 Previously
12 Grafted: Her.
13 Metheglin
18 Cape Horn native
24 Activists
25 Peeler
26 Immerse
27 Thomas Tryon novel: *The* _____
28 Calliope
29 Thor's wife
31 Finial
32 Classical dramatic farces
33 Bewildered
35 Nocturnal carnivores
37 Imagine
40 Custom
41 Weir
46 Disclose
48 Bridge hand
51 Italian poet
52 Divot
53 Swathe
54 Assistant
55 Assemble
57 Lawyers' patron saint
58 Vend
59 Irish Gaelic
60 Wound
63 Notes: Mus.

CROSSWORD No. 7

There is an immediate difference noticeable between this and the plain British puzzle: obscure words (including proper nouns), abbreviations and prefixes are all OK. In fact you might even expect to find clues such as 'Room to swing _____ ' (with the answer A CAT!).

Quiz and general knowledge puzzles

People who enjoy quizzes often enjoy clues which depend on knowledge that may not be found in an everyday dictionary. A clue like the one below (from *The Daily Telegraph* of 25 May 1967) is one which will send many happily scurrying to a dictionary of quotations:

[1.2] 'Has, having, and in quest to have, _____ ' (Shakespeare Sonnets) (7)

Did you know that the answer is EXTREME? If you didn't know, you might have worked it out from E _T_ E _ E.

This is a *quotation clue*, which could be regarded as a particular type of *quiz clue* or *general knowledge clue*. Here is another quiz clue, which relies on the solver's general knowledge:

[1.3] Wife of Ahab, King of Israel (7)

You probably won't need a concordance to arrive at JEZEBEL.

General knowledge puzzles have become increasingly popular in recent years, offering families an opportunity to take down an otherwise little-used atlas from the bookshelf. We conclude this chapter with a puzzle from *The Sunday Telegraph*. As with most general knowledge puzzles there are many proper nouns in the answers—and that atlas could be useful.

CROSSWORD No. 8

ACROSS

1 Small group acting within a larger group (6)
4 Dorset port and seaside resort (8)
8 Fine parchment prepared from animal skin (6)
9 Rare flightless New Zealand rail (8)
10 Plant of the ginger family used in making curry powder (8)
11 Any doxology that begins with this word (6)
12 Japanese dish of very thinly sliced meat, vegetables and seasonings (8)
13 Any of the 50 sea-nymphs who were daughters of a Greek sea-god (6)
15 Samuel's mother (OT) (6)
18 Float supporting one in the water (8)
20 _____ Currie, former MP (6)
21 Traveller in a hot-air balloon (8)
23 Species of shrike with black-and-white plumage and a reddish-brown crown (8)
24 _____ Town, non-League town with a reputation for giant-killing (6)
25 Person picking or harvesting flowers or fruit (8)
26 Ivy genus of the Aralia family (6)

CROSSWORD No. 8

DOWN

1 Small cat-like carnivore (5)
2 Nationality of a native of Bogotá (9)
3 Region of ancient Palestine (7)
4 Measurement of the cooling effect of moving air (4-5, 6)
5 Long, usually curved, Turkish dagger (7)
6 Deprive of strength or resolution (7)
7 The business of a farmer (9)

12 Fishing port on an inlet of the Baltic in northern Germany (9)
14 Legendary English outlaw during reign of Richard I (5, 4)
16 Sir Henry _____, poet, author of "Drake's Drum" (7)
17 Moorland shrub with purple flowers (7)
19 Frederick _____, author of "The Day of the Jackal" (7)
22 City with two universities in NE Oklahoma (5)

2

The Basic Crossword Grid

Checked and unchecked squares

Although the clueless crossword above is very simple we can use it to define certain terms:

1. The letters C, T, W and N are in squares that belong to both across and down answers. These are called *checked squares*.

2. The letters A, O, E and I belong to only one answer each and these are in *unchecked squares* or *unches*.

3. The words CAT, WIN, COW and TEN are of course the *answers*. When you come to solve a more difficult puzzle with its own instructions you may come across a word that denotes the answers as they appear on the diagram. That word is *lights*. Unfortunately this term is also used to refer to individual letters within words (as C, A, T, O, E, W, I, N here). The particular meaning is usually obvious from the context, but I now avoid using 'lights' wherever possible.

4. The central square is a blank and the whole crossword has a *blocked diagram* or, as we might also say in crossword parlance, a *blocked grid*.

All the puzzles in Chapter 1 were on blocked grids and for most of the puzzles there was a high level of what we might call *checking*. In Puzzle 7 the checking was in fact 100%.

04 dope, drug, foil, grab, nick, take	(Richard), **Laue** (Max Theodor Felix von),
05 bribe, catch, check, get at, pinch, seize, steal, swipe	**Mann** (Thomas), **Mott** (Sir Nevill Francis), **Néel** (Louis Eugène Félix), **Rabi**
06 arrest, buy off, collar, defeat, hinder, pilfer, snitch, thwart	(Isidor Isaac), **Ross** (Sir Ronald), **Rous** (Peyton), **Shaw** (George Bernard), **Ting**
07 disable, warn off	(Samuel Chao Chung), **Todd** (Alexander,
08 knock off, threaten	Lord), **Tutu** (Desmond), **Urey** (Harold
09 frustrate, hamstring, influence	Clayton), **Whit** (Patrick), **Wien** (Wilhelm),
10 intimidate	**Yang** (Chen Ning)
12 incapacitate	05 **Agnon** (Shmuel Yosef), **Aston** (Francis
13 interfere with	William), **Bethe** (Hans Albrecht), **Black**

Nobel Prize

▶ *Names of Nobel Prize winners:*
- 02 **Fo** (Dario), **O** (Kenzaburo)
- 03 **Lee** (Tsung-Dao), **Paz** (Octavio)
- 04 **Belo** (Carlos), **Berg** (Paul), **Best** (Charles Herbert), **Bohr** (Niels Henrik David), **Bll** (Heinrich), **Born** (Max), **Buck** (Pearl Sydenstricker), **Cela** (Camilo José), **Cori** (Carl Ferdinand), **Dale** (Sir Henry Hallett), **Duve** (Christian René de), **Gide** (André), **Hess** (Victor Francis), **Hess** (Walter Rudolf), **Hume** (John), **Katz** (Sir Bernard), **Koch** (Robert), **Kuhn**

(Sir James Whyte), **Bloch** (Felix), **Bosch** (Carl), **Bovet** (Daniel), **Bragg** (Sir Lawrence), **Bragg** (Sir William Henry), **Braun** (Ferdinand), **Bunin** (Ivan), **Camus** (Albert), **Chain** (Sir Ernst Boris), **Crick** (Francis Harry Compton), **Curie** (Marie), **Curie** (Pierre), **Debye** (Peter Joseph Wilhelm), **Dirac** (Paul Adrien Maurice), **Doisy** (Edward Adelbert), **Eliot** (Thomas Stearns), **Esaki** (Leo), **Euler** (Ulf Svante von), **Fermi** (Enrico), **Gabor** (Dennis), **Golgi** (Camillo), **Grass** (Gnter), **Haber** (Fritz), **Hesse** (Hermann), **Hubel** (David Hunter), **Klerk** (Frederik

An extract from *Chambers Crossword Dictionary* which might be handy for a general knowledge puzzle.

Now look at the puzzle below:

Here the checked squares contain C, T, O, E, W and N, and the unchecked squares contain A, R and I. Letters are kept apart by a bar rather than a block and this is known as a *barred diagram* or *barred grid*.

Most crosswords are in fact blocked puzzles, but the Small Crossword of *The Daily Express* is a definition-type puzzle with a barred grid. As we shall see, most advanced puzzles use barred grids, and the reasons for this will become clear later in the book.

Over the page is an early example of the plain, blocked puzzle. In fact it was the first crossword published in *The Daily Telegraph* on 30 July 1925, and you might like to have a go at it.

CROSSWORD No. 9

From the *Daily Telegraph* 1925

ACROSS

1 Author of 'Childe Harold'
5 Author of tales of mystery
8 Will reveal the hidden
13 Incursion
14 Elizabethan sea-rover
16 Lily
17 Succulent plant
18 Useful in haymaking
19 Nap
20 Where cricketers are trained
21 A distinguished order
22 Adverb
23 Chinese coin or weight
25 A seaside pleasure
28 Cut
30 Soothing; product of Gilead
34 A blemish except in a billiard ball
35 Shakespearian character
37 A word from the motto of the Garter
39 A seaside implement
40 Where Sir John Moore died
41 Travellers' haven
42 Selvage
44 Part of a ship
45 First name of famous American author
46 Unadulterated
47 Petition
48 Beverage
53 King of the Amalekites, who came 'delicately'
57 Military abbreviation
59 That is
60 A measure
63 Cromwell's 'Empty bauble'
64 Island home of an ancient civilisation
66 The germ of a building
67 A volcano
68 Guarded by eunuchs
69 Kind
70 Visionaries
71 Applied to anything perfect
72 A people with unalterable laws

DOWN

1 Often 'snatched from the burning'
2 A seat of learning is the key to this
3 Tumult
4 Poems
5 Bears the burden of youth
6 Tree
7 Supplements
9 Transported
10 Air (mus.)
11 An annual festival
12 A fish
14 Fall
15 Greek god of love
24 Mythical founder of a great Empire
25 Country of Europe
26 Not so well
27 Pronoun
28 Indian lemur
29 A district in South London
31 Conjunction
32 River of France
33 Can pick and strike
34 Note of octave
35 First name of famous Highland outlaw
36 Unit
38 An explosive
43 Thank you
45 Exist
49 A king, both first and sixth
50 A German word not used on Armistice night
51 Consider
52 Depressions
54 Bars and is often barred
55 A skin affliction
56 Changed by motorists
58 Rock
59 Also
60 Recess in a church
61 Lump
62 Would apply to the upper atmosphere
65 Before

CROSSWORD No. 9

B	Y	R	O	N		P	O	E			X	R	A	Y	S
R	A	I	D		D	R	A	K	E			A	R	U	M
A	L	O	E		R	A	K	E	R			P	I	L	E
N	E	T	S		O	M		S	O			T	A	E	L
D					P		R		S						T
	S	W	I	M		L	O	P		B	A	L	M		
S	P	O	T		R	O	M	E	O		S	O	I	T	
O	A	R		C	O	R	U	N	N	A			I	N	N
H	I	S	T		B	I	L	G	E			B	R	E	T
	N	E	A	T		S	U	E		B	E	E	R		
J					H		S		S						D
A	G	A	G		O	C		I	E		A	C	R	E	
M	A	C	E		C	R	E	T	E		P	L	A	N	
E	T	N	A		H	A	R	E	M		S	O	R	T	
S	E	E	R	S		G	E	M		M	E	D	E	S	

-OR-E

Opening up the grid

Was there anything you noticed about the grid for Crossword No. 9? The symmetry? Yes, of course—the grid would look the same if it were turned upside down, a feature we will notice in most grids. (This particular grid will also look the same if turned sideways and if reflected in a mirror.) But what else did you notice? What I noticed was that no sooner had I put a few words together than I came to a stop and had to start again. If you look at the grid carefully, you will see that there are in fact no less than nine crosswords all isolated from each other in the one square. This sort of thing wouldn't be too popular with crossword editors today because one of the requirements of a grid is that all the answers should be interconnected. Totally isolated parts won't do! Times change of course and when we look at p.31 of the *Daily Telegraph 50th Anniversary Crossword Book* we see the grid below from 1928 (a grid still used today incidentally).

When we come to p.172 you will see that the 1928 clues are slightly cryptic, but for the moment let's look at the grid and compare it with the grid for Crossword No. 9. Two features are notable:

(i) The average length of a solution has increased considerably and the number of clues has been reduced substantially. Two-letter solutions have gone, and we have four long solutions of 13 letters each. Crossword No. 9 has 82 clues; the puzzle three years later has only 32 clues.

(ii) In the 1925 puzzle nearly all the white squares are checked, whereas the 1928 puzzle shows a grid where alternate letters are checked. The 1925 puzzle has a 'closed' grid with lots of solid white; the 1928 grid has a latticed appearance, being a much more 'open' grid. In 1925 you had to solve barely more than half the clues to finish the puzzle; in 1928 you had to solve them all.

We will be looking again at grids in Chapter 12, and you will see that even the 1928 grid has its weaknesses, but for the moment let's recognize what an advance it is over the previous one.

That's enough on crossword grids for now. It's time to look again at clues. In fact, it's time to go cryptic.

3

Beyond the Simple Definition

Double definitions

The first *Daily Telegraph* puzzle (Crossword No. 9) had lots of short words of the type that quickly became hackneyed. The solver of the twenties must soon have realized that 'poems' = ODES, 'thank you' = TA, and 'before' = ERE. Yet even in this puzzle there is a hint of the cryptic in 2 down: 'A seat of learning is the key to this'. The setter is inviting us to think of Yale University and a Yale lock; and he has offered us something a little more interesting than 'An American university'. Now, as it happens, I don't find this a very sound clue because Yale University can't really be the key to a Yale lock—but the setter's heart was in the right place! The Yale clue has a descendant in the modern puzzle called the *double definition*.

An example of the double definition clue might be this:

[3.1] University name on key (4)

The answer is YALE because it is both a university and the name on certain keys. This may not be a very exciting clue, but it shows a degree of trickery absent from the plain clue. Had we wanted simply to offer two definitions on a plate we might have written 'University, name on key', but the omission of the comma is a legitimate trick and we might just be led astray for an instant to think of some poor Oxbridge undergraduate returning home after mid-night unable to enter his college.

Now here are some more examples of double definitions which you might like to try for yourselves:

[3.2] Broken part of body (4)

[3.3] Take notice of Gospel writer (4)

[3.4] Sombre mausoleum? (5)

[3.5] Tumblers producing spectacles (7)

The answers are BUST, MARK, GRAVE, and GLASSES. In [3.5] the two definitions are joined by a *linkword* 'producing'. This linkword helps the clue make sense, and it is justified because the word for 'tumblers' produces the word for 'spectacles'. More about linkwords in due course. Were you misled into thinking of the wrong meaning for tumblers and spectacles? Then you have been the victim of what I call the *misleading context*. The clue has provided you with a phrase about acrobats (the straightforward reading), but the *cryptic reading* has nothing to do with the circus: you are being given a coded (or cryptic) instruction to find a word with two meanings. Isn't that more interesting than 'Spectacles (7)'?

There is no reason why we should not string together a whole series of definitions, as the following clue shows:

[3.6] Left harbour gate bearing drink (4)

The solver may have visions of a sailor sloping off with his rum, but this is simply a series of five definitions for the word PORT.

The double definition can often be entertaining if one of the definitions is fanciful:

[3.7] Sad like the girl who's had a haircut? (10)

Here the answer is DISTRESSED, suggesting that this might mean having had tresses removed. Because this usage is fanciful the clue finishes with a question mark.

Here are two examples that yield phrases:

[3.8] Feeling very happy like the mountaineer who's climbed Everest? (2,3,2,3,5)

What phrase suggests that someone is either 'very happy' or at the highest point of Earth? Answer: ON TOP OF THE WORLD.

[3.9] Dismantle slate (4, 5)

Another misleading context, because 'slate' here means 'criticize', which like 'dismantle' means TAKE APART.

In the following clue one definition leads to a phrase and the other to a name:

[3.10] Footballer even more pleased than usual (8)

More than 'over the Moon'? 'Over Mars' of course. Marc OVERMARS was playing for Arsenal when I wrote this one.

Cryptic definitions

If it is possible to mislead with two definitions, it may also be possible to baffle the solver with a single *cryptic definition*. My children used to tease me with jokes like this: What do you take the lid off before putting the bottom on? This joke can be turned into a cryptic definition:

[3.11] You take the lid off it before putting the bottom on! (6)

Because this is an outrageous definition we allow ourselves an exclamation mark to warn the solver. The answer? TOILET!

Here's another one derived from a joke book:

[3.12] Will doing them make a scout or guide dizzy? (4,5)

Answer: GOOD TURNS.

We could perhaps define a SKINHEAD as follows:

[3.13] An extremely distressed youngster (8)

A definition such as:

[3.14] A letter demanding money for accommodation (8)

may suggest an unpleasant communication through the post until we remember that it is the LANDLORD (or LANDLADY) who lets out the accommodation. 'Letter' is one of a number of -er words often used in a misleading sense; you will meet others.

Here are some cryptic definitions, including one or two old chestnuts:

[3.15] A wicked thing (6)

[3.16] A jammed cylinder (5,4)

[3.17] Keen observer of gulls? (8)

[3.18] Presumably one doesn't run after it? (4,5)

[3.19] He was rushed almost from the start (5)

[3.20] 014? (6,5)

[3.21] Company car? (3-6)

[3.22] You won't necessarily see anyone till after this meal (10,5)

The answers to the last eight clues? CANDLE, SWISS ROLL, SWINDLER, LAST TRAIN, MOSES, DOUBLE AGENT (=2×007!), TWO-SEATER, and PLOUGHMAN'S LUNCH.

Notice how in [3.22] 'till' is a verb, not a preposition (*a misleading part of speech*).

The Times crossword has always been notable for its cryptic definitions. Here is one that gives the same answer as the last clue:

[3.23] What expert in share movement wants from the board (10,5)

And here are some, from *The Times* Jumbo, for long answers (which often have to rely on cryptic definitions if their clues are to be cryptic):

[3.24] Did he have spelling lessons? (3, 9, 10)

[3.25] Paper chain (10, 10)

[3.26] Honest but careless, these famous last words (7, 2, 4, 1, 4, 4, 1, 4)

[3.27] Factory skip? (7, 2, 8)

The answers are: THE SORCERER'S APPRENTICE, CONTINUOUS STATIONERY, FRANKLY MY DEAR I DON'T GIVE A DAMN (from *Gone With the Wind*), and CAPTAIN OF INDUSTRY.

Now you are invited to try a tutorial puzzle based on the ideas in this chapter.

CROSSWORD No. 10

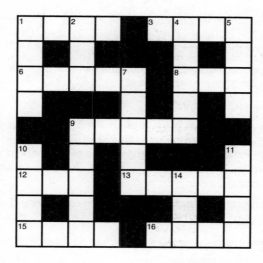

ACROSS
1 This girl is a ruddy gem (4)
3 Roasting device to sputter (4)
6 Marijuana? One notifies the police (5)
8 Six-footer working on a hill? (3)
9 Money for animal (5)
12 Beastly butter! (3)
13 Tree, one of greater age (5)
15 Red wine seen in the marquee perhaps (4)
16 Break? That will do for a card game (4)

DOWN
1 Newspapers showing student pranks (4)
2 Female supporter (3)
4 But it can also play forte! (5)
5 Lyle's partner is displayed in the gallery (4)
7 Parisian flower (5)
9 One like Brutus, upright type (5)
10 Ridge on the guitar may make you worry (4)
11 Holiday accident? (4)
14 Writer of this book, a studious type! (3)

4

The Anagram

From 'anag.' to anagram indicator

In Chapter 3 we saw how fiddling around with definitions could produce an element of 'crypticity' (if I may be allowed to coin a new word). But a word not only has a meaning—or more than one meaning—it has letters too, and these letters offer us many chances for word puzzling. One very popular way of indicating the letters is the anagram, and this is where we begin.

We are forty years on from Don Lemon and his book of puzzles, and we are looking at *The Daily Telegraph* crossword for 21 July 1932. Here is 7 down:

[4.1] 'Meet tired Pa' (anag.)

Although there are millions of ways of arranging these letters, it will only take a minute or two to come up with PREMEDITATE—and of course it may well prove easier if we already know some of the checked letters. Even so, there is something unsatisfactory about this clue because we aren't given any definition of the answer.

However, we must not be unfairly critical when considering clues of over 50 years ago—some progress has been made. The next clue appeared in 1947:

[4.2] Atom plaint farce (anag.) (Yet power can be controlled by it) (3, 2, 10)

This clue offers us an anagram and a definition—and it is a definition that tries to link up with the theme of the letters to be anagrammed (however vaguely!). The answer is ACT OF PARLIAMENT.

An improvement, yes, but this is still a bit on the clumsy side. How much more elegant is this 1973 *Telegraph* clue:

[4.3] Pure ice broken up for the fussy diner (7)

Here again we have an anagram but instead of ' (anag.)' we see the phrase 'broken up'. This phrase serves as an *anagram indicator*, telling us that the letters of 'pure ice' must be broken up to yield a word meaning 'fussy diner'. The answer is EPICURE.

In a 1960 puzzle we have this clue:

[4.4] Arrange to send port (6)

Here the anagram indicator is an imperative verb. We are told to arrange 'to send' so that we can get a word meaning 'port'. We've already seen that port has at least five meanings (p.27), and from the way the clue is worded we're probably thinking of an alcoholic Chrismas gift. In fact, however, the port is a harbour and the answer is OSTEND.

Anagram indicators are many and varied. Any words or phrases that indicate a jumbling of the letters will do, so long as the clues are grammatical and make sense: 'terribly', 'excited', 'mixed up' are all warnings to the solver that an anagram might be afoot. Now try this:

[4.5] Dicky came top (4)

Doubtless you will think of a clever boy called Richard who beat his class-mates in the examination. However, this is another example of the mislead-ing context because the *cryptic reading* of the clue has nothing whatever to do with a successful male. In the cryptic reading 'Dicky' is an adjective (not a proper noun) meaning shaky and shaky 'came' means an anagram of came. The answer therefore is ACME, meaning 'top'. Again we see an example of how a cryptic clue presents you with a series of words which are ostensibly about a particular theme, but you must ignore the theme and concentrate on the words as a series of cryptic instructions to lead you to the answer.

First steps in clue analysis

So far we have looked at two types of cryptic clue: the double definition and the anagram. In the following chapters we shall meet other types.

Before that, though, we are going to have a foretaste of 'clueology' to see how the coded instructions are put together. We are going to analyse all the bits and pieces that actually make up a cryptic clue and label them.

We shan't be doing this for *all* our clues, but if we do it now and then, you will see that there is some sense in the cryptic clue, even it it looks like gobblede-gook at first sight! Once you appreciate this, you will know what to look for in a clue when you try to solve it—and this is important.

Into clueology we go then, and first of all we take a look again at clue [4.3] and under its different parts you will see that I have placed some letters:

[4.3] Pure ice broken up for the fussy diner (7)

A stands for *anagram* and AI for *anagram indicator*. Together they form S, the *subsidiary indication*. L stands for *linkword* because it links the subsidiary indication to D, which is the *definition* (of EPICURE).

Already in the clues we have seen that A and AI can be the other way round and that L need not always exist, as is the case with:

[4.5] Dicky came top

Now it is also possible for D to come before S, as in this example:

[4.6] Fungus in a crag, I fancy

The linkword 'in' means 'consisting of' so we are being asked to find a fungus which consists of the six letters of 'a crag I' in a fancy way. The answer is AGARIC.

I hope you have enjoyed your introduction to clueology. What you now need to understand is that *the normal modern cryptic clue consists of a definition and subsidiary indication unless it is simply a cryptic definition.* An anagram is only one form of subsidiary indication, and we shall be looking at some others in the following chapters. In the meantime have fun with the puzzles below. Crossword No. 11 consists entirely of anagrams, so in each clue look out for the AI, the A and the D (and sometimes the L), Crossword No. 12 mixes in anagrams with the sorts of clue covered in Chapter 3. Sooner or later you will have to discern what type of clue the setter has laid before you. At this stage you should be able to recognize a few of the tell-tale signs, but as a help the anagram clues are asterisked.

CROSSWORD No. 11

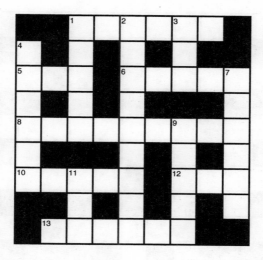

ACROSS

1 Duet is newly adapted (6)
5 Form of art shown by sailor (3)
6 Re tax — it could be more than is necessary (5)
8 Neat prose translated into universal language (9)
10 Aimed to upset TV, press, etc? (5)
12 Weapon destroyed gnu (3)
13 Modern centre, redeveloped (6)

DOWN

1 Use leather to lash unruly prats (5)
2 *Anti*-beer? I may become drunken! (9)
3 Devour tea possibly (3)
4 Master diverted little river (6)
7 Man out, swinging — what's the total? (6)
9 Weird thing in the dark (5)
11 Female creature featured in odd ode (3)

CROSSWORD No. 12

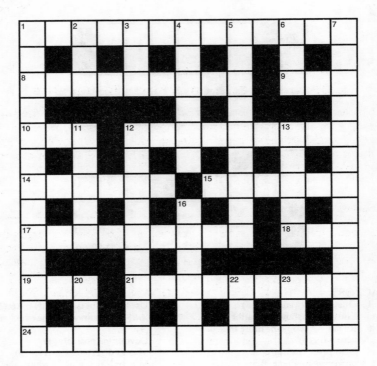

ACROSS

- 1 How competitors in dead heat cross the line, nevertheless (2,3,4,4)
- 8 Evangelist? He scores a couple of points (9)
- *9 Reg revamped work unit (3)
- 10 Distinguished airman is a card (3)
- *12 A pith gets messy in a food (9)
- *14 Hog, sir, is horrible, monstrous (6)
- 15 Elegance from Warsaw? (6)
- 17 Gymnast could be thinking the right way (2,3,4)
- 18 Prosecute a girl (3)
- 19 I will, badly (3)
- *21 Natural manure makes pod spring out (9)
- *24 Broken down floor, note, in historic building (5,2,6)

DOWN

- *1 A great school! I get excited – I'm very keen on ancient history (13)
- 2 Money container? (3)
- 3 The temptress when night approaches? (3)
- *4 Rat, say, could deviate off course (6)
- *5 More wrath upsets the gardener's friend (9)
- *6 Fish die in agony (3)
- 7 A period when youngsters come to a full stop? (7,6)
- *11 Greet funny little bird (5)
- 12 One who hangs up half a stocking support? (9)
- 13 Attempts scores in rugby (5)
- 16 Start to show to advantage (3,3)
- 20 Vulgar sound of cow (3)
- 22 In favour of person being paid (3)
- *23 Edward makes a bad end (3)

5

More Basic Clue Types: Charades, Container and contents, Reversals

In Chapter 4 we saw how the anagram and its indicator could be used as a subsidiary indication to a definition. We now start to look at a few ways in which a crossword setter can indicate the letters in the answer. For the moment we must leave the history of crosswords behind, and look at some modern examples.

Charades

Have you ever played the game of charades? In Act 1 someone drops the word 'hat' into the conversation; in Act 2 the word 'red' is dropped in; then in Act 3 someone tries to mention the word 'hatred' without you noticing. You have played this parlour game? Well, the *charade clue* is just like that; you define 'hatred' as 'hat' and 'red' and tell the solver to put the parts together.

[5.1] Headgear on communist evokes intense dislike (6)

(hat)   **CI**   (red)   **L**

└─────**S**─────┘   └──**D**──┘

CI is a *charade indicator*; the word 'on' is suitable for a down word. The *link-word* L means 'draws out' (i.e. 'provides').

Before we pass on to other examples note how the word 'red' is defined by 'communist'. This is a bit of *crossword jargon* and there are a number of such words that are great favourites with crossword setters. Another favourite is 'ant', which is often defined by 'worker'. You will pick these up as you go, but some of the more common three-letter ones appear in Appendix 1.

Now here are some more examples of charades:

[5.2] Man needs essential animal (6)

(Don)   **CI**   (key)

└─────**S**─────┘ **D**

giving don + key = DONKEY. Here is an alternative clue giving the same answer:

[5.3] Stupid person a university lecturer provided with solution (6)

⌐___D___⌐   (don)   ⌐___CI___⌐ (key)

[5.4] Discharge of lightning on a Lancashire town (6)

Here the 'discharge of lightning' equals 'bolt'; 'on' is simply equal to itself, 'on'; and the 'Lancashire town' is BOLTON. There is no CI in the clue; the parts just follow on.

Here is another clue with no CI:

[5.5] Expose record waste (8)

'Disc' ('record') plus 'lose' ('waste') equals DISCLOSE ('expose').

[5.6] Dental deposit? Use salt repeatedly (6)

You may use a salt water rinse for that stain on your teeth, but think too much along those lines and you'd be a victim of the misleading context. Think instead of 'salt' as a sailor and use 'tar' repeatedly to get TARTAR.

[5.7] Bridge over loch? That's cunning (8)

This is a down clue and 'arch' (= bridge) is 'over' (CI) 'Ness' (a loch). Such ARCHNESS from the crossword setter!

[5.8] It's very warm, the Spanish inn (5)

'Very warm' is 'hot', 'the Spanish' (i.e. 'the' in 'Spanish') is 'el', and an 'inn' is a HOTEL. Again there is no CI. This is a good moment to warn you that you can expect some simple *foreign words* in subsidiary indications. EL is another bit of crossword jargon. In addition, LE, LA, LES can all be denoted by 'the French'; 'of the French' would be DU; 'the German' is DIE, DER or DAS. We are concentrating on the grammar, but we are also picking up some vocabulary.

Container and contents

The charade clue gave us a formula A *plus* B equals C; *the container-and-contents clue* gives us a new formula A *in* B equals C:

[5.9] Vegetable to stick in the shelter (6)

CCI

Stop thinking about the wilting lettuce and start getting word-conscious! 'To stick' is a definition for 'gum'; 'the shelter' is 'lee'; 'gum' in 'lee' gives LEGUME.

[5.10] Finishing with a boxed ear—charming! (9)

CCI

When 'ear' is *boxed* by 'ending' we have ENDEARING. Have you guessed what I mean by CCI? It's the *container-and-contents indicator*! 'Holds' is a popular CCI and will often tell you what sort of clue you are dealing with:

[5.11] Girl holds information for business programme (6)

'Ada' holds the 'gen' for the AGENDA.

'Clutching' is another give-away CCI:

[5.12] Members clutching a rota—they insist on proper procedure (9)

'Members' here are 'legs' because we're thinking about members of the body, not MPs in the chamber—a nice piece of crossword jargon in a misleading context. 'A rota' is 'a list' and 'legs' clutching 'a list' becomes LEGALISTS.

[5.13] A jeer about music club being below par (2, 1, 8)

The word 'about' is a very common CCI. Put 'a taunt' about 'disco' and you have AT A DISCOUNT.

Another common CCI is 'around'. So too is 'outside'.

[5.14] Rubbish outside lair may suit this creature (6)

'Rot' outside 'den' is RODENT.

Reversals

Turn around the word 'peek' and you get 'keep'. This simple fact can be made the basis for a *reversal clue*:

[5.15] Have a little look round part of fortification (4)

RI

RI is the *reversal indicator*, telling us that when 'peek' (= have a little look) is put around (backwards) we get KEEP (part of the castle). You mean 'around' is an RI? I thought it was a CCI. Well yes, it could be either: ambiguity is what cryptic clues are all about!

For a down clue the reversal word could be said to go up, so 'up' is another RI, as in this example:

[5.16] Bear up: here's a ring (4)

Not 'Cheer up, darling, have a bit of jewellery!', but Pooh (Winnie-the-!) up to give HOOP.

Some words are of course palindromes, and so we could have a clue like this:

[5.17] To-and-fro action (4)

Write the word DEED 'to' (forwards) or 'fro' (backwards) and it is the same.

Sometimes the reversed clue can be ambiguous:

[5.18] Expert turned evil (3)

Read this as D, S and the answer is DAB; read it as S, D and it's BAD! (If the setter has offered you _ A _ with the first and third letters unchecked, he is no dab and is most certainly very bad!)

You now know about six types of cryptic clue: cryptic definition, multiple meanings, anagrams, charades, container and contents, and reversals. We've still got a long way to go before we've covered all the weaponry at the setter's disposal. Before we go on, however, it's time for you to consolidate what you know; so here's another tutorial puzzle.

CROSSWORD No. 13

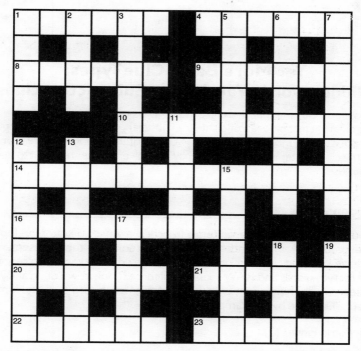

(The answer to 14 across is a well-known phrase even though not found in *The Chambers Dictionary*.)

ACROSS

1 Disease boy has got in fifth month (6)
4 Remarks not heard by fellow players when going around team (6)
8 Plump bird's grumble (6)
9 Cat bothered us more (6)
10 Russian cast? They work on a script (9)
14 Gentry receive guests here making Nanny retreat with rapture (5,8)
16 There's scope in the sultanate for a fervent royalist (9)
20 The curse of an old Egyptian city (6)
21 Repay artist on return (6)
22 American general arranging truces (6)
23 More than one door-keeper rushes around (6)

DOWN

1 Faces shown by simpletons (4)
2 Bring up jemmy, for instance — get the swag (4)
3 Wanted gentleman caught in the act (7)
5 Cost I worked out for philosopher (5)
6 Diana's noble disregard (8)
7 Laid importance on sweets being served up (8)
11 Material dug from pit comes to the surface (5)
12 Coasting aimlessly, uncertain of what to believe (8)
13 'These are corpses' vulgar fellow declares (8)
15 In the belfry they play doubles (7)
17 Death is solemn (5)
18 Revolutionary Dutch cheese produced (4)
19 Does funny poems (4)

Yet More Basic Clue Types:
Hidden words, Vocal clues, Subtractive clues

By now you can see that there are lots of ways of writing a cryptic clue by using different techniques to indicate the subsidiary indication. In this chapter we inspect some more weapons in the clue-writer's armoury. Note though that the clue-writer is not out to destroy the solver; rather he is out to tease and amuse.

Hidden words

If you take the letters of a sentence in order, a word will often be found lurking. To show what I mean, I invite you to consider the very sentence you have just read. Look at 'order, a word' and you may see ERA spanning the first two words and RAW spanning all three. Look at 'will often' and you can see LOFT. This phenomenon is the basis of the *hidden clue*, and it may best be illustrated by an example:

[6.1] Pub in Pinner (3)

    D HI HW

'Pub' is INN and it may be found in 'Pinner'.

The word 'in' is our HI (*hidden indicator*) and HW is the *hiding word*.

The word 'in' is also part of the HI in this clue, where the hidden word spans more than one word (HP = *hiding phrase*):

[6.2] Rat getting in among children? Egad—exterminate! (8)

    D ⌞___HI___⌟ ⌞_____HP_____⌟

The hidden word, meaning 'rat', is RENEGADE.

Another common HI is 'some':

[6.3] Some overenthusiastic kissing—one draws blood (4)

This is nothing whatever to do with a romantic love scene. 'Some (i.e. part of) overenthusiastic kissing' is TICK, a bloodsucker (defined by 'one draws blood').

The longest known hidden phrase occurred in a *Times* clue written by Brian Greer:

[6.4] Some job at hand? We'll soon see (4, 3, 5)

The 'see' in question is BATH AND WELLS.

Vocal clues

Vocal clues depend on how the answer sounds when it is spoken.

There are two sub-categories.

The *pun clue* relies on the fact that some words sound like others, e.g. PAIR and PEAR, HEIR and AIR. They are homophones, to use the technical jargon. Here is a pun clue:

[6.5] Feature of Scotland where there was a vicar, we hear (4)

The two words 'we hear' form a very common *pun indicator* (PI).

Where was there 'a vicar'? Bray of course, and it's 'Bray' that we hear when we get the answer which is a feature of Scotland—BRAE.

Can you find the PI in the following clue?

[6.6] Such a range of food is said to be satisfactory (4)

It is the phrase 'is said to be'. FARE sounds like 'fair' ('satisfactory').

One more:

[6.7] Shakespeare in speech? It should be precluded (6)

'Shakespeare' is the 'Bard'. What sounds like 'Bard'? BARRED, meaning 'precluded'. (Would you have spotted the PI?)

The *accent clue* relies on oddities of speech. Such a clue could also be regarded as a special type of two-definition clue. Here are some examples:

[6.8] Animal is warmer according to 'Arry (5)

[6.9] Correct, but in a refaned way? Scold angrily (4)

[6.10] A f-fellow somewhere in Jordan (5)

[6.11] Bird gettin' dressed for ceremony (5)

[6.12] Not thin and thuffering from a complaint (5)

In [6.8] 'Arry is an aitch-dropping cockney who talks about things being 'otter (hence OTTER). In [6.9] our awfully 'nace' person is never 'right' but 'rate', which prompts us to RATE him. [6.10] is a combination of an accent clue with a simple charade. Our unfortunate stutterer is unable to talk about 'a man'; instead he refers to 'a m-man' (AMMAN is Jordan's capital). In [6.11] 'robing' without the final 'g' leads to a bird (ROBIN) and in [6.12] our lisping (or 'lithp-ing') friend is 'sick' (THICK). Your author is quite fond of stammering and lisping clues, but some crossword editors eschew them on the grounds that they are offensive to the handicapped. Political correctness knows no bounds for some people, alas!

Subtractive clues

In several of our clue types we have been involved in adding words to other words or putting words into other words. In a charade, for example, the formula has been

A + B = C

Well, equally we can use the idea that

B = C − A

In the average daily cryptic the most common way of subtracting is by removing a head or a tail and the indicator is usually fairly obvious. Thus:

[6.13] Mama, topless, is something else! (5)

Concentrate on the words please, reader, not the misleading pornography! 'Mama' is mother. Remove the 'top' letter and we get OTHER. 'Topless' is a give-away *beheading indicator*: 'headless' is another. (The suggestion of 'top' means that this clue would probably be suitable for a *down* word rather than an across one, by the way.)

Here's a clue involving truncation at the other end:

[6.14] Endlessly talk about the field event (6)

This may conjure up a picture of a boring commentator at the Olympic Games, but you need to decode the words regardless of that unappealing image. Again, concentrate on the words, please. When 'discuss' is presented 'endlessly' it becomes DISCUS. 'Endlessly' and 'endless' are give-aways for this type of clue.

If words can lose their first and last letters, they can also lose their hearts:

[6.15] Get the better of the heartless monster (4)

The 'monster' is a 'beast'—remove the heart ('a') to give BEST, a verb mean-ing 'to get the better of'.

In a *very* sophisticated puzzle you might come across:

[6.16] University lecturer is   an ass   ignoring the solution (3)

└────D────┘ L (Donkey) └─SI─┘   (key)

'Donkey' minus 'key' = DON (SI = subtraction indicator), or even:

[6.17] Arousing affection, having had ear removed, dying (6)

(Endearing)   └─SI(i)─┘ (ear) └─SI(ii)─┘ └─D─┘

Answer: ENDING.

On that gruesome note we are ending this chapter, but not before you attempt another tutorial exercise.

CROSSWORD No. 14

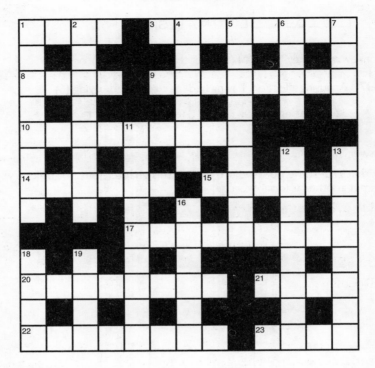

ACROSS

1 Animal sounding like an organ (4)
3 Philosophers? They can't thwim! (8)
8 Title held by certain American (4)
9 Vine-crop is exceptional in particular district (8)
10 Nun's dirge played for parting (9)
14 Looked only briefly — decapitated — killed with a spear? (6)
15 Terrible 'arvest — get desperately hungry (6)
17 A cake before the social function is more than enough (9)
20 Repertory company gets up musical repeats (8)
21 Side of blade useful for cutting 'awthorn barrier? (4)
22 Drunk one coming to entrance? Seek help from the law (8)
23 Requests jobs not using the head (4)

DOWN

1 Sincerely pious outside the home (8)
2 Booze inside worker — one to bring something up! (8)
4 Drug cut short a courageous girl (6)
5 Worked out a route and gave it out (9)
6 Wilderness shelters this eagle (4)
7 Left-wing Tories upset, in a sweat (4)
11 Exhilarating tale given twists (9)
12 See grand exploding bombs (8)
13 Young hares? Permits needed for catching at all times (8)
16 Treasure stored? Not completely, that's most certain (6)
18 Said of country life — it must put aside the past (4)
19 Heartless Jack, who couldn't eat everything, expectorated (4)

7

Non-word Elements in Subsidiary Indications:

Abbreviations and symbols, Numbers, Bits and pieces

Over the past four chapters we have looked at all the main clue types, but so far we have used whole words as building-blocks for the clues. We can, however, use letters or clusters of letters as we shall see below.

Abbreviations and symbols

Consider the word PRATTLED. This may suggest 'p + rattled', but can the setter indicate 'p' in a subsidiary indication? The answer is yes, because 'p' is short for 'piano' or 'quietly', so a charade clue might read as follows:

[7.1] Gossiped quietly in a fluster (8)

        (p)   (rattled)

D |___S___|

In the world of crosswords there are a vast number of common abbreviations, and you will find a fair number in Appendix I. This list is by no means exhaustive though, and one of the joys of learning how to solve is in coming to recognize the language of abbreviations and symbols.

In the clues that follow we can introduce only a small number in various types of clue.

[7.2] Miss West embraces novice man
Answer: MALE: 'Mae' embraces 'L' (= learner, novice).

[7.3] Good man, a sailor lying on bed, wounded (7)
A 'good man' is a saint (ST); a 'sailor' on this occasion is an AB (on other occasions he's a tar or something else!). Put it all together (in a down clue) to give STABBED.

[7.4] Bob has to study for the exam-buzz off! (5)
A 'bob' is (or was!) a shilling (= s); 's' + 'cram' = SCRAM.

[7.5] Slant in Conservative policy (7)
A simple charade: 'in' + 'C' + 'line' = INCLINE.

[7.6] Poet has edited religious education book (6)

This is a bit trickier. 'Religious education' = RE and an (edited) anagram of 'RE book' is BROOKE.

Asking the solver to form an abbreviation which is then incorporated into an anagram is regarded as fair only where the abbreviation is obvious. Even so it is a technique better left to the more advanced cryptics. On fairness and advanced puzzles, more anon!

Numbers

In crossword land we still use Roman numbers when convenient. Thus I (the roman letter) = 1 (the number), V = 5, X = 10, L = 50, C = 100, D = 500 and M = 1000, with of course the possibility of combinations. Thus:

[7.7] 100, very old and shut in (5)

And glad to get the Queen's telegram? Forget it! 'C' is a hundred; 'very old' becomes 'aged'. Answer: CAGED.

[7.8] Five hundred taking beer in the valley (4)

Just the sort of outdoor festival that might appeal to me! 'D' is five hundred. Add to 'ale' to get DALE.

[7.9] Around 50, it takes courage to get a sweetheart (7)

Just as well some of us are happily married. 'L' in 'daring' gives DARLING.

'Love' (from tennis) and 'duck' (from cricket) are useful speaking terms for zero which is regarded as the shape of O. Thus:

[7.10] The lady's love is a very brave man (4)

Answer: 'her' + 'O' gives HERO.

[7.11] Cricket ground where there's a duck, 5 and a 50 (4)

Answer: 'O' + 'V' + 'a L' = OVAL.

Bits and pieces

In this chapter we've seen two ways in which the crossword setter can get rid of odd letters. There remains a third, very important way. A letter can be defined by the position it occupies in another word. A few examples will suffice to illustrate this:

[7.12] Look at bee for example round end of cowslip (7)

The words 'end of' will tell us that we want the last letter in the word that follows, i.e. 'p'. Put 'insect' around 'p' to get INSPECT.

[7.13] Craftsman is good initially—then not working so hard (7)

'Initially' is a tell-tale word and 'good initially' gives 'g'. When the craftsman is not working so hard he is 'lazier'. Answer: GLAZIER.

'Finally' is also a tell-tale word:

[7.14] Climbing plant with flower finally providing fruit (4)

'Climbing plant' is 'pea'; 'flower finally' is 'r' ('r' being the last letter of 'flower'). Answer: PEAR.

Expect also to meet 'extremely' as in:

[7.15] Keep silent about extremely unmerciful prison system (5)

from *The Times*.

Here 'extremely' denotes the first and last letters of 'unmerciful' which put inside 'gag' leads to GULAG. Not everyone approves of such a use of 'extremely' though—can it really mean the 'extreme letters of'? The Ximeneans would say no. Who are Ximeneans? You'll find out in Chapter 11.

[7.16] Head of school, many years a wise man (4)

'Head of school' is 's'; add 'age' to get the answer: SAGE.

Initial letters can often be put together in a charade, as follows:

[7.17] Leaders of firm are terribly obese (3)

Take the three 'leaders' (leading letters) to get FAT. (Alternatively final letters may be joined together, but this is much less common.)

Now try this one:

[7.18] A bit of trouble with relation's reproach (5)

Not all crossword editors like 'bit of', but those who do take it to mean 'the first bit of', so 'a bit of trouble' is by convention 't'. Add 't' to 'aunt' and you get TAUNT. There's one other thing to notice about this clue. The apostrophe-plus-s combination denotes a possessive to give the clue sense, but means 'is' when we're thinking about the construction of the clue ('t' with 'aunt' *is* TAUNT).

Though bits, a head and an end always have single letters, a heart may have one letter or more:

[7.19] Chap with heart of steel, bit of a lion? (4)

The 'heart of steel' is 'e'; add it on to 'man' and you have MANE.

[7.20] Stupid fool in middle of road, beginning to fluster (3)

The 'beginning' to the word 'fluster' is 'f' and the 'middle' of the word 'road' is 'oa', giving OAF.

More on Crossword Terminology

The 'cross word puzzle' has become the 'crossword puzzle' or plain 'crossword'. But what about the 'realm' of crosswords and the people who participate in it? Could we agree on 'crosswording' and 'crossworders'? Maybe, but neither of these words has found a regular place in the dictionaries.

A word that was coined in the 1970s was 'cruciverbalism' (from the Latin *crux, crucis*, a cross, and *verbum*, a word). This means 'the realm of crosswords', and a 'cruciverbalist' would be someone interested in crosswords. The adjective is 'cruciverbal'. Happily all three words have made it into *The Chambers Dictionary* since the last edition of this book.

Cruciverbalists are of course in two categories: those who make up the crosswords and those who solve them. The latter are clearly 'solvers', but what about the former? The word 'compiler' has been much used, but suggests that puzzle construction only involves collecting the material together and underplays the aspect of creativity. What about 'composer'? This is quite good, but would be viewed by some as too grandiose. Many crossword contributors like to be called 'setters', since anyone making up a crossword is 'setting' a puzzle for the solver. 'Setter' therefore seems the ideal word.

Half-words can be useful to the crossword setter:

[7.21] Famous performer is semi-naked (4)
'Semi-starkers' is STAR.

So too can pairs of letters, as in:

[7.22] Leading couples in Chelsea actually hated dance music (3-3)
Add 'Ch' from 'Chelsea' to 'ac' from 'actually' to 'ha' from 'hated' and you have CHA-CHA.

Bits and pieces offer all sorts of possibilities. The clue-writer can, for example, take third letters from words, substitute one bit for another, or even move bits around. It would be impossible to catalogue all the various possibilities, especially since inventive clue-writers will find new ones. Some of the techniques are covered in Chapter 14 where we will look at advanced clues, but some of these clue styles are beginning to appear in daily cryptics, especially in *The Times*.

That's enough for now though. It's time to turn the page for another tutorial puzzle which has a number of clues incorporating non-word elements in their subsidiary indications.

7 ACI

ACIKNOR Koranic	ACINORT carotin	ACLLOOR corolla
ACIKNPY panicky	Cortina®	ACLLOPS scallop
ACIKPRT Patrick	ACINOSS caisson	ACLLORR Carroll
ACIKPSX six-pack	casinos	ACLLORU locular
ACIKPSY sick pay	ACINOST actions	ACLLOSU callous
ACIKRWW Warwick	ACINOTU auction	ACLLOTU call out
ACIKSTT stick at	caution	ACLLOVY vocally
ACIKUWZ Zwickau	ACINPRY Cyprian	ACLMNUY calumny
ACILLLU Lucilla	ACINQTU quantic	ACLMORU clamour
ACILLMS miscall	ACINRTT Tantric	ACLNOOO Laocoon
ACILLRY lyrical	ACINRTU curtain	ACLNOOR coronal
ACILMOT comital	ACIOPRS prosaic	ACLNOOT coolant
ACILMSU musical	ACIOPRT apricot	ACLNOOV volcano□
ACILNNY cannily	ACIOPSS Picasso	ACLNOPT Clapton
ACILNOR clarion	ACIOPTY opacity	ACLNORY Carolyn
ACILNOS Nicolas	ACIORRS corsair	ACLNOUV Vulcano
ACILNOU Luciano	ACIORSU carious	ACLNPSU unclasp
ACILNOV Calvino	ACIORTT ricotta	ACLNSTY scantly
ACILNOZ calzoni	Riot Act	ACLOOPP Coppola
Zincalo	ACIPRVY privacy	ACLOPSY calypso□
ACILNPY pliancy	ACIPSST spastic	ACLORSU oscular
ACILNTU lunatic	ACIPTUY paucity	ACLORWW Wroclaw
ACILNUV vincula	ACIQRTU quartic	ACLOTTW Walcott
ACILOOR air-cool	ACIRRTY carry it	ACLPRTY cryptal
ACILOPT optical	ACIRSST sacrist	ACLRSSY crassly
topical	ACIRSSU cuirass	ACLRSTY crystal□
ACILORX Lacroix	ACIRSTT astrict	ACLRSWY scrawly
ACILOST stoical	ACIRSTU Scutari	ACLSSTU cutlass
ACILOTT coal tit	ACIRSTY satyric	ACMNOPR crampon
coal-tit	ACISSSU Cassius	ACMNOPY company□
ACILPST plastic	ACISSTT statics	ACMNORY acronym
ACILPSU spicula	ACISSTU casuist	ACMNSTU sanctum
ACILPTY typical	ACISSTV sits vac	ACMOOPT Potomac
ACILRTU curtail	ACISTTU catsuit	ACMOOST scotoma
ACILRTY clarity	Tacitus	ACMOPSS compass
ACILRYZ crazily	ACITUVY vacuity	ACMOPTU camp out
ACILSTU St Lucia	ACJKKSY skyjack	ACMQTUU cumquat
ACILSUY saucily	ACJKLOW lockjaw	ACMSUUV vacuums
ACILTTY cattily	ACJKNNO jannock	ACNNNOS cannons
tacitly	ACJKNOS Jackson	ACNNNOY no' canny
ACILTUV victual	ACJKOPT jackpot	ACNNNUY uncanny
ACIMNOP campion□	ACJLORU jocular	ACNNORU Corunna
ACIMNOR Marconi	ACJMNTU muntjac	ACNOORS coronas
Minorca□	ACKKOOR cork oak	ACNOORT cartoon
ACIMNOS masonic□	ACKLLOP pollack□	ACNOPSU Canopus
ACIMNRU cranium	ACKLLOR Rockall	ACNOPSW snowcap
ACIMNTT catmint	ACKLLSY slackly	ACNOPTU act upon
ACIMOPT potamic	ACKLMOR armlock	ACNORRU rancour
Tampico	ACKLMOT Matlock	ACNORRY carry on
ACIMOST maticos	ACKLNOU uncloak	carry-on□
somatic	ACKLORW warlock	ACNOSSZ scazons
ACIMPRY primacy	ACKLPSU slack up	ACNOSTU conatus
ACIMRSU muscari	ACKMOTT mattock	ACNRRTU currant
ACIMSST miscast	ACKNNOS snack on	ACNRSWY scrawny
ACINNOR Corinna	ACKNORY Conakry	ACNRTUY truancy
ACINNOT contain	ACKNSTU unstack	ACNSSTU Sanctus
ACINNOZ canzoni	ACKOPRR parrock	ACOOPRR corpora
ACINNST stannic	ACKORRT rock art	ACOOPTT topcoat
ACINOPT caption	ACKPSTU stack up	ACOORTU touraco
paction	ACLLLOY locally	ACOOSTV octavos
ACINORR carrion	ACLLMMO Malcolm	ACOPRRT car port

Words marked □ can also be spelled with an initial capital letter

---

An extract from *Chambers Anagrams*, for those who are solving in a hurry perhaps.

CROSSWORD No. 15

ACROSS

1 Loud oriental celebration (5)
4 Start to tamper with gun — it's only a toy (6)
9 Girl about ten may receive radio waves (7)
10 Agents bringing food aboard (5)
11 Unusual combination of gunners and engineers (4)
13 One drawing southern vessel, *The Queen* (8)
14 Doctor, endless pain is something monstrous (6)
17 Be a chap like George and start to slay monsters (6)
19 To make one's way takes a very long time in these corridors (8)
21 Five — the age for a girl (4)
25 Make a song about the West — jazz? (5)
26 Grass pots are falling to bits (7)
27 Don't have all the lemonade, sister! Leave off! (6)
28 Happening that's not odd at the end of August (5)

DOWN

1 Learner in the amusement park shows instinctive skill (5)
2 Performer is a hundred — over the hill (5)
3 Look after what would now be about 4p! (4)
5 Badge labelled 'First Prize'? It's specially presented to steer (7)
6 Fifty trapped in conflicts — ways of escape needed (7)
7 Makes certain unfavourable judgements, the head having left (7)
8 Note 500 pairs perhaps on Noah's boat (4)
12 Tune is first class? Right! (3)
13 Star in revolutionary students union (3)
14 Deprived of top position (given drugs to capture record) (7)
15 Attacks a ship about to travel (7)
16 Fruit, very large, seen around the open country (7)
17 Public transport almost broken down (3)
18 Salt submerged in Antarctica (3)
20 Former prime minister in the garden (4)
22 Mountain-top home — Jane's taken around one (5)
23 Sailor not at home, abroad (5)
24 Some chap serving in part of church (4)

CROSSWORD No. 15

The Orchestration of Subsidiary Parts: Complex clues, Linking clues together

You now should be able to solve the following clues, recognizing a different type of subsidiary indication in each one:

(a)	**[8.1]**	Put up with a rude person (4)
(b)	**[8.2]**	Goose's mate ruined garden (6)
(c)	**[8.3]**	The French shelter is hidden (6)
(d)	**[8.4]**	Fast and quiet in sudden attack (5)
(e)	**[8.5]**	Show contempt perhaps—gratuities sent back (4)
(f)	**[8.6]**	Sea-eagle in her nest (4)
(g)	**[8.7]**	Despatched perfume we hear (4)
(h)	**[8.8]**	Senior is more daring, losing head (5)

The clue types are:

(a)	*Two definitions*	(answer: BEAR)
(b)	*Anagram*	(answer: GANDER)
(c)	*Charade*	(answer: LATENT)
(d)	*Container and contents*	(answer: RAPID)
(e)	*Reversal*	(answer: SPIT)
(f)	*Hidden*	(answer: ERNE)
(g)	*Vocal*	(answer: SENT)
(h)	*Subtractive*	(answer: OLDER)

Complex clues

Each of the eight clues above could be described as a *simple* cryptic clue (however hard it is to solve!). A *complex* cryptic clue on the other hand, includes some combination of more than one technique. Here is a random selection (keyed by the letters above):

(b,c) **[8.9]** Trails along with legs collapsing after wearisome task (8)

An anagram of 'legs' is 'gles'. Add it to 'drag' and we get DRAGGLES. If you like you can add the S/D notation to see how the clue works, but it's about time you understood the shorthand way that setters use to explain a solution. In this case the solution note would read (drag + anag.). Other notes will be explained as we go along.

(c,h) **[8.10]** The man has almost finished paved area around a plant (7)

Here the charade incorporates a subsidiary component which has been clued 'subtractively'. The man is 'he'; and 'almost finished paved area' is 'pati' (not quite a patio!) and around is 'c'. The answer is therefore HEPATIC (a liverwort). The note would read (he + pati(o) + c).

(c,d) **[8.11]** You get dry around bottom of tongue with an American disease (7)

You get 'TT' around 'e' ('bottom' because it is a down clue) with 'an' plus 'US': (e inTT + an + US) gives TETANUS.

(b,d) **[8.12]** Secular lot are somehow besieging politician (8)

Here we have an abbreviation inside an anagram: (MP in anag.) gives TEMPORAL. Alternatively we could have an anagram inside something else:

(b,d) **[8.13]** Palatable fruit nasty lice will get into (8)

Here 'nasty lice' = 'elic', and so (anag. in date) gives us DELICATE.

(b,c,d) **[8.14]** Sweetmeat—kitchenware contains a small amount, cool possible (5,9)

'Plate' contains 'a' plus 'inch' plus an anagram of cool, 'ocol': (a + inch + anag.) in plate gives PLAIN CHOCOLATE. In this clue we have the formula A contains BC, with both B and C placed inside A. However it is quite possible for A contains BC to mean 'A contains B, then add C' as in this example:

(b,c,d) **[8.15]** Mathematician worries terribly about Northern fisherman (6,8)

A strange bringing together of concerns? No matter—put an anagram of 'worries' around N, then add 'angler': (N in anag. + angler) gives SENIOR WRANGLER, Cambridge's best maths graduate. You, the solver, would have to sort out whether to put the fisherman inside the anagram or outside. This sort of ambiguity adds a distinct spice to a crossword clue.

(b,c,e) **[8.16]** Signified dire need after doctor returned (6)

Signified means OMENED and the clue works like this:

(MO, rev. + anag.)

(e,f) **[8.17]** Fairy coming back in dire pantomime (4)

Here we have to look for a word hidden in reverse, and it isn't too hard to spot PERI (hidden, rev.).

(b,h) **[8.18]** Bread in short supply—unusually scanty (4)

Take (anag. of brea(d)), i.e. an unusual presentation of a short rendering of 'bread', and you get BARE.

(d,e) **[8.19]** Chaps turned up in the American agency—it should be entertaining (6)

Our note would read (men, rev. in CIA) and the answer is CINEMA.

(c,d,e) **[8.20]** Women's Libber swallows man up, one man who'd fight (9)

Poor chap! The man is Dan (he could be Les or anybody else, but he isn't). When one (I) is added on and (Ms) Greer does her swallowing, the answer is GRENADIER. Our note would read (Dan, rev. + I in (Germaine) Greer). We add the bracketed Germaine, because Ms Greer may not be found in the dictionary.

Clearly we could find yet other combinations of our eight clue techniques, and you can expect to meet others not given here. Deciphering a complex clue is one of the joys of crossword solving.

Linking clues together

In most daily puzzles each clue is separate and independent. The solver has to manage (say) 28 or 32 clues and any linking occurs in the checking of the letters. Sometimes though a setter will attempt to find connections between *clues*. For example, successive clues may be linked together by three dots to suggest a common theme:

[8.21] Now for the give away (7) ...

[8.22] ... from me, perhaps, a Spaniard with gold (5)

The answer to the first clue is PRESENT, a simple two-meanings clue —which we would explain in the notes as (2 mngs). Who does a present come from? Answer: a DONOR (don + or). You may not yet have learnt that gold = or (the heraldic colour) or possibly Au (the chemical symbol), but I can't tell you everything at once!

Answers may spread across several words at different sites in the puzzle. This was a clue I used in the *Birmingham Evening Mail* (starting at 9 across):

[8.23] 9, 5 down, I across, 25 down, 27 across, 22 across. Claim of our paper—exceptional deal, this fine blend reveals many great things (2,3,3,7,7,4,2,3,8).

An anagram of the last eight words gives the catchline on the front page:

BY FAR THE LARGEST EVENING SALE IN THE MIDLANDS.

Sometimes there will be cross-referencing between clues all linked by a common theme. Thus, 30 across and 9 down could be linked as follows and the solver may be (mildly) misled into treating 9 as a number in its own right rather than a clue reference:

[8.24] 30. Looked after 9 somehow (6)

[8.25] 9. Separate revolutionary students in rising (6)

9 gives the answer SUNDER (red NUS, rev.) which can somehow give NURSED (anag.), the answer to 30.

This is a simple example. In some puzzles the cross-references can cover half the clues.

On the next page another tutorial. This time you have a complete 15 × 15 with a few complex clues thrown in.

Three Amazing Stories

The Times did not decide until 1930 to include a daily crossword, and when the go-ahead was given there was no one readily to hand to produce the puzzle. Robert Bell of *The Observer* was approached (he was producing the Everyman puzzle) and he delegated the task to his 28-year-old son Adrian. Adrian had never solved a puzzle before, let alone set one! He had ten days to learn and continued setting for over 40 years. Bell's identity was kept secret until a BBC interview in 1970. (Adrian's son Martin achieved fame as a broadcaster and white-suited MP.)

One of the early *Daily Telegraph* setters was L. S. Dawe. In 1944 he was visited by members of MI5 who pointed to six suspicious words in his recent puzzles: MULBERRY, NEPTUNE, OMAHA, OVERLORD, PLUTO and UTAH. These words just happened to be code-words for the impending D-Day. Dawe was fortunately able to show MI5 how his crosswords were constructed, thereby convincing them of his innocence.

A lady in Fiji completed a *Times* crossword in May 1966. The puzzle was published on 4th April 1932 and she had been working on it for 34 years!

Additional Challenge

Take the word PALE and see if you can use each of the clue types listed on p.52 to write a clue for it. The reverse clue can be a reverse charade *(e,c)*. For good measure, try two charades and a reverse hidden. Then compare your list with mine on p.79.

CROSSWORD No. 16

ACROSS

1 Band possibly took horses we hear—route going around city? (4,4)
5 Soul manifest in tipsy cheering (6)
9 Terrible collapse with love deserting—I'm in the operating theatre (7)
10 Fellows in the wrong causing anguish (7)
11 Bit of excitement with a glass of beer he had in frolic? A risky venture (4,2,3,4)
13 Mad artist's characteristics (6)
14 Lessons from the school chaplain? A source of help (8)
16 'Ostel allowed unlimited tea and food (8)
18 Smooth ambassador endlessly getting round (6)
21 Novel with Indian going to America? (5,3,5)
23 Conflict and bombast—what's the justification? (7)
24 Cunning one is turning singer (7)
25 Garden tool has some little worth when brought back (6)
26 Quietly abode—was in the chair (8)

DOWN

1 Concerning the answer you need determination (10)
2 Falls once more upset artist (7)
3 Hate made rip go wild in fit of passion—one should have to make amends (6,3,6)
4 Silver allows metal ornaments to be produced (6)
6 After meal a person gets lively making attempt to do something novel (6,4,5)
7 The scrutineer was a twister in the sixties (7)
8 'Enrietta, a painter (4)
10 Propositions from the session just over half way through (6)
12 Part of watch that isn't new (not seen in digital variety!) (6,4)
15 Start of storm—and oak perhaps will come down on top of the thoroughfare (6)
17 Order to forbid some who grab men turning up (7)
19 A long time before Edward got 'airy'? (7)
20 Examiner of films possibly upset crones (6)
22 Marbles must be given up—prepare for exam (4)

CROSSWORD No. 16

9

The & Lit. Clue

What is an 'and lit.'?

Unless you solve advanced crosswords and look at the solution notes, you are unlikely to come across the expression 'and lit.', which is conventionally written with the ampersand. This does not mean, however, that you are unlikely to meet an '& *lit.*' clue—and it is something rather special. Take a good look at this clue:

[9.1] No fellow for mixing (4,4)

Can you solve it? Where is the definition? Well, it reads like one, doesn't it? In that case, where's the subsidiary indication? Well, it could be that as well—perhaps an anagram of 'no fellow' (with 'for mixing' as the anagram indicator). In fact, all four words serve as both a definition and a subsidiary indication. This is indeed an anagram clue and the answer is LONE WOLF. If we use our S/D notation we can analyse the clue thus:

No fellow   for mixing

⌞__A__⌟ ⌞__AI__⌟
⌞_____S_____⌟
⌞_____D_____⌟

A clue like this, where S and D span the whole length, is known as an & lit. [9.1] is an 'anag. & lit.' Here are two more:

[9.2] I'm one involved with cost (9)

[9.3] What could give bang out at sea? (7)

The answers are ECONOMIST and GUNBOAT ('at sea' suggests confusion and is a very useful anagram indicator).

The & lit. doesn't have to be an anagram, though, as the following examples show:

[9.4] Part of it 'it an iceberg (7)

The 'hidden & lit.' gives us TITANIC.

[9.5] Leaders of various individual congregations (alternatively rectors sometimes) (6)

'Leaders' are first letters here. This 'initials & lit.' clue leads to VICARS.

A somewhat overused old chestnut is:

[9.6] One has gone into the church

'I in minster' & lit. gives MINISTER.

For a 'rev. & lit.' try:

[9.7] The reverse of a divine fellow (3)

DOG is the reverse of a god in more ways than one.

The 'semi & lit.'

Let's have a look at this clue:

[9.8] Denomination spreading abroad 'Christ doeth much'? (9,6)

The last three words may be spread abroad and we see that they are an anagram of METHODIST CHURCH. The first word is clearly a definition and yet the whole clue also gives a definition—an 'enhanced definition', in fact. We could analyse the clue as follows:

Denomination spreading abroad 'Christ doeth much'? (9,6)

where D^e stands for 'enhanced definition'. Since in this clue D^e and S overlap for much of the clue I will term this a 'semi & lit.'

We could attempt to turn this into a 'pure & lit.' by rewording it as follows:

[9.9] It spreads abroad 'Christ doeth much' (9,6)

Both clues are acceptable, although [9.8] is perhaps a little more helpful to the solver.

Some 'non & lits.'

Here is an attempt at an & lit. clue where there is no real definition:

[9.10] Andrew could become this (6)

This is a very bad attempt at an anag. & lit. to give WARDEN. Little Andy could become a bus conductor or a brain surgeon (or even a crossword setter!). The definition is somewhat remote, to say the least! But the clue becomes perfectly respectable (even if uninspired) when we stop trying to be too clever and put in a definition:

[9.11] Andrew could become a guard (6)

To finish with, a word on what & lit. *doesn't* mean! The origin of the phrase is much debated but it seems to stand for 'and literally'. This clue, & lit. tells us, is a configuration of letters *and* a literal definition. What & lit. does *not* mean is: here is a clue which simply gives you a piece of information which is literally true. Here is such a clue:

[9.12] Mint perhaps in gel? It can be refreshing (7)

The answer is SHERBET (herb in set). Anyone who has eaten a glacier mint can bear testimony to the truth of the clue, but anyone who understands the S/D analysis knows that this is *not* an & lit. clue.

This chapter brings us to the end of our survey of clues for everyday cryptic crosswords. We shall return to advanced clues in Chapter 14, but it is worth noting that some of these clue types do appear in everyday puzzles such as *The Times*. Take a breather for now though and have a go at the tutorial which follows. See how many & lits. you can spot.

CROSSWORD No. 17

Games and Puzzles **Competition winner by D. F. Manley, June 1977**

ACROSS

1 Rooms on view in publishing house favoured by crossword fans (8)

5 Difficulty can be severe, going around centre of maze (6)

9 There's mud — it's a messy sports ground (7)

10 Spiteful woman's dad was primarily a stooge (7)

11 Reptile upsetting a girl a lot (9)

12 Low in generosity to some extent, being in debt (5)

13 Two-faced crook who would spoil his ballot paper? (6-7)

16 True leader of rectors always to be found at the close? (5,8)

20 Something for ploughing an allotment? (5)

21 Disturbances due to unruly brute in horse race (9)

23 Resentment from someone ineffective having gone mad (7)

24 Girl, East European, is dance's centre of attraction (7)

25 Wine can make you reticent about sin (6)

26 Vague notions from learner in fashionable Cambridge college (8)

CROSSWORD No. 17

DOWN

1 Wise man taking vehicle around Bath perhaps (6)

2 I went ahead after girl helped (7)

3 Uses the telephone at that place in the pub — gets through finally? (6,2,3,4)

4 Set up a watch maybe — or relax (5)

6 Moon or a star? Ryle would get excited, being this (10,5)

7 Adult w-works vigorously—tries for new job? (7)

8 Imposing old ladies arrange bets (8)

10 Boat specified by Conservative pundit (7)

14 Offer no resistance, confess, having told fibs at first (3,4)

15 Editor, one turning up surrounded by journalists, takes the chair (8)

17 Dreadfully enraged nobleman (7)

18 Fierce character embracing love is a soldier (7)

19 Estimate the worth of a female twit? (6)

22 Tiny chap broadcasting, an Athenian (5)

10

Crossword Lingo

We have now covered all the main clue types that you can expect to meet in a daily cryptic crossword. Much of our attention has been focused on the grammar of crossword clues. In this chapter we are going to focus briefly on vocabulary. When faced with the series of words in a clue you need to know what to look for. You will ask yourself lots of questions: Are these words the definition? Is the setter telling us to put one word inside another? What does 'about' mean here? The comma comes here, but is this where the definition and subsidiary indication are divided? Why has the setter used a question-mark here? And so on.

Definitions

For the most part we have concentrated on subsidiary indications and taken the *definition* for granted. Take the word CAPTAIN. A dictionary definition begins thus: 'a head or chief officer: the commander of a troop of horse, a company of infantry, a ship, or a portion of a ship's company.' In providing a definition for a cryptic clue we can either (i) provide a *straight definition:*

[10.1] Commander with army in awful panic (7)

(TA in anag.)

or (ii) provide a *cryptic description* (based here on a cricket captain's function):

[10.2] 'Pa, I can't! That's wrong!' he may declare (7)

(anag. with the misleading context of George Washington?)

or (iii) provide a *definition by example:*

[10.3] Cook? Starts to prepare the added ingredients to be put into container (7)

(ptai in can with another misleading context-think of Captain Cook).

[10.3] shows us how the crossword setter's lingo often relies on *double meanings*. Vocabulary may be specially selected to mislead—but the clue is nevertheless fair.

Anagram and other indicators

It is not long before a crossword solver learns to recognize *anagram indicators*. There are hundreds of words at a crossword setter's disposal: 'strange', 'unusual', 'terrible' are common adjectives; also used are the corresponding adverbs ('strangely', etc). A setter may refer to 'a mixture of' something or talk about something being 'cooked' or 'ruined'. And so on. But beware of 'upset' which can indicate reversal in a down word.

'Upset' is indeed an ambiguous word as the following examples show:

[10.4] Light at night has upset these rodents (4)
Answer: RATS (star, rev.).

[10.5] Rats upset Russian emperor (4)
Answer: TSAR (anag.).

We learned in an earlier chapter that 'around' and 'about' are likewise ambiguous—even more so in fact. Consider these clues with 'about'.

[10.6] Banter about a fibber (4)
Answer: LIAR (rev. of rail).

[10.7] The manner shown by chaps about one (4)
Answer: MIEN (I in men).

[10.8] Fastening device about source of light (5)
Answer: CLAMP (c. + lamp).

[10.9] About to get single girl, being lax (6)
Answer: REMISS (re + miss).

In these four examples we see how the word 'about' can indicate two types of clue or be part of a subsidiary indication.

'In' is another troublesome little word, which the solver must learn to interpret:

[10.10] Girl found in cloisters (4)
Answer: LOIS (hidden).

[10.11] Mean not to go in the river (6)
Answer: DENOTE (not in Dee).

[10.12] Setter let loose in thoroughfare (6)
Answer: STREET (anag.) with 'in' simply acting as a linkword between the subsidiary indication and the definition.

You know now that 'we hear' means a pun and you will spot reversal indicators such as 'returning' and 'coming back' quite easily. Something 'getting' something might suggest a charade and something 'outside' something could suggest a container-and-contents clue. Recognizing the indicators, like everything else, comes with practice.

Some give-away words for short subsidiary components

Attempt a daily cryptic and you will enter a world preoccupied with directions (north = N, etc), numbers (hundred = C, etc), and a more-than-usual interest in the French (LA, LE, LES). American soldiers may have gone home after the War, but the good old GI still appears in the back pages of our papers. Indeed there is something of a military preoccupation with gunners (RA), engineers (RE), volunteers (TA) and so on. Crosswords may be square, but they often have sex-appeal (IT or SA) which may please a sailor (AB or TAR usually). A worker is regarded as less than human (ANT), but great consideration is shown to the doctor (DR, GP, MB, MD, MO—a health centre practice where you don't know which one you will get). Political neutrality is achieved with a fair balance between left (L) and right (R), though the Conservative (C) party has more seats in the grid than Labour (LAB) which still lags behind the Liberal (L) party.

If you want a longer vocabulary, look at Appendix 1. The bibliography (Appendix 2) also includes crossword dictionaries. It is impossible, however, to tell you everything—and I only hope that I haven't told you too much, for one of the joys of crossword puzzles is to learn the language for yourself. Time for another tutorial.

CROSSWORD No. 18

By Quixote from *The Independent*

ACROSS

1 Put upon others, little devil does wrong (7)
5 Old soldier detained in Newport Hospital (7)
9 Note friend hardly at all (9)
10 Virginia's not well inside the house (5)
11 Golf course—after a little time man gets a round in (5)
12 Mediocre journalist announced requirement to be trite (9)
14 Tar making one tarry! (7,7)
17 Where records of matches are kept (8,6)
21 Luminous fish, one six-footer! (9)
23 A green? He wants to _____ eco-disaster! (5)
24 Get to know Edward by name (5)
25 Thy crimes found out? The forensic bods use this! (9)
26 Give back to stock again (7)
27 Beast making the lady gasp at first (7)

CROSSWORD No. 18

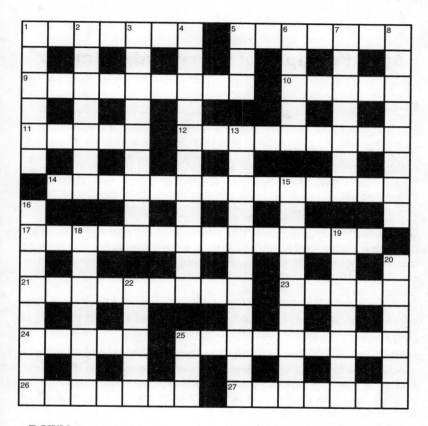

DOWN

1 Favoured friend, someone imprisoned (6)

2 Is this card game bridge? Yes and no (7)

3 I'll help make the meaning clear—but I can't mess about! (9)

4 We offer spectacular entertainment — see lad hop in air acrobatically (11)

5 Money received brings a little power always (3)

6 Sailors will hang around an avenue for a bird…(5)

7 …Henry's caught that peaceful bird (7)

8 Flag to be situated overlooking a road (8)

13 Some top chap spouted a lot of rubbish! (7,4)

15 Increase in business has someone in the family collecting francs (9)

16 A footballer from the cradle? (8)

18 Could they render airs with gut? (7)

19 Sounds like a dishonest boundah, a beast! (7)

20 One to keep trying — gets part of the way to the top, we hear (6)

22 Performed slowly in sullen tones (5)

25 Line needing to be heard? (3)

II

Basic Principles of Crossword Grammar

Fair Play

This is a book about Crossword English. Learning about different clue types is rather like learning about parts of speech—nouns, verbs, adjectives, and so on. By doing some analysis of definitions and subsidiary indications, we've learnt how to 'parse' a cryptic clue. Now it's time to look at Crossword Grammar. Normal English has its grammar; so too does Crossword English. Normal English has some rules and some areas of dispute; Crossword English is the same.

To trace the history of Crossword Grammar we must resume the historical account we left several chapters ago. It is now time to introduce three famous names. The first is Torquemada of *The Observer*. He is the setter credited with the invention of the cryptic clue. Born Edward Powys Mathers, he dominated the scene in the 1930s so far as very hard cryptics are concerned, but at times his puzzles were unsolvable. Torquemada was a genius who invented much of Crossword English, but it was left to others to codify Crossword Grammar. We shall return to him later.

While Torquemada was teasing *The Observer*'s readers in the 1930s another crossword setter was exploring new crossword possibilities in *The Listener*. Prebendary A. F. Ritchie of Wells Cathedral took the pseudonym Afrit (an Arabian demon), and he too on occasion was able to produce puzzles that attracted no correct entries! But Afrit was a pioneer, and when after the Second World War he turned his attention to the theory of crosswords he laid the foundation on which another great pioneer, Ximenes, was to build so successfully.

Torquemada died in 1939 and his eventual successor was Derrick Somerset Macnutt, a classics master at Christ's Hospital, Horsham, who took another inquisitorial name, Ximenes. Afrit and Ximenes can be regarded as the 'law-makers', the codifiers who brought order and discipline to a pastime that might otherwise have got out of hand. Their campaign began with Afrit's book of *Armchair Crosswords* which was published in 1949. In a preface Ximenes commends Afrit thus: 'The crossword world may be trivial, but like greater worlds it needs standards, and Afrit is the man to set them.' The next few pages contain an Introduction by Afrit which mentions *The Book of the Crossword*, an 'exhaustive treatise' which 'has not been written'. In his section on clues we discover Afrit's Injunction, appropriately culled from Alice (how appropriate indeed when Lewis Carroll was such a marvellous forerunner of the modern crossword setter!). This is what Afrit says:

> We must expect the composer to play tricks, but we shall insist that he play fair. *The Book of the Crossword* lays this injunction upon him: 'You need not mean what you say, but you must say what you mean.' This is a superior way of saying that he can't have it both ways. He may attempt to mislead by employing a form of words which can be taken in more than one way, and it is your fault if you take it the wrong way, *but it is his fault if you can't logically take it the right way.* The solver, for his part, is enjoined to read the clues in an anti-Pickwickian sense. This also requires explanation. To take a remark in a Pickwickian sense is not to take it literally; therefore, to read a clue in an anti-Pickwickian sense is to close the mind to the acquired metaphorical meaning of the words and to concentrate upon their bald literal significance. If you do so, you may find you are being presented with an anagram of the solution, or the solution is 'hidden' in the clue, or a bit of jugglery with its component parts is being done.

In other words: the solver who follows the structure of a clue literally should expect to discover a grammatical set of coded instructions leading to the answer.

A crossword clue is rather like a mathematical sum. The symbolism must be fair to lead the solver to the correct answer. The concept of fairness was further developed by Ximenes through his clue-writing competitions in *The Observer* and his book *Ximenes on the Art of the Crossword*. In fact the post-1949 developments now make many of Afrit's own clues in *Armchair Crosswords* look suspect! The debates about crossword grammar are still ongoing (and this book will undoubtedly contribute to them). Modern followers of the principles laid down by Ximenes sometimes call themselves 'Ximeneans'. For them there are definite rules of grammar that make a clue fair and they point the finger at crossworders who produce 'unsound', 'unfair' or 'non-Ximenean' clues. Your author is a Ximenean, but realizes that *some* non-Ximenean practices are not necessarily all bad.

It's time to look at some examples of fair and unfair clues.

Fair and unfair clues

Let's start with this one:

[II.I] Small pebbles—English (7)

This is supposed to give an anagram of 'English', namely SHINGLE, but the clue is a breach of Afrit's Injunction because the clue-writer has omitted an anagram indicator. This is a case of the *unindicated anagram*. The clue may be rendered sound by the addition of a suitable indicator:

[11.2] Small pebbles—possibly English (7)

might do. 'Possibly' is an anagram indicator. Here is an alternative:

[11.3] Broken English pebbles on the beach (7)

By no means a great clue, but a sound one, and this is important.

Here is a clue which may look all right at first sight, but which a Ximenean would regard as unacceptable:

[11.4] English mixture on the beach (7)

Two things are wrong here. For the Ximenean 'English mixture' cannot mean 'mixture of English'—it is simply ungrammatical. This is an example of an *unsatisfactory nounal anagram indicator*. Secondly 'on the beach' is an *inaccurate definition* leading to the wrong part of speech. An adverbial phrase (which this is) cannot be used to define a noun. Here is [11.4] rewritten:

[11.5] Mixture of English pebbles on the beach (7)

A clue such as the one following has all sorts of problems!

[11.6] Small pebbles possibly coming from the country (7)

This sort of structure has often been referred to as a clue to a clue and this particular example is an indirect anagram. The solver is expected to equate 'coming from the country' with 'English' and then work out an anagram. He may get the right answer from the definition and the checked letters, but to deduce 'English' and then work out an anagram is too much, because there are simply so many interpretations of 'from the country': 'Turkish' and 'bucolic' are just two! And of course any letters already in the diagram cannot easily be fed into the working out of the subsidiary indication. However, some would find the following clue quite defensible:

[11.7] Concerning what diet might become, it's seasonal (5)

Written by your author for the *Radio Times*, this clue was meant to suggest TIDAL (i.e. of 'tide', which is an anagram of 'diet'). Since 'diet' can only become two different words ('tide' and 'edit'), perhaps the clue may be deemed fair. [11.7] may perhaps be termed an *indirect definition*.

Here are three more indirect clues sanctioned by *The Times*:

[11.8] Country with its capital in Czechoslovakia (6)

[11.9] Novel sounds as if it will never be read (7,5)

[11.10] Half-hearted robber found in kitchen (7)

The answers are NORWAY (the capital in 'Czechoslovakia' being Oslo); FOREVER AMBER (it will never be 'red'); DRESSER ('robber' becomes 'rober').

Are these fair? Perhaps they are if you consider that they lead to unique solutions. I am not personally very keen on the indirect homophone (e.g. [11.9]), but it is common, and an unexpected clue type can add spice.

There is no excuse whatever for the following clue if the answer is supposed to be SHINGLE:

[11.11] What English could produce (7)

Here we have no indication of the definition—an *undefined answer*! Nor would there be any excuse if the length indication were (6) and the answer were supposed to be GRAVEL! The inexperienced clue-writer might argue thus: 'English could produce shingle, and gravel means shingle. What's wrong with that?' Let me tell you: i) there is no definition to the clue, and ii) the subsidiary indication leads not to the answer but to a clue to the answer. All very unsatisfactory!

Here are two further clues with unsatisfactory definitions:

[11.12] Brief affair with a lassie? (8,5)

The answer is supposed to be HIGHLAND FLING. This would be a clever idea for a subsidiary indication but the true meaning of Highland fling is Scottish dance and the clue presents an *inadequate cryptic definition*. It could be remedied by turning it into a double definition thus:

[11.13] Jock pursuing an illicit affair in a Scottish dance (8,5)

[11.14] HIJKLMNO (5)

This clue consists of the sequence H to O. Say 'H to O' and it sounds like 'H₂O', which everyone knows is WATER. This may seem ingenious, but to my mind this *indirect pun* is simply a nonsense. That sequence of eight letters simply cannot define WATER, and it does not pass muster in the same way that clue [3.20] does, in my opinion. I know that one or two crossword editors have quoted [11.14] as their favourite clue, but I must part company with them.

Sometimes a clue-writer will provide an *inaccurate definition*. One way of doing this is by *false generalization*. A couple of examples will suffice to illustrate this:

[11.15] Month in East for the saint (9)

clearly gives Augustine (August + in + E), but now look at this clue:

[11.16] Dreadful stain produced by Augustine (5)

The intended answer is SAINT, but this won't do because while 'saint' can define a particular saint (i.e. Augustine), 'Augustine' cannot define 'saint'. Because the saint (who produced this mysterious stain!) might have been Matthew, Mark, Luke or John, we must qualify 'Augustine'. Three common ways of doing this are:

[11.17] Dreadful stain produced by Augustine? (5)

[11.18] Dreadful stain produced by Augustine maybe (5)

[11.19] Dreadful stain produced by Augustine perhaps (5)

Another way of providing an inaccurate definition is by indicating an *incorrect part of speech*, and we saw an example of this in [11.4]. Here is another example:

[11.20] What's hidden by Fred afterwards? He must be stupid! (4)

The S part of this clue is straightforward. The answer is DAFT. But what about the last few words? They suggest a definition that is a noun rather than an adjective-say TWIT or FOOL. A clue-writer will often want to dress up his clue to make sense but won't know how to tie in the D with the S. In difficulty he adds extra words ('He must be'), then tries to convince himself that the clue is really quite good by sticking an *unnecessary exclamation mark* at the end (an additional fault in itself). When you think about it, clue [11.20] is indeed daft. If we must stick with this idea, though, and we want to produce a sound clue we could try this version:

[11.21] What Fred afterwards conceals is stupid (4)

Clearly an adjective must define an adjective, so presumably a noun must define a noun? Well, it's not quite that simple, sorry. Hold tight for the next few clues—we're about to get into deep water.

By convention, it *is* permissible for a noun to be defined by a verb, as in this clue:

[11.22] One party after another is really dead (4)

```
|_____S_____|  |___D___|
```

('do' plus 'do' equals DODO). Here the definition is understood to be:

[It] is really dead

with the 'It' understood.

However the clue could be unacceptable to Ximeneans without the 'is' since taking 'It is' on trust is simply too unfair—an adjective cannot define a noun. Similarly unacceptable would be this attempt at a hidden & lit. clue for SIMKIN:

[11.23] Among wines I'm king

An adverbial phrase is being used to define a noun and the clue should be recast to make it acceptable:

[11.24] It is among wines I'm king

This 1981 ruling was given by Azed, the successor to Ximenes, about whom we will hear more anon. What is interesting is that the 1972 Azed had no problem with clues like [11.24] (even awarding one a prize).

I warned you about deep water! It's time to move on, but first please look back to clue [11.20]. It gives evidence of the *redundant word syndrome*. Here is another clue that suffers from the same syndrome, and it is supposed to give the answer DORSET.

[11.25] Strode out to where Hardy lived (6)

The trouble is that 'to' fulfils no syntactical function in the clue. It is not a legitimate linkword between the S and D parts denoting equivalence (such as 'for' or 'in'); it is merely there to make the whole clue read better. A better version is:

[11.26] Strode out where Hardy lived (6)

Before we leave the subject of redundant words, let's take a fresh look at two clues from an earlier chapter:

[7.3] Good man, a sailor lying on bed, wounded (7)

The answer, remember, is STABBED (ST + AB + bed). Isn't the 'a' redundant? In a sense it is, but by a long-standing convention we may allow ourselves to introduce the indefinite or definite article when defining a noun.

[7.4] Bob has to study for the exam—buzz off! (5)

SCRAM consists of 's' + 'cram', and here we have defined cram by 'to study' in the way that a dictionary might. In fact the 'to' in the infinitive could be deemed redundant, but convention allows us to use it.

Now to another type of unfair clue. I call this the *overhidden clue*:

[11.27] Idle in the United States of America (4)

This hidden clue to ERIC (he of *Monty Python* fame) can't justify all those extra words where our comedian isn't lurking, so let's make it snappier:

[11.28] Idle in America (4)

If a crossword setter can put too many words in his clue he can also put in too few:

[11.29] Fred in a bad way? A mate is required (6)

An anagram of 'Fred in' suggests itself fairly quickly: FRIEND which means mate. But look carefully. The word 'in' is doing *double duty* as part of the phrase to be anagrammed and the anagram indicator. The clue should really read 'Fred in in a bad way'—it is 'Fred in' that is 'in a bad way', not just Fred. What about the right-hand side of the clue? After all I have said about redundant words, wouldn't 'mate' suffice? Yes—but the extra words can be justified syntactically. The solver is telling you 'You require a word meaning mate,' so the extra words do fulfil a function as a legitimate instruction to the solver. If we want to rewrite the clue soundly let's try this version:

[11.30] Fred in muddle. A mate is required (6)

At first sight this may look like another example of double duty: 'Fred in' in (a) muddle. Or it may look as though we have an unsatisfactory noun as the anagram indicator (see [11.4] above on p.68). But this clue can be justified: 'muddle' is an acceptable intransitive verb: the words 'Fred in' muddle, i.e. they 'potter about', to produce the answer.

Contrast [11.27] with this:

[11.31] Fred in difficulty—a mate is required (6)

A clue-writer might try to argue that 'in' is not doing double duty. The clue is meant to suggest that there is difficulty with the words 'Fred in'. This is not Mr Macmillan's 'little local' difficulty but a 'Fred in' difficulty. A true Ximenean will regard this as stretching the language too far: the clue suffers from the same fault as [11.4].

Here is another way in which an anagram could be improperly indicated:

[11.32] The East has lad striking a bargain (4)

The word 'striking' is the anagram indicator and we are supposedly asked to form an anagram from 'E' and 'lad' to give DEAL. The word 'has' is quite unfairly misleading however. It is true that East is somehow involved with lad in the anagram, but 'has' is grammatically misleading.

It's easy to make the clue sound:

[11.33] Eastern lad striking a bargain (4)

and

[11.34] Lad involved with Eastern bargain (4)

are both possible.

In [11.33] we have treated 'has' as a redundant word; in [11.34] we have integrated the anagram letters with the anagram indicator in a syntactically accurate way.

The unsatisfactory anagram indicator is a particular example of what we might call *word abuse* (for want of a better phrase). Types of word abuse are best illustrated by individual examples:

[11.35] An accomplishment indeed to be beaten (8)
This is supposed to give 'feat' in 'deed' = DEFEATED. Ximeneans say that 'indeed' in a clue does not equal 'in deed' (two separate words). Not all setters agree (alas).

Here are two clues with similar difficulties:

[11.36] Peruse in Gateshead—or somewhere in Berkshire (7)
The intended answer is READING ('read in g'), but Gateshead = G is taking too great a liberty with the language say Ximeneans (even if 'g' is head of the word 'gate'). Let's call this *unacceptable initial indication*. Here is a different form of the same problem:

[11.37] First man to have cut grass
Here 'first man' is supposed to indicate 'm', so that 'm' + 'own' = mown, but for a Ximenean this is unsound—'first man' simply cannot mean 'first letter of man', unlike 'man initially'. But there is another problem with this clue: 'mown' is defined as 'cut grass' whereas it really means 'cut'. This is another example of the redundant word syndrome. This time we have a *redundant object associated with a verb*.

What about this one from a daily newspaper:

[11.38] In chair first, one's getting gold tooth (7)
This is supposed to yield in + c + I's + or = INCISOR, but can 'chair first' indicate 'c'? I don't think so.

This clue shows another offence against the spirit of Ximenes:

[11.39] First chap, aged, frigid (4)
This time 'first chap' is supposed to indicate 'C', but grammatically this just doesn't work—'first chap' cannot mean the 'first letter of chap'. But it isn't difficult to write a *sound* clue:

[11.40] Leader of chaps, aged, frigid (4)
Not exciting, but an accurate clue for COLD.

Continuing on the theme of word abuse, let's look at the following clue:

[11.41] The cold season now in Bury (5)

This is supposed to suggest INTER ('winter' with no 'w'). The Ximeneans rightly assert that 'now' cannot equal 'no w' in a clue. Notice too that Bury has a capital B which it shouldn't really have. The false capital is a very minor offence (if it is an offence at all), but see how we can overcome the difficulty and the 'now' problem by putting Bury at the beginning of the clue:

[11.42] Bury in the cold season, no hint of warmth (5)

The 'cold season' (winter) with no 'hint of warmth' (w) gives INTER.

The same convention applies to 'hint' and words of that type as applies to 'bit' (see p.47). It should indicate only the first letter. Similarly with the tail. Ximenes has an amusing example of an unsound clue where this is not so:

[11.43] There's a horse in the stable with a lion's tail (8)

The answer is STALLION (stall + (l)ion), but as Ximenes says, 'Why should a lion have a tail three times as long as the rest of him?'

Middles must be precisely middles, too, says Ximenes, so this would not pass muster:

[11.44] Active learner at heart of Universe (4)

The supposed answer is LIVE (L + (Un)ive(rse)) but the heart of UNIVERSE is 've' or even 'iver', not 'ive'.

The next example is perhaps the most oft-quoted of all clues adjudged unsound by Ximenes:

[11.45] I am in the plot, that's clear (5)

The intended answer is PLAIN ('i' in 'plan'), but 'I' is the letter, not the pronoun. To overcome the deliberate ambiguity we can change the form of the verb and of course we can change 'I' to 'One'. Here are just some of the ways by which [11.45] can be rendered sound:

[11.46]

$$\left\{ \begin{matrix} \text{I} \\ \text{One} \end{matrix} \right\} \quad \left\{ \begin{matrix} \text{will be} \\ \text{must be} \\ \text{can be seen} \\ \text{should be} \end{matrix} \right\} \quad \text{in the plot, that's clear (5)}$$

Curiously enough, though Ximeneans do not allow the word 'I' to assume a personal status, a word or cluster of words can develop human characteristics:

[II.47] Rescue reviled drunk (7)

The word 'reviled' is 'drunk', i.e. in a disorderly condition, giving the answer DELIVER. Notice how 'reviled' is an adjective in the meaning reading of the clue and 'drunk' is a noun—but in the actual cryptic reading these parts of speech are reversed. This is a nice example of Afrit's Injunction.

Sometimes a setter will produce a double definition clue using meanings derived from the same dictionary headword:

[II.48] Leave vehicle in enclosed piece of land (4)

gives PARK using verbal and nounal definitions but this is a *spurious double definition* since the clue relies essentially on one word (unlike the clue for the many 'ports' we met on p.27). Similarly it would be less than ideal to use 'park' as a partial subsidiary indicator within a clue for 'park-keepers'.

One very common error is that of the *wrong direction*. Consider this clue for example:

[II.49] Dull poet coming back (4)

This is all right for an across clue but not for a down clue. The letters of 'bard' are reversed to form the answer DRAB, but they should go back in an across word and up in a down word. So a better version for a down clue would be:

[II.50] Dull poet turned up (4)

If for some reason a crossword setter had a brilliant clue involving 'up' (and 'back' would not do), he could change the grid by making all the across words down and down words across. A drastic measure, but one which your author has resorted to a few times.

In some crosswords you will find almost any Roman numeral defined by 'many' (L possibly, C, D and M certainly). Thus:

[II.5I] Many aged suffering from hypothermia (4)

Here, 'many' is supposed to suggest C (= 100); C + old = COLD. But by what criterion is a hundred equal to 'many'? Ximenes certainly didn't like this practice, and I don't think he would have liked this clue either:

[II.52] Note ancient brave (4)

Here you are presumably invited to take cognizance of a revered figure by his tepee, and B + old = BOLD. But a 'note' could be A, B, C, D. E, F or G (not to mention DO, RE, MI, FA, SO, LA, TI with all their variant spellings!). If notes are plentiful, so too are directions:

[II.53] Direction to have a meal—get a chair (4)

It's quite easy (S + eat = SEAT), but there are lots of directions if you box the compass from N, NE, round to NW. I haven't got a name for what is wrong with these last three clues. Shall we call it the *many/note/direction syndrome*?

Less common these days is a tendency to provide a *partial subsidiary indicator*, as in:

[II.54] Can be inside what's mythical (6)

Here 'can be' is supposed to be a definition of 'able' (which it isn't!) and 'able' is found in FABLED, but the 'f' and the 'd' are left unclued—which is unfair. This clue appeared in a national daily in the British Isles in August 2000. Can you believe it?

Next a few words on *punctuation*. You will already have noticed how the D and S parts of a clue can be juxtaposed without any punctuation (as in [II.47]). The Ximenean convention is to allow the omission of punctuation but not to allow inaccurate punctuation. This would amount to word abuse. The presentation of 'Gateshead' for 'gate's head' could be deemed an example of this, but there are other dreadful possibilities usually reserved for the more difficult cryptics with the words 'Punctuation may be misleading' in the preamble.

Watch out for this sort of thing:

[II.55] Stage love-in—Shakespeare setting initially? (6)

'Stage' is the definition for BOARDS (O in bard + s). The addition of the hyphen and the dash undoubtedly helps to make sense of a sequence of the six words, but this constitutes a case of unfair punctuation in breach of Afrit's Injunction. The clue must be recast to make it sound.

I have left until last the type of clue that is sound but meaningless. It is quite possible to write a clue which is fair under the conditions laid down in this chapter but which is still unsatisfactory.

[II.56] Floor covering fish—and Parisian! (6)

The answer is CARPET (carp + et). Yes, this is fair in terms of its construction, but in what context would this gibberish mean anything—and does the clue-writer hope we will enjoy this nonsense by adding an exclamation mark? Here is the *nonsensical clue*, and it is a type that many crossword clue-writers (especially novices) find difficult to avoid. Clues must make sense, or even semi-sense, but not *nonsense*.

Challenges to Ximenean standards

I have dwelt on the matter of fair and unfair clues at some length, and with so many clues on show I'd like to think that I've said all that needs to be said. Alas this cannot be so, for two good reasons that apply as much to crossword grammar as to English grammar generally: (i) grammar can never be a fixed prescription in any language and ideas will change; (ii) not everyone agrees with the rules laid down. Most of the principles I have outlined in this chapter would be taken on board by virtually every clue-writer, but not everyone will be bound by all the rules, whether those rules be laid down by Ximenes, Azed, or even Don Manley. Here then is an outline of where the main challenges to Ximenean standards lie:

(1) *The nounal anagram indicator.* Some would see 'English mixture' (see [11.4]) as an acceptable tatpurusha to denote 'mixture of English'. Expect to find this construction in *The Times*, for instance, where it is regarded as an acceptable grammatical construction. Incidentally Ximenes himself was happy with 'gin cocktail' for 'ING' and 'train crash' for RIANT, on the grounds that these two-word constructions had a meaning in terms of things being involved in a jumbling action, but some have suggested that in making this distinction the great man was guilty of a *categorical error*, since clues have to do with letters being mixed, not objects. More deep water, I'm afraid!

(2) *Other anagram indicators.* Although we haven't mentioned it, Ximeneans are happy with 'possibly' as an anagram indicator, but find 'perhaps' and 'maybe' too weak. Expect to find both these words, though, in the papers. There is also disagreement about other individual candidates for anagram indication with a number of marginal candidates such as: 'sort of' (no, say Ximeneans?), 'form of' (yes, say Ximeneans?), 'playful' (Ximeneans perhaps divided!).

(3) *Indirect clues.* While the extreme form of a clue to a clue would be shunned by all, some indirect clues, such as [11.8]–[11.10], might be deemed to add a little spice. Even Ximeneans might turn a blind eye.

(4) *Definition by part of speech.* In practice many clue-writers would be happy to have 'in India' as a subsidiary indicator written within a clue to BOMBAY even if the strict Ximeneans would prefer 'somewhere in India'.

(5) *Gateshead and suchlike.* Expect Gateshead = G. As a Ximenean, I'd be reluctant to give in on this one—but you should expect to see it. And expect 'many' for 'C' and 'note' for 'te' (the latter perhaps a very minor offence!).

(6) *Direction conventions.* Some would argue that clue [11.49] was quite satisfactory for a down clue on the grounds that clues are always written horizontally with vertically being introduced only when a solution is reconfigured on the grid. They have a point, *pace* Ximenes.

Why does Crossword Grammar matter?

We've spent a long time on crossword grammar and what constitutes a fair or an unfair clue. Does it all matter, you may ask? Well I think it does. To quote the master in *Ximenes on The Art of the Crossword* in his chapter on Cluemanship: 'I believe the principles laid down in this chapter can, if followed, make crosswords more satisfying.' Ximenes was a prescriptive grammarian, and prescriptive grammar hasn't been hugely in fashion these past thirty years. Isn't it the case, though, that the best writers of English have a command of English grammar? That grammar may well not be noticed by the reader, but a grammatically correct work will be more helpful to the reader than an ungrammatical one. Grammar may not be entirely prescriptive and it may not be absolutely rigid, but the best writers know what it's all about and how it can help their readers. The same goes for crossword setters and their solvers.

After all that, you are due another tutorial puzzle. The clues had all better be sound!

CROSSWORD No. 19

By Duck from *The Hamlyn Book of Crosswords No. 1*

ACROSS

1 The French doctor and essayist (4)
4 A cricket club's umpire saying 'Exit sir'! initially points the finger (7)
10 Possibly a group of extremist pop fans is coming around the party afterwards (9)
11 See nurse rummaging to some extent for fluid to inject (5)
12 See thin fragments in food being obtained beside a street—this sort of food? (7,8)
13 There's a shortage of salt passing through a plant (6)
14 A boy stuck in marsh plant used logic (8)
16 Whole large tin exploded (8)
18 Nothing in swimming pools? That's an anticlimax (6)
21 A long struggle. Representing us: Edward R. and a Henry (7,5,3)
23 Ignorant learner must have external restraint (5)
24 Firm newspaperman, anything but apathetic (9)
25 Relax almost completely in lodgings and introduce red herrings (7)
26 Artist left cathedral city (4)

DOWN

2 Rousing a fellow in a side-section of the building (9)
3 He produces booze in a little brown jug (6)
4 Satisfy an appetite perhaps with grilled sausage (7)
5 Actors we hear in the class (5)
6 Sign of future developments in London street appearing round top half of window, ghastly white (5,2,3,4)
7 The dog will reform someday (7)
8 Endlessly talk about a field event (6)
9 Party putting up for election makes 'class' the issue (6,8)
15 Tries messing about with wall—a difficult region for the home decorator (9)
16 A bloke at first opulent, losing head—the glory has departed (7)
17 Forcibly removes tar on pipes (7)
19 Violins producing sort of jazz on board (6)
20 Plant's a sensation with double dose of nitrogen in (6)
22 Mountain range, head of Glencoe—make journey round (5)

CROSSWORD No. 19

TEN CLUES FOR PALE
(see Challenge on p.55)

(a)	Whitish stake of wood.
(b)	Leap frantically looking ill?
(c)	Soft drink wanting in colour (p+ale). Friend needs a bit of expertise to make part of fence (pal +e).
(d)	Albert in Physical Education is not looking well, maybe (Al in PE).
(e,c)	Eastern circuit goes around wooden post ((E + lap), rev.)
(f)	Sup ales—partly making you lose colour? (pale, verb).
(f,e)	Wooden post in hotel apparently rejected (rejected = sent back).
(g)	Whitish bucket, we hear ('pail').
(h)	Bill coming out of palace looking ashen (palace minus a/c, a/c=account, bill).

12

More on Grids

In Chapter 2 we defined what we meant by checked and unchecked squares and we saw how the cryptic puzzle moved quickly from a closed grid to an open grid. It is time to look at grids in a little more detail and in doing so give you the chance to have a few more tutorials.

The most common size for an everyday cryptic is 15 × 15 and the grid will usually be based on the lattice shown below:

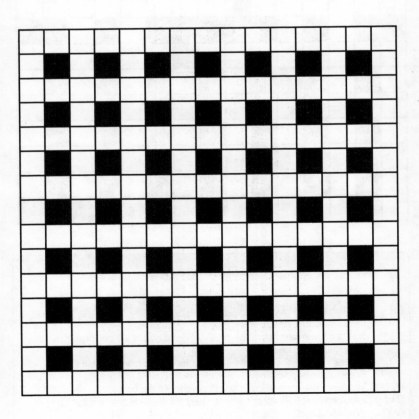

Extra squares will then be blocked out to divide words off and the result will usually be a puzzle of 28, 30 or 32 clues. The 28 formula is regarded as ideal because it offers four long words or phrases and a range of answer lengths. The *Times* crossword championship, however, uses puzzles of 30 clues, so that each clue can be assigned an equivalence of one minute during a 30-minute solving period. It is also possible to blank out the squares in either of these ways:

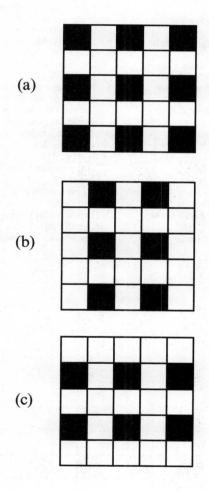

(a)

(b)

(c)

(Grid (c) amounts to the same thing as Grid (b) turned through 90 degrees.) The two puzzles which follow show grids based on these lattices.

CROSSWORD No. 20

By Quixote from *The Independent on Sunday*

ACROSS

7 No summer in guest-house would be complete without this cake (8)

9 Each flower is placed in dry kitchen vessel (6)

10 Dress is needed by the Spanish star (5)

11 Ate bits of nut ground extra small within fancy diet (8)

12 Lets out a secret and causes a problem in the kitchen? (6,3,5)

15 Useless beer—died after a couple of rounds (2-4)

16 What did Henry swallow? (Think of King, in pain!) (6)

18 Scientist to perform with hesitation when there's another (similar?) scientist around (14)

20 What 18 down could be? It's arrived (6,2)

22 There's little right in a fever—it makes one get heated maybe (5)

24 Soft further on in the day? That'll suit poor horse (6)

25 Disgusting mince pies—one rejected sample (8)

DOWN

1 Prefab in tract of land (parking included) (8)

2 Enclosure must be sound (4)

3 Fairy shut up to die (6)

4 Guns set up for animal to be hunted (4)

5 New gold chairs? Disgusting! (10)

6 You'll get wind when accompanying uninteresting person (6)

8 Endoscopy now helps surgeon remove it—Galen lost out! (9)

13 Reason US soldier is stationed in a particular place (10)

14 Amazon weapon? (9)

17 Domestic device makes runny marge set (3,5)

18 One provides cover by bringing in bread (6)

19 Upper section of pillar shows tribute (6)

21 Female artist needing work initially (4)

23 Endless dirt is unpleasant (4)

CROSSWORD No. 20

CROSSWORD No. 21

By Duck from *The Hamyln Book of Crosswords No. 4*

ACROSS

7 Builders, etc. hang around a monument in Scotland (9,6)

10 Symbol displayed by 'Arry's picnic basket at the seaside? (9)

11 Kind but terribly green (5)

12 Master to make a study of wine (5)

13 Rows with beet sown by middle of patch—and here's a place for the runners (3,9)

14 Airmen stayed up endlessly—a chancy business (6)

16 Powerful joke about Henry (6)

17 Form of art—while there's this there's hope (5,4)

19 Rascal in Society party (5)

21 Pervert asked for more (5)

22 Author—one to sample but only a minor literary figure (9)

23 Get very angry wanting insect removed from part of machine (3,3,3,6)

DOWN

1 Bring stillness to city area, bring stillness around (6)

2 Fairy appearing in October only (6)

3 Introductory comment—blame rep if it's wrong (8)

4 Advertisement in exhibition for spirit (6)

5 Father going to inn got drunk somewhere in Devon (8)

6 Riding up on the green, turn back (6)

8 Climb tricky with ice? A pity —faultlessness will be required (13)

9 Showing feeling for what a nice lettuce should be? (6-7)

15 Almost entirely deceitful Welshman, character created by Shakespeare (8)

16 Comes before President goes back (8)

17 Directions given to gent to begin journey (3,3)

18 Charge mischief-maker with upsetting trade union, leader of extremists (6)

19 Beetle making mark on seaman (6)

20 Hospital worker providing beer (6)

CROSSWORD No. 21

Sometimes a pattern will have different lattices clashing into one another, so that rows and columns appear to be dislocated. In the grid of Crossword No. 22, for example, there are examples of answers where two checked letters sit together and two unchecked letters sit together.

CROSSWORD No. 22

By Quixote from *The Oxford Times*

ACROSS

1 Some French bigwig in charge is tyrannical (8)

9 On the wing cloud is causing panic (8)

10 Band in the heart of New Orleans (4)

11 Warn that dear loony it spells out 'no hope' (5,7)

13 Beer for college servant (6)

14 Be hugging the monster? *I'd* get rid of the devil (8)

15 Flower Circle involved in arrangement for Easter (3,4)

16 Food cases with meat half one's own (7)

20 Leading character not what you'd expect—I may be confused with another (8)

22 Helical pairs formed life originally? (6)

23 River with waters swirling into specially designed hydroelectric plant maybe (5,7)

25 Two little islands in river (4)

26 Mocking lecturer in car is naughty (8)

27 Is the sacked worker not sure what to do? (8)

DOWN

2 It could make one hear with plug initially inserted (8)

3 Need MP retire if found out? Settle in advance (12)

4 You get a form of art in these, possibly (8)

5 Sack employee of NatWest? (7)

6 Rock has unpleasant smell—get basin for washing (6)

7 I am in city, a South American capital (4)

8 Laws providing conditions to restrict trade union (8)

12 Tie inspector—absurd office worker conscious of public image? (12)

15 Very good saint? Only if his mouth is sealed off first! (8)

17 Gold and fragrant substances as omens (8)

18 I care not about the response (8)

19 Ruler abandoned Roman church (7)

21 Member of sect: 'The most important thing is to oust the Conservative' (6)

24 Fighting dunce, a child who needs special care (4)

CROSSWORD No. 22

Whatever basic grid is used the setter should try to keep to certain standards of fairness:

1. *No part of the grid should be completely cut off* from another part of the grid (remember the nine mini-crosswords on p.23).

2. *The number of unchecked letters (unches) in an answer should be half of the total or less.* It won't matter much if 7 letters out of 13 are left unchecked, as here: _ R _ S _ O _ R _ V _ R _. Knowing that the answer should give you a football team (7,6) you will soon get BRISTOL ROVERS. In the grid on p.24, though, one may be left trying to solve e.g. 13 across with _ A _ E _ and this can simply pose too many possibilities for comfort. (It should be added that lattice (a) makes the observance of this convention easier than (b), (c) or (d) do.)

3. *The triple unch (and worse!) should be avoided.* This means that no answer should contain three consecutive letters not checked by crossing letters.

4. *Normally the grid should be symmetrical if given a half-turn* (i.e. through 180 degrees). Some grids also give symmetry if turned through 90 degrees. Sometimes a mirror symmetry will be preferred to a half-turn symmetry, as in the final tutorial puzzle for this chapter.

CROSSWORD No. 23

By Don Manley from *The Church Times*

ACROSS

1 Hymn tune which could make Sid feel sedate (6,7)
7 Wise man to draw breath in amazement on arrival (6)
8 Small number having happy Christmas (6)
9 Tempts everybody with devilish ruse (7)
11 Fellow of generous disposition—now there's good news for all...! (7)
13 Boy, 8 (4)
15 Love to people shown in a sign (4)

21 Anger so out of control—not fruit *of the Spirit* (7)
22 '...thou goest I will go' (Ruth 1: 16, AV) (7)
23 Relating to a morning service in which mum can feature (5)
24 Girl's song now being heard? (5)
25 Gin now on sale maybe to bring seasonal bonhomie? (9,6)
28 Cheap and ostentatious like Christmas tree decorations? (6)
29 Like the Pope, free from coarseness (6)

CROSSWORD No. 23

DOWN

1 God's messengers held by gang elsewhere (6)
2 Methodist preacher using rambling prose? (5)
3 Sin brings an element of terror (3)
4 Fashionable northern bar with limited accommodation? (3)
5 A chap may have red wine—but avoid the extremes! (5)
6 This night we celebrate as 24-singers—enlist for wandering around (6)
10 Vessel from Abraham's city, last thing found in excavation (3)
12 The family makes one of the three travellers stop short (3)

14 Strains go out from church musicians perhaps (9)
16 Bishop's cope is silly on friend (9)
17 Some rays are funny when placed round head of saint (6)
18 Letter from bishop of bygone days (spoken) (8)
19 Strange arch, very French, in cathedral city (8)
20 Alter introduction to 'Messiah' in arrangement for band (6)
26 Peter e.g. with yen to follow master (3)
27 Present, very big, put up on piano (3)

Ten clues to edit

Here are ten clues from published crosswords. Your task is to edit them to make them sound. When you have completed the task you might like to look at my analysis and compare your list with mine in the box on p.155.

1	Ate nuts in a way that produced lockjaw (7)	
	(Answer: TETANUS)	
2	Is that you among the cargo with the cat? (6)	
	(Answer: COUGAR)	
3	Salvia may be such a help in this way (6)	
	(Answer: AVAILS)	
4	Please sound like a victim (4)	
	(Answer: PRAY)	
5	A famous conqueror at the beginning (6)	
	(Answer: ATTILA)	
6	Ego clue provided by short poem (7)	
	(Answer: ECLOGUE)	
7	How Henry plays on board with his mother (5)	
	(Answer: HALMA)	
8	A six-foot long caper, I see (5)	
	(Answer: ANTIC)	
9	A Dior creation in most homes (5)	
	(Answer: RADIO)	
10	Bid a run to be used to free locks (7)	
	(Answer: UNBRAID)	

The Basic Advanced Cryptic Crossword

It is now time to progress from the everyday cryptic crossword to the advanced cryptic. We will be moving from blocked grids to barred grids, the clues will become trickier, and some of the vocabulary will become less familiar. For that you will need *The Chambers Dictionary*. Apart from being very good for everyday usage, *Chambers* (as we call it) offers a remarkable range of unusual words and ancient language that rarely survives in a single-volume dictionary.

This is not just a commercial for my publisher—*Chambers* is simply indispensable. Where else can you so easily find the probable misprint in Shakespeare (EALE)? Where else, in such a concise volume, can you find a supposed 'cross between a male yak and common horned cow' with ten different spellings (though some are male only, some female only)? If you don't believe me, look under ZHO in the big red book where you will also find: ZO, DSO, DZO, ZHOMO, DSOMO, JOMO, ZOBO, ZOBU, DSOBO. Also in its 2000-odd pages you will find everything from ancient words for 'grievous' (DEAR, DEARE, DEERE) and a Scotticism for a hanging clock (WAG-AT-THE-WA') to WORD PROCESSOR (a cryptic definition of a clue-writer?). If you pause to read *Chambers* while solving a puzzle, you may also find some quirky definitions in the best Johnsonian tradition: try ECLAIR and MIDDLE AGE for example.

As you progress to the barred puzzle you will need to learn the abbreviations in *Chambers*. You will still be meeting MA indicated by 'master', but that abbreviation may also be clued by Morocco, the International Vehicle Registration. Copper may still be Cu, but you had also better know that beryllium has the symbol Be. And so on.

Barred grids in advanced crosswords

The tradition of using bars was established in the early days of British crosswords and became the hallmark of Torquemada, mentioned briefly in Chapter 11. One of his puzzles from his 1934 miscellany *The Torquemada Puzzle Book* is shown below.

I provide the grid with the answer because in my humble opinion no one in his right mind should be expected to attempt a solution! By today's standards this is a work of misdirected genius with its unsound clues and difficult references. Note too the lack of symmetry and the reversed words which strike us as very odd.

TORQUEMADA PUZZLE

ACROSS

1 Bunny gets a head on him and becomes peevish
7 American law-giver sets a Scottish standard
12 Waited for by Brutus but not by Pilate
14 I wrote Terminations when I started and The Trimmed Lamp when I ended
15 *rev.* 36
16 I take those who do not take themselves
17 37's
19, 21 Confirm officially
20 City found in a town
23 I'm already fashionable and if you add the difference between six and sixteen I'm an erroneous overcoat
24 Genus of worms in a heretic
25 *rev.* French fleet in English waters
27 Shepherd's bad companion
29 11
30 You may discover us in a trick but you had better shake to make sure
31 34 dn
32 *rev.* Shortened
34 Relying on a large scale
38 Trim is my county town
39 Epitaph in bad verse
40 I can hold a candle—to 26

DOWN

1 Behead this old clothesman for a murderer
2 Bisected drawback
3 e.g. squire
4, 11 One boot that helped another to dish a cake
5 Clouded with brown from unfaces it
6 Walked on by people in coloured shirts
7 Solomon's eight-bottle man
8 *rev.* I said: "The purple flowers droop: the golden bee Is lily-cradled: I alone awake"
9 A German might associate this piece of lead with 22
10 Novelist not encouraged to write at Cambridge
13 *rev.* Scottish stout that becomes musty when it crosses the border
18 Next will help in
22 Should come after 27
26 *rev.* 29
28 *rev.* Noah's care has become anyone's old care
32, 33 All but the play by Maugham
34 31
35 My first is unchecked in 13 and my second in 11
36 *rev.* 15
37 One 17

TORQUEMADA PUZZLE

F	R	A	B	B	I	T	J	E	D	G	E
R	E	P	L	Y	N	H	E	N	R	Y	R
I	T	H	U	F	F	E	R	O	A	P	S
P	R	E	C	F	U	N	O	N	I	S	E
P	O	S	H	U	S	A	B	E	L	L	A
E	D	I	R	T	C	R	O	O	K	E	R
R	U	S	E	S	A	L	A	T	R	U	C
S	C	U	T	A	T	E	M	E	A	T	H
A	T	R	I	P	E	T	O	R	C	H	E

Notes

Across: 7. Two meanings. 12. Julius C., III, 2, 37; Bacon, Essays, Of Truth; 14. Henry (James), (O.) Henry; 23. Posh-teen, posteen; 24. Sabelli(i)a(n); 25. *rev.* French borrowing; 30. R-us-e, anag.; 39. T-R-I-P.-e; 40. Candelabrum when put to 26.

Down: 1. Jack the (f)Ripper; 2. Draw back; 3. Esquire; 4 and 11. Wellington, Napoleon; 5. Anag.; 6. And others; 7. I Kings, xii, 28; 8. *rev.* Tennyson, O., 28; 9. Trail; 13. *rev.* Two meanings; 28. *rev.* C-ark; 32 and 33. (The) Letter.

It would be very easy for us to write off this puzzle completely, but two aspects of it have survived: the difficult vocabulary and the barred grid. Clue-writing has become more disciplined, and this has allowed the difficult solution to be more solvable (thanks to the pioneering work of Ximenes); the barred grid has become more orderly. A typical 12 × 12 Azed grid is shown below.

The basic permitted parameters for the 12 × 12 plain puzzle were laid down by Ximenes in his book *On the Art of the Crossword*:

1.   Number of unches in a word:

       4 and 5 letters, 1 unch

       6 and 7 letters, 1 or 2 unches

       8 and 9 letters, 2 or 3 unches

       10, 11 and 12 letters, 3 or 4 unches

2.   Number of words in a barred puzzle: 36, usually with six rows and six columns containing one word and the other twelve two words. Four of the twelve one-word rows and columns will contain your four long words: the other eight will be reduced in length by bars to fit shorter words.

(In recent times however some setters of 12 × 12 puzzles have prided themselves on managing with as few as 32, 28 or even 24 clues.)

Note how the Ximenean formula leads to a tidy balanced-looking grid with no multiple unches. You can see that there is more checking in a Ximenean grid than in a blocked grid, and this is a distinct asset for the solver. Suppose you are faced with a clue such as this:

[13.1] Vegetable, very black inside—it grows in the tropics (6)
and you have all the crossing words to give you LEB _ E _ .

By the time you get that far you should be able to work out BB in leek = LEBBEK, but if you cannot you can always look up *Chambers*, find the only word that will fit and work backwards to see how the clue works. With L _ B _ E _ or _ E _ B _ K it would be a shade harder.

For the most part, clues in plain barred puzzles are similar in concept to those in blocked puzzles, but to give you a flavour of the different language due to *Chambers* here are some examples and answers all from Azed and his competitors (we shall look at the Azed competition again in Chapter 16):

[13.2] Pour out Jock's shin-bone soup (5)
Answer: SKINK which has two meanings—hence the note reads (2 mngs). Skink is a Scottish word for that form of soup—hence the label 'Jock's'. Jock is a familiar person in Azed.

[13.3] Zinc sulphide to mix with einsteinium (6)
Answer: BLENDE (blend + E). You've been warned about abbreviations.

The next clue won S. L. Paton first prize in Azed No.1:

[13.4] Before the heart ensnares one, one likes to go on a binge (7)
Answer: ORGIAST (a in or + gist). Note two things: (1) before = or, a rare usage which would be too obscure for the average cryptic: (2) one = a (quite justifiable but in less advanced cryptics 'one' = 'I' usually).

[13.5] Campaigner in old company holding steadfast to right (8)
Answer: CRUSADER (sad in crue + r, 'semi & lit.'). This too was an Azed first-prizewinner from M. L. Perkins. Note the use of 'old' for the obsolete word 'crue'. Many words in *Chambers* can be labelled 'obsolete', 'stale', 'traditional' or 'as before'. In this clue also note 'to' meaning 'beside', a useful throwaway in a charade.

[13.6] Gee surrounded by at least four more dashes (6)
Answer: SPANGS (g in spans). 'Gee' is a spelling of the letter 'g' (as well as a suggestion of a horse). Look our for el, em, es and others!

[13.7] Oily swimmer has success on lake—goodness me, born genius (9)
Answer: GOLOMYNKA for a down clue (go + L + o my! + n + ka). An interesting assemblage of obscure bits and pieces combining to make an

obscure word—but genius = ka is soon learnt with experience!

In advanced cryptics the answer often describes itself in the first person. This prize-winning clue from C. O. Butcher uses this convention to achieve an & lit:

[13.8] I form bulges erected on a defence's sides (9)
The answer is GABIONADE (I bag (rev.) + on a d e & lit.).

This *personification* goes back to the Victorian riddle (see p.4). This sort of thing is definitely allowed, even if the personal I cannot be allowed in the plan (see p.74)!

Solvers of an Azed puzzle will need to know that familiar words can take on unfamiliar meanings when used as indicators. If you are familiar with the hymn 'There is a green hill far away', you will know that 'without' can mean 'outside' as well as 'lacking'. Here's an example from Ximenes:

[13.9] Rural spot without excitement (8)
giving MOFUSSIL ('fuss' in 'moil').

Did you know that 'on' can mean 'getting drunk' and that 'over' can suggest a word being rolled over (i.e. reversed)? No examples here, but you will meet them soon enough!

From unusual words and unusual usages of usual words to unusual word order. Most of us think and write like this:

I hate people who flatter me with lies.

But a poet does not always write his sentences in the order 'subject/object/verb'. Thus William Cowper:

The lie that flatters I abhor the most.

And thus Will (W. J. M.) Scotland, an Azed prizewinner demonstrating another verbal art form, that of clue-writing:

[13.10] The jungly mass one cleaves (7)
The answer is MACHETE (anag. in m ace, because in fact 'the jungly' is cleaving 'mass one').

Finally a subtle pair of clues from Azed linked by leader dots:

[13.11] Cunning but timorous if losing head … (5)

[13.12] … To these fools, given which they would have heads (5)

[13.11] gives LEERY and [13.12] OAVES. Transfer the L from the first clue to the second and you would have 'eery' (timorous) and 'loaves' (heads). Clever stuff!

The time has come for two small tutorial puzzles. Then we must look at some of the more sophisticated clue types common to barred puzzles.

CROSSWORD No. 24

ACROSS

1 Poppy and a stone in Jock's gutter (8)
7 Greek character will shortly become invalid (4)
8 Arsenic arrives from geological formations (4)
10 Source of hope in troubled times? (6)
12 One in old age not yielding milk for Mac (4)
13 Fruit giving dog energy (4)
16 Man at table shows orange stain (6)
17 Unit attached to bit of sound (4)
18 Scottish boy shows spirit (not square) (4)
19 Watching over five couples on the floor? (8)

DOWN

1 Pa eats nut rudely rejecting superior old appetiser (8)
2 Flower that's tender, hurt when upset? Not entirely (4)
3 Bard puts touch of magic into E.lang. and E.lit. (7)
4 Master sermon amplifies a message from the heavens maybe (5)
5 One in love is secure (4)
6 Die with a tear destroyed in shoot out… (8)
9 …killed with gun outside American institute (7)
11 Workers appearing before newspaper boss complained as before (5)
14 Instrument with nothing in order (4)
15 Touches of obvious talent in crossword in 'The Listener' (4)

CROSSWORD No. 25

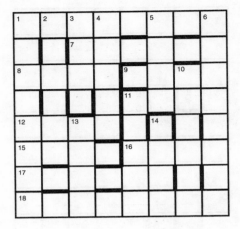

ACROSS

1 Plant tissue shows tree is 2000 roughly (8)
7 Dedicated man retired, no longer with us (6)
8 Bird's old garment (4)
9 Townsmen linger endlessly around (4)
11 Do is producing an old-fashioned racket (4)
12 What Jumblies went to *sea* in — or river we hear (4)
15 'urried along and declared (4)
16 Poet heard to be in prison? (4)
17 Girl gets hold of hard Azed — 36 lines of skilled writing? (6)
18 The old weaken and come in about to die (8)

DOWN

1 I am great, fantastic — superior's right! (8)
2 Beetle story upset Her Majesty (6)
3 Heartless bird's mutter (4)
4 Fallen angel, one with happiness curtailed (5)
5 Bird eating a wee portion (4)
6 A month in old Paris requires my French, second language, right? (8)
10 Cordyline has two birds in it (6)
11 Old city governor is in the city (5)
13 A bit of mutton to devour? (4)
14 Expert turned up admitting learner's lacking in literary style (4)

14

Advanced Clues

Ximenes once recommended that hard words should have easy clues and easy words hard clues. Much of the hardness in clues is due to the subtlety of wording, but there are clue types used in advanced puzzles that you are less likely to meet in the everyday cryptic. The examples that follow are culled from Azed puzzles and Azed clue-writing competitions in *The Observer*.

The moving letter(s)

In this clue type the solver is invited to find a word and then move a particular letter (or letters) to discover a new word:

[14.1] See me in N. European water, tail moving? (6)

N. European water is WASSER: move the tail (r) to get WRASSE. Note that an '& lit.' effect is also achieved since a wrasse is a fish.

[14.2] I disapproved of the unseemly skunk, tail foremost (4)

Move the c of atoc (a skunk) to the front to obtain the censor CATO.

The substituted letter(s)

Here you are invited to find a word and substitute one letter (or set of letters) for another. Thus in this clue:

[14.3] Vigorous? Love yielding to East in source of drowsiness (5)

We find a source of 'drowsiness' (poppy) and substitute e for o (love) to arrive at PEPPY (meaning 'vigorous').

Alternate letters

The solver is asked to discard every other letter in a clue such as the following:

[14.5] Outings in which you find chain keeps losing odd bits (5)

A ride on a shaky bicycle? Maybe—but forget the misleading context and remove the odd letters ('bits') from the 'chain keeps'. The result is HIKES.

The words 'odd bits' and 'even bits' usually give the game away but here is the technique given a new subtlety by Azed:

[14.6] Ancient Syrian one regularly placed among king and troops (8)

Place A alternately among R and MEN and you'll get ARAMAEAN.

In the following clue (which won a first prize for N. C. Dexter in a 1984 Azed competition) the alternate letters are anagrammed:

[14.7] By it 'truth' and 'lie' looked alternately interchangeable (11)

An anagram of BITUHNLEOKD is DOUBLE-THINK (another & lit. of course).

The missing-words charade

This type of charade is best illustrated by some examples:

[14.8] Opening gambit at parties is hard if shyness _____ inhibits one (7)

The first word here provides the definition. The remainder is a sentence into which you must insert some words which make sense. The words required are 'or if ice' ('ice' meaning 'reserve'). Put them together in a charade and the answer is ORIFICE.

[14.9] 'Adam's _____ ', said archaic Eve, very old crone? (6)

The answer is RIBIBE. Can you see why?

Sometimes the charade provides a 'letter formula' telling you how to get from one group of letters to another:

[14.10] Highland cattle put with this will become quiet (4)

The answer is NOUT (Highland cattle) because 'put with no ut' equals 'p' (an abbreviation for 'quiet'). A relatively unusual type of clue this, and the example given threw more than one solver when perpetrated by Azed.

The subtractive container-and-contents

This type of clue is a combination of techniques (d) and (h) in Chapter 8. Here's an example of my own, :

[14.11] This minor when put in bed is happy (4)

It's nothing to do with a compliant child when you read the clue cryptically. You want a word which when put in bed gives you 'blessed': hence LESS.

Here's one from Azed:

[14.12] What'll those enthralled like us in Market get? Mare's-nest (5)

The word you want, hidden in the 'mart' (or market) in 'mare's nest' is ESNES, who are enthralled as slaves. Quite simple really!

The composite anagram

The composite anagram was revived by Don Putnam in the (now-defunct) *Games and Puzzles* magazine in 1975. He described a clue from Afrit's book which read as follows:

[14.13] You could make this whale seem quarrelsome, but hold it up by its tail and it begins to laugh (7).

Forget the words after 'quarrelsome' and concentrate on the first seven words. Afrit is saying take 'this word for whale' plus 'seem' and you could make 'quarrelsome'. The answer is RORQUAL (hence the 'lau' in the reversal, the beginning (!) of 'laugh'). Quite soon after Putman's article Azed and *Listener* puzzlers were faced with the rediscovery of the composite anagram. The clue-writer was saying in effect 'If A won't form a decent anagram, I'll add B and define it as an anagram of C.' A way had been rediscovered of combining the anagram with the subtractive clue.

This type of clue normally appears as an & lit., as the following examples illustrate:

[14.14] Ecuadorans, broke, might produce a _____ and nothing else (5)

ECUADORANS is an anagram of 'a, _____ and, o'. The missing word is SUCRE.

[14.15] Some sprinkling with this could give a tame meal gusto (9)

This won B. Franco a first prize from Azed in 1977. The word 'some' has to be sprinkled with a word to give 'a tame meal gusto'. Answer: MALAGUETTA (look up its meaning in *Chambers* if you don't know it).

My own prize-winning Azed clue for PICKLE (which can mean 'steal') read as follows:

[14.16] Kleptomaniac: a man to _____ indiscriminately?

(Incidentally 'A man to pickle indiscriminately' is a rather good clue for KLEPTOMANIAC, don't you think?)

stay	bley	Esky®	ismy	espy	oosy	gazy
quay	fley	yuky	fumy	I-spy	posy	hazy
away	gley	paly	cany	nary	rosy	jazy
M-way	sley	waly	many	oary	upsy	lazy
sway	joey	ably	wany	vary	busy	mazy
tway	drey	idly	zany	wary	maty	vizy
baby	grey	rely	deny	scry	city	cozy
gaby	prey	ugly	reny	adry	mity	dozy
inby	trey	lily	miny	aery	pity	fozy
goby	stey	oily	piny	eery	doty	oozy
go-by	quey	wily	tiny	hery	arty	Z
toby	defy	ally	viny	very	duty	Geëz
upby	affy	illy	winy	airy	cavy	chez
orby	cagy	inly	bony	miry	Davy	trez
ruby	edgy	only	cony	wiry	navy	oyez
lacy	eggy	holy	mony	skry	wavy	phiz
pacy	bogy	moly	pony	dory	bevy	whiz
racy	dogy	poly	tony	gory	levy	friz
ricy	fogy	duly	puny	lory	envy	quiz
fady	orgy	guly	tuny	pory	movy	swiz
lady	hugy	July	awny	rory	yawy	Gënz
wady	achy	puly	gyny	Tory	dewy	lutz
eddy	ashy	ruly	ahoy	spry	nowy	Druz
tedy	caky	owly	pioy	'Arry	towy	jazz
tidy	laky	gamy	cloy	bury	waxy	razz

An extract from *Chambers Back-Words for Crosswords*, a reverse-sorted word list, ideal for the crossword fan who is stuck with (say) _ _ TZ: LUTZ is the only answer here, but it just could be RITZ!

The composite anagram does not have to be part of an & lit. clue; as in this case of mine 'very highly commended' by Azed near St. Valentine's Day:

[14.17] A little romance? Such fun with cryptic letters may show it is fourteenth.

In other words take a word possibly meaning 'a little romance', combine it with 'fun' cryptically to give 'it is fourteenth'. The answer comes out as HISTORIETTE (a short story). In the first of your next tutorial puzzles all clues are based on the clue types described in this chapter. Quite often though you won't find a single example of any of them, even in an Azed—but there are just a few in the full-size puzzle. Remember, too, that the setter will always be looking for a new and subtle way of telling you how to deal with the letters in front of you.

Time for two more tutorial puzzles.

CROSSWORD No. 26

ACROSS

1 Might _____ malfunction to make light smear? (5)

5 This snake with ring around is making grating sound (3)

8 Fragments to classify, first to last (4)

10 Work of art's loud, not soft and languishing (8)

11 Plans—utter odd bits showing what man's made of? (5)

12 Plundered—one gets a hanging (dead towards the end) (5)

17 Offering amnesty—a little time given for four (8)

18 Jock's cattle oddly shifting round—it's a habit (4)

19 An unseemly place like this could be nasty (3)

20 Bell sounds pierce, start to finish (5)

DOWN

1 Look fit selecting odd bits in the attic (4)

2 It's Bahrain: see _____ in this setting? (4)

3 Dot boozes with a touch of sadness coming to the fore (7)

4 See girl ruin tea—odd bits served (4)

6 Numbers switching ends in ecstasy (4)

7 Horror writer has a bit of ghastliness for his middle bit of book (4)

9 Special errand: _____ might be attracted to Mr Electron! (7)

12 Ogres half twisting into fabulous birds (4)

13 Lean sceptic may interject with _____ (4)

14 Write in _____ or ... alternatively presented as 'orient'? (4)

15 _____ ? It is possibly to sing (4)

16 Big _____ 'd produce bad sting possibly (4)

CROSSWORD No. 27

ACROSS

1 Look around mountain pass—it will have hard mass of igneous rock (9)

10 Chemical coming from a chimney in Glasgow? (4)

11 Black crew in underground layer (8)

12 Tropical dish maid can cook—not all right, fantastic! (9)

13 Strong liking for eating a bit of garlic and salad (6)

14 Black mineral has resistance? This will pierce a hole (5)

17 Feminine English woman's felt hat (6)

19 Small cask in pub attracting glance, not half! (7)

20 Hobo languishes holding a coin not worth much (4)

22 Advance payment for penniless pre-1971 poet (4)

24 Artist put back silk in cupboard (7)

26 You can't play cricket without _____ ball! This intruder's taken possession (6)

29 Praying not to get gee-gee as present (5)

30 Garbled matins—one only *appears* to pray (6)

31 A learner needs library service—never on a permanent basis? (9)

32 Cold sea bit tricky, around zero? Such may be the answer (8)

33 Account by army for the official minutes (4)

34 Softly touching woman—not entirely kind to be a grasper (9)

DOWN

1 Bean produced in the biologist's workplace repeatedly? (6)

2 A loser primarily, an 'orse not finishing sadly (7)

3 Water-carrier wasn't fit, with wooden joints somehow? (12)

4 In room a ghost lurks somewhere in Ireland (5)

5 Antiseptic appearing as yellow crystals—ten sufficient for the chemistry class? (8)

6 Wife featured in educational paper organised communities (6)

7 Mother 100—having modern technology around one is key to prolonging life (12)

8 I don't go to matins *and* evensong—what'll do for collection? (5)

9 A time in Israel with actors turning up (4)

15 Torment losing every other part—allowance for waste required (4)

16 Fish become frightened—I had *one* caught (8)

18 Be a success? Ali was with his (4)

21 Wine that's yellow I vote 'nasty' (7)

23 Where you'd see British go on jaunt—and the king? (6)

25 Some of the fens, earthed, dry up as before (6)

27 Fine French child for rude eruption after meal? (5)

28 Would a non-conformist Scot primarily inhabit me? (5)

29 Handle of kettle perhaps or bucket (4)

CROSSWORD No. 27

CROSSWORD DINNERS

Crossword dinners have been held in honour of *The Listener* and *The Observer* and one in 2001 was held to celebrate Azed MD and Listener (known as the Maddest Zeal Dinner for anagrammatic reasons). *Observer* dinners have celebrated Ximenes Nos. 100, 200, 500, 750 and 1000, Azed Nos. 250, 500, 750, 1000 (a lunch), 1300, and 1500 (the joint celebration with *the Listener* puzzle). The 'D-AZED' menu is shown below for the Azed 500 Dinner held in Oxford in 1981. The conventional menu is shown opposite.

D-AZED MENU

Ten common beers? No! (8,8)

* * * *

Eel's fins? Tell no fool! (6,2,4,6)

* * * *

A crab trifle left? Come often! (11,2,4,7)
Heat a cat-toe soup... (7,8)
...Ill at our tea? (11)
Boil croc (8)

* * * *

Mum's choice lemon cheese (we'd hot treat) (9,6,4,5,2,6)

* * * *

The finer men ate stiff cow-rind (6,4,5-6,5)

MENU

CONSOMMÉ BRETONNE

* * * *

FILLET OF SOLE NELSON

* * * *

CONTREFILET OF BEEF CLAMART

CHATEAU POTATOES

RATATOUILLE

BROCCOLI

* * * *

CHOCOLATE MOUSSE WITH CRÊME DE MENTHE

* * * *

COFFEE WITH AFTER-DINNER MINTS

Wine kindly provided by *The Observer*

15

Special Crosswords

All the crosswords so far have had normal clues (however complex) and the words have been entered in a normal grid. In a special crossword something is abnormal—either the form of clue or the grid. In extreme cases you may be faced with several forms of abnormality. There are a number of standard special crossword types and beyond that there are the 'special specials'! In this chapter we shall look at some of the well-known specials. In each case we shall look at the standard rubric which accompanies that type of puzzle and then illustrate with a tutorial.

Printer's Devilry

This form of puzzle was invented by Afrit (see p.66). Here is the rubric in its classical Ximenean form:

> Each clue is a passage from which the printer has removed a hidden answer, closing the gap, taking liberties sometimes with punctuation and spacing, but not disturbing the order of the remaining letters. Thus in the sentence *Now that it's so much warmer, can't I let the boiler go out?* MERCANTILE is hidden. The printer might offer as a clue: *Now that—it's so much wart, the boil : ergo, out!* Each passage when complete makes some sort of sense.

The clue Ximenes chose has an extreme case of shifting word breaks along the line. A PD clue with a simple break and no shifting letters is also possible, as in this beautiful example which won Mrs E. M. Pardo a first prize from Ximenes:

[15.1] Children taking piano lessons soon learn the sign ff (6)

The break occurs in 'ff' giving the undevilled version '… for a clef', and the answer is therefore ORACLE. In Azed competitions this additional advice is give to PD clue-writers:

N.B. Preference is given to PD clues in which breaks before and after the word omitted (before and after omission) do not occur at the ends or beginnings of words in the clue.

Hints to solvers. Sort out any obvious space shifts. Then try to find the point at which the clue looks strained and insert a pencil stroke. See if you can add new letters to the stranded letters either side of the stroke to produce a word which fits in with the theme of the clue. In the Ximenean example above you should be able to see 'the boiler go out'. In that context a 'wart' doesn't make much sense. By trial and error you might decide to break thus: war/t. In the context of the clue and perhaps with some help from checking letters you should arrive at 'warm' and 'warmer'. Then if all else fails, you can look up the 10-letter MER words in *Chambers Words* and work backwards. Solving PD clues can be very hard, but this tutorial puzzle offers generous checking and should present few problems.

CROSSWORD No. 28

Printer's Devilry

ACROSS

1 Royal Academy will only display the bet (4)
5 If you're going in for driving, Tess, son might help (4)
6 Got a big success? Banks should be pleased! (4)
7 In a gale you might see town (4)

DOWN

1 Towards end of game do play 'ere (4)
2 Sleep's needed by one living in busy street-bus? 'Tis impossible with traffic noise (4)
3 Cats are crossbred by American ranchers (4)
4 Ties—dress in the latest fashion (4)

Misprints

Misprint is a form of puzzle invented by Ximenes, and the rubric explains all:

Half the clues, both across and down, contain a misprint of one letter only in each, occurring always in the definition part of the clue: their answers are to appear in the diagram correctly spelt. The other half, both across and down, are correctly printed: all their answers are to appear in the diagram with a misprint of one letter only in each. No unchecked letter in the diagram is to be misprinted: each twice used letter is to appear as required by the correct form of at least one of the words to which it belongs. All indications such as anagrams, etc., in clues lead to the correct forms of words required, not to the misprinted forms.

The Ximenean rubric does not give an example of misprinted clue, but we can illustrate from Ximenes himself:

[15.2] Rummy sort of girl—see the old-fashioned bun (6)

The answer is GINGAL (gin + gal), and the misprinted word is 'bun' which should be 'gun'. It is a curious feature of the misprinted clue that it always makes much better sense than the so-called correct version!

Correctly printed clues are like any other clue but you need to work out by process of elimination where the misprint occurs.

Hint to solvers. Fill in unchecked squares in ink, but divide the checked squares diagonally, putting the across letter in pencil in the top corner and the down letter in pencil in the bottom, thus:

When you have settled the priority, work out the implication for the crossing words, inking in where possible. And if two letters agree, use ink straight away. Put a pencil line through each misprint in the clues, and beside the number of each misprint clue mark C (for *clue* misprint). If the misprint is in the grid or diagram, mark D (for *diagram* misprint). Thus a sequence may read as follows (supposing that 'work' is a misprint for 'word'):

Down

C1 ......work......

D 2.................

D 3.................

In each section of clues you will probably be looking for nine Cs and nine Ds. This may help you categorize some of the clues as you tussle with the last one or two.

In the tutorial puzzle that follows, checking is generous, which should be helpful.

CROSSWORD No. 29

Misprints

ACROSS

1 Here's a little to eat and a little to drink, dear (6)
7 Dagon has limb in the drink (6)
8 Jock's mysterious disease—the unemployed won't get it (6)
9 With five rings perform a touch of oriental magic (6)
10 Ale not bad? I get tight coming in (6)
11 Leaves again being terribly restless—ship sails off (6)

DOWN

1 Corn Street, somewhere in Bucks (6)
2 Dean produces sort of tract about the Old Testament (6)
3 Sheep perhaps beginning to play before long on mountain range (6)
4 Community work interrupts footballer (6)
5 Musical composition rendered by for example French artist, not English (6)
6 Claps a lot, one with half-century having been caught (6)

Letter to *The Observer*, 11 July 1971:

XIMENES

'It just won't do,' said the angel crew,
'To go on with our present compilers:
It's getting much harder for Torquemada
And Afrit can no longer beguile us.

'The judging, too, has gone all askew;
And the lists grow quite absurd;
A crafty sinner was last month's winner,
With God's clue only third.'

'I'm on your side,' St. Peter cried,
'I'd hoped for a V.H.C.,
And the last bit of luck for old Habakkuk
Was in 1953.'

So loud and long the heavenly throng
Debated some fresh nominees:
Then with one voice they agreed on a choice—
And sent for Ximenes.

N. C. Dexter (Oxford)

Playfair

The Playfair code was invented by the famous Victorian scientist Charles Wheatstone (you may remember his famous electrical bridge for measuring resistance if you took physics at school), but it was his friend Lyon Playfair who publicized it: hence the name. Used by the British Army in the First World War, this code is rather more difficult than the simple substitution code where one letter is replaced by another. Afrit it was who introduced Playfair codes to crosswords, and this is the now-familiar rubric using the sample code-word favoured by Azed:

> In a Playfair word square the code-word (in which no letter recurs) is followed by the remaining letters of the alphabet, I doing duty for I and J (see below).

```
ORANG
ESTIC
KBDFH
LMPQU
VWXYZ
```

To encode a word split it into pairs of letters, e.g. CR IT IC AL. Each pair is then seen as forming the opposite corners of a rectangle within the word square, the other two letters [at the corners of the rectangle] being the coded form. Thus CR gives SG (not GS which RC would give). When a pair of letters appears in the same row or column, the coded form is produced from the letters immediately to the right of or below each respectively. For last letters in a row or column, use the first letter of the same row or column. When all pairs are encoded the word is joined up again, thus: SGCICEOP. Answers to clues are to be encoded thus in the diagram. Solvers must deduce the code-word from pairings determinable by cross-checking letters, thus enabling them to complete the diagram.

This rubric nowhere states that the remaining letters are in alphabetical order, but this is always evident from the example. In a typical Playfair puzzle there are four words to be encoded. Often they are of six letters each with two pairs of letters checked for coding and one pair unchecked.

Hints to solvers. The first stage is to solve the Playfair clues—without help from any checked letters! Because of the lack of checking the setter should give you easy clues (e.g. a hidden word, a simple anagram, a two-part charade all help). For solving these codes Scrabble® tiles can be a great help, enabling you to shift around the letters more quickly than with pencil and paper. The setter should give you some straight line coding and once you can decide whether the straight line is a row or column you are well on the way. Remember always to point your diagonals consistently upwards or downwards rather than sideways (see the note about CR above).

If you come across a sequence such as PQR, you may reasonably assume that it comes horizontally among the remaining letters. This can be a great help. *Expect* to find XYZ on the last line—but beware the tutorial puzzle that follows!

CROSSWORD No. 30

Playfair by Duck from *Games and Puzzles* (see rubric on pp.112–13)
Coded words are asterisked

ACROSS

1 The Devil's old catalogue (6)
6 Hamlet, for example, is mostly tragic in retrospect (5)
10 That is associated with rugby (masculine, rough game?) (9)
11 Showing ribs weakened, lacking energy (7)
12 Front half of gym shoe can make you swell (4)
13 Somehow became lower once (6)
*15 Leave a club perhaps and join up again? (6)
17 Epic dual is thrilling (6)
18 Introduced quietly, showing embarrassment and hiding effrontery (8)
22 Organ's something awful—it may be full of sand (8)
24 Yarn found in old magazine? (6)
*25 Gate—it often falls on sports field in summer (6)
27 Local girl collecting seaweed in abundance (6)
29 One with little height, circling, came down (4)
30 Delay coming through old Czech province (7)
31 A number could be revolutionary in combat (9)
32 Remain b-bad, old, backward (5)
33 Inflicted injuries—horrific—with weapons (6)

DOWN

1 Not in sorrow as previously—start afresh (5)
2 Salt drink, sort of soup, taken about noon—Sal usually has it (9)
3 There's semblance of disorder as before with shortage of oil (4)
4 Plant with two currents? One must have *a*! (6)
5 French lady in ermine, etc.—they can provide material for heat (8)
*6 Mace-bearer has to live with raw deal (6)
7 Schoolboys' punishments — bottoms must turn over. It's a handicap (6)
8 Bitterness is slightly excessive? You can do this to wine (7)
9 New horses in mire are slithering around (6)
14 Restaurant's dreadfully lurid inside and lifeless according to Mac (9)
16 A pet lamb? Mickey isn't half taken in school (8)
19 Riding over Somerset ditch is likely to make you sneeze (7)
20 Man who supposedly demonstrates 'god-power' upsetting conventions in party (6)
21 Drawing no. 50 at least? (6)
*22 Inwardly hard, outwardly spiteful, inclined to gossip (6)
23 Region in South Africa where men were tough (6)
26 Mass of flowers round top of loom once used for weaving (5)
28 Dice game without name initially—did Caesar go to work on it? (4)

CROSSWORD No. 30

Letters latent

Here is the appropriate rubric:

> From the answer to each clue one letter must be omitted whenever it occurs in the word, before entry in the diagram. Definitions in the clues refer to the full unmutilated answers; subsidiary indications refer to mutilated forms to be entered in the diagram. Numbers in brackets show the full lengths of unmutilated words.

Then usually is added something like this:

> The letters omitted, read in the order in which the clues are printed, form an appropriate message/quotation from the *Oxford Dictionary of Quotations*.

Curiously a sample clue is rarely provided, but that is no reason for you to be deprived:

[15.3] Politicians monkey with society repeatedly (8)

The diagram (from Azed) shows that the mutilated form has five letters, so we are looking for a word with three letters the same, all missed out. The SI consisting of the last four words gives us 'sai' + S + S = SAISS and since '-ists' looks like a possible ending for a word meaning politicians, we try to find some way of constructing a word with three t's. There is one, STATISTS, so we put a T in the margin to contribute to the message or quotation.

The generous checking in the puzzle that follows should make your task reasonably easy. The missing letters spell out a name to which we must all be grateful, but there is one proper name missing from that book!

CROSSWORD No. 31

Letters Latent

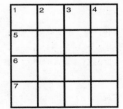

ACROSS
1 Burglars finally grab a bit (5)
5 Orchestra competely English (5)
6 Navy'd name rowing boat (6)
7 Measured part of carpet edge (5)

DOWN
1 Times for bringing up a sword (5)
2 Right and left, with hints of national tragedy, soften (6)
3 Tree, possible supplier of deal (5)
4 Jock's vaulted passage to shed (5)

A filler on fillers

This little article is a filler, an extra topic slotted in to fill an awkward gap. Some words in crossword grids could also be described as 'fillers'.

Imagine the crossword setter filling in the grid. At the outset, everything looks possible-nice long phrases (OVER THE MOON, OUT FOR THE COUNT), long and interesting words (STAGE-WHISPER, POWER-STATION). All too soon, though, the setter is faced with E _ T _ A. It has to be EXTRA, a word he or she has written a clue for several times before (usually something to do with an extra run at cricket or a jobbing actor). EXTRA is a filler, a word that the crossworder can't escape from. Here are some more five-letter words beginning with E in the same category: EASEL, ELAND, ELOPE, ENSUE, ERASE, ERATO, EVOKE. And what can you do with I _ A _ E? IMAGE, INAME, IRATE (and IRADE, if that isn't too hard a word). And look-here's R _ D _ O. Last time it was RADIO, so this time we'll fill in RODEO (oh, not 'rode' + 'O' again, please!). If you are a setter, beware of the five-letter words beginning with E! No one likes coming up with a sixth clue for ENSUE—one is bad enough.

Grids are, of course, to blame—but, as we have already noted, _ A _ E _ and _ R _ T _ would seem to offer the solver too many possibilities. No doubt about it—five-letter words are a problem.

There are fillers of other lengths too. Expect to find ELEMENT and EVEREST frequently, especially along the edge. And in barred puzzles you'll soon learn about EATH (an old word meaning 'easy') and the noun EALE ((Shak., Hamlet I, iv, 36) various conjectures, generally supposed to be for evil, but perhaps a misprint).

Dear solver, forgive the setters their fillers. Learn to regard them as old friends.

The Common Theme

Perhaps this is the most common of all special puzzles. The rubric simply reads as follows:

The unclued answers have something in common.

(Sometimes the word 'lights' is used instead of 'answers', but since this word has also been used on occasion for actual letters, I have avoided using it in this book.) If you finish solving all the clues you might be left with a set of unfilled answers as follows:

CAL _ IO _ E, CLI _ , ER _ TO, EUT _ RP_, _ ELP_ MENE, PO _ YH _ _ _ NIA, TE _ PSI _ HOR _ , THA _ IA, _ RANI _

It should not be difficult to spot that these are the nine muses (Calliope, Clio, Erato, Euterpe, Melpomene, Polyhymnia, Terpsichore, Thalia, Urania). The common-theme puzzle is the simple diet for weekly *Spectator* solvers, and one of mine follows. The grid (one of a number supplied by *The Spectator*) isn't exactly Ximenean, but it is reasonably fair, given the vocabulary being used.

CROSSWORD No. 32

Looking Up by Duck from *The Spectator*

The unclued answers have something in common. A clued answer could be said to have given them a start.

ACROSS

9 Going in for comp again and making deeper impression? (10, hyphened)
14 Boxer landed one short (3)
16 Part of empire—gold carriage (6)
18 Some benzole ICI supplied—oily (5)
20 Burning is contant hazard known to Lloyd's (7, hyphened)
22 Interferometers and other things assigned to Head of Science (7)
24 One (late) taken aback by certain heavenly bodies? (7)
25 Tangle—what fools must finally suffer (5)
26 Valley with coal-dust, black (5)
28 Terrible ordeal around noon in controversial play (7, two words)
31 He may travel in it over it unconsciously (7)
33 Cowper's work has Greek character endlessly blue (7, two words)
37 Dead serious crime? Answer's hanging (5)
39 Stale vinegar is penetrating fish—end of meal (6)
40 Narrow projecting part 'urt (3)
41 Ixtle's been woven and elastic (10)
42 Secluded lanes with hollow tree among other trees (6)
43 Wyatt rejected eminences—magistrates (8)

DOWN

1 Blades in country cycle, dress and hat carefully arranged (13, hyphened)
2 Go off having relaxation without hint of anxiety (5)
3 Punch is nothing after sharp pain (6)
4 What's in poisonous air showing up somewhere in Paraguay (5)
6 Alluring commander is incompetent (7)
7 Boy to remain cuddling Dad, upset (6)
8 Some bypassed Amsterdam—to go here? (4)
10 What's this—is seen possibly? (6, two words)
11 Bird in wavy bit of déshabillé with few people around (9)
12 Mean women fool these society suckers (13)
13 Canine sight—peer hard (8, hyphened)
15 Beautifully thin having eaten nothing (7)
21 Element of thrillers produced by South American writers with energy (8)
29 Obliquely, like philosopher (6)
30 Rivers in depressed old pasture (6)
32 Bring down medic—to free from pain going round (6)
34 Soft, pure, terribly superior (5)
35 Prison dance (5)

CROSSWORD No. 32

Theme and Variations

A development of the thematic puzzle is the theme and variations puzzle, for which the rubric is as follows (the numbers may vary):

> Four theme words have something in common. Each of them has two variations connected to it, though the nature of the connection differs with each set of variations.

In the puzzle some of the clues read 'Theme-word A', 'Variation of A', and so on. To give you some idea of how this works, here is a listing of some answers from an early Azed puzzle:

Theme: Four stomachs of ruminants

Theme-word A   Rumen. Variations: Lions, Wasps (R.U. men)

Theme-word B   Reticulum. Variations: Bonnet, King's hood (alternative names, see *Chambers*)

Theme-word C   Bible. Variations: Vinegar, Breeches (names of famous bibles)

Theme-word D   Read. Variations: Solve, Study (definitions)

A theme and variations puzzle appears as No. 54 on pp. 202–3.

Carte Blanche

With this sort of puzzle you are presented with a blank grid or diagram, usually 12 × 12, and asked to fill in the bars as well as the letters. Instructions are in the form:

> The symmetry of the diagram is such that it would be the same if turned upside down, but not if given a quarter turn. The proportion of checked to unchecked letters is about normal. The clues are in their correct order.

In other words you have a normal Ximenes/Azed grid of 36 clues with the usual conventions on the number of checked letters (see p. 94).

Hints to solvers. You would be well advised to avoid using the printed grid initially. Start solving the puzzle on a large sheet of squared paper, until you have defined the tops of the grid's two sides. Concentrate very carefully on the first three or four across clues, and a few down answers will suggest themselves. When you are able to fill in a bar, fill in the one symmetrically opposite. Remember the *n*th across clue will be in a symmetrical position with the *n*th counting from the end, but the same is not true of the downs. By the end of the sixth row of the grid there should be space for nine across clues since there are usually 18 in total.

gaff¹ *gaf*, *n* a hook used *esp* for landing large fish; the spar to which the head of a fore-and-aft sail is fastened (*naut*). — *vt* to hook or bind by means of a gaff. — *adj* **gaff'-rigged** (of a vessel) having a gaff. — **gaff sail** a sail attached to the gaff; **gaff'-topsail** a small sail, the head of which is extended on a small gaff which hoists on the top mast, and the foot on the lower gaff. [Fr *gaffe*]

gaff² *gaf*, (*slang*) *n* a low-grade or cheap theatre; a fair; a house or other building, *orig* as the site of a burglary; one's private accommodation, apartment, flat, room, pad, etc. [Origin obscure]

gaff³. See **gaffe**.

gaff⁴ *gaf*, (*slang*) *vi* to gamble. — *n* **gaff'er**. — *n* **gaff'ing**. [Origin obscure]

gaff⁵ *gaf*, (*slang*) *n* humbug, nonsense. — **blow the gaff** to disclose a secret, to blab. [Prob connected with **gab²** or **gaff³**; cf OE *gegaf-sprǣc* scurrility]

gaffe or (*rare*) **gaff** *gaf*, *n* a blunder. [Fr *gaffe*]

gaffer¹ *gaf'ər*, *n* *orig* a word of respect applied to an old man, now *archaic*, *dialect* or *derog* in this sense (*fem* **gammer**); the foreman of a squad of workmen; (*orig US*) the senior electrician responsible for the lighting in a television or film studio; a master glass-blower. [**grandfather** or **godfather**]

gaffer², **gaffing**. See **gaff⁴**.

gag¹ *gag*, *vt* to stop up the mouth of forcibly; to silence; to prevent free expression by (the press, etc); to choke up. — *vi* to choke; to retch: — *pr p* **gagg'ing**; *pa t* and *pa p* **gagged**. — *n* something put into the mouth or over it to enforce silence (also *fig*), or to distend jaws during an operation; the closure applied in a debate; a nauseous mouthful, boiled fat beef (*Lamb*). — *n* **gagg'er** a person who gags. — **gag'-bit** a powerful bit used in breaking horses; **gag'-rein** a rein arranged so as to make the bit more powerful. [Prob imitative of sound made in choking]

gag² *gag*, (*slang*) *vt* to deceive. — *vi* to practise deception or fraud. — *n* a made-up story, lie. [Possibly **gag¹**]

gag³ *gag*, (*colloq*) *n* a joke; a hoax; an actor's (*esp* comic) interpolation or improvisation of his or her part. — *vi* to introduce a gag; to joke, make gags. — *vt* to introduce a gag into: — *pr p* **gagg'ing**; *pa t* and *pa p* **gagged**. — *n* **gag'ster** (*colloq*) a person who tells jokes, a comedian. — **gag'man** a person who writes gags; a comedian. [Poss **gag¹**]

An extract from *The Chambers Dictionary*, showing lots of definition possibilities for the crossword setter.

CROSSWORD No. 33

Carte Blanche by Duck from *Crossword*

The clues appear in the correct order. Solvers are asked to fill in the bars (but need not bother with the numbers). Symmetry is such that the diagram would appear the same if turned upside down but not if given a 90 degree turn.

Clamorous priest stirred up the Northern worker
A talent to contain what's original, not going to an extreme?
Some speeches drag out in Shakespeare
Violent poetry translator's immersed in
Field of activity—what the book records in this place
River needs raised bank, removing rapid current in duct
Scottish observer—creeps nervously about, very Scottish
Poisonous plant from Uruguay, thin short one
Genus of monkeys—see returning missionary with one
The most evil character in Indian police station detained by security force
Part of opera: what's central in it?
Note aphis spurting... what comes from a _____ ?
Look in farm vehicle, see old peasant
Bashed lout in revenge
Communist always rejected Thatcher
The prize in old game
Onset of crisis and I go a greeny yellow
The pan is shaken in the specified place—is this a precious ore here?
Group of armadillos look heavy coming up round end of plateau
Animal in tangle with short tree, right between the branches
'To the garçon' (He got a _____ split up?)
Old woman wanting common time in the gutter
Aquatic organisms lunge uncertainly in canal
What the intrusive newsman says: Here's a monetary advance
As before, you should stifle onset of excessive laugh
Eye cut with lancet and chemical often used in cutting
What laugh may produce, we hear, spreads
Murmuring softly instead of loudly in excessive nicety
Marine creature from old civilisation kept in an American city
Certainly old Duck is not absurdly hard...
...Eagerly aimin' to provide what overstressed solvers need?
What you get in *Private Eye?* It bores
Porgies—what one receives aboard?
Low character in airship
Public shelter keeping out the cold...
...Nevertheless one... one probably won't feel it!

CROSSWORD No. 33

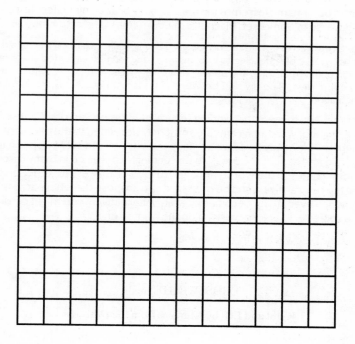

Right and Left

This type of puzzle was invented by Ximenes, who also set several examples under his other name Tesremos for *The Listener* (for the uninitiated, Tesremos is the reverse of Somerset, Macnutt's middle name). The rubric says all:

> Apart from I across, which is normal, each clue is really two clues, side by side but not overlapping, leading to two answers, one for the numbered space on the left of the central line and one for that on the right: the clue for either side may come first. The division between clues is not necessarily marked by punctuation.

Hints to solvers. It is worth spending several minutes on I across. Quite often it is a straightforward anagram clue and it may be related to the peculiarity of the right-and-left puzzle. Solve as many clues as you can in the upper half of the puzzle and expect the break to be cunningly concealed in many cases. If the worst comes to the worst, arrange clusters of answers together on one side of the central divide and be prepared to transpose the letters across the divide when everything becomes clearer. Alternatively you might consider using a copied grid before working on the printed one.

The puzzle below is one from Ximenes:

CROSSWORD No. 34

Right and Left by Ximenes from the *Observer*

ACROSS

1 Fruit bolter being terribly sick in rowing-boat (12)

6 Every one of these fish is to pass the Rear Admiral safe and sound — a close shave (6,6)

7 There's starchy stuff in half the arm-bone and in half the guts — in half of each more than a pound (6,6)

8 With pride old Nelly embraces an Apollo with a head of gold caught like Apollo himself on the rebound (6,6)

10 Slow down: there's a danger signal about road-surfacing with lumpy projections not firm edging second-class road (6,6)

12 This predatory bird hasn't quite got the dash to catch carp, or scarlet-backed carp-like fish (6,6)

16 Mum, a mercenary Venus, needs to be got up in the old, old way, i.e. long curls innumerable (6,6)

17 A thing which stands for Britain, with what's British in it, to provoke a shy creature around America (6,6)

18 Preserve one bed for each: this fertiliser is not quite at full strength (6,6)

19 A dark blue cloth — something unique I got in jumble-sale — a short yard, with a margin to spare (6,6)

CROSSWORD No. 34

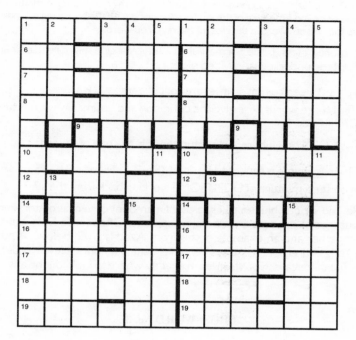

DOWN

1 Jet flyer crashes bridge — G.W.R. link with east disorganised: single line remains — verb. sap. (7,7)

2 It's the Cup — grand — half the second half's gone — all the tricks — blaze away — the ball's in — it's a goal (5,5)

3 Spanker's near me! I've terrible Latin, little Greek — I'll be kept in — not well up in courses about oxygen: we're downtrodden, but na tanned the noo (8,8)

4 I stagger along: I might remind you of the cricket tests — those paragons of patient effort (6,6)

5 Great violinist, having to give a recital among you, renders no less than fifty odd pieces (5,5)

9 A night-flier with strength to diminution can hardly fly at all — pulls up, being about to fit sails (8,8)

11 Saintly man in France has his prime interrupted by the Nine wild and eery busting the clerical domicile (7,7)

13 She'll advise you, for example, up the river to go slowly and take it easy with little work (6,6)

14 An Admiral, born to be on the water, that's to say a fatherly man where there are ships (5,5)

15 The organ stops: part of the woodwind has perished and rings sharper: some of the cellos elope (5,5)

Definition and Letter-Mixture

> In a DLM puzzle each clue consists of a sentence which contains a definition of
> the answer and a mixture of the letters (beginning with the beginning or ending
> with the end of a word in the clue) of the required word.

That, more or less, is the normal rubric. A typical clue might read as follows
(without the underlining provided of course!).

[15.4] I can't sleep 'cos I'm an insecure sort of person (9)

The first three words here give the definition and 'cosimanin' is a mixture of
INSOMNIAC.

Here is a DLM clue where the mixture ends at the end of a word:

[15.5] Tango theme is rendered by octet (9)

Can you see a mixture of EIGHTSOME working back from the 's'?

Unlike the strictly hidden clues, a certain amount of verbal 'cottonwool' is
encouraged to produce an interesting context. Often three DLM clues are
run together and an example of this from Azed is given below. A puzzle
consisting entirely of DLM clues becomes quite easy once a few words have
been put in, because you soon learn exactly where to look for the answer.

CROSSWORD No. 35

Radio Times by Azed from *The Observer*

Each 'programme synopsis' contains both a definition (one word or more) and a
mixture of the letters (beginning with the beginning or ending with the end of a
word in the clue) of the three words indicated by the clue numbers (in the
correct order). Both indications of the first word precede both indications of
the second, and so on. In each case either the definition or the letter-mixture
may come first.

ACROSS

1 ⎫ *The beat glides up.* George Melly
7 ⎬ shows how rhythm has been put
10 ⎭ on disc and film since the Beatles
were seen prancing through
Yellow Submarine land (8, 4, 10 (2
words))

11 ⎫ *What were we wearing?* A panel of
12 ⎬ fashion experts examines how to
14 ⎭ get back those old styles, i.e. rare
clothes from the clothes-horse, or
make copies of old garments ('U',
of course) (6, 5, 8)

17 ⎫ *The Stage is Set* (play). Country
18 ⎬ shepherd cannot refuse scheming
19 ⎭ city bird, abandons sheep, ewe
lambs and all, in exchange for the
inevitable lost innocence (6, 6, 6)

20 ⎫ *Lifting the veil.* In a downright
23 ⎬ uncompromising look at what is
25 ⎭ going on in a modern convent,
Rory Pinstripe seeks to explain
unceasing devotion to the 'habit of
centuries' (6, 6, 6)

CROSSWORD No. 35

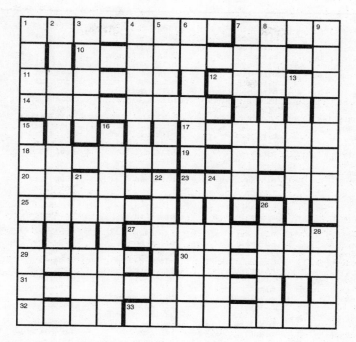

27 ⎫ *Pins and Needles.* See Charmian
29 ⎬ Purl knit a shawl from yak hair
30 ⎭ (matted) and sew a flimsy dress in
bombazine (her class assisting in
this) (8, 5, 6)

31 ⎫ *Punk — Inspiration or Babel?*
32 ⎬ Lower end of music scene
33 ⎭ scrutinised by Ted Grope, a
chap with no liking for glib
appraisals or easy slants (10, 4, 8)

DOWN

1 ⎫ *Comic Book Art — Pop or Op?*
2 ⎬ Examining the role of Superman,
3 ⎭ Penny Numbers checks on what
may be salvaged from the original
concept (4, 10, 5)

4 ⎫ *Lines in Maroon Ink.* Dundee poet
5 ⎬ Hamish Thible seeks to bare his
6 ⎭ soul and thus give a Gaelic ring to
the phrase 'go metric' (6, 6, 6)

7 ⎫ *A 'Pink' or a 'Purple'?* Giles
8 ⎬ Painter's talk is not so rash as to
9 ⎭ try to get at what liberalism really
means but it should help to clear
the system (8, 6, 8)

13 ⎫ *Everything About it is Unfeeling.*
15 ⎬ Representing show business in
16 ⎭ declamatory lingo, puts off the
comic mask, warning of that
elusive 'slot in the bill' (10, 8, 8)

21 ⎫ *New Arrangements.* A conducted
22 ⎬ tour through the maze of
23 ⎭ modern dance orchestrations by
that skilled Scot king of the
ballroom pas, Hew McOrnes
(6, 6, 6)

24 ⎫ *Here let me lie.* Panel-game in
26 ⎬ which contestants repair to the
28 ⎭ Truth Booth to see flagrantly
fictitious experiences dispensed
with as objects of fun (6, 5, 4)

B 8

beveller	-s	biparous		Blenheim		blushful
beverage	-s	birdbath	-s	Blennius		iest
bewailed		bird-bolt		blessing	- s	blushing	-s
bewetted		birdcage	-s	blighted		blustery
bewigged		birdcall	-s	blighter	-s	-iest
bewilder	-s, -ing	bird-eyed		blimbing	-s	boarding	-s
	-ed	bird-lice		blimpish		boarfish	-es
bezonian		bird-lime		blindage	-s	boastful	-ier
bheestie	-s	birdseed	-s	blind-gut		-iest
biannual		bird′ s-eye		blinding	-s	boasting	-s
biassing		birdshot	-s	blinkard	-s	boatbill	-s
biathlon	-s	biriyani	-s	blinking		boat-deck
bibation	-s	birthday	-s	blissful		boat-hook
biblical		birthdom		blistery	-rier	boat-load
bibulous		biscacha	-s		-iest	boatrace	-s
bick-iron		Biscayan		blithely		boat-song
biconvex		bisector	-s	blizzard	-s	boattail	-s
bicuspid	-s	biserial		bloating	-s	bobbinet	-s
biddable		bisexual		blockade	-s, -d	bobby-pin
bidental	-s	bistable			-ing	bobolink	-s
bien-être		bistoury	-ries	blockage	-s	bobstays
biennial	-s	bitchery	-ries	blocking	-s	bobwheel	-s
bifacial		bittacle	-s	blockish		bob-white
bifocals		bitterly		block-tin		bodement	-s
bigamist-s		bivalent	-s	bloncket		bodiless
bigamous		bi-weekly		blood-hot		bodywork	-s
Bignonia		Bixaceae		bloodily		Boeotian
bijwoner	-s	bizcacha	-s	blood-red		bogeyism
bilabial	-s	blabbing	-s	blood-tax		bogey-man
bilander	-s	blackboy	-s	blood-wit		bog-Latin
bilberry	-rries	blackcap	-s	bloomers		Bohemian
bile-duct		black-cat		bloomery	-ries	boldness
billbook	-s	black-fox		blooming		bollocks	-es, -ing
billeted		blacking	-s	blossomy	-mier	-ed
billfold	-s	blackish			-iest	boll-worm
billhead	-s	blackleg	-s, -ging,	blotched		bolt-head
billhook	-s		-ged	blotting	-s	bolthole	-s
billiard		*black-neb		blowball	-s	bolt-rope
billowed		blackout	-s	blowdown	-s	bomb-site
billyboy	-s	blacktop	-s	blowhole	-s	bombycid	-s
billy-can		bladdery		blowlamp	-s	bona-roba
bilobate		blah-blah		blowpipe	-s	bonassus	-es
bimanous		blamable		bludgeon	-s -sing	bondager	-s

An extract from *Chambers Words*, compiled 'for the benefit of all who play in fun or in earnest with words.'

Wrong number

This, perhaps, is the least common of the standard specials, and it is very hard to start off. Here is the rubric:

> Each clue includes a one-word definition of the word required at the number where it stands but belongs as a whole to a word of the same length elsewhere. Method recommended is to find, after solving a clue, a definition of the solution in one of the other clues to words of its length: this will show where the word is to go.

Here is a set of four clues with answers of the same length from a puzzle by Azed:

[15.6] 10 across Insects in cabbage—picker's covering one? (10)

30 across After round grimace, show start of husbandly love, iron crumpled vestment (10)

8 down Man, what bugs us in a love? Essentially the same (10)

11 down Like believer in thrift, aim on nil return in silver, take pounds (10)

The answer to the clue at 10 across is COLEOPTERA (cole + opter + a), and this is placed at 8 down, where 'bugs' is the definition. The answer to the clue at 8 down is HOMOOUSIAN (homo + anag.) which in turn is placed at 11 down, where 'believer' is the definition. The answer to the clue at 11 down is AGRONOMIAL (aim on O, rev. in Ag r L), which is placed at 30 across, 'husbandly' being the definition. The answer to the clue at 30 across is OMOPHORION (o + mop + h + o + anag.), and the only 10-letter slot left is at 10 across, which is confirmed by the definition 'covering'.

Hints to solvers. Focus on a set of clues of the same length and look for pairs of synonyms (e.g. insects/bugs in the example above), but be warned that the synonyms are sometimes well disguised.

See how you get on with the one from Ximenes over the page.

CROSSWORD No. 36

Wrong Number by Ximenes from *The Observer*

Each clue includes a one-word definition of the word required at the number where it stands but belongs as a whole to a word of the same length elsewhere. Method recommended is to find, after solving a clue, a definition of the solution in one of the 5 other clues to words of its length: this will show where the word is to go.

ACROSS

1 Grape contains centre of pulp, a conical body (5)

5 I'm from the isle—I'm too small to pull a coach (7)

11 I'm fleecing a bird that's swallowed champagne, perhaps: you can have a slice (7)

12 To take prolonged looks at a TV is to flounder (5)

13 The Navy in America are used in state elections (4)

14 Rail being far from broken is together in one piece (8)

15 East China must slough off N. America and welcome in minor officer, Turkish official (6)

18 What's divine about novelist revered a good bit (7)

21 Crown, and less valuable coins, contain a mineral coated with copper carbonate (9)

22 To intrigue disloyally with her is horrific, just a bit (9)

24 Held head in an awful state, covered with blood (7)

28 Have a crack at the French in the hollow (6)

29 Putter-in of good work in bar, being in debt, behaves like bird-fancier off to Gretna (8)

30 Aromatic condiment kept in pukka vases (4)

31 Fastener—here's part of the clasp right in view (5)

32 Meal dear in Paris: he'll pinch your pony and sock you (7)

33 Socialist votes stuck together—shows herd instinct (7)

34 The flower of creation, its appetites and its food (5)

DOWN

1 Unusual ernes in flight, to reach which one must cross part of the Channel (8)

2 The activity of a fly-by-night round that location could be learnt as the result of a pick-up (8)

3 If it luxuriates on a lawn, spray is in vogue (5)

4 Take sly measures lacing one tea with another (9)

6 Hiding-place on shore where seceding party receives envoy representing Navy (6)

7 This cherry split's nice, not 'arf—swell (6)

8 Affected by storm tortile tellurium is laminated (9)

9 Rising prima donna, wanting meals supplemented (4)

10 Make declarations and talk rubbish in the 'ighlands (4)

16 With endless rush I beat: my force fairly staggers (9)

17 She's in arch, short shows never filmed by BBC—they gave lots of people the sack (9)

19 ITV arias out of tune must have got the bird (8)

20 Once passionate wench in only part of garment (8)

22 Ham recipe is wrong—result's slimy, often salt (6)

23 Product of juice of red fruit spoils a metal (6)

25 Lobe of whale's tail's eaten mashed—that's lucky (5)

26 To separate brawlers, flushed with start of drink (4)

27 Economised—only half keen—in a limited edition (4)

CROSSWORD No. 36

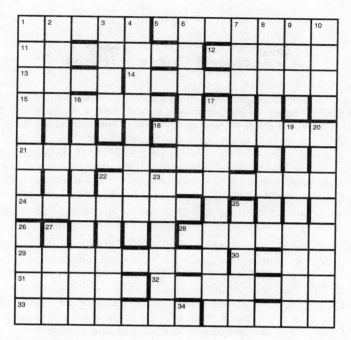

Other specials

In addition to the specials just described there are a number of other specials which have made repeated appearances. Some, though, are very much 'special specials'. A special special may exploit a different clue type, a different way of entering words on the grid, a different shape of grid, a requirement to highlight a mystery word or phrase in the grid, a request to fill in a key word or phrase beneath the grid—or even some combination of these. Some advanced solvers feed on such a diet of puzzles almost exclusively, and their needs are well catered for by the *Listener* crossword (now in *The Times* every Saturday) and the Crossword Club. Other specials currently appear in the Magazines of Saturday's *Independent* and the *Sunday Telegraph* ('Enigmatic Variations') and Azed devises some special specials from time to time in *The Observer* (especially at Christmas).

In difficulty such puzzles vary enormously, and the setter can overload the dice against the solver by leaving too many possibilities for the answer's mode of entry on to the grid. Special specials lie at the top of 'Crossword Mountain'. You must decide how high you want to go.

16

Crossword Competitions

Although solving crosswords is often a solitary occupation, it is possible to introduce a competitive element. Many periodicals limit their competitions to the level of chance, by inviting solvers to send in their solutions and then awarding prizes for the first three out of the hat. This at least reassures the editor that there is someone 'out there' solving the puzzles—though it is surprising how many of Afrit's *Listener* puzzles in the 1930s attracted no correct entries. The best competitions, though, must be those that have an increased element of skill. The best-known of these is undoubtedly *The Times* Crossword Championship in the newspaper (or on line). Here one has to solve a puzzle before progressing to a regional final and the national final. Speed and accuracy are the keynotes of this solving competition.

If *The Times* championship is the best-known competition, then *The Observer* clue-writing competition is probably the most significant in terms of 'good done for crosswords'. Started in 1945 by Ximenes, it continued until his death in 1971, then resumed under Azed in 1972. Solvers are required to solve the puzzle, then write a cryptic clue for a specified word (usually replacing a definition-only clue in the puzzle itself). Through the competition Ximenes developed the theory of cluemanship from Afrit's basic ideas to a fine art (culminating with the publication *Ximenes on the Art of the Crossword*). Azed is the pseudonym of Jonathan Crowther, who for many years was also an editor at Oxford University Press. He has carried on where Ximenes left off, and although he takes his name from the reverse of a Spanish inquisitor (the reverse of Deza) he is no more tolerant of latter-day 'heretics'!

Associated with *The Observer's* competition have been annual honours lists and periodic celebrations to salute the setter. As the competition now stands, the submitters of the three clues judged best by Azed are rewarded with book tokens and two honours points; the next 20 or so best are labelled VHC (very highly commended) and gain one honours point; and a further 70 or so are deemed HC (highly commended). A cup passes between first-prizewinners and a silver salver between annual champions. Prizewinners and VHCs are listed in *The Observer*, and in a competing year there are 13 competitions (12 monthly, plus one at Christmas when VHCs are awarded 'extra prizes'). Solvers can subscribe to a newsletter (called the 'slip') detailing successful clues plus a commentary from Azed on the competition, often with details of clues that didn't make it and why they didn't.

For the rest of this chapter we will look at some extracts from the slips, with the comments of Ximenes and Azed. As we do so, we will note one or two recurring names (among them Colin Dexter and his arch-rival Sir Jeremy Morse, whose name became associated with the famous detective). We will also see some clues which Azed wouldn't reward today (because required standards of soundness have become yet more rigorous). And we will note some interesting commentary on matters cruciverbal and otherwise. At some points you will see my own comments, daring to challenge some of the recent rulings by Azed, but these should not detract from the overall worthwhileness of the Ximenes-Azed competition in terms of upgrading the standards of clue-writing.

Ximenes

Ximenes No. 79

SALOME: I. Maj. B. W. Shepherd (Scarborough): Perplexed damsel wanting a head and requiring nothing more (amsel-o and literal mng.)...
...An interesting point of 'cluemanship' was raised by a regular and expert solver. Was 'insist' for 'in sist' without a hint of division, sound in the clue to SISKIWIT? ... the practice had better stop...

Ximenes No. 87

SISKIN: I. A. R. Fraser: Among wines I'm king

Author's comment. I'd be happy about this, but the latter-day Azed wouldn't, as we saw on p.71!

Ximenes No. 148

FILIBUSTER: I. A. N. Clark (Portsmouth): I rifle tubs at sea ... Mr Clark's *multum in parvo* is, I think, superb; he has brilliantly seized a rare chance.

Ximenes No. 159

SPANIEL: I. D. P. M. Michael: Lies curled up taking nap.

Author's comment. A lovely picture, but I don't think the way 'nap' is introduced would be judged sound by today's standards.

Ximenes No. 162

TITANESS ... 'A hardy girl to go against a goddess.' Unsound in many ways! It is meant for 'Tess anti' anag., but no anag. is indicated, the wording being vague and unhelpful: this is particularly unfair in an indirect anag., the actual anag. words not being given: on top of that Hardy loses its capital—this is deliberately unfair, as it cannot be a true clue; the converse process is allowable—a writer may give a word a capital for his own purposes without incorrectness...

Ximenes No. 229

MASCOT: I. C. Allen Baker (Milnathort): Up in the morning and with the sun and early bed is said to bring good fortune.... May I repeat what I have said before several times, that when I quote unsuccessful clues, I do so not to hand wooden spoons to the authors but to help not only the authors but the competitors, especially the newcomers.

Ximenes No. 275 (Printer's Devilry)

ESTOVER: I. J. B. Filburn: True! Man's fasts are inconsistent even with Lent here to inspire.... COMMENTS—375 entries, 354 correct... I must repeat two principles about devilled clues. (I) The formal sense must not be sacrificed to the devilled sense... (2) The hiding can be too well done. An example is 'A good coke heats water in no time'... Very difficult...no fun at all....

Ximenes No. 382

ABSTAIN: I. F. E. Newlove: Put a saint in a bath of Champagne and see if he does (bain, Fr.)... 'Lindwall is a kind of fast bowler whose deliveries may well put bats in a confused state of mind.' Here 'kind of fast may well put bats in a confused' gives a clue; the rest is irrelevant padding, which might be useful against Lindwall but has nothing to do with 'abstain'! This is flagrantly unsound.

Ximenes No. 425

TRAVERSE: I. R. N. Chignell: How gunners get a line on either side of the target (t-R.A.-verse & lit.)...' Look at those mountains! You can make your way across quite easily!' The sender should ask himself whether he would be likely as a solver to arrive at 'vet serra', so that it would provide an anagram to help him.

Ximenes No. 460

ASTONISHMENT (Misprints): I. H. S. Tribe: Open winder? Then no mats is shaken (wonder).... By the way, my wife assures me that Mr Tribe's delightfully neat clue presents a strong household hint... Indication of anagrams. There were a good many which I couldn't accept as sound, e.g. 'fraught','separation of','critical','it appears'.

Ximenes No. 634

BEDSTEAD: I. C. J. Morse: To lie still is not enough here: both sides of the sheet must be tucked in (be-d-st-ead '& lit.').... It seems clear that posting on Friday is no longer safe, even in London itself. One solver has written, he tells me, to the P.M.G. to complain, and has so far received no satisfaction but a brief acknowledgement.

Ximenes No. 647

MADCAP: I. E. Gomersall (York): Cake with nuts on top (cake = madcap, Chamb.).

Ximenes No. 690 [A 'trick' puzzle for I April]

ASCERTAIN: I. Miss D. W. Taylor (Worthing): Find the right answer? Sure—the first of April's over! (A-'s-certain) ... 263 entries, 229 mahoganies...the leg-pull was far, far more successful than I meant.

Ximenes No. 777

TAILOR-BIRD: I. N. C. Dexter (Corby): Fantastic warblers do it—sew leaves! Here's one among them (*anag. minus sew incl i & lit.*).

Author's comment: Faced with this clue, Azed would have reservations. He argues that the departing letters should be in the same order as they are in the word or phrases to be anagrammed, although they do not need to be contiguous. To make the clue acceptable, where 'w, e, s,' are leaving 'warblers do it' and not 's, e, w' he would probably suggest 'somehow sew'. It is arguable, though, that one could choose to make the anagram such that the letters would fall into the correct order ready to drop out. Readers may decide for themselves, but those entering Azed competitions will now know where they stand!

Ximenes No. 945

OBLITERATE: I. N. C. Dexter: (Biol.) Treat defective end of a tube (anag. plus e & lit.')... R. Postill: Wipe out Beatle and disorganised trio remains... [Mr Postill] says in his note 'out, vb'; that leaves 'blot' [sic] alone as the definition, and I don't think it will quite do without 'out'.

Ximenes No. 967

CREMOSIN: I. N. C. Dexter: Colour of the Skie, perhaps, with Morne [sic] breaking (*anag. '& lit.', F.Q. II, 3 'Early before the Morne with Cremosin ray'*) [F.Q. = Faerie Queene.]

Ximenes No. 1000

THOUSAND: I. C. J. Morse: Up-to-date product of X and C.... All the dishes on the 'Millenu' (and most of the speakers) began with M.... One thing I forgot to say, so I'll say it here—how greatly I appreciate the sporting way in which you never dispute my often doubtful umpire's decisions...

Ximenes No. 1115

FLESHPOTTERY: I. Mrs B. Lewis: Product of the Tory's pelf, snarls the prosy left (*anags. '& lit.': snarl = tangle*)... *COMMENTS—Just under 300 entries, nearly all correct. Was it too hot? Am I, quite unconsciously, becoming more difficult? Or were people upset by not finding Jethart staff (s.v. Jeddart)? This arbitrary omission of cross-references in C is annoying (and, I think, inefficient)....*

Azed

Azed No. 27

VINEGAR: I. J. P. H. Hirst: Given unconventionally for Jack's head (*anag. replacing t of tar & lit.; Jack and Jill*)

Author's comment: Should this be allowed? In 1988 Azed said no. He disowned his earlier judgement, claiming that it was unsatisfactory to define a noun by a past participle, which is effectively an adjective. One sympathizes with the wish to discourage setters from defining 'glass' by 'transparent', but if one can swallow [It] why cannot one swallow [It is] or [It was]? It could be argued, in fact, that the ellipsis of [It is] is more common than the ellipsis of [It] in the history of language—certainly this clue seems more understandable than the winner of Azed No. 701 (over).

Azed No. 70

... If the misprinted clue is as much a definition as its original it cannot be considered to be misprinted. Ximenes made the point in the slip to No. 1131 for those who keep scrap-books.

... I would always regard 'a bit of', 'a piece of' as coming from the front of the word....

Azed No. 92

BRAINWASH: I. L. May: Bust down reason? (bra in wash).

Azed No. 100

CENTENARIAN: I. D. F. Manley: An ancient the Queen may get excited (*anag. '& lit.', royal telegram*)... 'Azed achieves his for when he drives around Muswell Hill chased by two?' (EN TEN (N. 10) in CAR = I = AN (1 + 1 =2)). Dreadfully unsound, I'm afraid, and virtually unsolvable. There is no indication of the part of speech required; 'When he drives' will never do for 'car'; Muswell Hill is only one part of N.10; and 'two' for I + AN is surely unacceptable.

Azed No. 430

TEGULA: I. C. G. Millin: What the fiddler might have played on, in the film (*gu in tel* '& *lit.*' *'Fiddler on the Roof*')... Is a tela a film? I examined this question very carefully ... *Chambers* definition somewhat inadequate ... turned to the new *Collins English Dictionary* for the reassurance I needed ... Finally a reminder that I still have small stocks of Azed ties, all three colours. The price is now £3 each inclusive of V.A.T...

Azed No. 482

BODY-SNATCHER: I. C. J. Morse: Stiff collaring, that's my trade-shows what can be done by starch (*2 mngs and anag.*).

Azed No. 500

BEFOOL (with 2 extra D's): I. D. Ashcroft: Admass imperative: get fund at other's expense (*be-fool imp. form of am-ass*).... Very few of you noticed that the style of the down clues was such that they made reasonable sense with and without the superfluous D's.... The Azed 500 Dinner was a spectacularly successful affair... I look forward to meeting many of these friends at No.750.

Azed No. 662

BARGE-COUPLE: I. R. J. Hooper: Sawyer's contribution to topping story shows the lighter Twain (*barge-couple; ref. Mark T.*)... [This following clue] is probably the most unsolvable clue I've ever received. 'O Attic shape! Sounds like naughty Keats may have been involved in this.' Explanation (I quote): 'Quotation from 'Grecian Urn' by Keats. Naughty = no T. Keats without T sounds like KEYS. Keys open locks, as do couples on a barge.' Need I say more?

Azed No. 679 (see also Ximenes No. 275, p.134)

ESTOVER ('P.D.'): I. T. J. Moorey: 'Dry' minister organising party left-winger...

COMMENTS:—A mammoth entry—702 in all... I also failed to notice that Ximenes used ESTOVER as a P.D. competition word over 30 years ago (his No.275), and there are still regular solvers who remember that earlier occasion... the Ximenes competition attracted a much smaller entry.

Azed No. 701

BALUSTRADE: I. M. Barley: Bears cope? (*balus trade*, & lit. cope [1,2]) ...and in case anyone queries this yet again I do accept—and use—the device of a finite verbal phrase defining the subject of it understood...

Azed No. 904

VOETGANGER: I. J. F. Grimshaw: Boorish promenader's against reggae not being represented (*v.* + *anag.*)... An interesting point of principle arose in a number of clues using the appealing 'a Green Govt' anagram. Is wording along the lines of '... could produce a Green Government', with or without 'shortly' to indicate an abbreviation of 'Government', fair to the solver, or is it tantamount to an indirect anagram, involving a two-stage decoding process? I tend to the latter view (especially as 'Govt' is only one of the abbreviations given for 'Government', as least in *Chambers*). Repeated use has given acceptability to the convention of including in anagrams single-letter abbreviations indicated by the full form of the word abbreviated, especially when such abbreviations are in common use, but there is a difference, I think, between the practice and expecting the solver to unscramble larger and perhaps less familiar abbreviations... Comments welcomed.

Azed No. 917

HOOLIGANISM: I. M. Barley: Trouble Italy has looming (*anag. incl. I & lit.*' ref. *World Cup*)... I hope my choice will be seen as consistent with my remarks on the use of abbreviations in anagrams in the recent VOETGANGER slip. One or two solvers have expressed misgivings about the use of IVR abbreviations, expecially those rarely encountered on cars in Europe, but this one is surely common and familiar.

Azed No. 1000

ONE THOUSAND: I. D. F. Manley: The Sun. No. specially launched with a do (*anag. & lit.; ref. AZ 1000 lunch*)... it had to be ONE THOUSAND since Ximenes got competitors to clue THOUSAND... The celebratory lunch in Oxford was a joyous occasion blessed by beautiful weather...

Azed No. 1130

AGRESTAL: I. C. J. Morse: Ace fully laps remainder of the field (*a* + *rest in gal*) ...'Thriving in the Open perhaps, Sandy Lyle starts with a great shot'and 'Laager with Springbok leaders confused and wild?' I cannot accept that 'starts' and 'leaders' in these two clues can fairly or logically be interpreted as meaning the initial letters of the preceding phrase, any more than that 'fathead' can indicate the letter 'f'. It has been argued that 'car crash' can indicate an anagram of the letters of 'car' since in the real world that is what the phrase suggests (the crash of (a) car), but even that worries me and I prefer to steer clear of it.

Azed No. 1225

CURRY: I. C. G. Millin: Hot dish with shapely figure, right for form of plunging neckline (*r for V in curvy*)... I am not keen on treating the prefix UR- as if it were a word in its own right, as a number of you did, i.e. by defining it as e.g. 'original' with no indication of its part-word status.

Azed No. 1334

CATACHRESTIC: I. C. R. Gumbrell: In which fashion see the cold as 'artic' (*anag. incl c, c, & lit.; cf. arctic*) ...They probably fell foul of pre-Christmas delays, but I do urge you to send off your entries in good time and use a first-class stamp if at all possible.

Azed No. 1385

PANTRIES: I. R. J. Hooper: What maids must step into daily when apprehending dinner's close? (*r in panties & lit.*)... 'Botched repaints? Sounds like Ladas.' This is an instance of 'a clue to a clue', as Ximenes would have called it, with no actual definition part at all. (The fact that it's not difficult to solve is irrelevant.)

Azed No. 1467

CANAPÉ: I. D. F. Manley: First thing Cowper has paean about? (*C + anag. & lit.; ref. 'I sing the sofa' at start of The Task by William C.*)... it is in the *ODQ*. (A passing comment on this indispensable work of reference: I have copies of the second, third and fourth editions (1953, 1979 and 1992) but a fifth has appeared since, plus 'revised editions' of earlier numbered ones. All this making assertions about the source of quotations very difficult...)

The Azed competition continues to thrive, and the competitiveness is greater than ever. Your author continues to enjoy doing battle with N.C.D. and C.J.M. but the undoubted star of recent years has been Colin Gumbrell who won the annual silver salver for three years running between 1998 and 2000. There is just space for the clue with which C.R.G. took the lead in the 2000/01 championship:

Azed No. 1502

RAPPEL: I. C. R. Gumbrell: What's given by drum if end of truce is approved? (*app. for e in reel & lit.*)...The dinner to mark Azed No. 1500 (combined with the annual dinner for *Listener* crossword setters) was a most enjoyable event... I was greatly cheered by all the kind and enthusiastic remarks I received, and shall press on with undiminished vigour to keep you all amused for as long as I can.

17

Crossword Setting: a Case Study

Filling the Grid

So many people ask me how I go about setting a puzzle for the dailies that I've decided to let you in on the secret. I shall show you how to go about a 15 × 15 puzzle. I have been fortunate enough to set for *The Independent, The Independent on Sunday, The Guardian* and *The Times*. In each case I have a choice of grids so I had better choose one and find some letters to fit.

A *Guardian* grid (their no. 49) sits on my desk. Suppose I put MOTORWAY MADNESS at 1 across. With help from *Chambers Words* and a trusty old *Modern Crossword Dictionary* (the 1967 edition as it happens) I've soon got the outside answers written in.

```
┌───┬───┬───┬───┬───┬───┬───┬───┬───┬───┬───┬───┬───┬───┬───┐
│¹M │ O │²T │ O │³R │⁴W │ A │ Y │⁵M │ A │⁶D │ N │⁷E │ S │⁸S │
├───┼───┼───┼───┼───┼───┼───┼───┼───┼───┼───┼───┼───┼───┼───┤
│ I │███│   │███│   │   │███│   │   │███│   │███│   │███│ C │
├───┼───┼───┼───┼───┼───┼───┼───┼───┼───┼───┼───┼───┼───┼───┤
│⁹S │   │   │   │   │   │   │   │   │   │¹⁰ │   │   │   │ R │
├───┼───┼───┼───┼───┼───┼───┼───┼───┼───┼───┼───┼───┼───┼───┤
│ A │███│   │███│   │███│   │███│   │███│   │███│   │███│ A │
├───┼───┼───┼───┼───┼───┼───┼───┼───┼───┼───┼───┼───┼───┼───┤
│¹¹P │   │   │   │   │   │███│¹²  │   │   │   │   │   │   │ T │
├───┼───┼───┼───┼───┼───┼───┼───┼───┼───┼───┼───┼───┼───┼───┤
│ P │███│   │███│   │███│¹³  │   │███│   │███│   │███│ C │
├───┼───┼───┼───┼───┼───┼───┼───┼───┼───┼───┼───┼───┼───┼───┤
│¹⁴R │   │¹⁵  │   │¹⁶  │   │   │███│¹⁷ │¹⁸  │   │   │   │ H │
├───┼───┼───┼───┼───┼───┼───┼───┼───┼───┼───┼───┼───┼───┼───┤
│ E │███│   │███│   │███│   │███│   │   │███│   │███│ O │
├───┼───┼───┼───┼───┼───┼───┼───┼───┼───┼───┼───┼───┼───┼───┤
│¹⁹H │   │   │²⁰  │   │²¹T │   │²²  │   │²³L │   │   │   │ N │
├───┼───┼───┼───┼───┼───┼───┼───┼───┼───┼───┼───┼───┼───┼───┤
│ E │███│   │███│   │²⁴A │   │███│   │ O │███│   │███│ E │
├───┼───┼───┼───┼───┼───┼───┼───┼───┼───┼───┼───┼───┼───┼───┤
│²⁵N │   │   │███│   │ N │███│²⁶  │   │ R │   │²⁷  │   │ S │
├───┼───┼───┼───┼───┼───┼───┼───┼───┼───┼───┼───┼───┼───┼───┤
│ S │███│   │███│   │ T │███│   │███│ E │███│   │███│ H │
├───┼───┼───┼───┼───┼───┼───┼───┼───┼───┼───┼───┼───┼───┼───┤
│²⁸I │   │   │███│   │²⁹R │ E │ T │ A │ L │ I │ A │ T │ E │
├───┼───┼───┼───┼───┼───┼───┼───┼───┼───┼───┼───┼───┼───┼───┤
│ O │███│   │███│   │ U │███│   │███│ E │███│   │███│ A │
├───┼───┼───┼───┼───┼───┼───┼───┼───┼───┼───┼───┼───┼───┼───┤
│³⁰N │ O │ N │ C │ O │ M │ M │ I │ S │ S │ I │ O │ N │ E │ D │
└───┴───┴───┴───┴───┴───┴───┴───┴───┴───┴───┴───┴───┴───┴───┘
```

Nice finishing letters on the right-hand side, but the O at the bottom of 20 and the I at the bottom of 23 are less than ideal. Never mind—let's tackle 23 down straight away—LORELEI is an old favourite—in it goes.

Now I'll tackle 29 across keeping an eye on 21 down. An R would be nice to start with because TANTRUM could go in at 21 down. Out with the Franklin Spellmaster: R _ _ _ L _ _ _ E and press ENTER: REDOLENCE (horrible word), REGULABLE (even worse), REPULSIVE (*not* repulsive, but let's keep going), RESALABLE (not today, thank you), RESOLUBLE (mm, maybe), RETALIATE (best yet), End of list. RETALIATE it is. And so it goes on and the answers go in in the following order (if you want to follow them through):

7 down (ELABORATE), 22 across (GALLEON), 22 down (GHETTOS—check 'OS', not 'OES'), 24 across (ASH), 26 across (ENRAGES), 27 down (GRAIN). The nasty SE corner is done—let's go to the SW. 19 across (HIDEOUT—hope the U will be OK!), 20 down (OREGANO—what, again?!), 25 across (NUCLEON—it's time we had some physics!) and 28 across (IBIZA—horrible last time, no better now I've got to find a new clue). 15 down has several possibilities starting with 'addiction' but let's try SEDUCTION this time (didn't I clue 'addiction' somewhere else recently?). Better look at 16 down. Try TAU. Then 14 across (RESTATE), 3 down (REPLICA), 9 across: 'stamp something'? No, try SANDPIPER. If 4 down is APPEASE, 11 across can be 'partita' and 2 down 'tenor', but I've clued 'tenor' a lot recently. Try TON-UP and PAPRIKA.

Only the top NE corner to go! 17 across suggests EYEWASH, YEA? (18 down), and MIRACLE quickly follows at 5 down. 13 across is SOL. We're nearly there having shown a lot of FLAIR (10 across). Let's have American defence for a change (DEFENSE at 6 down). We could have 'concoct' or 'contort' at 12 across but let's have CONSORT. I've simplified the process slightly (there *were* a few blind alleys!) but not much. That took less than an hour and probably not more than 30 minutes.

The Across Clues

So on to the clues. I've got some ideas already, but one or two worries as well. Never mind. Let's try taking the clues in order and see how it goes.

1 across: MOTORWAY MADNESS. A clever definition and an anagram? Could be tricky. Let's think about a cryptic definition. Idiots who crash in the fog (and the innocent victim too) may be driving one minute and finding themselves at the pearly gates the next, so let's try:

The sort of idiocy that makes folk drive up to the pearly gates? (8,7).

9 across: SANDPIPER. Almost the same as 'sandpaper'. In fact, they'd sound the same 'down under' surely:

Bird sounding abrasive in Melbourne? (9).

10 across: FLAIR is L in fair. 'Fair' is 'blonde' and 'flair' is 'talent'. I'm going to take a chance with the feminists here:

Blonde, about 50, shows 'talent' (5).

11 across: PAPRIKA. Awkward letters here. 'Papa' looks nice but I don't like the 'rik'. A bits-and-pieces job I think:

Condiment makes Dad consume only half the rice, ending with 'Yuck!' (7).

12 across: CONSORT. A gift, this: con + sort. I don't suppose I'll upset too many *Guardian* readers with this:

Tory type, a tagger-on? (7).

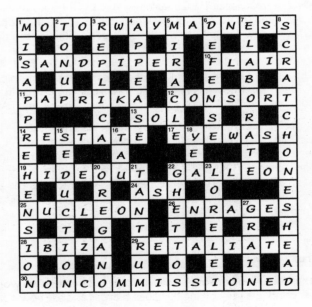

13 across: SOL. Isn't 'sol' an alternative for the note 'soh'? Yes, it is—and Sol means 'Sun' too. Not an exciting clue, this, but it's OK:

Note source of illumination (3).

14 across: RESTATE. Another charade, surely: rest + ate. Hmm, I think I've done that before, so let's try R + estate:

Once again affirm king must be given the property (7).

17 across: EYEWASH. I can remember a nice *Times* clue for this: 'English trees rot', I think it was (E + yew + ash). I'd better not pinch it. I'm saying the word to myself, desperately searching for a new idea and suddenly it sounds like 'I wash':

What sounds like claim to keep clean is nonsense (7).

19 across: HIDEOUT only differs from 'hideous' in the last letter. Ideally we should perhaps signal the exact substitution, but I think this clue is fair enough:

Den with nasty decor maybe changed finally (7).

22 across: GALLEON. Surely gall + eon, but how can we link that with a ship? Here's an idea which seems to work:

Rancour goes on a long time—one may have wanted calm waters (7).

24 across: ASH. A dull little word inviting a double meaning, but I've done that before. What about 'as H'? But how can we liken 'H' to wood? Simple!

Like rugby post made of wood (3).

25 across: NUCLEON. It's a particle in the centre of a nucleus, either a neutron (not charged) or a proton (charged). Try linking that to an anagram of 'on uncle'. No thanks! I'll go for a cryptic definition with a misleading context:

I play a central role, but I may or may not be charged (7).

26 across: ENRAGES. One of those dull seven-letter words ('element' is another, not to mention 'oregano'!) that keep cropping up in dense diagrams like this one. No good ducking it-time for an anagram. Whatever the definition, the answer could be as 'green as' could be. Let's try a theme of jealousy. To enrage X is to get X very cross, so here goes:

Gets very cross, being as green as could be (7).

28 across: IBIZA. A pain! Why did I allow it? Because I'm equally disenchanted with —'idiot' and 'idiom'. Since 'biza' is 'bizarre' minus 'rre' (= err, rev) and 'i' is a half of 'is', let's try something contrived and pass quickly on to the next clue:

Island is not half bizarre—go wrong turning to leave it (5).

29 across: RETALIATE. Only one anagram so far. Time for another:

Treat shamefully with a lie to wreak vengeance (9).

30 across: NON-COMMISSIONED. Oh, lousy word to define! Oh, horrible letters! Surely a candidate for a cryptic definition if ever there was one. Think for a moment! NCOs have stripes; COs have pips. Got it!

Give someone the pip and he won't be this any more (3-12).

The Down Clues

On with the Downs:

1 down: MISAPPREHENSION. Try an anagram. 'Perhaps' comes out nicely, and I quickly find 'some perhaps in in'. I'm going to be rather more devious than usual for this level of puzzle. Make 'in in' into 'double in' and use 'muddle' as a transitive verb. And of course 'perhaps' looks almost too innocent to be part of an anagram. The gerund definition should help though:

Some, perhaps, doubly in muddle, taking things the wrong way (15).

2 down: TON-UP. If I wrote 'ton' up, I would get 'not' surely? So if I suggest that the answer is a *clue* I can put the answer to the answer in the real clue! Who said I have a devious mind?

Not, as you would deduce, very fast (3-2).

3 down: REPLICA. My trusty *Chambers* defines this as 'a duplicate, properly one by the original artist'. Don't artists produce 'pics'? Here's an anag. & lit. then:

Real pic re-created (7).

4 down: APPEASE. I've clued this before, and obviously it is a + pp + ease. Looking in *Chambers* for a new twist I can't help noticing that 'ease' is quiet (n.) and 'appease' is quiet (v.)—not to mention p and p. If 'a' is one, the rest of the clue can consist of quiets!

One needs to get quiet, quiet, quiet—QUIET! (7).

5 down: MIRACLE. Not an anagram of 'reclaim' again, please, but I can see 'car, rev.' in 'mile' so let's try this, suggesting the latest model with the powerful brakes:

Wonder vehicle pulled up within the distance (7).

6 down: DEFENSE. It's not inconceivable that the boggy 'fens' would have a river round them and this time the *Concise Oxford Dictionary* helps me with the definition:

US military resources in boggy area with river around (7).

7 down: ELABORATE. The adjective looks slightly more promising than the verb from the definition point of view and an anagram comes easily (the fourth—we'd better not use many more!):

Complicated tale a bore spun out (9).

8 down: SCRATCH ONE'S HEAD. Phrases that offer a literal and a metaphorical meaning are a gift:

What can a person do without a comb? Be perplexed (7,4,4).

15 down: SEDUCTION. I've used s + educ(a)tion before but never 'du' in 'section'. Think of those naughty folk across the Channel:

Tempting act of the French in part (9).

16 down: TAU. Ta + u or T + Au. Not very interesting, let's face it, but it's almost 'taut', and we can conjure up a Saturday night in Athens with the retsina flowing ('retsina' is an anagram of 'nastier', did you know? I avoided it in 3 down):

Greek character little short of being tight (3).

18 down: YEA. Let's use 'indeed' as the definition and bring it alongside a statement of the obvious, so start with 'The old' for 'ye' and finish with 'indeed'. Then it's not too difficult:

The old will need a bit of assistance, indeed (3).

20 down: OREGANO. I've already grumbled about this. I suppose I've only got myself to blame. I'm going for O + anag. this time with October brought in for autumnal plausibility:

Herb leaves turning orange after beginning of October (7).

21 down: TANTRUM. So much French drink (tant + rum)? No, I must do something different. We haven't used a hidden word yet, have we?

Ill-temper brought by constant rumours (7).

22 down: GHETTOS. I'm getting perilously close to my maximum number of anagrams, but I can't resist 'get shot'!

Get shot going astray in slum areas (7).

23 down: LORELEI. I won't be the first (or the last!) to clue this by lore + lei, but we can't always be original!

Fabulous singer in folk stories given garland (7).

27 down: GRAIN. I see that this can be defined by 'fruit', something which we should encourage everyone to eat, of whatever age. Put in a 'perhaps' because it's possible to be a gran at 32:

Old lady perhaps eating one fruit (5).

So there we have it: 2 or 3 hours work, showing you how it's done. I haven't in any way saved up my best clues for this puzzle, and I haven't provided equal numbers of all types of clue (there are rather more cryptic definitions than usual, for example), but I hope it was enjoyable enough for *Guardian* readers on 25 January 1992.

The Complete Puzzle

Here is the puzzle, clues and grid together:

GUARDIAN CROSSWORD 19, 313

Set by Pasquale

ACROSS

1 The sort of idiocy that makes folk drive up to the pearly gates? (8,7)
9 Bird sounding abrasive in Melbourne? (9)
10 Blonde, about 50, shows 'talent' (5)
11 Condiment makes Dad consume only half the rice, ending with 'Yuck!' (7)
12 Tory type, a tagger-on? (7)
13 Note source of illumination (3)
14 Once again affirm king must be given the property (7)
17 What sounds like claim to keep clean is nonsense (7)
19 Den with nasty decor maybe changed finally (7)
22 Rancour goes on a long time—one may have wanted calm waters (7)
24 Like rugby post made of wood (3)
25 I play a central role, but I may or may not be charged (7)
26 Gets very cross, being as green as could be (7)
28 Island is not half bizarre—go wrong turning to leave it (5)
29 Treat shamefully with a lie to wreak vengeance (9)
30 Give someone the pip and he won't be this any more (3-12)

DOWN

1 Some, perhaps, doubly in muddle, taking things the wrong way (15)
2 Not, as you would deduce, very fast (3-2)
3 Real pic re-created (7)
4 One needs to get quiet, quiet, quiet—QUIET! (7)
5 Wonder vehicle pulled up within the distance (7)
6 US military resources in boggy area with river around (7)
7 Complicated tale a bore spun out (9)
8 What can a person do without a comb? Be perplexed (7,4,4)
15 Tempting act of the French in part (9)
16 Greek character little short of being tight (3)
18 The old will need a bit of assistance, indeed (3)
20 Herb leaves turn orange after beginning of October (7)
21 Ill-temper brought by constant rumours (7)
22 Get shot going astray in slum areas (7)
23 Fabulous singer in folk stories given garland (7)
27 Old lady perhaps eating one fruit (5)

GUARDIAN CROSSWORD 19,313

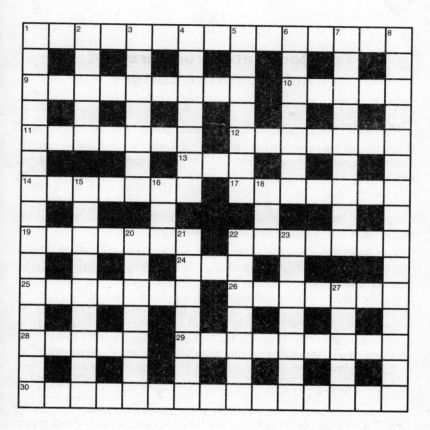

Postscript on Computers

This puzzle was set using pencil and paper. Nowadays many crossword setters (myself included) use a computer: to help look for words and phrases that will fit; to search for possible anagrams; and to format and print out the complete puzzle. A computer won't write decent clues though (yet?), so the use of software should be seen as a useful shortcut rather than as a cheating device—it is one stage on from the Spellmaster.

The use of computers is covered in Chapter 19.

18

The Complete Cruciverbalist:
Solver, Setter, Editor

The Complete Solver

In this *Manual* I've taken you through definition puzzles, 15 × 15 plain cryptics, and then suggested that you use your *Chambers* to tackle the 12 × 12 barred puzzles and eventually the advanced specials. The *Manual* is designed to help you do just that, and when you get to Chapter 20 you will be invited to romp up to the greatest heights. Inevitably, though, you may find the pace of the romp rather hard going, so use the newspapers to work out where you are as a solver and move up when you are ready.

The easiest 15 × 15 puzzles tend to be in the tabloid newspapers. Good starting-points in the broadsheets are *The Daily Telegraph* and *The Observer's Everyman*. Quixote puzzles in *The Independent on Sunday* are broadly similar to the Everyman puzzle but perhaps a little spicier if you're more than a beginner. Among the other broadsheets, the puzzles in *The Financial Times* and *The Independent* are of a very reasonable standard. So too is the puzzle in *The Guardian*, but this can vary significantly in style and level of difficulty, something which endears it to its fans. In recent years the most consistently good puzzle has probably been *The Times* crossword, although it (like many other dailies) continues to allow some non-Ximenean conventions which can jar. *The Times* Jumbo (a 27 × 27 blocked puzzle) has opened up new possibilities every Saturday, and the Saturday issue of *The Times* (with a definition puzzle, two blocked cryptics and *The Listener* puzzle) is a weekly must-buy paper for crossworders in the UK.

There are three Sunday papers offering 12 × 12 barred puzzles: Beelzebub in *The Independent on Sunday*, Mephisto in *The Sunday Times*, and Azed in *The Observer*. The Saturday puzzle in *The Independent* offers a relatively gentle introduction to the barred special and has plugged a gap between the plain 12 × 12 barred puzzle and the more difficult specials. Also recommended is Enigmatic Variations in the *Sunday Telegraph*, a puzzle which often resembles *Listener* puzzles of 20 years ago (when *The Listener* was generally much easier than it is today). Azed's specials are significantly more difficult than his plains, but generally not as hard as those published under the heading of the *The Listener Crossword*, now appearing in *The Times* Weekend Section on a Saturday. *The Listener* went out of business in 1990, but *The Listener*

Crossword lives on and continues to explore the frontiers of novelty and difficulty. Anyone who aspires to be a setter should ideally solve puzzles one level harder than the ones he or she sets (unless he or she is a *Listener* setter of course!). I would recommend that anyone who wants to be a regular 15 x 15 setter should enter the Azed competition, but at the same time recognize that the clue styles and vocabulary for daily puzzles will often need to be simpler. Incorporating an obscure abbreviation with an anagram for an Everyman-style puzzle would never do.

If you are in the USA look out for *Atlantic Monthly* (see puzzle no. 69 in this *Manual*) and *Harper's* (puzzles by Ed Galli and Richard Maltby Jr). These are barred puzzles. If you want the equivalent of a *Times* puzzle try *Games* magazine, edited by Will Shortz.

Ten Tips for Solvers

Here are ten tips for solvers:

1   Don't spend all day on 1 across! If I am solving a 15 x 15 standard cryptic, I read through the clues in order, spending no more than 15 seconds (roughly) on each and solving where I can. As I start on the down clues I can expect help from checking letters. After this first run-through I concentrate on clues relevant to a particular part of the diagram and follow wherever that leads.

2   Remember that the definition *should* always be at the beginning of the clue or at the end. If you can separate it out easily, the remaining words in the clue may suggest the clue type.

3   Hidden words and anagrams offer beginners the easiest start. Some crossword jargon shouts 'Anagram!'

4   Look out for other crossword jargon. Something 'going around' something may alert you to a container-and-contents clue. The 'worker' may well be an 'ant'.

5   Look out for opportunities to fill in individual letters on the diagram in pencil. The definition of a plural may allow you to fill in an 's'. Similarly you may see opportunities for 'ing', 'ed' and other common endings.

6   Learn to work backwards from the letters already filled in, i.e. solve *inductively*! Say to yourself 'The answer could be GRAMOPHONE, so will the clue give this answer?'

7   Don't be afraid to use a dictionary, especially when you are learning. It is *not* 'cheating'! In addition to a dictionary you may find other reference books helpful, especially a one-volume encyclopedia and an atlas.

8   If you get desperately stuck, have a break. Let your brain tick over on 'automatic pilot' and after a night's sleep the answer may be obvious.

9   If you fail to finish a puzzle, try to learn something by reading the answers.

10   Keep a sense of proportion, and don't let solving crosswords dominate your entire existence!

The Complete Setter

The would-be crossword setter has to face two challenges: (i) locating an outlet for puzzles, (ii) doing a decent job.

I must say a word about (i) first. When I was a teenager setting puzzles for the *Radio Times* I received a letter from the crossword editor of *The Daily Telegraph* returning my puzzle and telling me that 'Fleet Street is not normally reached in one leap'. Quite so. There have been one or two spectacular under-20 crossword setters since then, but on the whole you must work your way up. It is just possible that *The Modern Lady's Weekly* (my invention) may want a puzzle, or the *Agricultural News*, but don't think you can start with *The Times*. That way lies disappointment. Look for openings, local and national, but recognize that you're at the bottom of the ladder. If the only way to get on the ladder is to set a definition puzzle for *The Barchester News*, go for it.

Let's suppose that you're going to set a 15 × 15 puzzle. Perhaps it's for the good folk of Barchester or perhaps it's for your college mag. I suggest that you (like the solver) need ten tips.

Ten Tips for Setters

1   Get the grid settled first. If you want to devise your own grid, take note of the points I make in Chapter 12. As a novice, though, you would do better to used a grid from one of the dailies (but preferably not one of those which has five-letter words with only the second and fourth letters checked). Experienced setters can make up the grids as they go along and choose them to fit the selection of long words and phrases they want to use. This is the ideal situation—something the complete setter should eventually aim for. Ideally your grid should have answers with several different lengths. Words with 3 letters are not often used but they do provide an opportunity for the 11-letter answer that is otherwise likely to be forgotten.

2   Keep a good stock of resources, including dictionaries, encyclopedias and reference books.

3   Use a pencil, and be careful about word endings. There aren't many 9-letter words ending in J, so be prepared to use an eraser and don't be stubborn.

4   Use an interesting variety of words and phrases and fill in the long answers first. Avoid words that are boring to define and/or difficult to break up (e.g. STRENGTHLESS). You will often be forced to have dull words, but there is no need for you to make life difficult for yourself. Make sure that any phrase used is standard, i.e. either in the dictionary, in common parlance, or well known as a title. YELLOW SHIRT is not acceptable, but YELLOW FEVER is. YELLOW SUBMARINE wouldn't have been acceptable before it became a Beatles hit, but it could be appropriate in some crosswords (if the crossword editor allows song titles).

5   If you are setting for a periodical and dealing with a crossword editor, you must know what he or she does and doesn't allow on the grid. Several dailies will not allow the names of living people on the grid, for instance, and *The Times* doesn't like names of products or 'words with unpleasant or non-drawing-room associations (e.g. leprosy, semen, carcinoma, incontinent)'. For a 15 x 15 puzzle you will want your *Chambers*, but also use the *Concise Oxford Dictionary* to check that you have an 'everyday' word if in doubt.

6   As you write in your words and phrases, log up a few ideas on how you will clue them later on. If you have ten words that can only be clued by anagrams, you could be in trouble. For the sake of variety you will only want about half a dozen anagrams at most.

7   When you write your clues, put into effect all the principles outlined in the *Manual*. Ask yourself these questions for each clue:

> Is the definition fair?
> (Could I substitute the answer for the definition in a sentence?)
>
> Is the subsidiary indication fair?
>
> Can all the words in the clue be justified?
> (What about the linkword(s)?)
>
> Does the clue as a whole make some sort of sense or is it only a zany mixture of subject, verb and object?
>
> Don't try to be too clever. Err on the side of simplicity, and don't write a 'clue to a clue'.

8   Check your crossword carefully and get it checked by others if possible. If you know someone else who is a 15 x 15 solver, ask that friend to try and solve the puzzle. When you check your puzzle, check one thing at a time—the clue numbers, the clues, the numbers in brackets. You can easily make mistakes by trying to check everything at once.

9   If you are having your crossword published by a crossword editor, try to establish a dialogue if possible. The editor may be able to help you, but (if you've read the *Manual* carefully) you might even be able to help the editor. If an editor doesn't like your clue, do not allow him or her to inflict a non-Ximenean alternative if you can help it. Instead suggest a new clue yourself. You may want to ask to see proofs.

10 If you publish crosswords regularly, you may get much less reaction than you had hoped for. Solvers often overlook mistakes, so don't get too many hang-ups about them. They are much more likely to complain that a puzzle is too hard. It's one thing to set a really hard 'advanced' puzzle, another to set a 15 x 15 standard. You don't want your puzzles to be a push-over, but in the contest between setter and solver you must expect to lose graciously.

It is just possible that some readers of this *Manual* will want to go on to set advanced puzzles. For a 12 x 12 Azed-type puzzle, study once again Chapters 13-16. If you do set advanced puzzles for a periodical, you will almost certainly be able to choose your own grid and you will have the freedom to shift bars around to get the words to fit—this can be a great help. If you move on to advanced specials, you will need to have lots of original ideas or gimmicks. You will have the opportunity to construct imaginative new grids with letters entered in fanciful new ways, and you may even invent your own type of clue. Not many of you may get that far, but specialist publications such as that of the Crossword Club will take puzzles from all comers solely on merit—and *The Listener* puzzle in *The Times* is still open to all. There will always be room for new talent.

The Crossword Editor

Not many readers, I guess, will become crossword editors, but a few at least will become crossword setters who have to deal with editors, so it may be useful to reflect on the editor's role. The job of the editor is twofold:

(i)   to ensure that a fair and accurate puzzle appears in print;

(ii) to keep everyone happy (as far as possible).

To take point (ii) first. There are, of course, the solvers to be kept happy.

Inevitably some will from time to time complain about a puzzle being too easy or too hard, so it is a matter of keeping most of the solvers happy for most of the time. But it is also a matter of keeping the setters happy too. As an editor one may well need to rewrite clues, but one needs to be sensitive to the feelings of the setter. As in all areas of publishing (and this is something I have learnt in the day job!) authors and editors need to establish mutual respect. So let's have ten tips for crossword editors, shall we?

Ten Tips for Editors

1   Establish ground rules with your setters about your channels of communication. How would you like your puzzles submitted? Do you want the setters to provide notes? Do you want submissions by e-mail? Will you send proofs? And so on.

2   Establish ground rules with your setters about matters of style by providing written notes. You may wish to give guidance about such matters as which dictionaries to use, and you may wish to discourage certain practices. Many crossword editors now recommend *Chambers Crossword Manual* rather than attempt to write their own book about types of clue, etc!

3   Establish an understanding about 'ownership' of the final puzzle. Will you wish to rewrite clues or ask the setter to? Will you want to put your rewritten clues in print under the setter's name or pseudonym and will the setter be happy if you do? Do you want a protracted dialogue with your setters, or is time so short that you have to impose 'the editor's decision is final' at a fairly early stage?

4   Look after your setters by representing them to the periodical for which you are working. This may mean asking for a pay rise for them or making sure that they receive a free copy. One essential requirement is that you have the courtesy to tell your setters when their puzzles will appear.

5   When you receive a puzzle you can do one of two things: either (i) try to solve it on a blank grid (something you should always ask for by the way) or (ii) check out the clues against the solution. Option (i) is the ideal but you may find yourself wasting time if the setter is new and unreliable. A quick inspection using option (ii) can often (alas!) lead to a rejection with minimal time loss.

6   Even if you go for option (i) above, you should check out the puzzle using option (ii) subsequently. Before you look at the clues look at the grid. If it offends you, you must decide whether it is redeemable or not and who is to do any redeeming—you or the setter.

7   After looking at the grid look at the words on the grid. Again, face the redemption issue. You may decide, for example, that a crossing of a junction at the N of TENOR and NO HAIR can be redeemed by changing NO HAIR to MOHAIR and TENOR to TIMER. (And, yes, I have seen NO HAIR as a phrase in a puzzle!)

8   Faced with a clue you have three options: (i) leave it, (ii) amend it slightly, (iii) rewrite it. If a clue is sound and sensible (and hasn't appeared recently), you are best to leave it (option (i)) unless you can think of a small amendment which will add a touch of gloss (option (ii)); you may prefer someone to 'shelter' in a tent for example rather than to 'be located' in a tent. Only make the change if (a) it adds finesse or (b) it renders an unsound clue sound. Go for option (iii) if the clue is grossly unsound or doesn't make sense. Try to avoid substituting your own clue just because you think it's better than the perfectly adequate one submitted—save that for your own puzzles.

9   When you have been through the whole puzzle, look at the clues as a whole. Are there more anagrams than you would like and if so might you want to replace some of the clues? Do you really want right = R to be used *three* times? And so on.

10   Know your solvers. Know your setters. Know the editor of the periodical you are working for. Talk to them. Meet them. Be nice to them.

The Social Dimension

Solving and setting crosswords can be a lonely occupation—and that can be one of its attractions. But it doesn't have to be like that all the time, as many Azed solvers will testify. If you can, find others with whom you can discuss your ideas, and you may help each other up Crossword Mountain. For the truly complete crossworder the social dimension is essential.

Ten clues edited

(see Challenge on p. 90)

1 The clue would be sounder with 'that produced' changed to 'that's produced' or 'that produces'. Even then it makes little sense and 'lockjaw' is a *give-away definition*. To preserve the idea behind the clue the editor might change this to:

   Eat nuts? From such one might get disease (7)

2 There's a lot wrong with this clue: for starters, 'you' does not equal 'u', nor is there an anagram indicator. To preserve the cat and the cargo I would suggest:

   Cat you finally found hiding in cargo—naughty! (6)

3 Here the definition suggests a noun (some sort of help) rather than a verb. How can 'salvia' be linked to 'avails'? Perhaps through some idea of an aromatherapeutic preparation, so let's try:

   Preparation of salvia is effectual (6)

4 When I attempted this clue I didn't know whether to put in PRAY or PREY. And is the definition accurate anyway? I don't think so. Let's try this:

   Victim is heard to make supplication (4)

5 This is an example of a *partial subsidiary indication*. It's all very well to indicate the 'at' bit of ATTILA but what about the rest of the clue? Perhaps the clue should be rewritten, but let's try to preserve the 'at' with:

   Invader at front of tower—one starts to look anxious (6)

6 Is 'provided by' strong enough as an anagram indicator? I'm not convinced - and I'm not convinced by the sense of the clue either. But perhaps this edited version is *slightly* more plausible:

   Damaged ego—clue provided by short poem (6)

7   Try doing an S/D analysis on this one! The definition is sandwiched
    between bits of subsidiary indication and the 'How' at the front is
    supposed to make the clue more readable and the definition
    stronger. Now we've all heard of alma mater but who (apart from
    the author—see my dedication) had a mater called Alma? Let's try
    this:

    Henry faces girl in a board game (5)

8   An 'ant' is sometimes a 'six-footer' but again the definition has been
    sandwiched in the middle. Also note that 'see' and 'C' is a bit
    advanced for a daily paper (in which this clue was found). Let's try:

    Six-footer, one about to join in caper (5)

9   You know my views on nounal anagram indicators, but I am sure
    many crossword editors would let this through because soundness
    will inevitably increase inelegance—and after all, we've all clued
    RADIO (and RODEO!) every possible way, haven't we? Well, let's
    preserve 'Dior' at any rate with this:

    Special creation of Dior includes a device that has people talking (5)

10 I'm not at all sure what this clue means, but apart from that it is
    victim of the *unwanted-object-of-the-verb syndrome*. 'To unbraid'
    means 'to separate the strands of' according to my *Webster*, the
    only one of my non-OED dictionaries to include the word. So 'to
    free locks' is 'to unbraid locks', not simply 'to unbraid'. 'Locks' is the
    'unwanted object'. It's a marginal word, but let's say we allow it. Let's
    try:

    Free from entanglement—bird Una released (7)

    Not a brilliant clue, but notice how useful 'free' is here as a word that
    is a verb in the definition but appears to be an adjective in the
    overall context of the clue. 'Multi-part-of-speech' words are
    extraordinarily useful, as are words like 'put' and 'set' which retain
    the same form in the past tense and as past participles. Some
    things I must leave you to discover!

19

The Use of Computers

The computer revolution

When the second edition of this book was published in 1992 computers really didn't feature—apart from the Franklin Spellmaster. Since then there has been a revolution. Computers can now help setters to format their puzzles, and even (as we shall see) begin to help solvers work out clues. And then there is the Internet.

Using the computer to set puzzles

Computers can now be used to fill grids with words and phrases extremely quickly. A 15 × 15 puzzle can be filled in a matter of seconds and there is also the possibility of course of storing clues on a database (inside the computer or out). This led one national newspaper in the nineties to try an experiment. They filled in the grids and recycled their setters' clues, offering a fee for new clues to be added to the database. Word got out as it was bound to, but solvers too noticed a certain staleness—and not all the setters were that happy either. Sanity was restored, but that isn't to say that some of the setters couldn't use the computer quite sensibly.

There are currently two main products on the market for setters. The one I use for 15 × 15 daily cryptics is called Crossword Compiler 5 and it is produced by Antony Lewis of 16 Townley Road, London SE22 8SR (on the Internet at www.network.demon.co.uk). This particular program allows for the construction of blocked puzzles and then offers a choice of Autofill (to fill a whole grid) or Autofind (to choose a word or phrase). Autofill tends to give hackneyed (and frequently unwanted) solutions and is best for difficult corners when most of the letters are in the grid already.

Try Autofind with _ E _ R _ _ _ _ and you will be offered BEARABLE, BEARABLY, YEARNING under 'Default', BEAR ARMS and GET ROUND among the Compounds and Phrases. HEBRIDES and NEBRASKA among the 'Cities' (an inclusive geographical term) and even HEBRIDIT under Finnish (if you really want it). There are no birds meeting this formula. When the answer has been entered a clue window is available with a useful anagram button. Thus MOONLIGHT SONATA offers a whole range of anagrams beginning with ANTHOLOGIST MOAN and moving through to the more musically promising NOTTINGHAM SOLO A. Good setters will use the Autofill, Autofind and Anagram facilities selectively, and check out the acceptability of the vocabulary carefully. They will also add their own vocabulary outside the database of this particular program. And there is still the little matter of writing good sound clues, of course. That said, Crossword Compiler is a great asset for formatting, filling and anagrammatizing—a very useful additional tool. Also recommended is the Sympathy program on offer from Ross Beresford at Bryson Limited, 10 Wagtail Close, Twyford, Reading RG10 9ED (visit www.bryson.demon.co.uk). This is particularly good for advanced cryptics using barred grids with 'harder words'. It is not possible to mention all the features of these two excellent programs, and readers are recommended to visit the websites. For either program you will need a PC; there are no Apple Macintosh versions available.

Computer solving

Using a computer to set a puzzle is one thing; using it to solve clues is surely another! A very bold attempt, however, has been main by William Tunstall-Pedoe with his Crossword Maestro (available from PO Box 395, Cambridge CB3 9 PJ and featured at www.genius2000.com). One keys in a puzzle and tries out the clues, with varying degrees of success. I tried out Crossword No. 17 in this book. After a few outright failures it solved 5 across as HAZARD with a confidence level of 95% and told me that 'az' placed inside 'hard' is 'hazard'. I wasn't convinced with the 31% confidence level for PAPER TOWELLING at 13 across, but a nice straightforward clue at 17 down gave GRANDEE with a 99% confidence level. As letters were filled in, the suggestions became better but the puzzle needed a human brain for completion. The program is excellent on simple clues, though, and could be recommended to beginners as a way of trying to understand some of the basics. Crossword Maestro is great fun and an impressive achievement.

The Internet

Put 'crossword' into your search engine and you will find tens of thousands of sites, largely devoted to definition products from America. For British puzzles you can visit the newspaper sites for *The Daily Telegraph* and *The Times*, but if you want something more than just the puzzle I would recommend *The Guardian* site (www.guardian.co.uk) which offers additional support material and a chatline. The print version of the daily puzzle prints out nicely too.

For serious solvers of advanced cryptics the best place to start on is *The Crossword Centre*, an interactive and hugely entertaining website run by

Derek Harrison at www.crossword.org.uk. Among other things this has an Azed section, competitions, a message board, a book list, and excellent links to other sites. There is also a link to Crossword Utility, a freeware program for composing grids with blocks or bars.

Are computers a threat?

The answer must be yes and no. Yes, because if they are relied on too much, some of the joy of intellectual achievement in both setting and solving will disappear. And yet no, because a computer might produce some doggerel verse, but it can never be a Wordsworth—and I'm sure the 'Crossword Wordsworths' will be around for a while yet.

No, too, because a computer can save time on some of the more laborious processes without any loss to the ultimate quality of the clues. And no if only because it is now so easy to create a file and zap it by e-mail to the crossword editor rather than print, package and post!

Perhaps one should, however, finish with a word of caution about puzzles that are virtually impossible to solve in the armchair but become easier using the search facilities of a computer. One day we may live in a paperless world but until that happens I hope that those who want to solve difficult puzzles will still be able to do so with a pencil, a pen and (if necessary) a few decent reference books beside the armchair.

20

A Crossword Romp

This final chapter contains 54 puzzles ancient and modern. Some are easy; some are hard; a few might seem impossible. They have been chosen within three different categories: (i) 'historical' puzzles, (ii) representative puzzles of the modern era, and (iii) some of my own puzzles reprinted for a larger audience. Since I am writing the book, I had better contribute at least half the puzzles overall, but this proportion by no means reflects my significance as a setter! Not all the clues printed here will necessarily match Ximenean standards (though I hope my own will not be found wanting); but all the puzzles should have something interesting about them, so I hope you will enjoy the romp.

Nos. 37–40 take us back to the early days. No. 37 was a discovery in a second-hand Oxford bookshop while I was writing the earlier chapters of this book. In 1924 C. Arthur Pearson of WC2 published a book of 'word squares', but these were in fact primitive crosswords. Our No. 37 was Word Square No. 12. The individually numbered squares, overlapping words and unclued pairs (e.g. 49–50) are evidence of a new word-puzzle form coming alive. The idea of a pretty picture was taken up by Torquemada and his first puzzle in *The Observer* (No. 38) illustrates the feelers which the Sunday paper was putting out to its readers. Subsequent puzzles featured a marionette, 'all the world's a stage', 'Mrs Porter and her daughter' and other intriguing themes. Notice how many of the clues offer something a little more challenging than a straight definition (with a misleading context in the very first clue). No. 39 shows an early example of a Bible crossword from the *Sunday Companion* of 1 May 1926.

No. 40 takes us back again to the early days of *The Telegraph* with a full version of the puzzle promised on p.24. No. 41 was my first published cryptic crossword from the *Radio Times* in 1964, and I offer apologies to solvers who weren't watching TV in those days. Clue scrutineers should be warned that I hadn't yet discovered Ximenes.

We turn now to *The Times*. No. 42 is by Mike Laws, the current crossword editor, who prior to his appointment set puzzles under a number of pseudonyms for other papers (as the solution to this puzzle will reveal). No. 43 is one of my own puzzles.

Unlike *The Times*, *The Guardian* discloses the names (or at any rate pseudonyms) of its setters. One well-loved setter who died in 1998 was Alec Robins who masqueraded as Custos and we see his work as No. 44.

For many years Alec Robins was one half of Everyman of the *The Observer*, and in that capacity he helped Ximenes write his book before writing one of his own (see p.325). He was the Ximenean's Ximenean, and produced an output high in quantity and quality. For many years the other half of Everyman was Miss Dorothy Taylor, who used to enter Ximenes competitions under the pseudonym of her sister-in-law, Mrs B. Lewis (hence the name of Inspector Morse's sergeant). No. 45 is one of her puzzles. The current Everyman is Allan Scott, whose weekly puzzles can be recommended. There are, of course, a number of 15 x 15 blocked puzzles in the Sunday papers, and I appear every week as Quixote in *The Independent on Sunday*. No. 46 introduces a type of vocal clue not yet covered in this book, the *spoonerism clue*.

According to *Guinness World Records*, the world's most prolific setter is Roger F. Squires. To *Guardian* solvers he is known as Rufus, but he sets puzzles for many papers and periodicals, including *The Financial Times* (No. 47). No. 48 is also from *The Financial Times*. It is by Quark, who is Eric Burge, an experienced setter and a successful clue-writer in Azed competitons. He also sets for the *The Guardian* as Quantum. The most popular *Guardian* setter is the octogenarian Araucaria (Revd John Graham) whose puzzles are often extraordinarily inventive and entertaining. Araucaria is certainly not a member of the Ximenean party. This can infuriate those 'on the other side of the house', but there is nevertheless much to admire. Try No. 49 for Araucaria—and look out for his bank holiday specials.

Prospective setters may find it difficult to place their puzzles in the London dailies, but some years ago the *Birmingham Evening Mail* welcomed all comers. One of my own puzzles appears here as No. 50. My pseudonym 'Duck' comes from Donald Duck, in line with my philosophy that ultimately crosswords should be fun rather than inquisitorial.

One of my favourite puzzles as a teenager was The Skeleton in the *Sunday Express* (as exemplified in No. 51). It is a particularly interesting puzzle for anyone wanting some early lessons in how a grid can be constructed.

Nos. 52–55 are all puzzles of mine published by Quality Magazines, first with *Quiz Digest*, then with *Tough Puzzles*.

Our final blocked puzzle is from Afrit's *Armchair Crosswords*, the book which began with the famous Injunction. No. 56 looks old-fashioned to us now, in terms of both the grid and the clues. Afrit was too early to be Ximenean, but was Ximenes himself a Ximenean? You will soon be able to judge that for yourselves!

We now move from blocks to bars. No. 57 is a plain from the very early days of Ximenes (his No. 27 from the forties). I have chosen it partly because of the clue at 16 down which won W. K.M. Slimmings first prize. A lovely idea, but would it be mean to suggest that an adjective was here being defined as a noun? And what of the clues by the master in this puzzle? If 'Tennyson was not Tennysonian', then Ximenes was not Ximenean—in those early days at any rate! By modern standards rather less than 50% of the clues pass muster. In my view, though, this serves only to emphasize the achievements of Ximenes in formulating the rules and raising the standards through the fifties and sixties.

Nos. 58 and 59 are from *The Independent on Sunday*, coming from two different Beelzebubs. No. 58 is by Richard Whitelegg (the first Beelzebub, from 1989 until his death in 1995) and No. 59 is by one of his successors Michael Macdonald-Cooper, who is the crossword editor of *The Independent* and who shares the puzzle with Paul Henderson (see puzzle No. 66).

No. 60 is another 12 x 12 advanced cryptic, this time from Mephisto of *The Sunday Times*. Mephisto I who died in 1973 was Richard Kilner, Mephisto II (1973 - 1995) was Richard Whitelegg (see puzzle No. 58) and Mephisto III consists of Chris Feetenby, Mike Laws (see puzzle No. 42) and Tim Moorey (seen here). This puzzle is remarkable for having only 24 clues in a 12 x 12 grid.

Richard Whitelegg's exact contemporary at Cambridge, Jonathan Crowther, is (as you know by now) Azed of *The Observer*. His puzzles are mostly 12 x 12 but for variety he has introduced some 13 x 11 grids, as shown in No. 61.

A relative newcomer to the Sunday advanced cryptic scene is *The Sunday Telegraph*. Crossword editor James Leonard has run a series of special cryptics under the title Enigmatic Variations since 1992. We meet him here as Rustic in puzzle No. 62, and in puzzle No. 63 your author appears in his latest guise (as Giovanni). Enigmatic Variations puzzles are roughly at the same level of difficulty as *The Listener* puzzles of the 1970s and 1980s, but over the past ten years (as we shall see anon) *The Listener* has moved on to levels of greater complexity.

Nos. 64 and 65 are also two of my puzzles from a magazine of the 1970s called *Games and Puzzles*. Its crossword editor Don Putnam broke new ground in crossword journalism and there is nothing like it now in the magazine racks of our newsagents, alas. Don continues as Logodaedulus of *The Guardian*.

The Independent's Saturday magazine offers a special advanced cryptic puzzle every week. It moved into this territory in 1987, even earlier than *The Sunday Telegraph*. The level of difficulty is quite variable. No. 66 is a puzzle by Phi (Paul Henderson) and No. 67 attracted no correct solutions before the closing date, although one or two arrived late. I would maintain that the puzzle is quite solvable, so you may like to see if you can succeed where others have failed!

For the next two puzzles we cross the Atlantic. No. 68 is by Stephen Sondheim, better known for his musicals. Sondheim used to solve *The Listener* crossword with Leonard Bernstein while they worked on *West Side Story*, and he did much as a setter to further the cryptic crossword in America in the sixties. This narrative type of puzzle was probably invented by Torquemada. No. 69 is the 'Puzzler' from *The Atlantic Monthly* for November 2000. Each month Emily Cox and Henry Rathvon produce a fine crossword.

Stephen Sondheim is one of about fifty 'top crossworders' who receive a crossword each Christmas from Apex (the setter of No. 70). 'A Puzzle Each Christmas' has been circulating for 30 years, but the name Apex comes from 'Ape X(imenes)', something which Eric Chalkley began to do when he bought Ximenes' book. Apex has also set puzzles for the *The Guardian* and *The Listener*. One member of Apex's band is Michael Freeman, who contributed puzzles to *The Listener* and has his own monthly puzzle in the *New Statesman* (No. 71). Salamanca, as he is known, is a particularly inventive setter, but like Araucaria he worries orthodox Ximeneans.

The Listener crossword began unpromisingly on 2 April 1930 with a 'musical crossword'. One clue was 'Last three letters of Christian name of a great composer'. The answer (without notes) was IAN—presumably from the Sebastian of J.S. Bach. Mr I. Cresswell of 40 Hamilton Road, Colchester, provided the only all-correct solution but he didn't get a prize. The first pseudonymous setter appears to have been Doggerel, but the running was soon taken up by Proton (A. McIntyre) and Afrit. Before the Second World War prizes were often given to all winners, but the setters of a pre-Ximenean era confessed in print that they could not always gauge the appropriate level of difficulty.

Afrit's first 'Printer's Devilry' was first published on 2 June 1937 (No. 72). Some breaks came at the end of words; unrelated pairs of words are to be inserted; the checking is not as good as it looks because of unclued letter pairs; and there are numerous references to literature. Despite these difficulties there were 30 correct entries. Can you solve the puzzle? I couldn't, but reading the solution was interesting! During the War, *The Listener* introduced an easier (and rather poor) puzzle every other week; Afrit (none too pleased) dropped out but re-emerged after the War.

Thanks largely to the work of Ximenes, *Listener* puzzles have become more even in standard and difficulty. The number of competitors has doubled since the puzzle migrated to *The Times*, and entries for the easier puzzles are close to a thousand. Nos. 73–82 are example of *Listener* puzzles. Zander is Alec Robins (whom we have already met); Hen is Vince Henderson; Virgilius is Brian Greer, who has more recently enjoyed a spell as the crossword editor of *The Times*.

No. 78 by Mass (Harold Massingham) reminds us that crosswords need not be 'square', in any sense of the word. Look out in the *Listener* puzzle for all sorts of shapes, including hexagons. Mass also sets for *The Independent* and for many years appeared in *The Spectator*.

No. 79 is undoubtedly the hardest puzzle I have managed to complete. Published in *The Listener* to celebrate the Queen's Silver Jubilee, it provided me with over 20 hours of alternate frustration and enjoyment. It is three-dimensional, and I suggest you make a box. Leiruza (A. E. Hughes) has produced a number of puzzles involving knight's moves. No. 80 by Law is also a difficult puzzle but great fun. The champion *Listener* solver in 1989, who won the Solver Silver Salver, thought it the best puzzle that year and accordingly awarded Ross Lawther the 'Ascot Gold Cup' at the annual *Listener* Setters' dinner. (Though donated by the setter Ascot, it is not made of gold, nor is it a cup!) No. 81 is in the opinion of many the most brilliant *Listener* puzzle ever to appear. The setter John Grimshaw (known to solvers as Dimitry) claimed to have knocked it up very quickly when no one else had come up with a New Year puzzle. Without giving anything away, I would advise solvers to use a pencil rather than a pen. Columba, the setter of No. 82, is Colin Gumbrell, whom we have already met in the Azed competition. This is another brilliant puzzle, although anyone who knows about chess will find the moves somewhat less clever than those of a grandmaster. Nos. 81 and 82 were also Ascot Gold Cup winners.

And so, finally, to Ximenes and Azed. Nos. 83–85 are three Ximenes specials. His No. 1000 is an early letters latent puzzle and No. 1200 marked the end of the Ximenes era. It is 30 years since Ximenes died, but his final puzzle is much closer to the modern Azed puzzle than it is to the plain puzzle we looked at earlier. That is a mark of Derrick Macnutt's great achievement, an achievement which I celebrated in a special puzzle ten years after his death (No. 86).

Azed has brought his own style to crosswords with new clue types and even stricter rules. But being stricter about the rules does not mean being a killjoy and in the two specials of his own invention shown here (Nos. 87 and 88) we see a witty and playful spirit at work. In 1977 Azed's solvers contributed to *The Azed Book of Crosswords* (now out of print). Nos. 89 and 90 formed a tribute to Azed by myself and my Bristol office colleague Merlin (Richard Palmer). One or two of the clues do look dated, and the value of the top prize has risen to £30. My friendship with Merlin goes on, though. Azed too goes on, and so does the enjoyment of crossword puzzles. Long may that be so.

8 _A_I_H

```
          savingly                papillae      AITS  Calixtus      AKIL  backfill
          takingly      AILM  Panislam                haliotis      AKIT  backlist
AIHD  banished      AILN  carillon      AITY  papistry      AKLE  dark-blue
      famished                papillon      AIUA  Caligula      AKMN  marksman
      ravished                vanillin                capitula      AKND  darkened
      vanished      AILR  caviller      AIUD  fatigued      AKNN  Hakkinen
AIHE  Lapithae                variolar      AIUE  latitude      AKNO  talk into
      Pasiphae      AILS  bacillus                manicure                walk into
AIHM  Havisham      AILW  Ladislaw                vaginale      AKNS  markings
AIHS  Laoighis      AILY  facially      AIUL  habitual      AKNW  mackinaw
AIHY  garishly                labially      AIUN  taciturn      AKOB  back-comb
      lavishly                racially      AJIT  banjoist      AKOD  back-load
      rakishly                radially      AJNG  mah-jongg                Mark Todd
AIIA  basilica      AIMN  kakiemon□     AJRE  Marjorie                pack-load
AIID  pacified                talisman      AJRM  marjoram      AKOE  backbone
      ramified      AINA  hacienda      AJRS  zanjeros                banknote
      ratified      AIND  maligned      AKAD  backhand      AKOK  hack-work
AIIE  Catiline      AINE  patience□               backward      AKOL  bankroll
      laciniae                radiance                backyard      AKOM  backroom
      Latinise                salience                parkland                darkroom
      Latinize                sapience                parkward      AKON  back down
      maritime                valiance      AKAE  back-date                mark down
      maximise                variance                Jack Cade                mark-down
      maximize      AINL  national      AKAH  backlash                pack down
      sanitise                rational                backwash                talk down
      sanitize      AINR  maligner                Balkhash      AKOR  back-door
      satirise      AINS  MacInnes      AKAK  backpack      AKOT  jackboot
      satirize      AINY  malignly                hark back      AKPN  backspin
AIIK  basilisk□               radiancy                talk back      AKPR  larkspur
AIIL  familial                saliency      AKAL  talk tall      AKRE  Valkyrie
AIIM  basidium      AIOA  Danilova                walk tall      AKRL  mackerel
      Hasidism                Manitoba      AKAS  Walkmans      AKRO  jackaroo
      Latinism      AIOD  manifold      AKBY  Hawke Bay                jackeroo
      nativism                marigold□     AKCE  backache      AKRP  backdrop
      pacifism      AIOE  baritone      AKDP  tanked up      AKTE  hackette
AIIN  magician                camisole      AKDY  markedly      AKTN  pack it in
      Maximian                varicose      AKED  backveld      AKTP  backstop
      Parisian      AIOI  yakitori                Bankhead                pack it up
      pavilion      AIOM  ramiform                hawkweed      AKTR  marketer
      Tahitian                variform      AKEL  back-heel      AKTY  basketry
AIIR  familiar                vasiform      AKES  dankness      AKUS  sackfuls
      pacifier      AIOS  calicoes                darkness                tankfuls
AIIS  papilios                manitous                lankness      AKUT  bankrupt
AIIT  Hasidist      AIOY  palimony                rankness      AKVR  talk over
      Latinist      AIRE  caviarie      AKET  backbeat                walk over
      nativist      AIRM  variorum                dark meat                walkover
      pacifist      AISN  Taliesin                rack-rent                walk-over
      satirist      AISS  radiuses      AKGR  packager      AKWY  back away
AIIY  facility      AITA  Jacintha      AKGS  packages                hark away
      nativity      AITC  sadistic      AKHP  talk shop                pack away
      rabidity      AITD  satiated      AKHT  backchat      AKYD  hawk-eyed
      rapidity      AITE  Jacinthe      AKHW  talk show      ALAD  galliard
      salinity                Mariette      AKIE  backbite□               halliard
      sapidity                Mariotte                backfire                kailyard
      validity      AITL  parietal                backside                railcard
      vapidity                sagittal                hawklike                tailband
AILA  Daniella      AITN  Hamilton                mark time      ALAE  fail-safe
      radialia                Pakistan                Parklife                malleate
AILC  Cadillac®     AITR  banister      AKIG  cackling                palliate
      Pauillac                canister                darkling                tailgate
AILE  Danielle                ganister                rankling                talliate
      mamillae                radiator      AKIH  bank-high                wayleave
      maxillae                varistor                jack-high      ALAH  Paul Nash
```

Words marked □ can also be spelled with an initial capital letter

CROSSWORD No. 37

From The Word Square Puzzle Book (1924)

HORIZONTAL

1–14	Pertaining to the Church
12–17	The young of cows
18–23	Wild sheep of Nepaul
22–24	Refuse (noun)
25–27	Low marshy land
26–31	Unfriendly disposition
32–37	An intimate acquaintance
38–41	A kind of vermin
47–48	One of the bovine genus
54–56	An expression of affirmation
57–59	A girl's name
60–62	Part of the verb 'to be'
66–68	Nothing
69–72	A common beverage
73–76	To cause to fall
77–79	A snare
83–85	A kind of tree
87–91	Pertaining to the law
92–95	A heavenly body
95–97	A strong-smelling plant
100–103	A valley
105–109	An appointed meeting
110–115	To select
116–120	The top room of a house
122–127	To impress
128–133	A kind of poetic foot
140–142	To go astray
143–151	A section of the Government
152–154	Diminutive of Henry
155–157	Part of a clergyman's address
158–160	A loud sound
159–166	Guiltless
167–168	Latin for 'and'
171–172	An obsolete pronoun
173–179	A one-horned animal
182–184	Opposed to no
186–191	An ambassador
190–192	A beverage
196–200	A sailing vessel used for pleasure
200–212	Having four seeds
205–209	Frog spawn

VERTICAL

1–122	To set free
2–55	To convey
3–100	Cut or hewn
5–36	An age
7–24	A pronoun
11–25	The title of Kipling's famous poem
12–75	An edible grain
15–107	Affected by visions
16–64	An element
17–133	Having feelings in common with another
37–70	Accomplished
49–74	Dread or veneration
55–135	Compliant
57–69	A Jewish month
64–183	To revive
89–125	A pledge
90–126	In the manner of (in music)
92–116	A spring of mineral water
94–118	Practical skill
109–195	Sensible to slight touches
110–196	Austerity
124–172	To obey
134–196	Truth
135–171	A colour
137–182	A pronoun of plural number
143–200	A full-grown person
144–187	To partake of food
146–189	An ancient native prince of Peru
148–191	A square measure
165–207	The back of the neck
166–208	Produced by the lachrymal gland
179–206	A card game

CROSSWORD No. 37

1	2	3	4	5	6	7	8	9	10	11	12	13	14	15	16	17
18	19	20	21	22	23	24				25	26	27	28	29	30	31
32	33	34	35	36	37						38	39	40	41	42	43
44	45	46			47	48				49	50			51	52	53
54	55	56		57	58	59			60	61	62		63	64	65
66	67	68		69	70	71	72		73	74	75	76		77	78	79
80	81	82												83	84	85
86	87	88	89	90	91						92	93	94	95	96	97
98	99	100	101	102	103						104	105	106	107	108	109
110	111	112	113	114	115						116	117	118	119	120	121
122	123	124	125	126	127						128	129	130	131	132	133
134	135	136												137	138	139
140	141	142		143	144	145	146	147	148	149	150	151		152	153	154
155	156	157		158	159	160	161	162	163	164	165	166		167	168	169
170	171	172		173	174	175	176	177	178	179	180	181		182	183	184
185				186	187	188	189	190	191	192	193	194				195
196	197	198	199	200	201	202	203	204	205	206	207	208	209	210	211	212

CROSSWORD No. 38

Crossword: I.—Feelers by Torquemada from the *Observer* (1926)

ACROSS

1 Point was
7 Crux of 'Wrong Box'
14 A poulpe
15 61 across was
16 Adamsonia digitata
17 Cape in Tripoli
18 Greek fire prefix
19 Allow
20 Preposition
22 British Dominion (init.)
24 Plaything
25 Poet of husbandry (init.)
27 Worth half heels
29 In reference to
31 Very, very hard
32 N.B.
36 Infinitive of 43
38 Right-hand (abbrev.)
39 Interjection
40 Jewish ruin
41 Frenzy
44 This in tongue of 5
46 Saves suitor expense
47 Little in 32
48 Wrote 'Bury Fair' (init.)
49 My sons were sons of Belial
51 Depart
53 Before steamers
54 Sudden
56 Card game
59 We shatter sleep
61 Fabulous voyager (pop. spelling)
64 An Archbishop of York
65 Recovers
66 1578 Spanish book on drugs was this
67 Lie close... in tins

DOWN

1 Jemima's father
2 Higher than king (anagram)
3 Halt
4 Tristram's uncle
5 Thin in Bordeaux
6 Best of three games
8 Should not indulge in 37s
9 Inquisitive
10 Vetch
11 Arab chief
12 Excludes some 20s
13 Stage paper
17 Livingstone and Stanley did
20 An invertebrate
21 Seville Nights
23 A constellation
25 Contains a widow
26 I doubt it
28 Suited to anserine converse
30 63 is
33 Half a farewell
34 Citation makes me a sale
35 Evening when good
36 Prefix of duality
37 Unready part of speech
42 Diary of 53
43 Part of 36 across
45 Downy Roman... female
49 Break out
50 Flows into Danube
52 Am olefiant
54 Island of Schleswig
55 Brothers of business
57 More than one one
58 With 37 on the way
59 Defeated Zerah
60 On London trams
61 Hundredth of yen
62 Kinds of money desirable
63 Dose without circle

CROSSWORD No. 38

CROSSWORD No. 39

'No Man can Serve Two Masters' from *The Sunday Companion* (1926)

ACROSS

1 One of the Apostles
6 Where Ahab went (I Kings xviii.)
12 Two
13 Conjunction
14 Of (Fr.)
15 Part of fish
17 Spoke to our Lord (Mark xii.)
19 A group of scientific rules
21 Recline
22 Males
23 Lieutenant (Abbrev.)
25 Wickedness
26 Took a chair
28 Point of the compass
29 Matchings
32 Cries of fear
34 Flying creature
35 The raising of taxes
37 Cover
39 The definite article
42 Supposing
44 Cowshed
45 Used by bricklayers
47 Royal Institute (Abbrev.)
48 To soil
50 Where Samson dwelt (Judg. xv.)
52 A wilderness (Gen. xxi)
54 Town in Somerset [!]
55 Brought by Mary (Mark xvi.)
57 Thrown about
58 Bottom part of a ship
60 Small pocket case
61 Asset
63 Harm
66 Those who hone
67 Parentless boy or girl
68 In front of the door
69 Increase
71 Method of cooking
72 As well as

DOWN

1 Raincoat (Abbrev.)
2 Dries thoroughly
3 Prefix meaning three
4 Using certain garden tool
5 Irish
7 Enemy of Saul (I Sam. xiv.)
8 Wife of Haman (Esther v.)
9 Period
10 Ages
11 Nickname for lion
12 Religious song
16 Occasional winter occurrence
18 Without seeing
20 Twisted by age
24 Small label
25 Form of address
27 Do up
28 Above us
30 Small bird
31 Slope of hill or mountain
32 Father of Enos (Gen. v.)
33 First woman (Gen. iii.)
36 Small bits of straw
38 Rage
40 A mountain (Num. xx.)
41 The leper (Matt. xxvi.)
43 Move by breeze
44 Undergrowth
46 The scribe (2 Sam. viii.)
47 Unusual
49 Father of Bezaleel (Exod. xxxi.)
51 Town in Mesopotamia, besieged in the War (reversed)
53 Required
54 Heavy blows
56 Mount given to Esau (Deut. ii.)
57 Seen in the sky
59 Plural of 23 across (Abbrev.)
60 Poem (reversed)
61 Talk to
62 Method or rule
64 Cast out by Zebul (Judg. ix.)
65 Finishes
68 Written folios (Abbrev.)
70 Perform

CROSSWORD No. 39

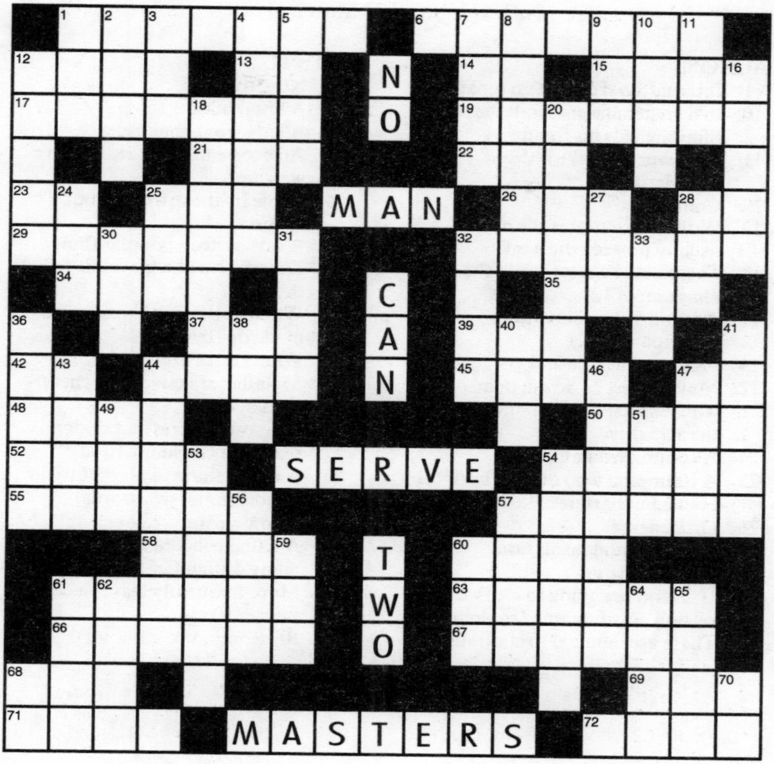
NO
MAN
CAN
SERVE
TWO
MASTERS

CROSSWORD No. 40

Daily Telegraph, 17 March 1928

ACROSS

1   International courtship repatched
10 In a bigger age colossal; the frozen tundra yields his fossil
11 However you take it this is stimulating
12 Confesses
13 With regard to this the nods usually precede the winks
14 These may suggest fun in the anagram of 12 across
17 Adoration travels with this cry
18 'Lip riot' (anag.)
19 As to manner, casual
22 May suggest 23 down, or an orator whose speciality is quantity rather than quality
24 A coming woman
25 A champion who did not burn his boats, but bartered them
26 Girl's name
29 Darkness and insulation characterise it
30 Use it before going to see that hair-raising play Dracula (hyphen)
31 These are inimical to continuity

DOWN

2   Nutritive seeds
3   A blind pilot
4   A lady from Shakespeare
5   An occasion when big ears are welcome
6   Made by those who favour a motion
7   A favourite in popular films
8   Descriptive of a plausible fellow (hyphen)
9   Whereat things of beauty are made up (hyphen)
15 What cooks need to do
16 Metallic adjective for a cheap loud-speaker
20 The sort of hope that seldom reaches a consummation
21 A useful thing to present to the importunate (two words)
22 'Show rip' (anag.)
23 A rising concern that presents many difficulties for the directors
27 More frequently leaves a church than enters it
28 Bird

CROSSWORD No. 40

CROSSWORD No. 41

Radio Times Crossword by D. F. Manley (1964)

ACROSS

1 Doctor refuses to work for TV series (10)
6 Writer distinctly lacking in warmth (4)
10 Animal in a most eerie context (5)
11 Comedian puts Scottish mountain before New York eminence (5,4)
12 What's my line? I must be absorbed by a measuring device (6)
13 Holidays for two opposites, Gilbert and Sullivan? (7)
15 Right back to 10—putrid! (6)
16 It's on in wild parts of Canada: a gigantic reptile (8)
19 Lamb sees, oddly enough, how to start a meeting (8)
21 We should return to make a song about a household job (6)
24 Bird box leads to quarrel (7)
26 A trail suited to the Lone Ranger (6)
28 Notices by-product is unfit for TV or radio (9)
29 Livid singer with 5. (Tricky? Not altogether) (5)
30 Famous gallery in the States (4)
31 Lawyer gives drink to mother and child (5,5)

DOWN

1 Not associated with the Rolling Stones (4)
2 Poets rate these as dramatic musical performances (9)
3 Work for the home? (7)
4 & 20 Merry lot bore being tortured for actor (6,6)
5 Recognise Ron? He is moved to become a comedian (3,5)
7 Carmichael turns to the navy in Scotland (5)
8 Novelist has long way to travel for TV series (5,5)
9 Most of my rod has strange powers (6)
14 'My Word!' A really outstanding writer is needed for this (5,5)
17 Northern issue can lead to hindrances (9)
18 Note the soft whistle employed by a glass maker (8)
20 See 4
22 Listener who has read about drink (7)
23 Quiet hen in the field perhaps (6)
25 As before, radio is something well worth having (5)
27 Actor born in America is V.I.P. in Scotland (4)

CROSSWORD No. 41

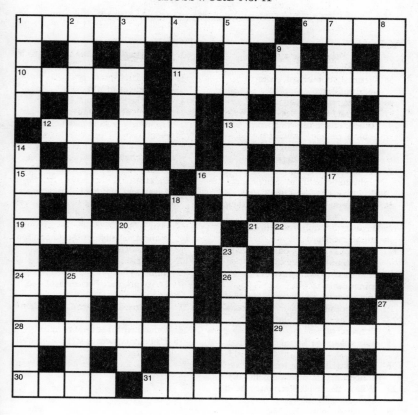

CROSSWORD No. 42

The Times Crossword 21,533 (September 2000)

ACROSS

1 Jester, one about to appear in royal house (6)

5 I'll miss gin, perhaps—almost none in diluted drink (8)

9 Fleming's agent used to keep physically fit (10)

10 Rebecca's son returned from exploit, penning article (4)

11 Oriental's pranks catching a Northern European (8)

12 Some of the crew is dominant—result of experience? (6)

13 Bond reported in from part of Asia (4)

15 Time in the capital with an ardent supporter (8)

18 What char may do, linking up with other char in a plant (5,3)

19 Get filled up, where drivers start to join motorway (4)

21 In conversation, show resentment of a wedding (6)

23 Tank designed for Siamese fighters? (8)

25 Mix red and yellow at first? I might (4)

26 Italian writer using reason concerning the environment (10)

27 What's needed to keep one's head above water? (8)

28 Law broken in other-worldly Hants town (6)

DOWN

2 Misguided aeroplane losing way in comic entertainment? (5)

3 So is butter sincerely recommended? (9)

4 Could he have taken a risk, ill-advised, about English? (6)

5 Obviously lacking instruction (4-11)

6 Infection's grown nasty inside raised edge (8)

7 Hair given very French style at first (5)

8 Disappear, having fallen out over a tape (9)

14 Asking about second person's health (3,3,3)

16 Almost call in popular opinon for face-to-face meeting? (9)

17 Rascal observed keeping friend quiet (8)

20 Strike about to become isolated (3,3)

22 Time to encapsulate Catholic's proud character in writing (5)

24 Person with 12 supporting University's custom (3)

CROSSWORD No. 42

CROSSWORD No. 43

By Don Manley (unattributed and edited by Crossword Editor) from *The Times*

ACROSS

1 Irrational fear may be seen in sinister pout (12)
9 Sea-going cutter? (9)
10 Female left-winger accepted by soccer authority (5)
11 Use some beef for this (6)
12 Strong supporter (8)
13 Hell can bring this! (6)
15 Having political divisions — the fashion in Panama perhaps? (8)
18 Where to have a pint after Choral Evensong naturally? (8)
19 American beauty queen is a married woman (6)
21 Their strange period establishing historical tradition (8)
23 Creepy-crawly goes back in the bath on return? (6)
26 Letter selected initially as a source of enlightenment (5)
27 Greek character, girl, is received by royal personage (9)
28 Remark about Post Office beginning to slip is not daft (6,6)

DOWN

1 Pay out to retain us — or deal thus with payment if broke? (7)
2 Top of prison twice used for demonstration! (5)
3 Bird touching bread put out on street (9)
4 Tour to rush along, missing nothing (4)
5 Islander will get brown going around Haiti possibly (8)
6 Dyke builder has left refuse (5)
7 Colours afresh material with bad stain (8)
8 Business alliance allowed Rex and Bill to get turnover (6)
14 Start of summer leading to nudity or revealing wear (8)
16 Read out story with quiet ending (9)
17 Jacks start to cheer their leading vessel (8)
18 Let fags do their worst? It's fashionable to get *healthy*! (6)
20 Little people should be shut up — right little devils! (7)
22 Trunk can come out of roots (5)
24 One who deduces God's existence from the swirling tides? (5)
25 What's in Palm Sunday's collection for distribution on Maundy Thursday? (4)

CROSSWORD No. 43

CROSSWORD No. 44

Guardian Crossword No. 15,000

Literal Transplants by Custos (20 February 1978)

The answer to each Across clue must have one of its letters removed before entry in the diagram. In each case the excised letter should be written instead alongside the word's clue. When this operation is completed the 26 transplanted letters, when read in clue order and added to 8 Down, will make an appropriate headline.

Definitions in these clues refer to the full, unmutilated answers (number of letters given in brackets); subsidiary parts lead to the mutilated forms to be entered in the diagrams. The first clue of each pair refers to diagram A, the second to diagram B. Each of the Down clues is really two normal clues printed side by side, never overlapping, one leading to the answer in diagram A and the other to that in diagram B. The division is not necessarily marked by punctuation, and either A or B clue may come first.

ACROSS

5   Nobleman, top-drawer, I found among ruins (7)
     Boring love I'd rejected in backward group (7)

6   Attendant, having pinched £2, gets sack (7)
     Sends back mother after being captured by Communists (7)

9   Exams, including English, are severe trials (7)
     Tolerated first of kids in family (7)

10 Fixer needs ceremony, one that conceals his true nature (9)
     Unadulterated back-pedalling by heavyweights leads to outbursts (9)

11 Bankruptcy for the band (5)
     A religious representation, a favourite one (5)

12 English clothing with a ring of dots around the edge (11)
     What sounds like costly and better type of headgear (11)

13 At length in favour of having area left in backyard (12)
     Plastic pressed so to become a diner's utensil (7-5)

18 Strait-laced in the end, blushing about it, given a sharp rebuke (11)
     Why let a mob run riot? It's reprehensible (11)

21 A four-wheeled carriage that's cast in precious stone (5)
     £100 is about right for the waiters' collection of tips (5)

22 Foreign girl has to write name when receiving a ring in one (9)
     An undertaker, I'm in cart after a mix-up (9)

23 Servant, one who hurries about excitedly (7)
     Doubles partners, perhaps, met running about court (7)

24 Putting things precisely? That's tremendous (7)
     Live within confines of southern railway, in sedate fashion (7)

25 Separate company suffers setback in disreputable resort (7)
     Felt hats, for when going about the East (7)

DOWN

1   Recommended getting a pleader to pass inside by means of a minister (8;8)

2   Laced stuff with which teachers' leader gets children drunk—see, dead drunk (6;6)

3   Long after the plane-trip makes frivolous petitions about having searches (8;8)

4   Fellow with skill made up a hymn tune, in the morning, after start of bardic festival (6;6)

5   Doctor, getting right on to a sovereign's deadly wound, carrying Edward round vessel (6;6)

CROSSWORD No. 44 – Diagram A.

7 Poem, produced by child with toil, still in existence, to be included in next anthology (6;6)

8 Being fuddled with claret, extolling a medium during a heat wave (11;3,8)

14 Watched William's diving ducks—watches Thomas getting duck caught by the legs (3-5;8)

15 Our sot, tipsy, holding party in the open air, solemnly poured out wine, gaining freedom, losing 'er (8;8)

16 Smack during a quarrel is hardly the sound of a frolic among Civil Service office workers (6;6)

17 Refuse, causing a disturbance, to follow closely master's principles (6;6)

19 Right joint to be constantly annoying a girl who needs help when grabbed by chaps (6;6)

20 Brewing tea, try indefatigably to jabber rubbish that diverts brides (6;6)

CROSSWORD No. 44

The clues are repeated here for convenience

ACROSS

5 Nobleman, top-drawer, I found among ruins (7)
Boring love I'd rejected in backward group (7)

6 Attendant, having pinched £2, gets sack (7)
Sends back mother after being captured by Communists (7)

9 Exams, including English, are severe trials (7)
Tolerated first of kids in family (7)

10 Fixer needs ceremony, one that conceals his true nature (9)
Unadulterated back-pedalling by heavyweights leads to outbursts (9)

11 Bankruptcy for the band (5)
A religious representation, a favourite one (5)

12 English clothing with a ring of dots around the edge (11)
What sounds like costly and better type of headgear (11)

13 At length in favour of having area left in backyard (12)
Plastic pressed so to become a diner's utensil (7-5)

18 Strait-laced in the end, blushing about it, given a sharp rebuke (11)
Why let a mob run riot? It's reprehensible (11)

21 A four-wheeled carriage that's cast in precious stone (5)
£100 is about right for the waiters' collection of tips (5)

22 Foreign girl has to write name when receiving a ring in one (9)
An undertaker, I'm in cart after a mix-up (9)

23 Servant, one who hurries about excitedly (7)
Doubles partners, perhaps, met running about court (7)

24 Putting things precisely? That's tremendous (7)
Live within confines of southern railway, in sedate fashion (7)

25 Separate company suffers setback in disreputable resort (7)
Felt hats, for when going about the East (7)

DOWN

1 Recommended getting a pleader to pass inside by means of a minister (8;8)

2 Laced stuff with which teachers' leader gets children drunk—see, dead drunk (6;6)

3 Long after the plane-trip makes frivolous petitions about having searches (8;8)

4 Fellow with skill made up a hymn tune, in the morning, after start of bardic festival (6;6)

5 Doctor, getting right on to a sovereign's deadly wound, carrying Edward round vessel (6;6)

7 Poem, produced by child with toil, still in existence, to be included in next anthology (6;6)

8 Being fuddled with claret, extolling a medium during a heat wave (11;3,8)

14 Watched William's diving ducks—watches Thomas getting duck caught by the legs (3-5;8)

15 Our sot, tipsy, holding party in the open air, solemnly poured out wine, gaining freedom, losing 'er (8;8)

16 Smack during a quarrel is hardly the sound of a frolic among Civil Service office workers (6;6)

17 Refuse, causing a disturbance, to follow closely master's principles (6;6)

19 Right joint to be constantly annoying a girl who needs help when grabbed by chaps (6;6)

20 Brewing tea, try indefatigably to jabber rubbish that diverts brides (6;6)

CROSSWORD No. 44 – Diagram B

CROSSWORD No. 45

Observer Everyman

ACROSS

1 River's sudden dash (4)
3 Elude me not—in short—I'm part of the clockwork (10)
9 A lot of paper's about before noon (4)
10 Owner of the land given away with a packet of cigarettes? (10)
12 Take back what you said about a pamphlet (7)
13 Scowls for those that shine? (7)
14 What a kiss did for Sleeping Beauty was a revelation (6,3,4)
17 High flown Greek ode—you won't be surprised if you have it (13)
21 Chorus? Don't! (7)
23 Street in a capital without a bit of litter—it's all in here (7)
24 Rocks in the Channel make tea in France almost superfluous (3,7)
25 A big blow for a girl, ending of romance (4)
26 Sadie's back and chaps get in the way, pestering (10)
27 A theologian's tots (4)

DOWN

1 Night on the heath over, one may expect some developments here (8)
2 Best fare cooked with love for Sunday lunch? (5,4)
4 Extend term of imprisonment (7)
5 Virginia's turned an awful green—Nemesis? (7)
6 Students of household management and cheap fare (7,5)
7 Invest 500 in the Revenue (Revolution's off) (5)
8 The endless run of a songbird (6)
11 Petermen pose no threat to bathers (4-8)
15 Piece of furniture for the team managers (9)
16 Why one gets small portions from the girl in the canteen? (8)
18 The realm of working domestics (7)
19 This veg is no longer fresh, dear boy (3,4)
20 Child that's been in the water—right in, the imp (6)
22 Father, always the liberator (5)

CROSSWORD No. 45

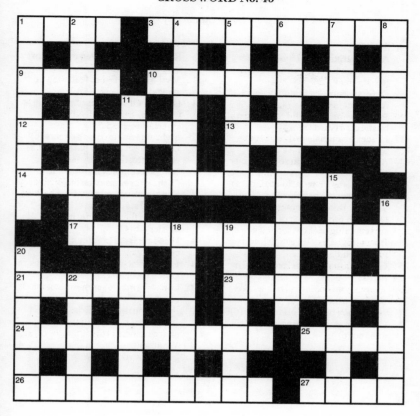

CROSSWORD No. 46

The Independent on Sunday by Quixote

ACROSS

1, 5 Actor delivering bad news from Little Bighorn, Spooner-fashion? (6,6)
8 Reverse sequence that may delay fulfilment in business (4,5)
9 Such may bring an end to prisoners by the courtyard (5)
11 Leader of animals in drama? (4)
12 Spanner no good for a car? (10)
13 A cop went berserk in southern city (4,4)
15 I struggled with tenacious plant (5)
17 A disguise said to help (5)
19 Torn anorak—go in jumper (8)
22 One with broad range of knowledge sorts catalogue (10)
23 Psychologist mostly rubbish and not much good! (4)
25 Germanic boy with a cross to bear (5)
26 There's some point in Irish worker moving around (9)
27 Notice boy heading off to green (6)
28 Great American character with guns at hand (6)

DOWN

2 Release snake trodden on by short member of family (7)
3 Mythological figure featuring in ancient horoscopes (4)
4 Door a 'wit' vandalised in Channel—supposedly for light entertainment (5,3)
5 Fighting female traps gunners (6)
6 Like a towel around bather that's very interesting? (9)
7 Oedipus complex is evident in Catholic organisation (4,3)
8 Rent for mooring may be shown on financial statements (4,7)
10 One who fears nothing in a battleship (11)
14 Freedom from bigotry can sway an elector (9)
16 Is potential giant-killer perhaps giving trouble? (8)
18 Girl—former lover man took by conquest (7)
20 Sweet murmuring (7)
21 Informer I brought in to make charge in court (6)
24 What you may get in booze—striking flavour (4)

CROSSWORD No. 46

CROSSWORD No. 47

By Roger Squires from *Financial Times*

ACROSS

1 They involve a shift in one's beliefs (6)
4 Insisted upon or abandoned? (4,4)
9 Penthouse let on a new arrangement (4-2)
10 Pretty useless object? (8)
11 Allow the Spanish poison to be brought back (6)
12 I'm off food and water (8)
13 This hat is out of date (3)
14 Put out in West winds (6)
17 One side of Glasgow (7)
21 Information a girl found in Switzerland (6)
25 The best-known surviving creature? (3)
26 Any crest may indicate it (8)
27 They grip and hold on in the last resort (6)
28 Ointment said to be used by the Royal Family (8)
29 He is or could be a shopkeeper (6)
30 Political favours? (8)
31 Stable companion? (6)

DOWN

1 It sounds highly unnatural (8)
2 Very frightened, I take a short rest before I can reorganise (2,1,5)
3 He expects people to put up with him (8)
5 Where you may find a sailor on the way (6)
6 Rising payment for the artist (6)
7 Key batsman? (6)
8 Growing anger? (6)
12 When people may collect in the streets (4-3)
15 The German uprising is serious (3)
16 A work unit (3)
18 Begin to fix a fight (3,5)
19 A lemon is strangely sweet (8)
20 TV's pop group? (4,4)
22 A bend in the road (6)
23 Climbs and balances (6)
24 Company guard (6)
25 First form (6)

CROSSWORD No. 47

CROSSWORD No. 48

By Quark from *Financial Times*

ACROSS

1 It's always sharp but can be shaken (7)
5 Brook's bird? (7)
9 A novelist to study, we hear (5)
10 As sheet-worker I go on the attack (9)
11 Fashionable although bound to be wet (2,3,4)
12 Arsenic layer is rather grey (5)
13 Give view round tree (5)
15 To raise collection get change in position (9)
18 Dress gone—taken to the cleaners, lost? (9)
19 Sequence seen on the road (5)
21 I, fool, getting torn paper (5)
23 Stop, pal—the game is up! (9)
25 Indicative of the firm that's shaky? (9)
26 Looks in, it is said, for an award (5)
27 Compiler going back on transactions in river? That's outrageous (7)
28 Petition in town centre attracts many (7)

DOWN

1 Got in trouble with river endlessly whirling (7)
2 Narrow escape? Close it! (4,5)
3 Iceberg sticking up, partly revealing bird (5)
4 Traffic hold-up on the way to the factory? (9)
5 Collection of twigs seen in clearing (5)
6 Might be encountered in The Old Curiosity Shop (4-1-4)
7 Scattered shale can be bind (5)
8 Train followers (7)
14 Try to keep balance dancing on some ice (9)
16 One who's likely to get lines (9)
17 The city pitch is among a number providing fruit (9)
18 Emphasise in French warning about end of EEC (7)
20 Heater wire could be iron (7)
22 Allowed in certain public items (5)
23 Invent one away in an island (5)
24 Not working? Take up subject to change (not English) (5)

CROSSWORD No. 48

CROSSWORD No. 49

Alphabetical Jigsaw by Araucaria (*Guardian*)

Method: Solve the clues and fit in the solutions wherever they will go

A   bell that rang elusively in part (7)

B   ship on the wrong river gets more smart (8)

C   bond where churchmen to a junction come (6)

D   instrument left out of celli – drum? (8)

E   the Dark Lady, topless, is way out (6)

F   woodwork tool when worry was about (7)

G   like an old tree sculptured by Legrand 97)

H   first of all invading famished land (7)

I   should bring interest at Mass as priests (11)

J   girl – yes (Ger.) – catch terriers (men, no beasts) (7)

K   sounding wanted, after may be rolled (7)

L   in security, state bird of old (8)

M   major route which City's fans (say) enter (4,4)

N   false clue is innate – group round a centre (8)

O   act too much: where's re-mi-fa in tune? (6)

P's   only round about the rug too soon (11)

Q   leave when obligations have been paid (4)

R   music's ear return without what's laid (6)

S   dog or bitch? Dog's tailless, split in six (6)

T   nethermost, ate piece the heat to fix (10)

U   house with rows in sunset, not the Pope! (10)

V   – by the left! – contains some drink or dope (4)

W   vole: hence Watson's dad's docked slips (5-3)

X   Persian king who punished waves with whips (6)

Y   in Colne Valley, place he madly wrecked (7)

Z   oxide, red, is citizen's effect (7)

CROSSWORD No. 49

CROSSWORD No. 50

Birmingham Mail Special by Duck, 1 March 1982

ACROSS

1 One working out the taxes makes masses sore but not me (8)

6,11,24 Dn, 28: have got jug at home – heed our rollicking. (Dai may sing this) (5,2,1,4,5,7)

10 Awful spite shown by the French in communication (7)

11 See 6 Across

12 Tooth? Not sweet rejecting bit of treacle (5)

13 Club having records on? Then it's sure tricky to talk! (9)

14 Timid chap, person pestered with kids? (3,5)

16 A witty saying about something very small (4)

20 One's 'green', vying? This may be in evidence (4)

21 Daniel's no wound leaving a ———— —! (5,3)

24 Pet has gone back to the street, girl! That's absolutely right! (4,5)

25 Lager would make this composer drunk (5)

27 Aged men tremble when mate is near (3-4)

28 See 6 Across

29 Appointed meeting to put good man to the test? (5)

30 Walk to Northern Territory? It's sounding harsh (8)

DOWN

2,15 Dad's said 'Vanity!', spoiling this time of celebration (5,6,3)

3 Former wife, frightful rioter, creating a scene outside (8)

4 Sporting course—sea comes up—waver round (8)

5 Negligent concerning a girl (6)

6 Dwarf without foot on part of sundial (6)

7 Received from ancestors, it is put in abode (9)

8 Escape from eastern lord, end of servitude (5)

9 Oxford college where they'll celebrate tonight? (8)

15 See 2 Down

17 This country? My anchor is fixed here (8)

18 Bird's evening booze? (8)

19 Silly men, beginning to embrace, she had entangled (8)

22 Narrow passage of water without bends, we hear (6)

23 For a painter irritating experience has entity (6)

24 See 6 Across

26 Presented information about four in Ancient Rome (5)

CROSSWORD No. 50

CROSSWORD No. 51

Sunday Express Skeleton

In the Skeleton Crossword the black squares and clue numbers have to be filled in as well as the words. Four black squares and four clue numbers have been inserted to give you a start. The black squares form a symmetrical pattern; the top half matches the bottom half and the two sides correspond. So you can fill in 12 more squares at once to correspond with those given.

ACROSS

1 Bible man with very little time to take a snack

4 Act oddly in providing food for one of the tribes

9 Money man able to achieve a flying turn

11 Last post dispatched by someone seeking business

12 Carry gently a short distance past Heathrow terminal

13 Embarrassed grandee in a passion

15 Means of making notes or backing a horse

16 Show it's wrong to be back in a depression

17 Your lot won't admit it's different inside

20 Nag a newcomer

22 Feeling it's a long way round Mile End

23 Real inciter of mischief going straight

24 Make further use of personal mobility

25 Islander organising a quiet upheaval beyond the city limits

DOWN

1 It might be longer if Tom got elevated on hot air

2 If not in the water one might give you sauce

3 It indicates the number approved for inclusion

5 The man who finds a way to move with difficulty

6 People afloat sounded pleased with themselves

7 Chalky having got it in the neck as a songster

8 Jack and Alan worried about trade union having eight members

9 When food comes up mostly fat he goes in for takeaways

10 Can it be right to find a thriller writer pedestrian?

13 It's the last thing one hopes to gain

14 Several light out when there's no drink

18 Praise what was formerly a different lot

19 Girl in a state looking after the kids

21 Being so taxing it's a departure from frivolity

22 Light-headed? Not a bad description

CROSSWORD No. 51

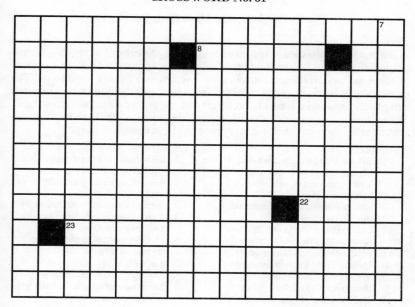

CROSSWORD No. 52

Misdirected Letters by Duck from *Quiz Digest*

A letter which should have appeared once in the answer to 5 across has turned up in the answer to 1 down (no other similar letter appears in 1 down). The same mistake has occurred in the answers to 7 across and 2 down, and so on. The subsidiary indications in the clues (*eg* anagrams) and the numbers in brackets refer to the mutilated forms to be entered in the grid; definitions are normal. When you have completed the crossword, you will find that the misdirected letters, taken in order, spell out an appropriate three-word message.

ACROSS

5 Clown, disgustingly idle beast (8)

7 Charm shown by backward-looking sultanate, primitive civilisation (6)

9 Russian exchange has leader of diplomats upset (7)

10 Marshal on far side of hill in old-style combat (6)

11 Bird with gloomy look evident around Early English church (6-3)

13 What makes crime soar disastrously (4)

14 Ugly woman's house somewhere in Surrey (6)

16 Piece of rag in wrong position (6)

18 Smooth beat (4)

19 Exceptional saint, inwardly so keen he is (9)

22 Enslave heart madly with hint of love (6)

23 Sheep with a twitch that's sudden (7)

25 One to expel a boy (6)

26 Fleet Street area rumour—leader in *Express* is obscure (8)

DOWN

1 Sounds of pain from gunners caught up in battle (6)

2 Something extra good in Paris to exploit (6)

3 B-brightened up—but not well (4)

4 Trade Union basis for action may undermine nation... (8)

6 ... Give money perpetually to terminate dispute? (6)

7 Let Athens get adapted for Olympic contestants? (9)

8 Fabulous creature at sea intended to embrace marines (7)

12 Manager joining firm is chap who may get waxy (9)

14 In the country sit in bar getting drunk (8)

15 Racing vehicle with some pinking? OK. A retuning is needed (2-5)

17 Unusual herons somewhere near water (6)

20 Agitating Miss Proll's right let down (6)

21 Finally forgot a quote—must be unsaid (6)

24 Sound of animal in desolate area (4)

CROSSWORD No. 52

CROSSWORD No. 53

Numerical Sequence by Duck from *Quiz Digest*

Some of the answers are harder than others! *Chambers 20th Century Dictionary* [now *The Chambers Dictionary*] could be useful.

ACROSS

1   3 (7)
5   Get big belly around with 'piggy' food that's on board (7)
9   Setter's gone wrong—tries again (7)
10 Sees the stars perhaps making visits (5,2)
11 Badly burnt, have become hazel-coloured (3-5)
12 7 (6)
14 Evilly influenced, a crude nurse needs to be reformed (5,1,5)
17 Smashing hotel (Hotel West) provides everything (3,5,3)
20 2 (6)
21 Bob not at home, having to go round supermarket—the way to get ice-cream in tubs? (5,3)
23 10 (7)
24 5 (7)
25 Oak, *eg*, chopped by a boy? It's criminal (7)
26 This mending makes Ming everlasting (7)

DOWN

1   9 (8)
2   Soft laxity like this is something that sounds commonplace (8)
3   Insecure, lacking heart—right? Pay me for security (7)
4   Unconstrained gate—it's favourable for progress (4,6)
5   1 (4)
6   Get no healing from an amateur? (7)
7   Insist upon having a bit of hair sticking up (6)
8   8 (5)
13 6 (10)
15 4 (8)
16 Good man speaks, speaks hesitatingly (8)
17 Germans munch a lot, we hear (7)
18 An older, decrepit man (7)
19 Start of university term, it seems, is to get modernised (6)
20 Travel to spot—see one expected to come? (5)
22 Some god, I (Norse) (4)

CROSSWORD No. 53

CROSSWORD No. 54

Theme and Variations by Duck from *Quiz Digest*

The four unclued theme words have something in common, and each has two variations. The four pairs of variations are related to their theme words in various ways, but both members of a pair are related to their theme word in the same way.

Theme word A: 27 across **Variations**: 12 across, 5 down

Theme word B: 3 down **Variations**: 19 down, 30 down

Theme word C: 13 across **Variations**: 20 across, 15 down

Theme word D: 16 down **Variations**: 26 across, 6 down

ACROSS

1 Greeting—it needs musical instrument (6)
4 Thrashes bat, slams spin (8)
9 Reprieve or annoy again? (7)
11 Can noisy? Then get lubricant, wrapping (7)
14 Shallow judgment only half formed (4)
17 Formal record touching the heart of the matter with hesitation (8)
18 Bit of wood to advance slowly? (5)
22 A sharp blow comes back, then a high ball comes back in a curve (8)
28 Wind in most of summer month (4)
31 Escaping number I rescue going west (7)
32 S American city has rest disturbed—by them? (7)
33 Road most messy? Use these coming home (8)
34 Fish Katharine's brought aboard (6)

DOWN

1 One making great effort—*eg* Peter on the water (7)
2 Left with a sharp pain, permanent (7)
7 Black substance the man had acted like a balm (7)
8 It's not heard to be golden (7)
10 One more for the team (6)
20 PS. Nudes are dreadful—keep out of office for a while (7)
21 Head of celery and eggs served up—a party hors d'oeuvre (7)
23 Let up on becoming rich (7)
24 Painters in dire straits (7)
25 Earth maybe putting energy initially into vegetable (6)
29 Business is steady (4)

CROSSWORD No. 54

CROSSWORD No. 55

Instruments by Duck from *Tough Puzzles*

Seven of the across clues are normal, but their answers must be transformed before entry in the grid. The remaining across clues have normal definitions, but their subsidiary indications refer to the form in which they are to be entered in the grid, that is, with one letter omitted. These letters, taken in order, give the name of the man desirous of the transformations to the other across answers. Solvers must decide to which type any particular clue refers. Down clues are normal.

ACROSS

1 Gravity to pitch into the trough of the sea one returning aboard
3 Being one of those called to decide damage?
9 After crash sends around box (black)
10 Bed—a bit of underwear needed by Virginia. A warm relaxing place? (2 words)
11 Instrument cut Italian flower first
12 Resolve but do show hesitation
14 A year's end, relaxing without energy, informal
16 Being without confidence should be praised somehow
17 Dignity of cardinal leading to bloody enmity
18 When most sent out various distributions
21 Infantry regiment—back half of it retreats
22 Brave appeal with exceptional pride
26 I supposedly get good results in the field or I sprint—versatile!
27 Uproarious noise—record by wiggling Rod
28 Artist steams angrily
29 Restrain river

DOWN

1 To produce drink mix two parts of lemon juice (no ice) with drop of port (5)
2 Thieves caught in country—egg-stealers? (5)
3 Ship's captain with father on the golf course (7)
4 She tells tales—cute senora, rambling (10)
5 German oil? (4)
6 Sailor's behind (5)
7 A little boy tucking into cereal like a cow? (8)
8 Dismisses bank workers (8)
13 Colleagues with zero assets, ruined—American agency brought in (10)
14 Telling your grandmother ...? (8)
15 Neighbourhood with endless sin and weapons (8)
19 Refuse to employ Marxist philosopher (7)
20 Rebel big just below the waist? (5)
23 Marks, singular cricketer (5)
24 Fine comic (5)
25 100 square metres—that's one (4)

CROSSWORD No. 55

CROSSWORD No. 56

From *Armchair Crosswords* by Afrit (1949)

ACROSS

1 Givest tips, from which the caddies receive what's coming to them (8)

10 You know your A.B.C.? Then the bet's off and you'll have to write this in as one letter (5)

11 A view which you may enjoy bareheaded, or in your hat (8)

12 Only a hundred left? It must be divided in two then (5)

13 The telegram you send to your wife, perhaps, when she's away. Quite mad, of course! (4)

14 Describes what you will recognise in a twinkling, making the rest all look silly (7)

16 It's no good trying to make this more difficult. There's nothing to see except air (6)

18 You'll have to put back a lot more than a pound whether you pay it or not (4)

20 A bit more strenuous than golf: a course of it would straighten that slice (9)

22 You need this to get a bite with, though the fish won't be large (9)

24 No one can say it's a clear case even if they're up your sleeve (4)

26 He gives me pain, as Simple Simon might have said (6)

27 A. had something on, and it's all helped (7)

30 Keeps the home fires burning? Get that idea out of your head! (4)

32 Whoever gets slain won't find it as hard as these (5)

33 This is obstinately difficult, but then it's half Irish (8)

34 A fisherman might lose one if it were shorter, but it's a disgrace to lose it altogether (5)

35 The whole of it is only part of it, so there must be a bally contradiction in it (8)

DOWN

2 Tax-collectors do, and you can't say it isn't right (5)

3 A policewoman, no doubt; anyway, she takes a nine (5)

4 He did a lot of speaking in public, but Brother Aldous has caught him up and gone on longer (6)

5 When he's good he's very, very good; but it's the very devil holding a married man in Paris! (9)

6 What brings you to town? Oh, the market shows an upward trend (4)

7 Remember that it isn't only youth that may follow hounds, and you'll guess it, however well it's wrapped up (7)

8 If internal combustion must be taken on spec. as a particular remedy (8)

9 There's a tangle at first, but the hair is all right afterwards. If you can't guess it now, you'll be on to it before morning (8)

15 Since the money-box is broken, replace it with a cheerful air (4)

17 It has long been a popular form of collecting, but not altogether lately (9)

18 It's plain at half the price, but what don't you care about it? (8)

19 In the same way, you won't have to suffer fools gladly (8)

21 See which way the cat jumps, and then you can exercise it (4)

23 Glides away, making you turn pale (7)

25 If we anticipate evil, sure enough it's in the ship's biscuit (6)

28 The result of employing too many cooks. It brings your heart into your mouth (5)

29 If an artist ever wants a pound, he can raise it with ease (5)

31 Gives an imitation of split peas (4)

CROSSWORD No. 56

CROSSWORD No. 57

By Ximenes from *The Observer*

ACROSS

1 Scene of a council—a rotten fiasco (6)
6 Had a long range, though out of breath (6)
11 Does this Prince? Ask 'ens wot's 'ad it! (6)
12 'Dope' Riley took this risk (5)
13 Mad Chloe gets spasms of overcrowding (8)
14 Philip keeps them brushed back (4)
15 It sounds as if it went to the head of *Le Malade Imaginaire* (9)
18 Australian brushman's Xmas dinner, luv? (7)
19 She loved one of whom there's some talk (6)
20 One of the 28; a 'cunning old' dog? (6)
22 Nogs of it are mixed (and with it) (6)
25 Hamlet grudged a penny for this bomb (6)
27 One of these agricultural implements won fame in the War (7)
29 I'm a rum plant myself, but my eponym's son's is even madder! (9)
31 Crop that will nearly make you mad (4)
32 Lord of Antioch gives Muse a dud cheque (8)
33 Hoard, a German submarine drama? (5)
34 The popinjay's jesting seems illegal (6)
35 It's no good saying that this acid can't be helped in the Bible (6)
36 Ira, the Victorian rowing coach! (6)

DOWN

1 For water on the knee try minced carrot (6)
2 Thrilling for the very young! (5)
3 Provided Hebrews with plenty of cabs (4)
4 *Bêche-de-mer* is mostly boring (7)
5 Stanza, put in Canada by Mr Weller? (6)
6 A windjammer starts this strife (6)
7 German tutor, a little French at heart (9)
8 All but the bun is held before it (8)
9 Dark blues take it out of fun for Lent (6)
10 Outsiders don't give the truth in answer (6)
16 Not the course a bull takes, to the discomfiture of a man in red! (9)
17 Cockney non-chemist's epithet for the skin of a living cow? (8)
21 Well known mound, etc., in algeria (7)
22 (2 words) Make a mess of the purist (6)
23 The very image of a limbless wire (6)
24 Look at the colour of the poor child! (6)
25 Expresses contempt for tall hats (6)
26 Kipling says you are more so, Madam (6)
28 Well equipped to take Romans for a ride! (5)
30 The Artful Dodger's mail-post (4)

CROSSWORD No. 57

CROSSWORD No. 58

By Beelzebub from *The Independent on Sunday*

ACROSS

1 Find another berth before entering ancient harbour up north (6)
8 To steal about pound is robbery! (4)
11 In trouble then, everybody in debt, they say, would be in slavery (10)
12 What's crazy about having a go? (4)
13 Form practice no longer is to work out amount (6)
14 Romany drinking bowl lets ice fall out (4)
15 Metal enclosure for bullock could be poison (5)
16 In outrageous code you have to detect spirited tyranny (12)
20 High cloud runs between Channel Islands and country further west (6)
22 Alarm caused by a bloomer going round bend (6)
24 Flounders, say, have the room at sea—for floundering! (12)
25 What's new in distinctive character of frogs and toads? (5)
27 With heavy knife, how far do Chinese go to get staves from it? (4)
29 I'd come for treatment from him! (6)
30 Burning sun, till no longer seen (4)
31 It could make square bashing a long treat (10)
32 Dagger of kings is here (4)
33 Isolated length is atop cathedral (6)

DOWN

1 They are left in air and used for shooting (7)
2 Employer's present during course—nervy if a student finally leaves (12)
3 Dark area of shiner in part's roughly concealed by drunk (8)
4 Cunning's working for a Greek magistrate (6)
5 Scot, say, accepted as species (4)
6 The Spanish tufts, old fashioned clotted hair style (8)
7 Fleeing debtors would, having left in appropriate guise (4)
8 Do Irishmen say it to ask for occasional Scotch? (7)
9 Wanting different cut a girl has range to be fit for farmers? (12)
10 Little space after scouring out of glacial valley (4)
17 He's God's gift to love with activity in that place (8)
18 Embroidery material showing a Frenchman holding head (8)
19 Endless hunt round Romania that is resulting in doubts (7)
21 Majestic mound in Arabia needing external support (7)
23 Flying lemur's surprised cry sucking in worm! (6)
25 Running thus, a donkey may drop tail? (4)
26 Caught breaking in at one? There'll be official proceedings! (4)
28 Grandfather's at all Scottish lochs without reactions locally? (4)

CROSSWORD No. 58

CROSSWORD No. 59

By Beelzebub (Michael Macdonald-Cooper) from *The Independent on Sunday*

ACROSS

1 Skips across square, over melting snow (5)

5 Cotyledon twice pruned, blossoming famously (7)

10 Extravagantly promote grass, engaging expert associated with a plant family (12)

11 Terrace seen in the evening long ago, anciently ageless (6)

12 Condensed version of Chapter One given in present summary (6)

13 Uncomfortable, slipping in, getting drink for a penny? (9, 3 words)

15 Letter in Greek Testament delivering censure (5)

17 Lecturer, no chicken, about to leap, bounded clumsily (8)

19 Simpleton taken in by claims of the advertisement (8)

24 Corolla leaf inverted in campanulate plants (5)

25 Three fare dodging on Charon's route? (9)

26 London local authority with no hospital treating patients successfully (9)

27 See costermonger work to engage attention (6)

28 Silver bell brings scurrying porters down to rear of college (12, 2 words)

29 Levy about to be adopted by eastern country ultimately cancelled (7)

30 Tried earnestly to comprehend electromotive force (5)

DOWN

1 Dresses woman in hosptial with last of bandages (7)

2 Gory pheasant unsuitable for vegetarians (12)

3 Start to talk about writer's publisher (6, 2 words)

4 Barrel organ in street played with energy (9)

5 Having decorative line old engraver initially included? (8)

6 Meretricious paintings held within confines of Tate Gallery (5)

7 Leave from airstrip (Macedonian) heading northwards (6)

8 Relaxed freedom a flower vendor's assimilated going around South Africa (12)

9 Those who agree bard's disputed usage must be raised (5)

14 Guard commander to follow monarch in Spain—clear? (9)

16 Turning up in factory, choose ceramic article (8)

18 Act including song put off (7)

20 Form of litre, not English, a measure used in Scotland (6)

21 It's up on central Arran—a Scottish address (6)

22 Worry sheep, possibly (5)

23 Way round deserted sandy tract (5)

CROSSWORD No. 59

CROSSWORD No. 60

Sunday Times Mephisto by Tim Moorey (September 1998)

The Chambers Dictionary is the reference for
all solutions except proper nouns

ACROSS

1 Writer's cutting chap busy with neat design? The opposite (12)
9 Bear out sailor going astray (10)
11 Turnover locally comes from fee including Net working (8)
12 Browning to press sword in jest (12)
13 One leaving French city borders (5)
16 Flan cooked inside to continue Italian standard (8)
17 Number in defeat upset previously (8)
19 Sort of acid in clubs that's left round back (5)
20 Ecologist pal terribly concerned with crop damage (12)
21 Sign at home saying "independence for Thailand" (8)
22 Noël's skirting a street to the sea (10)
23 Get tight and firm to be serious (12, two words)

DOWN

1 Bending when touched wrongly prompts oath about origin of Indian (12)
2 Ring about special deal for riding cycle around US (8)
3 Pressure keeping back repair (12)
4 Bird's hard tip showed up image about right (8)
5 Lots of high-pitched noise created by Paddy's verbal items! (5)
6 Con French fellow out of money—that's against one belief in France (12)
7 Extremely bad about time in prison cell with Scot (10)
8 Paper girl snorting cocaine gets a lesson (12, two words)
10 *Punch*, for example, repeatedly seen trying wit! (10, two words)
14 *Sun's* upset about handout and put out early calls to the contrary (8)
15 Common sickness to take hold? Not the first to produce fags (8)
18 Very original cover on ace book is what Chambers gives you (5)

CROSSWORD No. 60

CROSSWORD No. 61

By Azed from *The Observer*

The Chambers Dictionary (1998) is recommended

ACROSS

1 Yesterday's game or beef cut, very much a problem (13)
10 Gang leader hanged horribly after odd job (10)
12 Strong drink produced from empty barrel, Irish speciality! (4)
13 Reptilians stripped lime trees (5)
14 Murderous look instilled into corps (6)
15 Key financial date certainly followed by split (7)
16 What Adam *couldn't* be, great at restraining missus (not half)! (8)
19 Leader of number in race swerved (5)
21 Scots learning nothing, backward, in college (5)
23 Here's a tip: little over half teaching's retained by dull fellow (8)
24 'Sh!' I wail. 'That's awful language' (7)
26 Doctor binding bones for anti-terrorist service (6)
29 Suffer shipwreck, vessel's stern getting stuck in narrow sand bar (5)
30 Homeless pauper died in house (4)
31 Butterfly or egret a peke disturbed (10)
32 Do they earn top commission, distributing nameless purse? (13)

DOWN

1 Auntie comes up holding duck or old gull (4)
2 Driver of camion? *Huile* flowing round one runs (7)
3 Valuable ore, carbon, worker struck in hole mined (11)
4 African chief, one clad in leather (4)
5 To kill with a grenade one Scots tossed in is frightening (7)
6 Criss-crossing vessels get very wet on centre of ocean (4)
7 Hubris Hera's dealt with, pair imposing order on top? (11)
8 Entry point following this is left (5)
9 BA getting Cambridge place, very local (7)
11 Form of tiger's-eye, deposit in hot springs (9)
13 Something filling Conchita cooks? (4)
16 Approves bale on SS? (7)
17 Turkey heading skyward for fowling-net (7)
18 Ornamental shelf on board (7)
20 Ghanaian dialect term for 'taunt', 'upbraid' (4)
22 Purgative type of pepper? It bucks one up (5)
25 Albanian money, legal stuff we hear (4)
27 Retsina one may make lone parties squiffy (4)
28 Blue feathers (4)

CROSSWORD No. 61

CROSSWORD No. 62

Enigmatic Variations for *The Sunday Telegraph*

About...? by Rustic

All clues are normal. Solvers should determine what this puzzle is 'ABOUT...?', and highlight the example on which it concentrates in the completed grid. *Chambers* (1998) is recommended, but does not give two proper nouns.

ACROSS

1 Buildings excellent and stacks reported
5 Firm at first sponsored groups of Japanese wrestlers
9 I landed in one by skill
10 Old Abe could be on?
12 Syrian cloth enswathes a French patriarch
13 Aesop, for one, is writing about absolute nonsense mostly
14 Brussels found here support diet
16 To that extent baseless rambling can be evaluated
17 Centre to clean in forbidden picture
23 Laminated stage curtain at first upset one among the gods
25 Squinting as scimitars flashed round start of battle
28 Australian comes in to tap absorbent African trees
29 American bread is sliced and suited to the Middle east?
30 Fanatical Scots afraid to embrace bisexual
31 Bothan run for viticulturist
32 Attempt to trap bishop with ecstasy is subject to legal hearing
33 Bismuth in fouled oasis—no life there
34 Scabs formed round edge of eyes produce inflamed swelling

DOWN

1 Peevish female doctor takes temperature
2 Anonymous old lady swallows shilling—ridiculous
3 Final bit of colour in black can be washed out
4 Bring back West Indian girl in charge of vermilion colouring
5 Ship pays the penalty outside the deepest parts of the sea
6 Put an end to one type of worm climbing among remains
7 Lips and tops of legs are bruised in argument
8 Incited nervous date to accept wager
11 Look after small piece of paper petals
15 Infant girl swallows arsenic infusion initially for parasitic infection
18 Active boars roaming around Thailand—they intrude and take over?
19 Strong rope round top half of sturdy fellow like Boswell (according to Johnson)
20 Society members note prohibitions include island
21 Talks at length to confound leader of sceptics
22 Startle sister with table ornaments
24 Flustered subahdar drops one small piece of sponge
26 Chatter that is beginning to surprise simpletons
27 Ohio boy upset about a derisive cry

CROSSWORD No. 62

CROSSWORD No. 63

Enigmatic Variations from *The Sunday Telegraph*

No. 327 'Differences' by Giovanni

In some of the squares the letters from across and down solutions clash. In those across clues leading to a solution in which there is no clash there is a redundant word, and the initial letters of the redundant words spell out an indication of how to deal with the 'DIFFERENCES' produced by the clashes. *Chambers* (1998) is recommended.

ACROSS

1 Black bits hard to shift in porcelain basins put outside (9)
8 Aromatic fragrance in herbal anti-inflammatory medicine (4)
12 Sailor John going to sea came into view indistinctly (6)
14 Cold region with volcanic rock penetrated by engineers (4)
15 American help around North Atlantic being retracted (6)
16 Inhaler bothered about lung's rupture (7)
18 Hutton supreme at the crease, No. 1 in his country (5)
19 Trumpet's change of pitch playing true note (E) (6)
20 Mammal with long hair had meal sheltering (7)
21 Course admittance (6)
22 Cheated again with Ace of Hearts or Diamonds? (6)
24 Pal sins more wrecking theory of spiritual responsibility (11)
27 Knight absorbed by cause aroused interest once (6)
32 Drink slowly at leisure—half of splendid half pint drunk (6)
33 To recover—fantastic miracle! (7)
34 Article in one unusual book of travel (6)
35 Feeble basket replaced (5)
38 Imprisoned swallows sung, let out (7)
39 See some ass in school eat extra salt (6)
40 Wicked person shortly returning to show neighbour fist (4)
41 Gold coin of yesteryear—from time with Queen (Regina) (6)

42 Scottish goblin lounging in boat (4)
43 A little work could make one excessively testy—ease off! (9)

DOWN

1 Old intellectual boasted to the audience (4)
2 Holy place that's inspirational to some extent (4)
3 Copper disc, perhaps, fixed into medieval instrument (7)
4 Fritter time after being bouncing with energy (7)
5 A theologian induced to be like a bad egg (6)
6 Animals with great desire to get into laughs? (6)
7 Former cabinet to excel having contained the Right (6)
9 Italian poet with nothing to lose, privileged type (6)
10 Abandon any number, creating ferment (6)
11 Aussie bird fellows discovered round garden path in front of hospital (9, hyphenated)
13 Single photo excited expert in animal migration? (11)
17 Donkey in animal shelter losing tail (5)
19 Surer after accident, fellow is on the up again (9)
23 Old poem about love written on a vase (5)
25 Bad sport to lose without hint of pleasantness (7)
26 Consonant—it's an "r", "p", possibly? (7)

CROSSWORD No. 63

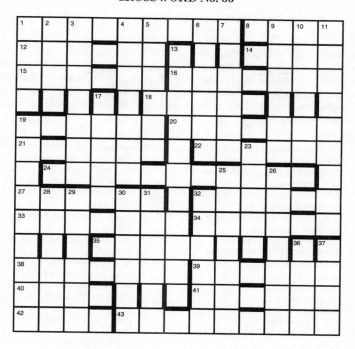

28 This fisherman's said to be less mad (6)
29 Fuss about a US serviceman being slow (6)
30 Widow's vessel lined with bit of extra white lead (6)
31 At university the man's about to get a break (6)
32 Vegetable collects prize in game (6)
36 Ultimately restores script line, right? (4)
37 Mark off one note and the one below it (4)

CROSSWORD No. 64

Next-door Neighbours by Duck from *Games and Puzzles*

Clues are normal but each solution is to be coded in one of two ways – either by taking the next letters in the alphabet or by taking the ones before (A follows Z). Thus FAG is entered as either GBH or EZF, and EZF could also be the code for DYE (the other possibility being CXD). Half the words are 'coded forwards' and half 'coded backwards'. Solvers must decide which code applies to each clue. *Chambers* is recommended.

ACROSS

1 Alloy in strange coin is all right (10)
9 Uranium in geological formation produces grin (5)
11 See Rolls-Royce—the ultimate in flashy transportation (5)
12 Ridge in part of Sussex—around Hassocks primarily (5)
13 Drags back for a pause? (5)
14 Missionary's old coin—catch (4)
15 Strain to express regret, we hear (3)
17 Brute issuing expression of disgust, getting a pair (5)
19 Poor house—one with a rodent (5)
22 Song about a valley (3)
23 Gin—homely way of getting Jock high (4)
24 Shoot chap in Devon? (5)
26 French vineyard and container for wine (5)
28 I'll have chanted about going to court (5)
29 Signal from British Prime Minister going West (5)
30 Salt—I'd eat it on bit of ham minced up (10)

DOWN

1 Laze around? One's immersed in rum and lemon, claret (10)
2 Go well together, get a local victory (5)
3 Hot old ale could make you spin round (4)
4 Plant, yellow one, given to child (5)
5 Brood of a nuthatch? No thank you (3)
6 Old backgammon? Wait to roll (5)
7 Gin, Alice? No, that's awful, it makes you numb (10)
8 Tribal woman with endless croak (5)
10 Bob's neck, something short and fat (5)
16 Kick old crank (5)
18 Everything's fine with a religious animal (5)
20 Part I of Shakespeare, volume given to relation (5)
21 See awful rot about an old city (5)
22 Batting? Illingworth's out—this weather doesn't help batsmen (5)
25 Tungsten embedded in another metal, something very similar (4)
27 Take for example Mr Maudling? (3)

CROSSWORD No. 64

CROSSWORD No. 65

Empty Pockets by Duck from *Games and Puzzles*

Each solution must have a word omitted before it is entered in the diagram. The missing words have something in common.

Both the definition *and* the subsidiary indication refer to the unmutilated solution.

ACROSS

1 O, a dunce will need it somehow! (9)
4 Jane? Inwardly English and very good, is outwardly not at all attractive (7)
7 Learner in art I mus' work—to become this? (10)
9 Heroic woman opposing subversive army activity (6)
10 Hampshire water, not fresh, provided by old spring (6)
11 Apparently I, bound by an ancient vow, will be most fortunate (8)
12 One lunatic somersaulting in a convulsive fit and going around naked? (8)
15 Crop to grind etc. when cut (6)
16 Marches past as red revolutionary (7)
18 Cooking apples out on the table as a matter of course (9)
19 Seemingly remove a barrier for protection (7)
20 Disparages exercises we hear (7)

DOWN

1 It's sensible having the top flat it seems (11)
2 Plain yellow record book with name entered in (8)
3 Ransack hotel's inside—in Scandinavia somewhere (7)
4 Condemned lover created by Continental writer—not half frightened (9)
5 Dazzlingly live deans e.g. gave gospel message (11)
6 Despatched about a hundred tree-trunks, dry through—sources of sweet smell (12)
8 Young member of family, girl gobbling short dinner, getting ill (10)
13 Commanding fairy in pain after initial application of iodine (8)
14 Harsh-sounding singer? Yes and no! (6)
17 Location with top class inside? (6)

CROSSWORD No. 65

CROSSWORD No. 66

Treasure Hunt by Phi from *The Independent Magazine*

The grid is a treasure map: north is at the top, and the treasure is marked in the usual way. Letter clashes between Across and Down answers in some squares (and only these) are to be considered directions. Starting at the clash in the top row and moving thence from clash to clash will reveal which of the possible sites conceals the treasure. Solvers should shade this square. One spelling (of a word not in *Chambers* 1988) is historically accurate; one proper noun appears only in an etymology.

ACROSS

1 With a bit of fructose added, this dish is prepared from bland nuts! (12, hyphenated)
10 One went off course, dropping velocity, and came back (8)
13 Source of wine knocked back by female, say, going round about (5)
14 Train former journalists (7)
15 Firm's current days for business (5)
16 Scots to predict the outcome? Odds are not right (4)
17 Tackled the garden—the man would have nothing planted in (4)
19 The cloth getting cut in circles (7)
21 It contains original features of Elian style, for instance (5)
22 Woody will appear round a disreputable house (5)
24 Noted plunger has 2,000 on the spot in one part of contest (7)
26 Spurs, say, needed for harnessed horses? (4)
27 Mournful cry is the last you get from happy bird (4)
29 Provide weapons as before—clumsy marine drops one (5)
30 Sport workshop the French subject to regulations (7)
33 Statesman, say, getting vote—one in 10 (5)
34 Old Scots rulers study music and literature, say (8)
35 Bit of kit needed in playing as in Centre Court, ultimately? (12, hyphenated)

DOWN

1 Announcement of wedding for girl in Bahamas (5)
2 Former husband clearly embraced by mysterious nude, with no alibi? (11)
3 Return, taking away fruit harvest (4)
4 Movie on TV service held up—only end of movie's respectable, on reflection (8)
5 One abandons theatre floors—you'll see me in the gods! (4)
6 Part of farm shelter housing a pig (7)
7 Love's revolutionary when one's embraced a nymph (5)
8 Use SRN to redefine these? (6)
9 Terminology from computing method one rejected, repeated in symbol mostly (7)
11 Put in other words, let's narrate in a new way (11)
12 British, with hesitation, to become part of US fraternity? (4)
18 No meal is ground from this (8)
19 Birdie? Introduction of curtailed round permitted it (7, hyphenated)
20 Left in marks showing gaps in popular wines (7)
23 Siren: knockout bit of naughtiness, morally loose internally (6)
25 Everything I'm capable of is curtailed by witchcraft (4)
26 'Raise skill' on the spot for this answer! (5)
28 Minimum delay that one's involved in (5)
31 Door-keeper shuts out hard drug addict (4)
32 Report shows barristers getting £1,000 (4)

CROSSWORD No. 66

CROSSWORD No. 67

More or less! By Duck from *The Independent Magazine*

In some of the squares the letters in the across and down answers clash. These squares should be filled in to accord with the shape they make, and a final mark should be added at an appropriate intersection of two grid lines. Answers include an acronym and an abbreviation-cum-acronym.

ACROSS

1 You don't like something? Blow it! (9)
7 Two-thirds of composer's church work cut (4)
11 Competent man who was murdered, we hear (4)
12 Indian revolutionary trailing behind a governor (6)
14 Mineral with iridium and one containing gold (7, two words)
15 Disreputable support (4)
16 Flat-topped hill in Rome, say (4)
17 Refuses to recognise ogre involved with sin (7)
18 Damaged port in Croatia (5)
20 Excellent gallery fabric (7)
21 In RAF I'd operate device to assist safe landing (4)
22 Violin not initially used for jazz (4)
24 Go wrong entering narrower road (3)
26 Not attacking fiends, Eve may be led astray (9)
30 Dose of radiation to produce fluttering? (3)
32 Object I stumbled into, rolling over (4)
33 Bet with a Fiver perhaps, nothing less (4)
34 Charge for transporting paintings etc in secure container (7)
35 Page by playwright brings expression of disgust (5)
37 Strange glen—and it's south of the border for such! (7)
39 More than one bird screams head off (4)
41 Terribly ill—by end of day a sort of white (4)
42 Footballer in match? (7)
43 Observe water in liquid or gaseous forms presumably (6)
44 Poet's time in uniform (4)
45 Small person's beginning to cry (4)
46 Ornamental covering required? Find the man to talk to (9, hyphenated)

DOWN

1 King helps to make sorties (5)
2 Look in the Home Counties for this fruit (4)
3 Boarding-house as an element of social security? (7)
4 Swell can make vessel sink in lake? On the contrary (5)
5 Specially note Eastern member on old ship (7)
6 Teased like a tramp? (6)
8 Listen to nearly all the soccer team cheer (7)
9 River 'ome (4)
10 Keep quiet, hold back (8)
13 Pious claptrap as a result of European division (6)
15 Provision of meals—almost completely pig (4)
19 Tree to waste away (4)
21 Expensive coat beneath which may be ornamental trim (8)
23 Small island offering excellent time (3)
25 List set of old books held by academy (4)
26 Fancy silver being found in one pit! (7)
27 Go quietly with endless poverty around (6)
28 Like a kilt that gives man appeal primarily (7)
29 Retsina that's gone off is not so nice (7)
31 Host is always jolly inside (4)
32 Some cloth that is needed! (6)
35 Become bloody—having been this? (5)
36 Navy invading was getting cautions (5)
38 Name US President as symbol of victory (4)
40 Upsurge of wickedness is not recorded (4)

CROSSWORD No. 67

CROSSWORD No. 68

Murder Mystery by Stephen Sondheim from the *New York Magazine*

'I **40A**(3) we're **39D**(3) here,' said the Inspector. He was standing in the jungle-like **1D**(12) of the **6D**(9) of the late Sir Leonard Feisthill, **19A**(4) while adviser to the Secret Service Department of **11D**(12) and setter of the weekly crosswords in its house organ, *The Secret Service* **3D**(6). He was speaking to Lucius I. Feisthill, the deceased's nephew, Dr. Nathanael Parmenter, his medical adviser, and **37A**(3) LaFollette, his secretary: 'Last week we had a **18A**(3) that Sir Leonard was about to denounce someone close to him for selling state secrets to the **33D**(5). His **35A**(6) was to publish the traitor's name—in **21A**(4), perhaps—as a warning to the betrayer to cease his nefarious activities. But it looks as if he was **13A**(6) at his own game, for here he lies, **2D**(4) in the back. I suggest we step into the study, where the victim's flight from the murderer began, to **40A**(3) if his desk will **44A**(5) us further clues.' None of the suspects dared **5D**(4) the suggestion and they **39D**(3) followed him, walking carefully around Sir Leonard's **1A**(7).

The walls of the study were lined with books on classical antiquities, Sir Leonard's only reading **7D**(6). (Hidden behind some of them was his famous collection of pornographic one-**20D**(7).) Among the **38A**(6) furnishings (Sir Leonard was a devotee of the decorative **37D**(4) and **25D**(7) on nothing) was a large African desk, acquired in the **26A**(5). On it were a glass of **30A**(3), his well-thumbed copy of the **45A**(7), his rusty typewriter, a thin **16A**(7) of ferric **12A**(5) all over it, and the crossword reprinted on this page, which was to be published the following week. The only other **8D**(4) was an unfinished pencilled work-sheet of Clues for it, as follows:

> Gun Bogart might have used in 'Born to Say No'
>
> Stare and see parts of the mosaic!
>
> Alternative finish for a Biblical witch? Quite the reverse!
>
> Call for help gets nothing for fair.
>
> Plan in retrospect to help if you put on weight.

'A four-letter, five-letter, six-letter, seven-letter and an eight-letter word,' murmured the Inspector, no **29D**(6) at puzzles himself. 'Odd... well, no **7D**(6).' In the **42A**(6) room, **39D**(3) that could be heard was a ladylike **22D**(4) from **37A**(3) and the rasp of a **43A**(5). The Inspector lit his pipe and suddenly turned.

'Miss LaFollette, Sir Leonard had a reputation for being quite a **41A**(3). How well did you know him?'

'Quite well,' the **32D**(5) replied. 'We first met **34A**(3) years ago at one of those literary **36D**(4). **10D**(6) summer it was, I remember, the trees all gold – '

'Her favorite color,' sneered Lucius, trying to **7A**(5) her innocent tone.

'In your **23A**(3), you **9D**(8)!' she screamed—inaccurately, for Lucius was by no means stupid.

'**15A**(6) on,' the Inspector cautioned.

CROSSWORD No. 68

'**37A**(3) is right,' the Doctor put in with his characteristic Vermont **28A**(5). 'I was treating **27D**(6) for a ruptured **31A**(4) at the time—he had chronic trouble with his back.'

'But not with his head,' mused the Inspector. 'Sir Leonard was a man who **4D**(7) himself quickly to any situation and I'm convinced that somewhere in this puzzle is an indication of the murderer's identity, made perhaps even in his presence but too subtle for him to **40A**(3) and therefore destroy.' He gave the puzzle and Clues a moment's study, then whistled softly in realization. 'Now I **40A**(3),' he said, and promptly arrested one of the people in the room.

Whom did he arrest, and what was Sir Leonard's method of accusation?

CROSSWORD No. 69

Puzzle Quote by Emily Cox and Henry Rathvon

(The Puzzler from *The Atlantic Monthly*)

Answers to clues are to be entered acrostic-style, but column by column from A to M. When every square is filled, the diagram will contain a quotation (slightly amended) from the book *Chambers Crossword Manual*, by the British puzzle writer Don Manley. Answers include one capitalized word.

CLUES

A   Going west to help at school sporting venues (13, 6, 1, 3, 8, 11)
Order French article in *Sex Appeal* (9, 2, 4, 10)
The person speaking with army cop's kid (12, 7, 5)

B   Perennial worry about a heading in the wrong direction (3, 13, 9, 11, 7, 4)
Colonel's first love covered by popular picture (5, 2, 12, 8)
Encounter trailer in French and Italian (10, 6, 1)

C   Bad rep that is true possessed by no Conservative (12, 6, 1, 3, 7, 10, 5, 8, 11)
Carefully peruse eastern volcano's peak (2, 4, 13, 9)

D   Trim Parisian's original old letter (11, 2, 3, 6, 8)
Cause damage to engineer's extreme terminal (4, 7, 10, 13)
Proceed north when carried by United (12, 1, 9, 5)

E   Before 50, develop an aggressive tone (10, 11, 2, 3, 4)
Prison guard ignoring southern company (9, 8, 13, 5)
Military's van is west of town in film (1, 12, 6, 7)

F   One caught in calls for counterfeits (1, 7, 10, 13, 5, 8, 2)
Eighth letter in "Theodore" provided a clue (9, 3, 6, 12, 11, 4)

G   Engineer to push for result (6, 4, 2, 12, 11, 1)
Fleet securely positioned (10, 7, 8, 5)
Fall behind the French gunner's maiden (3, 9, 13)

H   Making a cut in capital for auditors (3, 1, 7, 11, 13, 9, 12)
Heat of battle, and odds of match (2, 10, 4, 6, 8, 5)

I   Lead against one hundred in deserts (1, 2, 13, 9, 7, 11, 4)
Union gets into plot, after I'm inspired (8, 10, 6, 12, 3, 5)

J   Offense hedges about bomb warning (9, 5, 2, 13, 8)
Royal Engineer in control (1, 6, 10, 12)
Blame my friends and me after round number (4, 3, 11, 7)

K   New dons carried omen (11, 9, 5, 8, 13, 12, 2)
Stooge keeps time in a blunt way (4, 7, 6, 3, 10, 1)

L   More unpleasant friend of the French in *Witness* (6, 5, 2, 9, 10, 12, 13)
Southwestern warriors hurt after a President's inauguration (7, 1, 11, 4, 8, 3)

M   Items in disorder left aboard ship (5, 7, 4, 1, 10, 8, 12)
Sailor's back from the Orient after the first (6, 13, 11, 9, 3, 2)

CROSSWORD No. 69

A	B	C	D	E	F	G	H	I	J	K	L	M
1	1	1	1	1	1	1	1	1	1	1	1	1
2	2	2	2	2	2	2	2	2	2	2	2	2
3	3	3	3	3	3	3	3	3	3	3	3	3
4	4	4	4	4	4	4	4	4	4	4	4	4
5	5	5	5	5	5	5	5	5	5	5	5	5
6	6	6	6	6	6	6	6	6	6	6	6	6
7	7	7	7	7	7	7	7	7	7	7	7	7
8	8	8	8	8	8	8	8	8	8	8	8	8
9	9	9	9	9	9	9	9	9	9	9	9	9
10	10	10	10	10	10	10	10	10	10	10	10	10
11	11	11	11	11	11	11	11	11	11	11	11	11
12	12	12	12	12	12	12	12	12	12	12	12	12
13	13	13	13	13	13	13	13	13	13	13	13	13

CROSSWORD No. 70

University Challenge by Apex from *Games and Puzzles*

Clues are either Definition and Letter Mixture or Printer's Devilry. Solvers must discover which is which. DLM clues each contain a definition (one word or more) and a mixture of the letters (beginning with the beginning or ending with the end of a word in the clue) of the required word. Example: 'Why has the sea-going captain upset the Question-master?'; Answer: GASCOIGNE (SEA-GOING C...). Printer's Devilry (PD), each clue is a passage from which the printer has removed a hidden answer, closing the gap, taking liberties sometimes with punctuation and spacing, but not disturbing the order of the remaining letters. Example: 'Is the question 'Mice?' asked the Principal of Somerville.' Answer: ASTERN ('Is the Question-master nice?' asked the Principal of Somerville.) Each passage when complete makes sense. At the end of an exciting contest the Chairman, who had asked all the questions without batting an eyelid, added up the scores (two points each PD, one point each DLM) and announced that a replay would be necessary.

ACROSSBRIDGE

1 How does Euripides encourage the writer of tragedies? (9)

10 Why does a bride have tows after a wedding? (7)

11 Why is the poem a goer in the front row? (5)

12 Who relinquished the kilt to teach Scots a lesson? (4)

14 Which racehorse always bolted when the stabs were opened? (6)

15 How often did Lely visit the buxom beauties of Hampton Court? (6)

18 When did the kangaroo get a footing in Australia? (7)

19 Why did the malignant sprite keep ill-treating the Water Babies? (6)

20 Do all footballers report swear in contrasting colours? (6)

21 Why shouldn't the Cobble rub standard rubbers on? (6)

23 Which dramatic critic said 'This wreath is best!'? (6)

25 In which month were the seven veils chosen for dancing? (7)

28 Which Indian asked if he could have the chapter because he was full up? (6)

29 Who swam out every morning to collect alms in Scotland? (6)

30 What will all the idle hands do in a dispute? (4)

31 Which gambler always entered for a set never won? (5)

32 Why did the kind-hearted wardress lather dinner? (7)

33 Which dramatist in Eire is updating the plays of George Bernard Shaw? (9)

DOWNBRIDGE

1 Why has poet most of the Tories against him? (5)

2 Who outwitted the Red Villain in Lear's Book of Nonsense? (6)

3 Which TV Publicity Agent said 'Tow or tar wood below you!'? (9)

4 Which of the beneficiaries of a will said 'Is the Mall yours?'? (6)

5 Who was the most threatening of all Guy Fawkes' confederates? (4)

6 Who accused the strange Mr. Otis of poisoning his daughter? (8)

7 Why did the reputable firm give the biggest raise? (6)

8 Which well-known flirt gazed and winked at the poet laureate? (10)

9 Would Ophelia have loved ads like Hamlet? (6)

13 Which General gave his brave horse wine after every battle? (10)

16 Why does inferior cheese put some rats off? (9)

17 Why are the top pieces of a lantern light always obscured? (8)

CROSSWORD No. 70

21 What should one use to prevent worming over a garden? (6)
22 Why is the bruiser at fun facing everyone? (6)
23 Do you know that ass trying his luck on Mastermind? (6)

24 How does a revolving index help one to read a dial? (6)
26 Who relaxes with Margery on the see-saw? (5)
27 At what time did the mound own the clock? (4)

CROSSWORD No. 71

Automania by Salamanca from *New Statesman*

Three types of clue are encountered: i) Who For; punning or definitive hints are given as to suitable owners—e.g. dog-lover (ROVER): ii) Used Cars; clues treat answers in their subsidiary forms as though they are locked inside a car (total length indicated) while defining the real answer only: iii) Scrap; each clue contains a definition of one or more words and a hidden jumble of the answer, the answer in each case being entered with an extra letter to make another real word, the extra letter being the 'bonnet' of one of the cars used in ii, the remains of that car also to be found as a hidden jumble in the clue.

WHO FOR

1Ac A boulevardier (8)
1D   The DIY golfer? (8)
3   An astronomer (4)
5   A Covenanter (7)
7Ac A glutton? (4)
9   A Caribbean? (6)
10   A grass (4)
22   A geologist (8)
23   The forgetful (5)
24Ac The drinker/driver (6)
24D A simpleton (2 words, 7)
31Ac A circus performer (6)
32Ac The drinker/driver (6)
32D An old-fashioned girl (4)
33   A sportsman (4)
39   A fighter ace (8)

USED CARS

7D   Ghostly old English learner drivers with big bird in road smash (12)
8   Flying one got cut, ovine perhaps, of deer (15)
12   Author to live secure mostly (8)
14   Well-built small dog's brown, a wild hound, see? (14)
16   Devil grasped by head lama after gold deer (10)
17   Girl showing pain mostly is aged, decrepit (11)
18   Fail to hold what's threadlike one time (8)
19   Praise specially huge lump of wood, i.e., as I chopped (12)
21   Lord in court has game in hand perhaps (8)
25Ac Bird season for turning coalman out (11)
26Ac Tree: one's to spot one in mud (9)
27   Burgundy eleven study (7)

31D Pal flew in patterned flight (8)
35   Learner to choose one different role (8)
38   Have an advantage, being gowned in e.g. dress (9)

SCRAP

2   Driving made pleasant at this school (3)
4   Going to pass, I'd use signal correctly (3)
6   Drove excitedly and once gave a yell (4)
11   Pressed, pedal would go down to the bottom without a hindrance (4)
13   Local man that carries blood to save noble (4)
15   Tool vital for measurement of axle load (3)
20   Driver, one going over six acres (3)
25D Made engine rods go smoothly inside lorry (5)
26D Good drivers are ones that listen and look (4)
28   Tangle caused by the Rolls crashing initially (3)
29   Birds fare badly on these roads (4)
30   Avoid bad language, do! (3)
34   Employ lorries up in Bolton (3)
36   Many chaps taking the final test now (4)
37   A battered Beetle stuck in a trench (4)

CROSSWORD No. 71

CROSSWORD No. 72

Printer's Devilry by Afrit from *The Listener* 1937

The lights are complete words which were originally 'hidden' in the clues. It is to be presumed that the compositor, seeing that certain consecutive letters spelt a word or words, removed them and closed up the gap, sometimes taking a further liberty with the spacing and punctuation, but not altering the order of the letters. There is only one break in each clue, and the lights show the omitted letters in their original order.

ACROSS

(1) See 26D. (4, 7D) ' "Surely", said I, "surely that is something at my wine!" ' (7, 13D, 42D) Some numbers in Swinburne nest at Ely, kindly friend. (11) ' "Pooh!" trilled a linnet, and each dew-note had a lilt'. (12, 10) An article of faith is not merely an opinion bet. (16) 'Ah, wasteful woman, she that may on her own self sown price!' (18) 'The grey sea and the long band, the yellow half-moon large and low'. (22, 14, 36D) 'Something… moved a poet to prophecies – a pinch o' guarded dust'. (24, 39D) In robore fasces. (25) Asters go out, cricket comes in. (27) 'Here tone is music's own, like those of morning birds.' (28) 'My laver flags, and what are its wages?' (30) The party when parting had heard the curlew's knell. (32, 21D) The bad land is little but dear. (34) In olden days two fat people on one leg called for no remark. (38) 'The cliffs of England stand glimmering, and vain the tranquil bay'. (41) How shall poet's soul stand rapt when 'throughout the music of the suns is in her soul at once!' (43) See 31D. (44) Being a fashionable damozel, the stars in her hair were seven. (45) The concourse lulled to sudden silence awed my speech. (47) See 31D. (48) See 46D. (49, 17D) 'Shepherds feed their flocks by shallow river falls, melodious birds sing madrigals'.

DOWN

(1) 'Nor amid these triumphs dost thou scorn the humble glow-worms to adorn'. (3, 35) 'The dense hard passage is blind and stifled that crawls by a turn to climb'. (4) Errors oft in the stilly night break your slumbers. (6, 2) May the big never distinguish many merchantmen! (7) See 4A. (8) Some were here, some there, and the rest where? (9, 19) 'A good boy am I' makes Jack Horner's pie to *my* mind. (13) See 7A. (14) 'Will there be children in their hall for ever and for ever?' (15) 'Nor will occasion want nor shall wed with dangerous expedition to invade Heaven'. (17) See 49A. (20) Ascend we now, find foot-holds, cling to the rocks above. (21) See 32A. (23, 29) 'And that smile like sunshine (shall) dart into ma heart'. (26, 1A, 5) 'And not bows: only when daylight comes, comes in the light'. (27, 33) 'O the eternal sky, full of light and of dignity!' (31, 47A, 43A) 'Fatigued he sinks into some pleasant lair of wavy grass, an air and gentle tale of love'. (36) See 22A. (37) A nod or a beck, a quip or youthful jollity – which do you prefer? (39) See 24A. (40) 'Let a Lord once own the happy lines, how it brightens!' (42) See 7A. (46, 48A) Aspirer 'with slow but stately pace kept on his course.'

CROSSWORD No. 72

CROSSWORD No. 73

Justyn Print by Zander from *The Listener*

Each clue in italics is the imaginary title of a new book by an unknown author. Solvers are asked to deduce the authors' names from the broad hints given by their titles: e.g., if one such title was *The Broken Window* (3,5), the author's name might be EVA BRICK. Apart from several proper names, all words are in *Chambers 20th Century Dictionary* [now *The Chambers Dictionary*]. The unchecked letters of the authors' names make up the following new book title: UP HILLS, BY AL PING.

ACROSS

1 See 50
5 Tax associated with square vessels (4)
9 It goes to a Scotswoman's head a great deal, we hear (5)
13, 36A *Drake's Hammock* (5,8)
15 Breath-sweetener offered by a child, round, swallowed by copper (6)
17 A drama out East, with one after a wild ox (4)
18 Source of a varnish that takes a heavy knife to impair (5)
19, 55 *The Sprawling Metropolis* (5,6)
20 A cake-decorator in a quick-service restaurant (4)
21, 37 *Left in Suspense* (5,6)
23 This act is wicked and spiteful (7)
25 See 28
28, 25 *News From De Southland* (6,2,5)
31 Fatty tumour caused by taking marijuana into the mouth (8)
34 Gift with built-in resistance element (5)
35 It's a day's work to check vessel coming into Strait (5)
36 See 13
37 See 21
39 Frontal surfaces appear to be reflected around the upper end (7)
41 One who's late can cross this river—or can he? That's questionable (7)
47 Suit having the tail in front is a bore (5)
50, 1A *Getting A Move On* (4,5)
52 Old-fashioned case from which to obtain quiet drink (5)
53 Quintet, having a crude violin, becomes indistinct (5)
54, 30 *De Bestest Band What Am* (4,9)
55 See 19
56 See 52D
57 Advance payment about right for a beastly home (5)
58 Earth dug out and thrown up reveals rejected English child (4)
59 Holy building at Mecca, a double one, attended by leaders of bedouin Arabs (5)

DOWN

1 Payment in old shillings and pence diminished in Milton's time (6)
2, 42 *Tudor Banquet* (9,5)
3 Bitter drug that forms oxygen in drinks (5)
4 Margaret rings one with a lasso (5)
5 See 47D
6 Type of fibre cloth, usually striped, laid on Mac's drive (5)
7 See 9D
8 Beetle caused endless panic, landing on a baby's head (6)
9, 7 *Stay Where You Are* (4,4)
10 Funny hat, one originating in an Asian country (4)
11 A Glaswegian buys, and—up, by the sound of it? (5)
12 Hector achieving peaks of heroism under fiercest fighting (4)
14 Type of cereal that gives one endlessly passionate ardour (3)
16 Defensive apparatus fitted with spikes around battered portal (7)
22 See 38
23 Bond drops in for a cheering drink (3)
24 A month to live—start to tremble, getting het up about it (6)
26 Weel supplied wi' bawbees, I'll lodge in the better room (4)
27 Energy, having for basis a power emanating from the supreme deity (3)
29 Small flock of sheep you've to convey round river (4)
30 See 54A

CROSSWORD No. 73

32 Enraged, losing normal composure (7)

33 Stale cattle fodder, almost entirely (3)

36 A letter that's got lost without the end being lost (3)

38, 22 *Continental Breakfast* (6,6)

40 Find an easterner, used to the high life, with an unusual turn of phrase (6)

42 See 2

43 Malingerer is sullen, being without work ultimately (5)

44 Musical pipe accompanying English tale of yore (5)

45 Group of African peoples that has no beggars (5)

46 Mother in trouble looks up the serpent-witch (5)

47, 5D *Teenage Party* (4,5)

48 It's nitrogen in the Strait that makes the Scots yawn (4)

49 Frenzied shout given by woman embracing love (4)

51 Mixed fruit I lug all over the shop (4)

52, 56 *Incognito* (3,2,3)

CROSSWORD No. 74

Heart Transplants by Duck and Hen from *The Listener*

Each answer must be given a new heart: the word that would naturally belong at the heart of another answer. Each clue contains (in any order) a definition of the 'pre-transplant' answer, a subsidiary indication of the 'pre-transplant' answer and a one-word definition of the new heart. *Chambers 20th Century Dictionary* [now *The Chambers Dictionary*] is recommended. Ignore one accent.

ACROSS

1 Cavalcade quite miserable round Scottish city boundary? (7)
6 Copper had news of explosive beside a road (5)
10 Bed one pal improvised, part of horse shelter (9)
12 One with pain curtailed thanks god (4)
13 Coin box, one in Italian city (5)
14 Whale? Money, we hear—no small amount—applaud! (8)
16 Corn, peel and suet cooked round plaice (12)
19 River tide that floods, swamping matter (limonite) (6)
21 Hard worker has not aged (4)
22 Vessel—note it by Channel Islands reversing (4)
23 Grandiloquent, reactionary judge imprisoning man shows excessive feeling (6)
24 Lu has my apron on, home protection (12)
28 Going round valley a little kid came to coin (8)
30 American place of massacre—in a short time, look—nothing! (5)
31 Site to be changed if this place is squalid (4)
32 Street in almost complete collapse, business centre before simplicity (9)
33 Spike sneering bitterly, blue about heartless exposure (5)
34 River with dye, see, spoiling fish, tree (7)

DOWN

1 Stay motionless? Old tablets set up twitch (5)
2 One at far post, waving to us, coming in vestment (9)
3 A foreign flower contest, old-womanish (5)
4 Ol' voter converted, a Conservative swinging round to the left course (12)
5 Party racket in bed-sitter or tenement (5)
6 Story-books—this chapter's all about joint rulers (12)
7 Evil Sarah harbouring anger when upset in a row (8)
8 English drinking cup's short gold letters (4)
9 Removes chemical product from animals, street being messed up with lead and sulphur (7)
11 Stain on one good man, judge maybe (6)
15 Court submission about to interrupt the accused's plea (9)
17 Superior trooper running wild—one driving out native fellow? (8)
18 Oxalis is sure to upset innards finally—they give out (7)
20 Engineers standing still begin to rest (6)
25 Look around—a learner beat man on his own territory (5)
26 In criticism revolutionary student hammers governor (5)
27 Chair, bottomless yielding one, exists (4)
29 Sloth? Get out of bed, rebel! (4)

CROSSWORD No. 74

CROSSWORD No. 75

Hydra by Duck from *The Listener*

The 11 unclued lights are words which have something in common and which have been processed in a similar way. *Chambers 20th Century Dictionary* [now *The Chambers Dictionary*] is recommended.

ACROSS

11 People giving a refund for old collars? (8)
12 Strong chap sets one on edge (5)
13 Soon like a member of the Lords? (5)
15 A mostly sharp fruit (4)
16 We've some priceless oil! (4)
20 The EEC's confused about Germany's word to describe more than one German female (8)
23 Fails to justify unfilled tummies (6)
27 The man (lay worker) to get blunt (8)
29 Fillets, A1, eaten with excitement (7)
32 Onset of fever leads to a hospital note (3)
33 One-time flighty girl's engagement is fun (3)
38 Row about what's right? Judge required (5)
39 Simpletons, leaderless lot (6)
40 Bird hot with love? (8)
47 Wench shows desire bringing a touch of sexiness to the fore (4)
49 Swearword from the pastoral Henry (4)
50 To kick old copper's heartless crime (5)
51 Priest, a help for alcoholic chap (5)
52 One making a loan to leading character of Cowper? (8)

DOWN

1 Bird in California has sense to grab revenue (7)
2 Half peruse morning papers? (4)
3 Relation *not* 13, doddery (4)
4 Such primarily may have troughs (5)
5 Rough point in throat (4)
6 'Ellenic poet's dry measure (4)
7 Plant needing heat for brew (4)
8 Born in endless poverty (3)
9 Card game has fool taken in by wager (6)
14 Style of building, in short, is roguish (4)
17 To heal in oldentimes hand would conceal bit of old plant (8)
22 Cad's to hide as before (4)
23 Liz's letter to the Hebrews (4)
25 Socialist sets upset leaders of National Executive initially (6)
26 Discarded stakes—could be used around north for plants (4)
28 Rag sort of bandage triply wrapping one (4)
30 Indispositions caused by drinks we hear (4)
31 Instrument not half abused (4)
35 Plant with flower cracking a road up (7)
36 Australian beast in prison we hear (6)
37 Grass, rank when decomposed (4)
41 Worm wriggling round earth's surface may be seen on lawn (5)
42 More than one such guild could be gripping (4)
43 Cart may turn up here (4)
44 Goat-antelope—with head hung down it might appear to be a deer (4)
45 Boozy party for English after victory (4)
46 One wants the reverse of non-sweet sweets (4)
48 Kick and drag audibly (3)

CROSSWORD No. 75

CROSSWORD No. 76

Menu by Duck (*The Listener* Crossword, March 1994)

Duck offers this puzzle in eager anticipation of tonight's Listener Crossword Setters' dinner. Each Across clue contains a superfluous word. Taken in order, the initial letters of these words spell out a rudimentary menu with three courses and a final drink. Each Down solution must be processed before entry on to the diagram according to a thematic treatment suggested by one of the courses. It may help to know that the 'first course treatment' predominates and that only the final course can be said to have been consumed. Any ambiguity in the entry of some of the Downs should be resolved by a quotation in the 3rd (but not 4th) edition of the ODQ that is passed (appropriately) around the table. *Chambers* (1993) [now *The Chambers Dictionary*] is recommended.

ACROSS

1 Insignificant people given title of honour, servile politicians (7)

7 Tenor's excellent in oratorio's meaty part (5)

12 Watchmaker's unit with unusual stuff sealing in bit of glass (5)

13 Fellow practically strangled by fabulous bird (oriental love story) (7)

14 Magnificent fool, not English, wept north of the border (4)

16 Distant mount obfuscated isolated group of Scottish country buildings (8)

17 Straight article, serious first to last (3)

19 Strangeness with English? Pen translation—pen hesitantly (6)

21 Hold-up with explosive on street—one's inhaled fumes (5)

23 Member of tribe in Augustine's order gets only half religious (5)

26 Tinware punctured by hard uranium pin (5)

29 Detectives maybe using Irish bodyguard to protect provider of info (8)

33 Use illumination to divert motorway traffic meanly (8)

35 Sabbath display of irritation—tough sermon! (5)

36 Birds, senior, flying without abundant energy (5)

37 Little monster, one coming out of water-vase (5)

41 Antique pistol cap, a fragment not gold (6)

42 Disgusting music request one put at the end (3)

43 Bird loses tail carelessly in chalk hollow (8, 2 words)

44 Principal mine tunnel obstructed (4)

45 Abject fool, prodigal following society (7)

46 Leg of famous horse (5)

47 Gazelle runs in a crooked line—that's not new evidently (5)

48 Old knight erratically trailing female for food (7)

DOWN

1 Discourteous disregard shown originally in old tricks

2 Kindled wood garden half destroyed provides

3 Beast, one beset by growths singularly nasty?

4 Material isn't suitable for a new golf-ball? No

5 Agent tours city area on condition set down as required

6 Meteorological aid produced by novices

8 Final issue is thick—edition needing *very* severe pruning

9 Condition of hopelessness in which number may be embraced by French mistress

10 Explosive noise from castle—enormous castle finally destroyed

11 Chinese coin has safety mark, shield

15 Without Italian or Asian money

18 Cool one dish that is liable to be hot

20 Treat Europeans roughly? They're pushed into the water

CROSSWORD No. 76

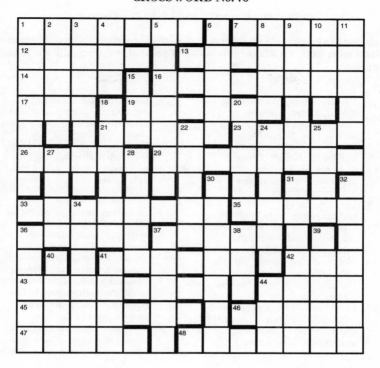

22 Production of badly torn pages, yah? *Not* a practice needed in offices

24 Drink heavily when producing poems

25 Horn band makes a croaky sound

27 Open a charity bazaar

28 Boundary trees

30 Sought cover as before with unruly adolescent in pursuit

31 One in struggle with rival lover shows the strain

32 Plundered on account of getting old

34 Colour I discovered in shrub

36 Old fool not right in class

37 Insert wrongfully—nothing fits somehow

38 Dishevelled remnant under control

39 Cold lady hoarding masses of things? A miserly type

40 Decoration fancifully wrapped, almost concealing everything

41 Grave danger? Search for holy books

44 Crisis gone—no more strain

CROSSWORD No. 77

Mixed Doubles by Virgilius from *The Listener*

Each clue has two possible solutions, thus each pair of clues yields four answers. Solvers must work out where these go—it is decided alphabetically where each one appears.

ACROSS

1 Usually nothing can be seen in this—but negro's in view/ Transport flier from here—it gives harassed flier help, going round (8)

6 Sort of suit North or South might lead for this island?/ Do some scratching in sporrans, perhaps—remove quarters outside and it's left over (4)

9 Give clear bit of encouragement—you might have it on horse/ As done in Scotland, produce a bit of witchcraft, parking in sea-tangle (4)

10 Not concluded yet, and put into view—without use of crook?/ Dancing walk produced by one who's staggered (4)

11 Completed—a bit of paper work (it precedes the start of tippling)/ One attracted by male swan, almost kept under control (3)

12 Rum else Madeira or Curacao is, left at end of bottle/ Name for girl, is this? Look back in Biblical legend for answer (4)

15 Eel's first (and second) in Italian fishing-place—it's little use as wages these days/ I display vacancy, with an extreme of eccentricity—mouth's opening here (4)

16 Article with a point—are women left this?/ A result of manipulating enough of electorate? That might shock you (3)

18 Rod may be used for me, or Kipling's master/ Mature, at end of life, moved to one side in Cumbernauld (4)

20 River in which Oxford college's dumped last of hock? Just the opposite/ I'm true royal chap—prince for a Russian community (4)

21 Used for observations rarely (third letter made plural)/ Inert material—use this, also, as lights' contents, perhaps (4)

22 Faults in red items uncommonly required/ Walter wanting fifth part upset, it's clear—I go into sea near Dover (8)

DOWN

1 Sort of neat, to shape course for fish/ Spot an edge, last put inside in a fairly bad condition (8)

2 Small part of old language, literally a vowel/ River making appearance at centre of Firenze (4)

3 Female I watched (out West) and I associated with sexiness?/ Up country in S.A., dispatch first letter in practice (3)

4 Girl's married name to a certain extent/ What rivers may come from, though poet's lost source of brook (4)

5 I uphold what's been laid down—e.g. it's all in order/ Tapered wood holding pole when in action—got from wine casks? (8)

7 It's associated with an unusual girl/ Result of instinctive impulses in South-East part? (4)

8 Easy, in a way, for party after end of debating/ Device for catching side in piece at end of boot (4)

13 Behaves amorously—see a bit of England (South)/ Ultimate of sites originally, soon inaccessible since in Scottified environment (4)

14 Not working with energy, one takes set without last letter/ Seen in noble regalia, in different version of 'Lear' (4)

15 Not favourable weather required to start producing ore under regulations/ Musical female (4)

CROSSWORD No. 77

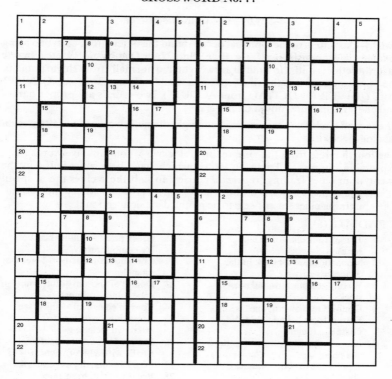

17 Designed to give sharpness in argument—you'll observe only second to change/Don's last English North-East river (4)

19 Bit of food we passed up? Not a great amount in proportion/Some suitable region to plough (in accepted English long given up) (3)

CROSSWORD No. 78

I-Spy by Mass from *The Listener*

Twenty-four letters of the alphabet occur round the outer circle, each one being diametrically opposite itself (e.g. R at 3 and 27; or Q at 15 and 39; etc.). In one case, the letter is initial to a radial answer entered normally from rim to pupil; in the opposing case it is the first letter of a jumble of an answer, e.g. QEVIUR from *Q*UIVER (or QCITAU from AC*Q*UIT). Two radials are proper names and one a Latin plural not in *Chambers*.

The second circle from the rim contains eight thematic words of six letters each, reading clockwise.

The fourth circle from the rim, reading clockwise, contains five words of an expression continued by those letters which have been *misprinted* in the twenty-four clues leading to *normal* entries. In half these clues the misprint affects the definition part; in the others it affects the subsidiary indications. The remaining clues for answers to be jumbled are conventional.

RADIALS (6)

1 Try sex for a change: it'll grate on Jones
2 Monastic place for cats: Father divided by cost
3 Woolly gelding, sow and most of stock
4 Double German craving?
5 Extract from ballad in old, old Castalian tongue
6 Like a swine dropping new penny in a phenol
7 Toothy construction mounted above round cote
8 Caught US General consuming endless oil
9 Who once deceived is ardent, we hear, with the Queen
10 Sword and plates are kept here, it's said
11 One unformed barrow for Jock getting right
12 Scottish king's evil pointless yarn
13 Worker chiselled on the inside, tilted antique
14 Guess old type's making a will
15 Wood man in distance in drizzle
16 Greet return of copper packing-ring
17 Deity has power with horrific clipped head
18 Spine of arch is forked elaborately
19 A smile *can* be seen in a visor
20 Turning dotty about me with pithy sayings

21 Greek priest swallows heartless lay humour rarely
22 One who stands in record breaking attendance
23 Domes of antiquity quite round in appearance—almost
24 Coax lo'ed one into kinky lace
25 Annoying losing face to an unknown, belching
26 Personal likeness for eastern t-trifle with a bit of yoghurt
27 Like Panama, dry as pea-stalks
28 Bruce up first, to sustain
29 One hard at it, (and, for Spooner, what he's unlikely to do!)
30 A Red header in play—or back-heeling
31 Look, register's backed and bound clumsily!
32 Roil, ring and shake
33 Wild zebra crushing Eastern farrier against wild beasts
34 She's out of breath (after blasting a lot?)
35 Arabic bird, shapely in manner of chest
36 Gets to register end of dyspepsia
37 A metallic monoxide counter unknown with tantalum
38 Deity, in wood, burned as tray exploded
39 Injure, snare recoiling like weasel
40 Goddess, with a palm, king suits

CROSSWORD No. 78

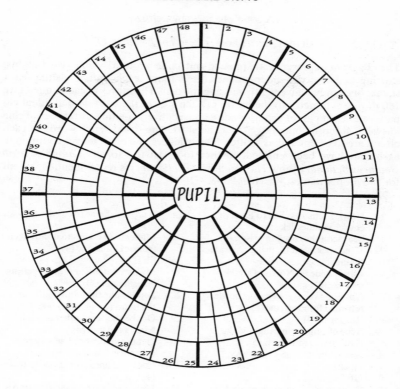

41 Cope with American notable Centaur
42 Kicks and struts around North
43 They're ruts: one limps round one
44 Spirits must have gravity, landlords
45 Dissembler returns concession whole

46 Luke has disorderly rooms with entrance to tombs
47 Rectifiers for features of shells
48 More than one rubs e.g. glass boss, edge of lens

CROSSWORD No. 79

A double harness by Leiruza

All the Queen's horses from *The Listener*, 1977

The diagram represents an opened-out cube around which two knights, starting at 1-1, make independent closed tours, each knight visiting each square once only, conveniently missing the date. The moves of each knight give 180 degree symmetry to the halves of each side of the cube, and an identical pattern to each pair of *opposite* sides, consecutively spelling its respective clue answers, stopping one move from the start. The five 3-letter words in each circuit are to be entered as written. Thirty letters and eight moves common to each tour have been entered, further to assist the solver. *Chambers 20th Century Dictionary* [now *The Chambers Dictionary*] is recommended, except for two proper names, viz. clues 23- & -21.

CLUES

1– Hawk's rein attached to Eastern church candlestick (5)

2– Scot scratches back in prison (4)

3– Wind socks as told, using separate threads

4– Rarely rode up North to attack, we hear (4)

5– Nothing taken from native bottle returned for medicine (4)

6– Rash firm (4)

7– Type of ringworm caught in the forest in Eastern parts (5)

8– A shark to rub the wrong way, Noel! (5)

9– GET

10– What the accoutred knight did, when late? (6)

11– Trap some tame shrew (4)

12– AGE

13– DEY

14– Viewer takes in first newsletter with old–fashioned grin (5)

15– Local food supplied by meat shops (4)

16– ERR

17– To be inconstant can stir up anger (5)

18– French sketch is ruined without first and last numbers (7)

19– One day's work in Scotland, to get a saint's mausoleum? (5)

20– Spenser's temper is a hindrance (5)

21– Cheater comes back a month short over bet! (5)

22– Tidy kine (4)

23– A portrait painter solely, but not very good (4)

24– It is pure shame to cover with wax (7)

25– Malay boat comes to different end from a Dutch one (4)

26– SUE

27– Malay boat has new prow getting lakeside salt (4)

28– Sounds like the bunny–girl part of the joint! (6)

29– On the sheltered side although the heart's not in it (4)

30– Get the vinegar on the way back, otherwise I must go in (5)

31– Foot's last product is said to scare! (4)

32– Perhaps the zip required to trap a Turkish bobby (7)

–1 In France I deliver a blunt javelin (5)

–2 Fixes the price of brandies and soda (4)

–3 RED

–4 The brat to catch one in (4)

–5 Spenser's hair was hearsay! (5)

–6 Sporting combination of brass and wood, of course (4)

–7 EAU

–8 Even if stale, beer gets no soaks back (5)

–9 Stable to a degree, was fitted with drains (5)

–10 This vessel has speed when there's nothing in it (4)

–11 Some transient Shakespearian offspring (4)

–12 Meaningless kink (4)

CROSSWORD No. 79

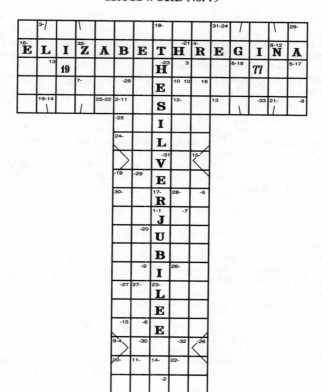

The crossword grid spells out **ELIZABETH REGINA** across the top row and **HESILVERJUBILEE** down the vertical column.

-13 Short violent blow naturally causes traumas (7)

-14 DEE

-15 High note or *not*—a note! (4)

-16 An abyss has no sun going over to truly speak of (4)

-17 Reckon the term of life from tree (4)

-18 Without song, French zany son shows over–excitement (6)

-19 Sandarac tree around about here? Or a little behind? (6)

-20 Take in, for example, Solomon's common NCO (5)

-21 It's hard to be in this German district (5)

-22 Was this impudent person once very clever? (4)

-23 The Bard's carrion eater in an earthy environment (4)

-24 Sallow skin (4)

-25 Head back and double in Paris (4)

-26 Artists' frame pointed South towards the East (6)

-27 Loki's daughter freezes screw–propellers

-28 GAS

-29 Tangles with Swedish money (4)

-30 For blackcurrants and the like, car is best thrown away (5)

-31 With no returned sale, evaluates old cellar (5)

-32 I *must* be absorbed by Dane to condescend to take in Shakespeare (5)

-33 GAY

CROSSWORD No. 80

A Three-Pipe Problem by Law from *The Listener*

The grid represents the floor of a room with peculiar plumbing. Three pipes, α, β and γ, enter at the top and leave at the bottom, but the routes they take are circuitous, to say the least, and it is not known which outlet corresponds to each inlet.

Each square contains two sections of pipe joining the midpoints of its sides, in one of three configurations:

1   ⊞   2   ⟋⟍   3   ⟍⟋

(N.B. In configuration 1 one section passes above the other – they do not meet.) The 24 re-entrant sections around the outside ensure an uninterrupted flow.

The alphabet has been divided into three groups, one corresponding to each configuration, and one letter is to be entered in each square in such a way that a) the appropriate pipe configuration is below each letter, and b) each of the three pipes traces out a series of words from inlet to outlet (note that the re-entrant sections have no letters). The starting squares of these words are given, numbered in the top left, top right and bottom left corners for pipes α, β and γ respectively.

Three types of clue have been used, the type for any particular word being determined by the group to which its initial letter belongs. Words with initial letters in group 1 have normal clues; those with initial letters in group 2 have definition-and-letter-mixture (DLM) clues, each of which contains a definition and a mixture of the word's letters, beginning and/or ending at a word-break; while those with initial letters in group 3 have clues with a misprint of one letter in the definition part. Each letter of the alphabet appears as the initial letter of an answer at least once: thus the letter-groups may be determined and the path of each pipe traced.

It will be seen that the final clue for each pipe is not given. The correct letters in the misprint clues, taken in the order in which they are presented, spell out an exceptional clue, which can be read as either normal, DLM or misprint, and so leads to three answers as required—though which corresponds to which pipe is to be determined.

For clarity, the internal pipe sections need not be shown on the completed diagram, but the solver is asked to identify the outlets corresponding to inlets α, β and γ by lettering them appropriately.

Two apostrophes are to be ignored, and punctuation may be misleading. *Chambers English Dictionary* [now *The Chambers Dictionary*] is recommended.

PIPE α *(numbers in top left corners)*

1 Spenserian casket material, seen in use a little (4)
2 Give up fur: money is the real essential, ultimately (4)
3 Mede, frozen, miswrites timeless edict (4)
4 Pitiful Scot – locally, he has not many round about – it's acceptable (5)
5 The poor thing's lost – 'Come here, Daisy' (4)
6 A blind child must certainly wear a bib (5)
7 Quiet of old, uninterrupted by noise (5)
8 Scottish child's coy: dress is back to front, right? (4)
9 Compound found in tap water needs removing – wads might do (6)
10 Audibly apprehend large amounts of wit (4)
11 Ghana's where this officer's found – crazy one breaks rule on return (7)
12 I adjudge Spenser's in a bad mood (6)
13 Henry's gold, extremely luxurious togs (5)
14 Colloquially, *thou's* certainly acceptable (*thou* for *thee*) (5)
15 Being tense inwardly (3)
16 Map of Slavonia shows us Sweden in Iran – confused? (7)
17 Actor dressed as cowboy for rodeo scene (4)
18 Endlessly arrogant old fool leaves dregs of mail (7)
19 Ian's door is shut, yet not locked (4)
20 An old dish, but as bonny as they come (5)
21 Take in backward idiot in game (4)
22 (6)

PIPE β *(numbers in top right corners)*

1 Particle which may be formed by lots of electrons with one beside (3)
2 Fixed up uncle – married without him in the country! (6)
3 Began to be ruthless (4)

CROSSWORD No. 80

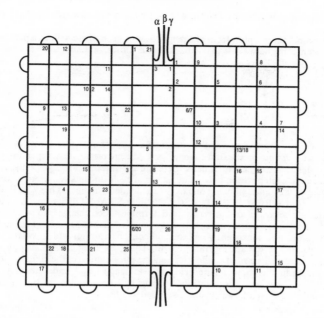

4 Carpet material causes flirt to become ten times as bad, initially (8)
5 A theologian returns to the East with books of mythology (4)
6 Embroider a tale with cunning and resourcefulness (4)
7 Evil spirit is not to be believed (4)
8 Subdue a West Indian Negro that's escaped (5)
9 Spade, perhaps, used to excavate coal in the early stages (3)
10 It takes three men to plant a tree (4)
11 Be careful with the garland – it's fragile (3)
12 Dry sherry's 60% I see! (5)
13 Horticulturist initially requires one local germen (3)
14 Settee in unoccupied building has insignificant person on it (5)
15 Do you dislike plums? I don't! (4)
16 Open country exposed to the elements (3)
17 Carry the books home, finally (4)
18 Queer bloke displaying ornament (8)
19 Holy man's put out in slammer (7)
20 See me somersault in the river – I may be old, but I'm free! (5)
21 Scots, shorn of southern latitude, with initial antagonism to English (4)
22 Old leap – note – into a creek (5)
23 Part of crab will open slightly (5)
24 Cloth covering for racket in common use (7)
25 Local stone cap set awry before (5)
26 (6)

PIPE γ *(numbers in bottom left corners)*
1 Old coin creates a buzz of interest (3)
2 Heavenly model, driven by dogs, hid from detestable, headless weird (6)
3 Squirrel's nest found in the farmyard (4)
4 Rilke enters the fold in Aberdeen (4)
5 Slow disdain in Perth evinced by tailless lizard (4)
6 Sh! Music's ending (3)
7 Glees about backward fools on the outside (6)
8 You must quickly escape – a soldier is coming (5)
9 The crowd pressed forward with threatening and rude gestures (5)
10 It's a very *rara avis* that will dress *after* dinner! (5)
11 Become thin by not eating fat (4)
12 Run and ring noisily of old (4)
13 Mick, though ancient, causes giant's head to drop (4)
14 Seeds, skimming, risk confusion with roots of other plants (6)
15 Gay part of life spent in laughter? Just the reverse! (7)
16 (6)

CROSSWORD No. 81

New Year's Resolution by Dimitry (*The Listener* Crossword, January 1994)

In plain hunting, the simplest form of change ringing, each of the bells in a peal follows a regular path moving between lead and back. For instance, on four and on five bells:

1234	12345
2143	21435
2413	24153
4231	42513
4321	45231

and so on.

It is convenient to think of this as the continual swapping of successive pairs of bells in positions 1&2, 3&4 etc on the first change, 2&3, 4&5 etc on the next, repeating until the original order is restored. For n bells there are 2n different arrangements, each bell having struck in each position twice. The letters of each clue answer are to be treated as bells, the light to be entered being one of the subsequent changes. Thus CROSSWORD might be entered as RCSOWSROD, RSCWORSDO, SRWCRODSO etc. No clued word is ever entered unchanged and solvers must determine which change is to be entered.

In accordance with the quotation which will be revealed in the unclued lights, one letter of the alphabet must be consistently replaced on entry by another which, where checked, appears normally in the appropriate crossing entry. Each clue contains one inserted word which must be discarded to allow normal cryptic solution of the clue.

Solvers should further hunt in the grid for a message which indicates how to find Dimitry's first New Year's Resolution. Solving will be speeded up by realising the singular contribution made here by the discarded words.

Chambers (1993) gives a number of abbreviations used here not in the 1988 edition. It does not, however, contain one (in 1988) used extensively in this puzzle. 26D is a simple compound (in Webster). Unclued lights can be of one, two or three words.

Dimitry's second Resolution will be indicated later and only in obedience thereto should solvers complete the diagram.

ACROSS

1 Indians escort couple round shying horse to Washington south (7)

6 Ooh! Food brought over's not hot—picnic dip, Adam? (6)

10 Eniac put short measure on non-odd number (6)

12 Young moth (coiled) inbreeds with one at first in old bud on rotten tree (8)

14 Feelings conveyed by one mocker I caged in very best when time's served out (5)

15 Create colourful image where you can see "Pommie galah" overlie "British Drongo" progressively with time (5)

18 Shrieve, turning back response in the antechoir (4)

19 "Grease" appearing gangly in Galatea Art Club (9)

21 Fool set a vasty current flowing in reverse after a bit of naughtiness (5)

24 Original *Sea-lily* packet-boat rebuilt as a merchant lighter (5)

25 Closely maintaining track I had won, evanish loco hidden in empty siding (9)

28 Instrument from eastern town: enterer playing strain (6)

32 What can be used to assault rhombic cleavages to cut therein (5)

34 Estate keeps gowan but acacia mutated (5)

35 Being unruly at orlop, United Nations in charge of ships (6)

36 Confused hard Greek, Iastic, deletes 'European' and gets in a pickle (7)

37 Made turbulent *Revolutionary Etude* entering slick material? (6)

38 Chops rent entry list—name's lacking sixpence (7)

DOWN

1 Fruit tree: wrest off currants and I ran away (6)

2 One can see very independent genii care how the power ends (6)

3 See fish wheel unhappily in bilge (5)

4 Disheartened quiet around joint after

CROSSWORD No. 81

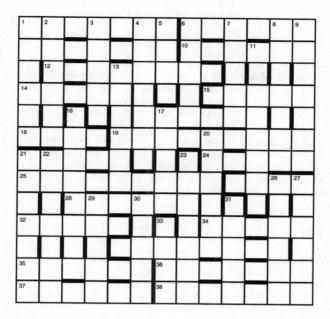

removal of small Jack O. Weekes group (7)
5 Move to right side on warhorse with it in leap (4)
6 Slip in a genuine bell-like instrument (5)
7 Cavil at asbestic calcium removed and replaced with acceptable substitute for one ceiling (5)
8 Take for instance disease of bronchi—I'll educe mean cluster at one point again (7)
9 Perhaps SAS rebel may scheme afresh in Eastern lair (7)
11 Time I'd caught some off over—I slog when I'm in! (8)
13 What's old in unchanged yeve or Ind's last of language of Milton (6)
16 Convincingly ebon quality man found on bit of lignite in company with unknown quantity? (8)
17 One with arcane powers like Gagool-Iai-do champion's overcome by old knowledge (5)

20 Power of deep one confined in bad antre goes to damnation primarily (6)
21 SA flier takes half errant spree (plus criminal sentence!) (7)
22 Badly torn in East Persia—thin layers of paper (7)
23 The turbulent avalanche: col on mountains will get you this (7)
26 Following end of earache stout female's requiring the services of a couple of chaps (6)
27 Death when given out deters loud man on board (6)
29 Scots disperse: I and numberless clans in furore repine (5)
30 Mounted scot tried reins (5)
31 End of monastic fare following 'hard rock' peevish complaint (5)
33 Shut out? Better use old interjection! (4)

CROSSWORD No. 82

A Marvellous Game by Columba

(*The Listener* Crossword, October 1998)

Clues are in two groups, representing White and Black in the game of chess annotated below. Each clue is associated with a piece or pawn that moves at least once in the game; solvers must determine which piece is associated with which clue. Each answer is to be entered on the board in accordance with the sequence of squares occupied by the piece it represents. For example, the first letter of the answer to the White Queen's clue should be entered in square d1, the second in e1, the third in c3 and so on. In a hypenated word, ignore the hyphen. Each clue contains one superfluous word. The initial letters of these words, taken in clue order, reveal the source of what will be seen to develop in the course of the game. The conclusion to this should be entered in the line below the board. One answer is a common abbreviation; two are proper names not in *Chambers*.

THE GAME

1 e4	d5	**2** c4	g5	**3** Bd3	dxe4	**4** Bxe4	Bg7
5 Na3	Bf6	**6** Rb1	Bd7	**7** b4	Na6	**8** c5	Bd4
9 Kf1	Rc8	**10** Qe1	e5	**11** Bb2	Ne7	**12** Bf5	Nxc5
13 bxc5	g4	**14** Bd3	Be3	**15** Bd4	Nf5	**16** Bb2	Be6
17 dxe3	g3	**18** Be4	Nd4	**19** fxg3	Ne2	**20** g4	Ng3+
21 hxg3	Qd7	**22** Bd4	exd4	**23** Rh6	Qa4	**24** Rf6	Qb4
25 Bg6	hxg6	**26** ex4	Rh4	**27** g5	Rg4	**28** Qc3	Bc4+
29 Ke1	Be2	**30** Rb2	Bf3	**31** Rc2	Qb2	**32** d5	Rc4
33 g4	Rxc5	**34** Rb6	Ra5	**35** Qxc7	Qxa2	**36** Qc4	Rc6
37 Rxb7	Rb6	**38** Nb1	Rb4	**39** Qf1	Rc4	**40** Rxc4	Rb5
41 Rc8							

WHITE

Make toes fit in clenching gym shoe

Emits cry of objection, perhaps, since boxing horribly hard

Enisle rum, half-vanished group of related plants

What's employed in keeking, granny?

Meat Muslims may eat, accepted in Arab dinner

Restlessness of oblique type, rabbit Alice engages

Dog salmon, carrion for Jock about loch

Flower line has entangled life

Poor Nigel's to quit, after absorbing hour, with queen lost—surpassed in striking

How much doubled rooks' leader benefits, once on the far side

Explosive deep-red wine throwing out head of Edinburgh yagger

Settlement of what Artemis is due as superior

Hollow enclosed part of howe made neat

BLACK

Actor's tips? "I follow director's cue"

Deity evolving tea rose

Clement, eleven PM, on the sheltered side, keeping dry

Drag round soldier, Will's escort initially shier

Ditch marled fruit enclosure

Male, note, altered colouring

Stringed instrument, in a mess, roadman adjusted

Science fiction volume concisely reported cup-shaped structures

Chess champion enthralled, speaking about sacrificing piece

Fabulous tree out of one Lebanese rises

Thrash with loud sound

CROSSWORD No. 82

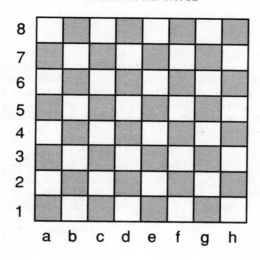

CROSSWORD No. 83

On The Wagon by Ximenes from the *Observer*

Ximenes (in Lent) invites solvers to join him in substituting soft drinks for hard in the answers to the ten italicised clues: thus *ransacked* might appear as RANCOCOAED, *lauwine* as LAUWATER, *Martinique* as VICHYQUE. The definition parts of these clues, and the bracketed numbers at the end of them, refer to the original words; but subsidiary portions, such as anagrams, reference to part of words, etc., refer to their 'softened' forms which are to be entered in the diagram.

ACROSS

2 *Buttercup: see same among a tangle of vegetation, pale, about beginnings of Oct. and May* (7,5)

9 Badly off, without a start—that's dreary in Glasgow (5)

10 Total battle produces a call to surrender (7)

13 Products of the soil, mixed, are stored here (4)

15 Sweat goes through it, to make a careful study (4)

16 *Very good reversed Indian pillar, all of a piece—a memorial* (10)

17 That hurts! Stop! That hurts just the same (That's like what may come out at the dentist's) (8)

18 Ill-founded pleas will do (5)

19 *It's a marauder: fight back in the confusion* (8)

20 *Ingenuous and a novice? Quite the reverse: I wake people up* (5)

24 Small vehicle, in a restrictive space, may sting you (5)

28 Revolutionary gripped by Irishman or marauder (8)

29 *Ten injured – keeping cool – makes car move on* (6)

31 Tear open one bank of the Tiber of old (4)

32 The old port must be made to go round (4)

33 Opposing Territorials between Genoa and Milan (7)

34 A few drams helpful for forgetting fevah when full of the warm south? (5)

35 *M.D. wanted: you'll find M.D. alone here, harassed* (6)

DOWN

1 *Rolly couple here, rocking wildly—I'll sell tracts* (10)

2 *'U' old ruffian, ancient bird, with grasp of the turf* (6)

3 Stuffs the last of the infantrymen in trenches (6)

4 Take a quick look up and down in Princes St (4)

5 Having a bend—here's a thing to drink out of (6)

6 In Latin you and I have grasped the reverse of badly Cicero & Co. (6)

7 Leaves that could well be moist (5)

8 A mere number, a corporal: his name's not given (6)

11 *Secretary's job—the pay-rate's absolutely rotten* (11)

12 To make a searching enquiry about a fuddled toper is an employer's right (8)

14 Let's have an aid to calculating—I almost get bogged in sexagesimal arithmetic (8)

21 She's one to relax—she often spoils children (6)

22 A 'U' Frenchman is seen in skill over love (6)

23 Matthew Arnold's watery husband of a human bride has to flirt with one (6)

26 *To choose, in brief, glorification of principle* (6)

27 Unjustifiable delays keep one in longer (5)

30 Label bag, inside, last stop before Waterloo (4)

CROSSWORD No. 83

CROSSWORD No. 84

Letters Latent by Ximenes (No. 1000)

Someone somewhere claims (as Ximenes couldn't dare to when this series started) to know of '—— .... ——'. Each of the two blanks represents 4 words (18 letters); the dots represent 4 other words in the middle of the quotation which are disregarded here as irrelevant. The 36 relevant letters in turn should really occur (in some cases more than once) in the 36 answers to be entered in the diagram, the first in **1 ac.**, the second in **6 ac.**, and so on successively in the right order up to the last letter, which should occur in **30 dn**. But these letters must all be omitted, wherever they should occur, when the answers are entered. Definitions in the clues refer to the full, unmutilated words; subsidiary indications, e.g. anagrams, references to parts, etc., refer to the mutilated forms to be entered in the diagram. Numbers in brackets show the full lengths of unmutilated words.

17 is a compound word in Webster, not in Chambers; **20** is the Greek form, given in Chambers as a derivation, of a Latinised word; one answer is a prefix.

ACROSS

1 Rough-tongued red revolutionary about in Feb. (8)
6 Expand old railway—augment, perhaps, as before (7)
10 Sid got wild, gripping club, stubborn as before (13)
12 Greek money down—a quid short: the unit system (8)
13 Groans, tetchy, losing heart, inclined to grumble (7)
14 Returning east likewise was sweet (5)
15 Pop singer—wrong transactions curtailed (7)
16 Snakes like consuming a satisfying finish (9)
17 Ties can, when broken, make a law void (8)
23 They cause variations: choosed—that's wrong (9)
24 Ornamental vessel, incorrectly centred (8)
26 Premier returning in state, waterlogged (6)
28 Squabbles shortly following in certain conditions (5)
29 Concentrated, with a distinct aroma, we hear (7)
31 Beauty queens? They always get left (8)
32 It helps the crystal-gazer to see heroics, love, gold in a cache returned (12)
33 Eskimo conjurer in strange occultism (8)
34 Bird gets half dose of the cat with severity (7)

DOWN

1 Clasps in grief—O, O, O, O, O .... (6)
2 A bribe—dollars, apparently (9)
3 Officer gets commendation, derived from calculus? (6)
4 Relay high spot—hare all over the place (9)
5 Salt—it's multiplied by one pinch of Jock's (8)
6 I'm hippy: off with constable's headpiece (7)
7 Ruddy Scots dove up a tree—or Scots cuckoo (7)
8 (2 words) We're in slapstick—dress up, act madly (11)
9 The man overcomes trouble without any guidance (8)
11 Filmy green plant—fibres rent all to pieces (11)
18 Heere's the best of luck, little birds (8)
19 Unmechanized cultivator, pipe with prominent ridge (8)
20 With no S.A. wild youth, uppish, harbours mites (8)
21 Powerful car—girl unwell inside (8)

CROSSWORD No. 84

22 Something orthorhombic, even including a monkey (9)
25 This introduces something hairy, waving a torch (6)

27 Big city wise, one hears, about rising purpose (6)
30 Sharp rebuff—certainly not, little sir (5)

CROSSWORD No. 85

Legsin Cricotas by Ximenes (no. 1200 in the *Observer*, 1972)

Today's puzzle, the last to be composed by Ximenes before his death, marks the end of an era. The brilliance of its diagram composition and the ingenuity of its clues combine to show the compiler at his most inspired.

The 21 initial letters of the words ACROSS, when correctly shuffled, form a 3-word Single Acrostic appropriate to the number of today's puzzle. Every word is in *Chambers 20th Century Dictionary* [now *The Chambers Dictionary*].

ACROSS

1,23 (3 words) HQ makes dolt err, scoring duck (18)

5 Jovial chap—tipsy veteran by end of bar (8)

11 Is one, a sticker, sent back? That's divine (7)

12 Bill O'Reilly's last two: he has to sweat (5)

13 Club has last of tail in, and there's a spot (5)

15 A player catches Hill—it's the Guv'nor (6)

16 No-ball? Accuse then—hand over for penalty (9)

17 Old province puts one in the air, wildly (7)

18 Eat away part of the wicket, chaps (4)

22 One in a tour shows Mac in a good light (7)

23 See 1 across (13)

25 Overseas hero, X, produces a screamer (7)

29 A Surrey batsman back: once went in first (4)

31 Opening, stumped in Fifty club's reverse (7)

33 Ray going after club's feminine supporter (9)

34 Ere a collapse, returning, might miss stump (6)

35 Am run out, take off pads (5)

37 Gil—— bowled fast: observe wreckage (5)

38 Rest bat here very badly (7)

39 We look fine in the middle—pegs ne'er upset (8)

40 Ray's batting—it's sticky (5)

DOWN

1 We amuse—a lot of cricket among the trees (9)

2 Flighty opener's caught in gully, 50 (6)

3 Youngster put up in order—pulse noticeable (3)

4 Made a test 100—was worth weight in gold? (6)

5 Slow—encourage to go for low catch? (7)

6 Tourist gets six—one right over the hill (6)

7 Spinning—rubbish: a century about one (8)

8 See 'im in a knock that's uppish—it's usual (5)

9 Boundary up—batting when he's round's fast (8)

10 Hendry out—he's out—it's under a ton (4)

14 With a briliant pair set up, playin' in (9)

19 These diggers are tidy craftily led players (9)

20 Old game trio on a tour (8)

21 I am what's wanted in a bad spot, a cutter (8)

24 More than one third man at Perth? Without hesitation, that's stupid (7)

26 Men from overseas: slip in silly miss (6)

27 He who gets out is down on maker of appeal (6)

28 Ray taken in by shooters—long, hard test (6)

30 Saw an Indian cutter in maturity (5)

32 Lure towards short leg (4)

36 Dinna rin—bear up as before (3)

CROSSWORD No. 85

CROSSWORD No. 86

Tribute by Duck from *Crossword*

The clues are of two types: **1 Letters Latent** (L). From the answer to each clue one letter must be omitted wherever it occurs in the word before entry in the diagram. Definitions in the clues refer to full, unmutilated answers; subsidiary indications refer to the mutilated forms to be entered in the diagram. Numbers in brackets show the full lengths of unmutilated words. **2 Misprints** (M). Half of these clues contain a misprint of one letter only in each, occurring always in the definition part of the clue: their answers are to appear in the diagram correctly spelt. The remaining clues are correctly spelt: all their answers are to appear in the diagram with a misprint of one letter only in each. No unchecked letter in the diagram is to be misprinted; each letter appearing where two words cross is to appear as required by the correct form of at least one of the words to which it belongs. All indications, such as anagrams, etc., in clues lead to the correct forms of words required, not to misprinted forms.

The diagonals 1–37 and 10–36 spell an appropriate message.

ACROSS

L 3 He engraves lines around about piece of wood and ridge (11)

M 11 Diplomat's concluding words (5)

M 13 Caste once, to cease without god (6)

M 14 Bit of overstrain has mother closing exhausted eye (8)

L 16 Observe number—put it in! (7)

M 17 Secluded old offices set back (6)

L 19 Returning to look for tall plants (5)

L 20 Lent goes out with ultimate in jollity immediately after (6)

M 21 Filthy spectacle taking man aback initially (7)

M 23 Butler taking care over connection on drain? (7)

M 25 Hands cut off—is severe reproof putting disciple off? (5)

L 28 Fine, dry (5)

L 31 Most Excellent name that is recollected by solvers primarily? (7)

M 32 Jock's building-site shows his building material perhaps round about (6)

M 33 Geller? Trick has endlessly mysterious power (8)

M 34 A holy Frenchman, it seems, rare as before (6)

M 35 Suppress not completely novel idea (5)

M 36 Being sure offer a prominent position (10)

DOWN

M 1 Dan-Air is company flying a particular class of planes (10)

M 2 The old wonder at the present-day morass? (6)

M 4 Scientist's answer to 'What'll make the world go round?' perhaps! (10)

M 5 Song about e.g. sergeant in place of massacre (7)

M 6 Find new cork for liqueur half gone (5)

M 7 Resin in a source of gold (6)

M 8 Words from blown up cads? (8)

M 9 Volume discharged from Severn exceptional in eagres (5)

L 12 Woody tissue—what could be 'elmy'? (5)

L 15 Unusual screen around this French church, grotesque projection (11)

M 18 See this A1 performer producing rats? (8)

M 22 It's odd getting upset over a shower? Pestilence as before (7)

M 24 Succeed in getting pike fried (outside Scotland) (6)

M 26 Become wearisome aboard ships (6)

M 27 English snipe to get away safely (6)

M 28 Show excess feeding in the motel (5)

L 29 One scrapes—yen to get endlessly austere? (6)

L 30 Fibre, one sow turned up (5)

CROSSWORD No. 86

CROSSWORD No 87

Eightsome Reels by Azed for *The Observer*

Each numbered square in the diagram is surrounded by eight blank squares. All clues lead to words of eight letters and these are to be entered in the squares around their appropriate numbers, clockwise or anticlockwise, beginning anywhere. Solvers must determine where each word begins and the direction in which it is to go. The 12 unchecked letters at the corners of the diagram could give CLERK MAN HOME.

1   Curiously skeletal ponds?
2   Cask gents dealt with, metal
3   Siberian folk making sun guest unexpectedly
4   Custon embodied in song, musical
5   Colouring old fiddle? Stick around
6   Old tiara, mysterious, accepted by court
7   Units of force spun load out of control
8   Tracking ducks in high water
9   Translated an Ugric name regardless
10   They could be struggling in course
11   An adherent, I strove laboriously with king
12   Sex appeal in girl after bit of play, revealing occupation
13   Variable weight: ___ as dispence?
14   Soldiers in dark blue? They were open to bidders
15   Worthless shed duck enters for acorn meal
16   Dacha in Spain, possibly
17   Tingler perhaps even excited when hugged by social failure (2 words)
18   Optional US course: small college backed it, taken by foreign pupil
19   Old-style American diuretic that improves skin color (nothing less) (2 words)
20   Ten hours in flight from Australia?
21   Whereon to greet the lady after a call?
22   Tail caught in seed-drill?
23   It's thoroughly English to sell what's won wrongly
24   Purchase paper money in US bank
25   Crew replacing people in crowning Malay vessel
26   Blatant rubble
27   Military equipment War Dept returned in African capital
28   Wear out repeated source of furniture wood
29   River engulfed in swirling wet sand? Seine and suchlike
30   Stopper unusually rare bottles to settle
31   Money pool for fine fabric
32   A couple of eccentrics, what no society visitor could do without? (2 words)
33   Did crawl, swimming for chance to compete without qualification (2 words)
34   Ewe in fold tires? ___ set one ailing, possibly
35   Those lacking aim get feet caught by spinners, typically
36   Preacher, Sunday: 'Sin involves lucre mostly'

The Chambers Dictionary [1993 at time of puzzle] is recommended

CROSSWORD No. 87

	1		2		3		4		5		6
	7		8		9		10		11		12
	13		14		15		16		17		18
	19		20		21		22		23		24
	25		26		27		28		29		30
	31		32		33		34		35		36

CROSSWORD No. 88

Spoonerisms by Azed from *The Observer*

Half the across and half the down clues lead in their definition parts to Spoonerisms of the correct answers to be entered. Subsidiary indications in these clues lead to the correct answers themselves. In the remaining clues the definition parts have been distorted by one Spoonerism per clue. Subsidiary indications in these clues likewise lead to the correct answers. Spoonerisms may be either consonantal (e.g. MENHADEN/HENMAIDEN) or vocalic (e.g. BUNTING/BIN TONGUE) and may be accompanied by changes of punctuation.

The Chambers Dictionary (1993) is recommended but does not give the compound at 22. One other answer is an acronym.

ACROSS

3 Liquor at hand, get tipsy, horribly sated within (10)
10 Purchase food—cake, bit crumbly (7)
11 We Scots backed Ireland, not English—Scots drill and cheer (5)
12 Rural Dean clothed in American sack bleeds (4)
13 Barrels derrick put out stack money (8)
15 Coop, long, to try as cot (4)
17 Stealing two types of neckwear (6)
18 Had a nap beside piano, turning silent round it (6)
20 Old knight (Scots line) sullied title with pugilism (9)
22 Gatting barred's had group (gutted) distraught with this (9)
25 Soak, to thieve, reversed blood ties (6)
26 Show moderation before one last bit of fish here with chips (6)
30 Max in laurels won with fish (4)
31 Low troop disrupted spiritless discussion (8)
32 A beer almost like Roddy's beer (4)
33 Hill with few taking in Uruguay is centre for climbers (5)
34 Wham sensation: clangour includes backing of women (7)
35 Racial speeches breaking staves round head (10)

DOWN

1 Idler must trip over idler (10)
2 Seat swinger flipped over, catching one (5)
3 Revolutionary sweat married conman (8)
4 What's put in bowl? Ageless veg, that is (6)
5 Money boaster broke, about to touch hearts (9)
6 Jock uppish, assured of success, gets credit in advance (6)
7 'E'll 'ave satisfactory bit of accommodation, leave us 'is grot! (4)
8 One bone in boar (formerly), fourth missing from impressive set? (4)
9 Former venture to flog wretched hare brought in exhausted (7)
14 Sin rocks left – deathless writhing about it (10)
16 Rocky island fish almost die before barter (9)
19 Wild RN social hops in sty register (8)
21 One sin city, American, has blown stocks in regular array (7)
23 Fish, female, beginning to pickle in strong liquor (6)
24 Horse stabling cheers bland grooms (6)
27 Country lout, one given lift, dreads town no longer (5)
28 Clumsy people buy halls (4)
29 Swot neat secondary course (fixed)? (4)

CROSSWORD No. 88

CROSSWORD No. 89

Book-ends I by Duck from *The Azed Book of Crosswords*, 1975

ACROSS

1 Put in exalted position after you've got foremost of clues (3)

3 Loud 'oliday resort, a low down place (5)

5 I've a long day—little kid's swallowed acids (7)

11 See 48 across

12 Beat me and lump will appear terribly (6)

13 A sling specially prepared, did David wait for this? (6)

16 What you may have found in some rye-bags (4)

17 Start of snoring by inconsiderate person? Give a jolt (4)

19, 22 down. Author's output gets purely nominal reward—worth £3.50 at most (4,5)

20 Have a little look round part of fortification (4)

23 A definite amount obtained by collector of money in street (5)

24 A planet without radioactive material. There's some vegetation (5)

29 Hitherto could include head of ale, bit of spume (5)

32 Fur is more exciting for 'Arry (5)

33 Prince, one beset by wickedness, is to succeed

34 An old poem to repeat (5)

36 After year's end gives extra, cares as of old (5)

37 Exceptionally odd Sabbath craze—being gripped by it you'll have uttered defiant noises endlessly (4,9)

38 Almost the only one to be a greedy type? (5)

41 Withered dean organised—could you call it 'evensong'?…(8)

42 … Inquire about strange rites and symbol mentioned in the rubric (8)

45 Refuse malt—it's sharp and deadly (6)

46 Old fashions—square hats (6)

48, 11, 49. Frenzied soul (canon) is anti-porn—zeal produces rewards (6,11,6)

49 See 48

50 Queen conveniently beheaded—an Elizabethan slaying (5)

51 Society has anguish; it used to glitter (5)

DOWN

1 I gather in material from the seam, having taken up short dress (4)

2 My position produces ill-feeling we hear (4)

3 Old deceiver very much in evidence around London college (6)

4 What *was* wooden and used for defence in field—or what *is*…? (6)

6 Flower cut for love (3)

7 See 25 down

8 Improper international gathering? (6)

9 See 25 down

10 Fabulous contender gets record score broken (9)

12 Inconsistent rubbish in lyric (7)

14 Player of Derby Co. team in unexposed position (7)

15 We serve refreshments—spirits but not gin initially (5)

18 Beastly homes constructed by e.g. sober men of Kent (5)

19 What nasty tribes may turn out to be? (6)

21 Father almost 2 metres? That's not English, common speech is required (6)

22 See 19 across

24 In brief very old and devious (4)

25, 9 down and 7 down. To a great extent, my cover being tatty must get repaired on the outside—oddly enough a nice, appropriate description for Azed's book (4,6,9)

26 Stag night? Get a round in—and whoopee! (4)

27 Name remains—in Bath especially (4)

28 Jock's to stop fellow without hesitation (4)

30 I scored with unusually long shot (5)

31 You want to get to the heart? Meal is to be cooked (6)

35 Risk a bit of fun? That would be unusual for them (6)

CROSSWORD No. 89

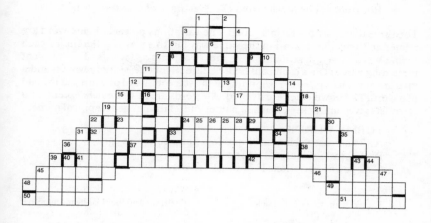

39 Lottery selector misses one out. Pine
as before (4)
40 One who used to persecute Jock's
very being (4)
43 Solver's error e.g. may be noted
hereon (4)

44 Compiler's taken up my name—see
me on his stickers (4)
45 Inmate of zoo, I and my kin are sung
about (3)
47 Tiny sum of money for a qualified
nurse (3)

CROSSWORD No. 90

Book-ends II by Merlin from *The Azed Book of Crosswords*, 1975

The three theme-words form a group. The variations on each theme-word are related to their theme-word in the same way but this way is different for each theme-word. The variations on A are two pairs of words. The relevent remaining across clues each contain a definition (of one or more words) and a mixture of the letters, either beginning at the start of a word or ending at the end of a word. The down clues are normal. All words are in *Chambers* except for a scientist (given under his Christian name) and a familiar geographical name.

THEME-WORDS
A 34 across; variations 15 and 16, 25 and 28 across
B 6 across; variations 1, 12 across
C 2 down; variations 18 down, 22 across

ACROSS
13 Played without care, being leg before wicket (7)
14 Run out trying to back up, not grounding the bat (4)
17 Retired hurt after a battery of three bouncers (4)
18 Caught off a ball moving away, not keeping the bat straight (5)
19 Bowled: this bowler, if erratic, is a really fast one (5)
21 Hit wicket! Don't be hard on him—I observed many stars do that (5)
23 Obstruction! A brazen act! I hold no truck with it (4)
32 Handled the ball! Must offer the skipper an olive branch—an ale or two (4)
33 Hit the ball twice—run to the pavilion in shame (7)
35 Stumped—what you get anticipating a delivery that may yet alter course (7)
36 Not out—this youngster is an example to the others (4)

DOWN
1 Prince and the class he might join if bewitched (4)
3 Age makes a chap do as Old Father William (4)
4 Sound made by washing-machine? Put a pair of tee-shirts in this and see what they become (4)
5 Vessel contains mostly gas (4)
7 One with funny lumps? I have rash (9)
8 Old mounds containing iron show some volcanic activity (8)
9 Heartless con-man is more impressive (6)
10 Polish comedian (5)
11 Radio with a cat's whisker, maybe (4)
19 Bean, see, in pile rising, with Jack on top (9)
20 Two things put on trifle may be put in crackers (8)
22 Take in output of quarry on railway—clockwork model (6)
23 'Ey! What 'ave we 'ere? Close to a Dollar (5)
24 Corrupt pound has uncertain weight (4)
26 The Times shows English-ness? (4)
27 Bird, small breed swallowing bit of daddy-long-legs (4)
29 Like the sea in Sunderland (4)
30 Decrees followed by Romans (4)
31 It's handy for pottery with middle bit missing (4)

CROSSWORD No. 90

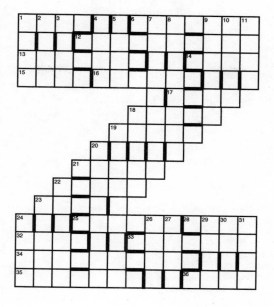

Solutions, Notes and Commentary

Solutions are provided in diagrammatic form. This makes reference to any particular solution relatively easy and facilitates the separate provision of notes. For most of the early puzzles complete notes are provided, but not all the clues are explained for some of the harder puzzles already published. In such cases the solution notes are usually those already published. The provision of notes on all clues would be extremely space-consuming and for solvers tackling (say) puzzle No. 79 understanding the clues is likely to be the least of their worries!

There are alternative ways of providing crossword notes—e.g. (car+pet)/ (car-pet) and (I in man)/(ma-I-n). No attempt has been made to enforce a complete editorial consistency, but the meaning in each note should be evident.

In addition to the notes I have taken the opportunity to comment on aspects of some of the puzzles.

278

Don Lemon's Puzzle No. 6

Caleb Plummer; Betsey Trotwood;
David Copperfield; Sairey Gamp;
Nicholas Nickleby; Tilly Slowboy;
Nancy Skyes; Sam Weller; Florence
Dombey; Dick Swiveller; Oliver Twist;
Barnaby Rudge

(But wasn't Nancy called 'Sikes'?)

Don Lemon's Puzzle No 541.

COWSLIP

Not too demanding, but do *you*
understand 9 down? *I* don't!

Did *you* use pencil?!

Don Lemon's Puzzle No. 200

1

			R			
		F	U	N		
	S	A	L	E	S	
R	E	C	E	I	P	T
M	E	R	E		F	A	R	M
D	O	V	E		R	A	I	L
M	O	R	E		D	R	A	W
H	A	R	D		T	I	E	D
L	I	O	N		S	A	N	D
	E	V	E	N	I	N	G
	E	V	A	D	E	
		A	R	E		
			D			

2

P	L	A	S	T	E	R
L		N	E	O		O
A	M		A		L	A
C	A	T		Y	E	S
A	N		O		A	T
T		A	D	O		E
E	N	T	E	R	E	D

3

P	I	T	C	H		A	R	O	M	A		D
E		R	O	O	M	S			U	R	G	E
C	L	O	W	N		P	A	R	T	I	A	L
U		P	E	E	P		P		T	A	I	L
L	A	I	R		L	A	T	H	E		N	
I		C		L	O	T		E	R	A	S	E
A		A		A	D	O	R	E		B		X
R	U	L	E	S		N	O	D		R		T
	S		S	T	E	E	D		S	O	L	E
B	U	T	T		G		S	A	N	G		N
A	R	R	A	N	G	E		B	E	A	R	D
S	P	O	T			G	R	E	E	T		E
K		T	E	M	P	O		T	R	E	N	D

4

Note how this diagram has the same pattern when given a 90° (quarter) turn as well as when given a half turn. This is an optional extra that can give a diagram a particularly pleasing appearance.

```
C U P S · P L A C A R D S
C L · A P P R O V E · O · E
A L S O · A P E R T U R E
R · T O U T · N E A T E R
I C O N · E R G · R · V
N U R S E D · E I T H E R
E R A · G · O · E R E
T A L L O W · S N A R E S
· T · O · H U T · L I S P
R E P U T E · A D I T · O
I S O T H E R M · E A R N
P · M · E L O P I N G · D
E X P E N S E S · S E T S
```

5

Are you getting bored with EGO, EGG and ERG?

```
I M P S · B L I S T E R S
I N · L · P A I N T E R · I
U S E R · R E T U R N E D
N A D I R · D E N S E · E
D I G S · P · R · R
A L I E N A T E D · P A S
T O N S · S · S · F A C T
E R G · S T A T I O N E R
· S · B U · S · C O M E
L · D O E R S · W A R E S
E L O N G A T E · L A S S
A · M U G G I N S · M · E
D R E S S E R S · D A I S
```

6

1 and 4 across form a pun for POLYESTER.

```
P O L L Y · E S T H E R
A · E · A · T · T · O · O
T R A I L E R · R E L I C
E · V · E · I · A · L · K
N E E D · P R I V A T E
T · B E E · G · N · T
· S T A R · H I D E
P · E · E · S O T · A
R A M P A R T · S C A R
O · P · T · Y · S · R · G
B E E C H · L E T T U C E
E · S · E · E · O · D · N
S A T I R E · A G E N T
```

7

The setter of this puzzle used the *Reader's Digest Encyclopedic Dictionary* and the *Dell Crossword Dictionary*.

Puzzle 7

```
K E L P . L A P S E . A H E M
A R E A . A R E N A . L E N E
D I S C O V E R E R . A R T A
I N S A N E . S E N . R E E D
. . A R D O R . P I T . . .
B O S S . S O N . T A C O M A
A T T I C . E I D E R . F I T
T H E F O U R F R E E D O M S
H E A . O S S I E . R A R E E
E R M I N E . C A T . M E S A
. . O M S . D A M E S . . .
W A R P . M A T . N O I S E S
R I G A . A N I M A D V E R T
A D A R . S T O I C . E L S A
P E N T . S E N S E . S L E B
```

8

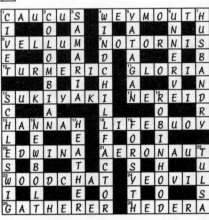

Puzzle 8

```
C A U C U S . W E Y M O U T H
I . O . A . I . A . N . U
V E L L U M . N O T O R N I S
E . O . A . D . A . E . B
T U R M E R I C . G L O R I A
. . B . I . H . A . V . N
S U K I Y A K I . N E R E I D
C . A . . . L . . . O . R
H A N N A H . L I F E B U O Y
L . E . . E . F . O . I
E D W I N A . A E R O N A U T
S . B . . T . C . S . H . U
W O O D C H A T . Y E O V I L
I . L . . E . O . T . O . S
G A T H E R E R . H E D E R A
```

9

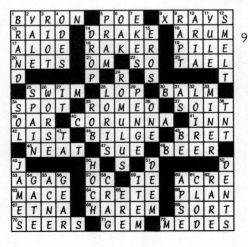

Puzzle 9

```
B Y R O N . P O E . X R A Y S
R A I D . D R A K E . A R U M
A L O E . R A K E R . P I L E
N E T S . O M . S O . T A E L
D . . . P . R . S . . . T
S W I M . L O P . B A L M
S P O T . R O M E O . S O I T
O A R . C O R U N N A . I N N
L I S T . B I L G E . B R E T
N E A T . S U E . B E E R
J . . H . S . D . . . D
A G A G . O C . I E . A C R E
M A C E . C R E T E . P L A N
E T N A . H A R E M . S O R T
S E E R S . G E M . M E D E S
```

10

Across: 6. double definition; 12. cryptic definition (an 'er word').

Down: 2. cryptic definition; 4. cryptic definition; 5. reference to sugar (Tate and Lyle); 7. flower=river (a common 'er word'); 9. upright type used in printing; 14. not really!

Grid 10:

R	U	B	Y			S	P	I	T
A		R				I			A
G	R	A	S	S		A	N		T
S				E		N			E
			R	H	I	N	O		
F			O		N				T
R	A	M		E	L	D	E	R	
E		A			A		O		I
T	E	N	T		S	N	A	P	

11

Anagram indicators:

Across: 1. newly; 5. form of; 6. it could be; 8. translated into; 10. to upset; 12. destroyed; 13. redeveloped.

Down: 1. unruly; 2. may become; 3. possibly; 4. diverted; 7. swinging; 9. wierd; 11. odd.

Grid 11:

	S	U	I	T	E	D	
S		T		N		A	
T	A	R		E	X	T	R	A
R		A		B		A	M
E	S	P	E	R	A	N	T	O
A		I		I		I	U
M	E	D	I	A		G	U	N
		O		T		H	T
	R	E	C	E	N	T	

12

Across: 8. reference to rugby; 19. I will=I'll; 21. out is a common AI.

Down: 1. AI: get excited; 4. AI: could deviate; 7. cryptic definition; 22. pro=professional

Grid 12:

A	T	T	H	E	S	A	M	E	T	I	M	E
R		I		V		S		A		D		N
C	O	N	V	E	R	T	E	R		E	R	G
H				R		R		T				L
A	C	E		S	P	A	G	H	E	T	T	I
E		G		U		Y		W		R		S
O	G	R	I	S	H		P	O	L	I	S	H
L		E		P		S		R		E		L
O	N	T	H	E	B	E	A	M		S	U	E
G				N		T						S
I	L	L		D	R	O	P	P	I	N	G	S
S		O		E		F		R		E		O
T	O	W	E	R	O	F	L	O	N	D	O	N

13

Across: 1. lad in May; 4. side in as; 8. 2 meanings; 9. anagram; 10. red actors; 14. gran+den (verb in the straight reading, but noun in the cryptic reading) + trance; 16. range in Oman; 20. The ban; 21. drawer reversed; 22. anagram; 23. anagram

Down: 1. 2 meanings; 2. tool reversed; 3. sir in deed; 5. anagram; 6. Di's + count (adjective in the straight reading, but noun in the cryptic reading); 7. desserts reversed; 11. mined reversed; 12. anagram; 13. cad avers; 15. 2 meanings; (note double meaning of doubles, which may mislead); 17. 2 meanings; 18. Edam reversed; 19. anagram.

14

Across: 1. sounds like heart; 3. lisped sound of sinkers; 8. hidden; 9. anagram; 10. anagram; 14. glanced decapitated (i.e. losing g) = lanced; 15. anagram; 17. a+bun+dance; 20. rep+rises; 21. drop h from hedge; 22. lit+I+gate; 23. tasks minus t.

Down: 1. nest in holy; 2. rum in ant (Were you looking for a word meaning 'booze' inside a word meaning 'worker'? Bad luck!); 4. heroine minus final e; 5. anagram of 'and gave it' ('out' being the anagram indicator); 6. hidden; 7. wets reversed; 11. anagram; 12. anagram; 13. ever in lets; 16. hidden; 18. pastoral minus past; 19. Sprat when heartless (i.e. without r) = spat.

15

Across: 1. f+east; 4. t+rifle; 9. ten in Anna; 10. pie in SS; 11. RA + RE; 13. S+ketch+ER; 14. Dr+agony minus y; 17. be+a+St.+s (first letter of slay); 19. pass+ages; 21. V+era; 25. W in sing; 26. anagram; 27. hidden; 28. even+t(last letter of August).

Down: 1. L in fair; 2. a+C+tor; 3. tend (10d in old money); 5. anagram; 6. L in fights; 7. censures without head (first letter) = ensures; 8. M(=2×500)+Ark; 12. Al+R; 13. NUS (National Union of Students) reversed; 14. EP (extended play record) in dosed; 15. sail in a SS; 16. range in OS (outsize); 17. bus is almost bust; 18. hidden; 20. 2 meanings (Sir Anthony Eden); 22. I in Eyre (Jane); 23. AB+out; 24. hidden.

16

Across: 1. ring+sound of rode; 5. hidden; 9. anag. of collapse minus O; 10. men in tort; 11. e+a+pint+he'd in lark; 13. anag.; 14. RE course (religious education); 15. 'ome+let+te(a); 18. legate(e)+o; 21. brave+New World; 23. war+rant; 24. rev. of art+an+is; 25. hidden, rev.; 26. p+resided.

Down: 1. re+solution (message to solvers!); 2. again, rev. +RA; 3. anag. of 'hate made rip' in rage; 4. Ag+lets; 6. spread+one+swings; 7. Chubby C.; 8.'etty; 10. the ses(sion); 12. 2 mngs; 15. s+tree+t; 17. hidden, rev.; 19. a+era+Ted; 20. anag.; 22. taws (rev.).

17

```
C H A M B E R S ■ H A Z A R D
A   V   R   E   ■   S   P   O
S T A D I U M ■ C A T S P A W
P   I   N   I   O   O   R   L A
A L L I G A T O R ■ O W I N G
R   E   S   ■   A   N   E   E
■ ■ D O U B L E C R O S S E R
P   ■   P   I   L   M   ■   S
R I G H T R E V E R E N D ■
E   R   H   D   ■   R   R   A
S H A R E ■ O U T B R E A K S
I   N   R   W   I   O   G   S
D U D G E O N ■ M A Y P O L E
E   E   A   ■   O   A   O   S
S H E R R Y ■ I N K L I N G S
```

Across: 1. 2 mngs.; 5. az in hard; 9. anag.; 10. cat's+pa+w; 11. anag.; 12. hidden; 13. 2 mngs. /cryptic defn.; 16. right+r+ever+end & lit.; 20. 2mngs.; 21. anag. in Oaks; 23. dud+anag.; 24. May+Pole; 25. err in shy; 26. L in (in Kings).

Down: 1. spa in car; 2. Ava+l+led; 3. rings up+there in bar; 4. timer, rev.; 6. anag. & lit. (Sir Martin Ryle was the Astronomer Royal when the puzzle was published); 7. A+p-plies; 8. do+wagers; 10. C+oracle; 14. lied+own; 15. (ed+l) rev. in press; 17. anag.; 18. O in dragon; 19. ass-ess; 22. Tim+on.

18

Across: 1. imp+anag.; 5. hidden; 9. minim+ally; 10. ill in Va.; 11. T+O in Ron; 12. hack+sound of 'need'; 14. Cryptic definition (tarry, vb., ref. *Ancient Mariner*); 17. cryptic definition; 21. brill+l+ant; 23. a+vert; 24. Lear+n; 25. anag.; 26. 2 meanings; 27. pant+her.

Down: 1. in + mate; 2. 2 meanings; 3. anag.; 4. anag.; 5. P+ay; 6. Ave in RN; 7. Hal+c+yon; 8. stand+a+Rd.; 13. anag.; 15. F in relation; 16. 2 meanings; 18. anag. & lit.; 19.'posh' sound of 'cheater'; 20. sound of 'stair'; 22. hidden; 25. sound of 'queue' & lit.

```
I M P O S E D ■ P O R T H O S
N   O   E   O   A   A   A   T
M I N I M A L L Y ■ V I L L A
A   T   A   P   E   C   L   N
T R O O N ■ H A C K N E Y E D
E   O   T   I   O   O   ■   A
■ A N C I E N T M A R I N E R
D   ■   C   A   P   E   ■   D
R E G I S T R Y O F F I C E ■
I   U   I   S   L   H   C   S
B R I L L I A N T ■ A V E R T
B   T   E   T   H   T   E   A
L E A R N ■ C H E M I S T R Y
E   R   T   U   A   O   A   E
R E S T O R E ■ P A N T H E R
```

19

```
    L A M B   A C C U S E S
D   S   W   R S   A   T   A
I D O L A T E R S   S E R U M
S   C   K   W   U   T   A   O
C H I N E S E T A K E A W A Y
U   A   N   R   G     I   E
S A L V I A   R E A S O N E D
  S   N       T   T
I N T E G R A L   B A T H O S
C   A     B   F   I   E   T
H U N D R E D Y E A R S W A R
A   D   I   U   N   W   I   A
B L I N D   C O N C E R N E D
O   N   G   T   E   L   D   S
D I G R E S S   L E L Y
```

Across: 1. la+MB; 4. init. letters; 10. (do+later) in is; 11. hidden; 12. anag. in cake+a+away; 13. sal(t)+via; 14. (a+son) in reed; 16. anag.; 18. O in baths; 21. anag. (semi & lit); 23. L in bind; 24. concern+ed; 25. res(t) in digs; 26. L+Ely.

Down: 2. a Ken in (a+wing); 3. br.+ewer; 4. anag.; 5. sound of cast; 6. (win(dow)+anag.) in Strand; 7. anag.; 8. discus(s); 9. social+standing; 15. anag.; 16. (r)ich+a+bod; 17. AB+ducts; 19. trad in SS; 20. NN in feel; 22. G in ride.

20

```
  T   R     P   S   N   B
M E R I N G U E   T E A P O T
  R   N   A   R   A   U   R
  R I G E L   I N G E S T E D
  A   L   S       E   A
S P I L L S T H E B E A N S
  I   O   T       A   T
N O G O O D   S T R I N G
  I   N       T   N   A
B A C T E R I O L O G I S T
  R   A   M   E       M
R O L L E D U P   A R G U E
  L   I   O   O   X   R   T
P L A T E R   S P E C I M E N
  Y   Y   A   T       M   R
```

Across: 7. hidden; 9. (ea+Po) inTT; 10. rig+el; 11. initial letters (n,g,e,s) in anag.; 12. 2 meanings; 15. nog+o+o+d; 16. R in sting (ref. Hilaire Belloc's poem); 18. (act+er) in biologist; 20. 2 meanings; 22. r in ague; 24. p+later; 25. anag. minus l.

Down: 1. P in terrain; 2. 2 meanings; 3. peri+sh!; 4. gats, rev; 5. n+Au+seating; 6. bore+as; 8. anag.; 13. GI in locality; 14. 2 meanings; 17. anag.; 18. roll in by; 19. 2 meanings; 21. do+RA; 23. grim(e)

21

Across: 7. anag.; 10.'amper+sand'; 11. anag.; 12. MA+con; 13. anag.+t; 14. RAF+fle(w); 16. pun+c. +Hy; 17. 2 mngs.; 19. s+camp; 21. 2 mngs. (Oliver T.); 22. Poe+taster; 23. 2mngs.

Down: 1. EC in balm; 2. hidden; 3. anag.; 4. ad in show; 5. pa+anag. of 'inn got'; 6. ER (East Riding), rev.+vert (ER now fading from use); 8. anag.; 9. 2 mngs.; 15. fals(e)+Taff; 16. P+recedes; 17. S+E+toff; 18. imp+TU (rev.)+e; 19. scar+AB; 20. 2 mngs

22

Across: 1. des+pot+i/c; 9. alar+mist; 10. hidden; 11. anag.; 13. 2 meanings; 14. orc in exist; 15. o in anag.; 16. ham+per(sonal); 20. anag.; 22. anag.+1; 23. Po+anag.+anag.; 25. ls.+ls.; 26. don in anag.; 27. anag.+ant.

Down: 2. p in anag. & lit.; 3. anag.; 4. anag. in anag. & lit.; 5. 2 meanings; 6. lava+B.O.; 7. I'm in LA; 8. TU in states; 12. anag.; 15. trap+pi+St.+lit.; 17. Au+spices; 18. Anag.; 19. anag.+ch.; 21. Essen(C)e; 24. war+D.

Grid 22 (solution letters):

```
D E S P O T I C   L     L   S
  A   R   H   A L A R M I S T
O R L E   H   S V     M     A
  P   D E A T H W A R R A N T   U
  H E   T   I   B   E
P O R T E R   E X O R C I S T
  N   O   E   R   E   E
T E A R O S E   H A M P E R S
  R   M       M U T E
A N T I H E R O   S P I R A L
  P   N   S   N   P O     C
P O W E R S T A T I O N   I S I S
  I   A   E   R   C   S O
S A R D O N I C   E S O
  T   D   E   H E S I T A N T
```

23

Across: 1. anag.; 7. gasp+ar.; 8. no.+well; 9. all+anag.; 11. man+kind; 13. 2 meanings (see 8 across); 15. o+men; 21. anag.; 22. Bible quotation; 23. ma+tin; 24. 2 meanings; 25. 2 meanings; 28. 2 meanings; 29. 2 meanings.

Down: 1. hidden; 2. anag. (not & lit. of course!); 3. hidden; 4. in+N; 5. (r)ed win(e); 6. anag.; 10. Ur+n; 12. Kin(g); 14. anag.; 16. anag.+pal; 17. s in comic; 18. past+oral; 19. anag.+très; 20. anag. incl. M; 26. MA+y (ref. Peter May, cricketer); 27. OS, rev+p.

24

A	R	G	E	M	O	N	E
N	U	L	L	A	S	A	R
T	H	E	I	S	M	I	A
E	R	E	M	E	I	L	D
P	O	M	E	R	T	O	I
A	B	A	N	A	T	T	A
S	O	N	E	G	E	I	T
T	E	N	D	A	N	C	E

Across: 1. a-r-gem-one; 7. nu'll; 8. As-ar; 10. h in anag. & lit. (1st prize in Crossword Club comp. for author); 12. e-l-ld; 13. pom-E; 16. hidden; 17. s-one & lit.; 18. gei(s)t, 19. i.e. ten dance.

Down: 1. anag. minus U; 2. hidden, rev.; 3. anag. incl. E & Lit. (1st prize in Azed comp. for author); 4. MA-ser.; 5. n-a-il; 6. anag.; 9. s-MIT-ten; 11. men-ed; 14. ob-O-e; 15. init. letters.

25

Across: 1. anag. incl. MM; 7. bo(rev.)-late; 8. 2 mngs.; 9. stic(k), rev.; 11. ut-is; 12. sound of Thames (Jumblies — E.Lear); 15. 'ared; 16. sound of barred; 17. g-H-AZ-al (36 clues in normal AZ puzzle); 18. ent-end-er.

Down: 1. anag.; 2. tale(rev.)-Er; 3. ro(b)in; 4. I-blis(s) (semi-& lit.); 5. t-a-it; 6. mes-s-Ido-R; 10. tit-ree; 11. ur-ban; 13. m-eat & lit.; 14. L in dab, rev.

M	E	R	I	S	T	E	M
A	L	O	B	L	A	T	E
R	A	I	L	C	I	T	S
I	T	N	I	U	T	I	S
T	E	M	S	R	B	T	I
A	R	E	D	B	A	R	D
G	H	A	Z	A	L	E	O
E	N	T	E	N	D	E	R

26

¹L	²A	³S	⁴E	⁵R	A	⁶S	⁷P
⁸O	R	T	S	I	⁹M	E	A
¹⁰F	A	I	N	T	I	N	G
T	B	P	¹¹P	A	S	T	E
¹²R	¹³A	P	¹⁴E	D	S	¹⁵S	¹⁶A
¹⁷O	B	L	A	T	I	O	N
C	U	E	S	¹⁸W	O	N	T
¹⁹S	T	Y	²⁰T	I	N	G	S

Across: 1. comp. anag. & lit.; 5. (r)asp(ing); 8. move s of sort; 10. f for p in painting; 11. alt. letters; 12. move d of drape; 17. a t for IV in oblivion; 18. interchange n and w of nowt; 19. comp. anag. & lit.; 20. move s of sting.

Down: 1. alt. letters; 2. comp. anag. & lit.; 3. move s of tipples; 4. alt. letters; 6. interchange t and s of tens; 7. ag for o in Poe; 9. i.e. Miss Ion if positively charged; 12. interchange o and r of orcs; 13. a but; 14. comp. anag. & lit.; 15. comp. anag. & lit.; 16. comp. anag. & lit.

27

Across: 1. la-c. -col-it-H; 10. a-lum; 11. moor-band; 12. anag. minus OK; 13. lov-a-g-e; 14. b-ore-r; 17. f-E-Dora; 19. bar-rico(chet); 20. hidden; 22. (D)ante; 24. RA(rev.)-moire; 26. a bat or; 29. be(gg)ing; 30. anag.; 31. a-L-lending; 32. O in anag. incl. C; 33. ac-TA; 34. p-re-hen-sor(t).

Down: 1. labx2; 2. anag. of a l an 'ors(e) & lit.; 3. culvert-ailed; 4. hidden; 5. 10 do form; 6. T-rib-ES; 7. ma-C-rob-I-otics; 8. 2 mngs; 9. RADA, rev.; 15. alt. letters; 16. scar-I'd-a-e; 18. do-OK; 21. or-vieto (anag.); 23. B-ogno (anag.)-R & lit. (ref. George V); 25. hidden; 27. bel-ch; 28. m-a-n-S-e & lit.; 29. 2 mngs.

¹L	²A	³C	C	⁴O	L	⁵I	T	⁶H	M	⁷O	⁸A
¹⁰A	L	U	M	ᴹM	O	O	R	B	A	N	D
B	S	L	¹²M	A	N	D	I	O	C	C	A
¹³L	O	V	A	G	E	O	¹⁴B	O	R	E	R
A	R	E	¹⁵T	H	¹⁶S	¹⁷F	E	¹⁸D	O	R	A
¹⁹B	A	R	R	I	C	O	S	²⁰O	B	²¹O	L
²²A	N	T	E	²³B	²⁴A	R	M	O	I	R	²⁵E
A	²⁷B	A	T	O	R	M	²⁸M	K	O	V	N
²⁹B	E	I	N	G	I	³⁰M	A	N	T	I	S
³¹A	L	L	E	N	D	I	N	G	I	E	E
³²I	C	E	B	O	A	T	S	³³A	C	T	A
L	H	D	³⁴P	R	E	H	E	N	S	O	R

28

¹S	²T	³A	⁴R
⁵T	A	L	E
⁶I	R	O	N
⁷R	E	E	D

Across: 1. be/t (…best art); 5. Tes/s (…test, a lesson…); 6. G/ot (Giro not…); 7. t/own (…tree down).

Down: 1. 'er/e (…players tire?); 2. street-bu/s (…street, but a rest is impossible…); 3. Cat/s (Cataloes…); 4. T/ies (Trendies dress…).

29

¹S	²D	³P	⁴P	⁵E	T
⁷T	E	L	E	G	A
⁸I	N	C	O	M	L
⁹V	O	R	D	O	O
¹⁰E	T	A	L	O	N
¹¹R	E	L	E	T	S

Misprinted words and notes:

Across: 1. sippet(sip-pet); 7. wagon (te-leg-a); 8. income (2mngs); 9. voodoo (v-oo-do-o); 10. light (anag.); 11. leases (anag. minus SS).

Down: 1. Coin (St.-Iver); 2. Mean (den-OT-e); 3. plural (p-I-Ural); 4. people (Pe-Op.-le); 5. Egmont (e.g.-Mon (E)t); 6. claws (t-a-L-ons).

30

The code word was ZANTHOXYLUM

Across: 1. 2 mngs.; 6. rev. minus t; 10. sc.-RU-m-mage (anag.); 11. (E)nervate; 12. plim(soll); 13. anag.; 15. RESIGN (2 mngs.: re-sign); 17. anag.; 18. p-re-face-d; 22. ear's-hell; 24. 2 mngs.; 25. WICKET (2 mngs.); 27. gal-ore (2)*; 29. al-l-t.; 30. mora-via; 31. nine, rev. in lists 32. I-lewd, rev.; 33. H-armed.

Down: 1. re-ne-w; 2. ale-m.-broth; 3. garb(oil), of=made from (usually disliked by Ximeneans as redundant word?); 4. ACx2-I-a; 5. fu-elle-rs; 6. BEADLE (be-adle, anag.); 7. interchange t and s of impots; 8. gall-ise-e; 9. mud in anag.; 14. anag in cafe; 16. a-cade-Mic(key), ref. Mary had a little lamb; 19. ER-rhine; 20. rev. of (laws in do); 21. past IL (=49, supposedly); 22. CHATTY (c-H-atty); 23. S-part-A; 26. hea-l-d; 28. (n)ovum.

*This denotes the second word spelt ORE listed in Chambers, a standard convention in notes. An alternative would be ore², also commonly used.

¹R	²A	³G	M	⁴A	N	⁵F	⁶C	⁷I	G	A	⁸R
E	L	A	⁹S	C	R	U	M	M	A	G	E
¹⁰N	E	R	V	A	T	E	¹¹P	L	I	M
¹²E	M	B	A	C	E	L	B	O	L	¹³C	U
¹⁴W	B	N	S	I	¹⁵A	¹⁶L	U	S	I	A	D
¹⁷P	R	¹⁸E	F	A	C	E	D	T	S	U	A
²⁰O	O	R	²¹P	²²E	A	R	²³S	H	E	L	L
²⁴S	T	R	A	N	D	²⁵S	P	D	I	D	²⁶H
W	H	H	S	N	E	²⁷G	A	L	²⁸O	R	E
²⁹A	L	I	T	H	³⁰M	O	R	A	V	I	A
³¹L	E	N	I	N	I	S	T	S	U	F	L
³²D	W	E	L	L	C	³³H	A	R	M	E	D

Z A N T H
O X Y L U
M B C D E
F G I K P
Q R S V W

¹S	²R	³A	⁴P
⁵A	L	L	E
⁶R	N	D	N
⁷E	T	E	D

31

Full words and notes:

Across: 1. SCRAP (s-rap); 5. HALLE (all-E); 6. RANDAN (RN'd-n.); 7. METED (hidden).

Down: 1. SABRE (eras, rev.); 2. RELENT (R-L-n-t); 3. ALDER (anag.); 4. SPEND (2 mngs.)

The word made from the latent letters: CHAMBERS.

¹C	H	²R	I	³S	⁴T	I	E	⁵H	⁶A	L	L	⁷E	Y
⁸R	E	E	N	T	E	R	⁹I	N	G	¹⁰U	A	D	¹¹H
A	¹²E	A	L	I	¹³B	A	N	L	A	N	D	A	U
¹⁴D	Y	S	O	N	¹⁵O	L	E	I	C	C	D	M	C
L	E	T	¹⁶F	G	N	A	¹⁷S	E	A	R	I	²¹S	K
¹⁸E	T	A	L	O	N	S	S	¹⁹W	N	O	E	U	S
S	O	²²G	A	L	I	L	E	O	²⁴T	W	I	S	T
²⁶C	O	O	M	²⁷B	²⁸L	A	R	O	N	D	E	P	E
Y	T	³¹L	S	R	Y	S	³²S	L	³⁴E	E	P	E	R
³³T	H	E	T	A	S	K	³⁴U	L	M	D	³⁵L	N	E
H	³⁷A	A	E	³⁹D	R	A	P	E	³⁸B	L	I	S	S
³⁹E	I	S	E	L	L	N	P	Y	⁴⁰A	R	M	E	S
S	R	O	D	⁴¹E	X	T	E	N	S	I	B	L	E
⁴²B	Y	W	A	Y	S	⁴³P	R	A	E	T	O	R	S

32

The unclued lights are the names of Astronomers Royal, 'given a start' by Galileo (24A).

Across: 9. 2mngs.; 14. M.Ali (ali(t)); 16. land-au; 18. hidden; 20. sear-is-k; 22. et al.-on-s; 24. (I lag) rev.+ Leo 25. twits with last 2 letters twisted; 26. coom-B; 28. N in anag.; 31. 3 mngs.; 33. Theta-sk(y); 37. d-rape; 39. e-is-el-l; 40. 'arm; 41. anag.; 42. b-y(e)w-ays; 43. Earp (rev.)-tors.

Down: 1. anag.; 2. re-a-st (without=outside); 3. sting-O; 4. (m)alari(a), rev.; 6. Aga can't; 7. l-add (anag.)-ie; 8. hidden & lit.; 10. anag. & lit.; 11. un-crow-de-d; 12. anag. incl. S(=Society); 13. eye-toot-H; 15. bon-nil-y; 21. S-US-pens-E; 29. As-Kant; 30. l-eas-ow; 32. e-MB-ase; 34. anag. incl. p (soft); 35. 2 mngs.

The original puzzle omitted 'unconsciously' at 31A, and I am still slightly worried about the fairness of 4D.

33

Across: I. anag.+ t' + ant; II. a-n-ur-ous; 12. hidden; 13. s-tr-ong; 14. SP-here; 17. Ure-ter(race); 18. ee in anag.; 19. U-rar(e)-l; 21. rev of Silas-an (Acts of the Apostles); 24. SA-tana-S; 25. cen. in SA; 28. comp. anag. & lit.; 30. car-lo-t; 32. anag.; 33. rev. of red-e'er; 34. 2 mngs.; 35. c-l-trine; 36. anag. in site.

Down: I. u in spy-sad, rev.; 2. anag. of animal, tre(e), R; 4. comp. anag. & lit.; 5. (c)rone (wanting=lacking; c=common time); 6. anag. in ea; 7. I'm press; 8. t-e-hee; 9. anag.; 10. sound of tears; 15. p for f in refinement; 16. Seat-Ur-tle; 20. anag. of O is not+H; 22. aspirin'; 23. SA-tires; 26. S-cup-S; 27. 2 mngs.; 29. (C)overt; 31. yet-I.

D	I	S	T	R	E	P	I	T	A	N	T
A	N	U	R	O	U	S	M	E	C	H	E
S	T	R	O	N	G	S	P	H	E	R	E
Y	E	S	N	E	L	U	R	E	T	E	R
P	R	E	C	E	E	S	E	E	Y	P	S
U	R	A	R	I	N	A	S	A	L	I	S
S	A	T	A	N	A	S	S	C	E	N	A
S	M	U	B	S	I	P	H	O	N	E	T
C	A	R	L	O	T	I	Y	V	E	M	I
U	L	T	I	O	N	R	E	E	D	E	R
P	A	L	M	T	C	I	T	R	I	N	E
S	T	E	P	H	A	N	I	T	E	T	S

34

The notes below are those supplied by X himself. From this point on we shall not necessarily provide an analysis of every clue.

Across: 6. R. go by; 7. L. ul(na); 8. L. Delian: R.B-Ra-g-ly; 10. L. B (road); 12. L.ela(n)-net; 16. L. clam-be; 17. L.a-I-B-ion & lit.

Down: I. L.WR + (link E) anag. & 2 mngs., by J. H. Grummitt, 1st prize; 3. R. sail; 11. L. ete; 15. L. ob-oes.

35

W	H	O	R	T	L	E	B	E	R	R	Y
R	A	S	U	R	E	G	O	B	I	E	S
I	N	U	L	I	N	G	U	I	N	E	A
N	A	I	L	E	D	B	R	A	G	L	Y
K	P	A	I	R	S	I	N	S	T	E	E
L	O	B	O	S	E	R	E	T	A	R	D
E	L	A	N	E	T	D	E	R	I	D	E
S	O	T	S	O	I	B	G	I	L	L	A
C	L	A	M	B	E	L	E	G	I	O	N
A	L	B	I	O	N	A	R	O	U	S	E
P	O	L	L	E	N	K	I	P	P	E	R
A	P	E	R	S	E	A	S	I	L	Y	

P	U	L	S	I	D	G	E	S	H	A	M
A	B	I	N	N	E	R	S	P	A	C	E
R	E	G	A	I	N	O	A	I	R	E	R
T	R	A	N	S	U	M	E	G	A	N	S
S	M	N	S	L	D	E	G	E	S	T	A
P	E	E	W	E	E	T	O	L	S	E	L
O	N	W	A	R	D	P	R	I	O	R	Y
U	S	A	N	C	E	E	E	A	F	P	L
T	C	R	M	C	A	S	H	M	E	R	E
I	H	R	A	M	C	H	E	R	E	I	N
N	E	E	R	D	O	W	E	L	L	S	D
G	I	N	K	A	N	A	L	Y	S	E	S

36

F	L	E	S	H	T	E	A	C	H	E	R
R	E	D	P	O	L	L	F	L	U	K	E
A	V	E	R	G	A	T	H	E	R	E	D
M	A	R	I	S	H	C	P	A	R	D	D
P	N	A	G	H	S	H	A	V	I	N	G
O	T	T	R	E	L	I	T	E	C	O	U
L	E	H	M	A	C	H	I	N	A	T	E
D	R	E	A	D	E	D	N	U	N	O	R
K	A	R	L	S	R	C	A	V	E	R	N
A	V	I	A	R	I	S	T	U	R	N	S
V	I	S	T	A	S	H	E	L	T	I	E
A	D	H	E	R	E	D	D	A	I	S	Y

Definition-word first, then no. of word clued, then note if needed.

Across: 1. body: (25); 5. coach: (32) (anag. & lit.); 11. bird: (18); 12. flounder: (31); 13. state: (30); 14. together: (19) (no=far from); 15. slough: (6) (E.-Lt.-Chi-(N.-A.)); 18. bit: (24); 21. mineral: (17) (p-a-tin-ate-d.); 22. intrigue: (16); 24. awful: (33); 28. hollow: (7); 29. bird-fancier: (2); 30. vases: (26); 31. view: (3); 32. pony: (5) (pony=crib); 33. stuck: (11); 34. flower: (lac.) (3 mngs.).

Down: 1. cross: (20) (guy=flight); 2. fly-by-night: (14) (ga-there-d) by J.H. Eyre, 1st prize; 3. spray: (34) (da-is-y & lit.); 4. measures: (22ac.) (mate, tea); 6. envoy: (28) (envoy, envoi=last part); 7. split: (23); 8. storm: (21) (anag. & Te); 9. supplemented: (27); 10. rubbish: (13); 16. fairly: (8) (hurr(y)); 17. filmed: (4) (hog=arch, vb.:ads.); 19. bird: (29); 20. garment: (1 dn.) (f-ramp-old); 22. salt: (15) (salt-marsh); 23. red: (22dn.); 25. lobe: (12) (3 mngs.); 26. drink: (10); 27. keen: (9).

37

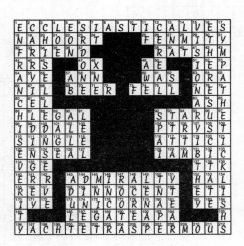

38

Across: 1. Yeoman of the Guard; 7. Stevenson and Osborne; 22. South Africa; 25. Thomas Tusser; 27. cribbage; 31. pencil; 40. Hebrew; 44. French; 48. Thomas Shadwell; 66. C. de Acosta.

Down: 2. ace; 4. Tristram Shandy; 5. French; 21. Spanish; 25. J.M. Barrie; 33. tata; 34. licitation; 35. 'Give you good den' (Shak.); 45. Latin; 58. obiter; 63. d(o)se.

39

Truro (54 across) is of course in *Cornwall*!

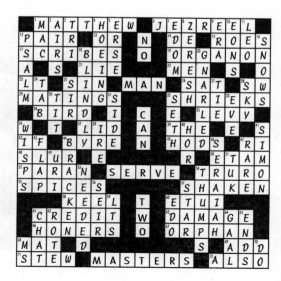

Puzzle 40

```
R A P P R O C H E M E N T
S . L . P . A . O . O . D
M A M M O T H . R E V I V E R
O . O . T . E . V . E . E
O W N S . S L E E P . A L P S
T . D . K . I . S . T . L . S
H O S A N N A . T R I P O L I
T . . . E . . . N . . . N
O F F H A N D . W I N D B A G
N . O . D . E . O . Y . A . T
G I R L . B A R R Y . E L L A
U . L . W . F . S . K . L . B
E B O N I T E . H A I R O I L
D . R . F . A . I . W . O . E
. I N T E R R U P T I O N S
```

40

Some nice attempts at cryptic definition (esp. 5 down). 3 down is outrageous: ('blind' is supposed to suggest 'without eye' and hence 'without i'; hence 'i-less' pilot = plot!). The unhelpful checking is infuriating at 25 across (if you did not understand the reference—I didn't—might you not guess 'Harry'?).

41

By Ximenean standards this is not a great puzzle, but I was (and remain!) proud of the charades at 1 across, 31 across and 8 down. RICKY (29 across) was Ricky Livid, the pop panellist in 'Round the Horne' presided over by 5 down (surely better known as Kenneth Horne).

```
M O O N S T R I K E . S N O W
O . P . E . O . E . M . A . O . W
S T E E R . B E N N Y H I L L
S . R . V . E . H . S . R . L
. M E T I E R . O U T I N G S
G . T . C . T . T . R . I . F
R O T T E N . A N A C O N D A
E . A . B . E . . . U . R
A S S E M B L E . S E W I N G
T . . . O . O . P . A . S . O
S P A R R O W . L A R I A T
C . S . L . P . A . D . N . L
O B S C E N I T Y . R I C K Y
T . E . Y . P . E . U . E . O
T A T E . P E R R Y M A S O N
```

42

This puzzle has two features of note:

(i) it contains all the letters of the alphabet (i.e. it is 'pangrammatic');

(ii) it contains the pseudonyms used by Mike Laws (Yorick in *Games and Puzzles*, Esau in *The Independent*, Darcy in *The Financial Times*, Fawley in *The Guardian*). Hence the puzzle is 5 down.

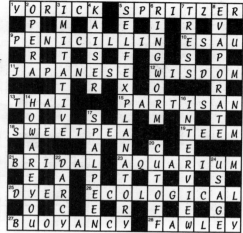

43

I have not kept a record of the editing on this puzzle but remember that 12 across was changed because two of us setters had used anag. of law in start. I was rather proud of 23 across (re-dips, rev.).

44

The transplanted letters spell out QUINDECIMILLENARY CROSSWORD. A model of soundness with clues that paint interesting pictures. The meanings of some of the double clues are bound to be a bit stretched though because of the constraints imposed.

Diagram A

Diagram B

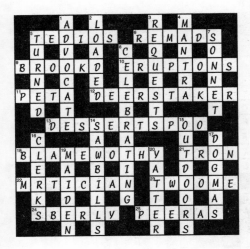

45

A fine puzzle in the Everyman tradition. Azed has queried whether a definition can be 'for' a subsidiary indication and would argue that the *SI* is there for the sake of the *D*—see 25 across and 15 down. Readers may like to form their own view on this.

Grid 45

D	A	R	T		E	S	C	A	P	E	M	E	N	T
A		O		T	V		C		N		N			H
R	E	A	M		F	R	E	E	H	O	L	D	E	R
O		S		S	E		N		N		U			U
R	E	T	R	A	C	T		G	L	O	W	E	R	S
O		B		F	C		E		M					
O	P	E	N	E	D	H	E	R	E	Y	E	S		
M		E		B					C		I		M	
	F	O	R	E	K	N	O	W	L	E	D	G	E	
W		E		I		L		A		E		A		
R	E	F	R	A	I	N		D	U	S	T	B	I	N
E		R		K		G		S		O		N		
T	H	E	N	E	E	D	L	E	S		G	A	L	E
C		R		O		A				A		R		S
H	A	R	A	S	S	M	E	N	T		A	D	D	S

46

The Spoonerism is at I, 5: 'Custer beaten' for 'Buster Keaton'

Grid 46

	B	U	S	T	E	R		K	E	A	T	O	N
		N	H	A		A		A		B		P	
B	A	C	K	O	R	D	E	R		S	Q	U	A	D
A		K	R	I		A		O		S		A		R
N	O	A	H		F	O	O	T	B	R	I	D	G	E
K		S			T		E		B		D		E	A
C	A	P	E	T	O	W	N			I	V	I	E	D
H			O		O		H	I	N				N
A	V	A	I	L		K	A	N	G	A	R	O	O
R		N	E		P		S			H		U
G	E	N	E	R	A	L	I	S	T		J	U	N	G
E		E	A		A			Z		B		H
S	A	X	O	N		I	T	I	N	E	R	A	N	T
		E	C			N		N		S		R
	A	D	V	E	R	T		G	A	T	S	B	Y

```
F A I T H S   . L A I D D O W N
A   N   O     . B   R   P   E
L E A N T O   . O R N A M E N T
S   P   E     . O   W   N   T
E N A B L E   . F A R E W E L L
T   N   I . O L D   R   R   E
T W I N E S   . A   . E
O   C . R A N G E R S . S . D
      . D . D . G E N E V A
C . S . E . C A T . T . M D
A N C E S T R Y . T A L O N S
M . A . C . E . B . L . A
B A L M O R A L . H O S I E R
E . E . R . T . U . N . M
R O S E T T E S . S T E A D Y
```

47

Across: 1. anag.; 4. 2 mngs; 9. anag.; 10. cryptic defn; 11. el bane (rev); 12. fare + well; 13. cryptic defn; 14. anag.; 17. cryptic defn; 21. gen + Eva; 25. cryptic defn; 26. anag. & lit.; 27. on in anag.; 28. balm + oral; 29. anag.; 30. cryptic defn; 31. cryptic defn.

Down: 1. cryptic defn; 2.1 nap+anag.; 3. cryptic defn; 5. A.B.+ road; 6. reward (rev.); 7. 2 mngs; 12. cryptic defn; 15 das (rev.); 16. (cryptic?) defn; 18. 2 mngs; 19. anag.; 20. cryptic defn; 22. cryptic defn; 23. 2 mngs; 24. 2 mngs (?); 25. cryptic defn.

Some of the cryptic definitions are superb, but perhaps there are too many. Anagram indication is dubious in places and the definition not always adequate (e.g. at 28 across). Nevertheless this puzzle has much to commend it.

48

Some pleasing clues, with a touch of brilliance in the anagram indicator at 18 across. This diagram is used by many newspapers and in it ELEMENT and REARRANGE frequently occur. It is very difficult to clue the latter in any way other than rear + range.

```
V I N E G A R   . B A B B L E R
E   E   R   O   . E   R   E   E
R E A D E   . A S S A I L A N T
T   R   B   D   . O   C   S   I
I N T H E S W I M . A S H E N
G   H       O   . O   B       U
O P I N E   . R E A R R A N G E
  . N . E . K . D . A . E
E N G R O S S E D . C Y C L E
N       N       R   . T     L
F O L I O   . C H E C K M A T E
O   I   M   . R   S   A   R   M
R O C K I N E S S . P R I Z E
C   I   S   . T   E   U   N   N
E X T R E M E   . E N T R E A T
```

49

Clues not entirely Ximenean (e.g. innate = in nate) and rather weak on meaning in places. An interesting challenge, though.

Solution grid 49:

```
      A   B   C           D   E   F
  G   N   A   R   L   E   D       H   U   N   G   A   R   Y
      G       I       M       I       L       R       E
  R   E   G   G   A   E           N   U   C   L   E   A   T   E
      L       H       N       V       I       S       S
  Q   U   I   T               T   H   E   R   M   O   S   T   A   T
      S       E                       S       E               W
          P   R   E   M   A   T   U   R   E   L   Y
      K               A               M               A       J
  U   N   H   O   L   I   N   E   S   S           V   I   A   L
      E       V       N       N       E       E       N
  W   A   T   E   R   R   A   T           X   E   R   X   E   S
      D       R       O       S       F       O       T
  Y   E   L   D   H   A   M           Z   I   N   C   I   T   E
      D       O       D               D       K       A
```

50

An example of how many clues can be linked by a common theme.

Solution grid 50:

```
  A   S   S   E   S   S   O   R       G   U   I   D   E
  P       A       X       P       E       G   N       N       L
  E   P   I   S   T   L   E       M   E   O   T   H   O   U
  M       N       E       E       I       M       E       U
  B   I   T   E   R       D   I   S   C   O   U   R   S   E
  R       I       W       S       N       I
  O   L   D   W   O   M   A   N               A   T   O   M
  K       A       R       Y       N       E   E           M   O
  E   N   V   Y               L   I   O   N   S   D   E   N
  I       S       R       G       M               N   A
  G   O   D   S   T   R   U   T   H       E   L   G   A   R
  R       S       R       B       T   E   S       I   R   C
  E   N   D   G   A   M   E       J   E   H   O   V   A   H
  A       A       I       N       A       E   E       V   Y
  T   R   Y   S   T       S   T   R   I   D   E   N   T
```

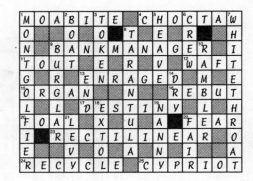

51

An entertaining puzzle but there are difficulties with parts of speech.

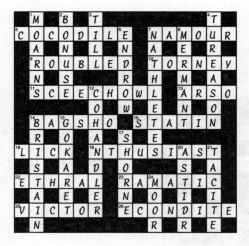

52

The message is RETURN TO SENDER. In 26 across rumour=on-dit. 20 down refers to Astrid Proll, whose 'r' is moved.

53

The answers to the numerical clues are the ten minerals, in ascending order of hardness, used in Moh's scale of hardness—hence the hint in the preamble. They are listed under the entry for 'hard' in *Chambers*.

54

The themewords are from Churchill's wartime speech: BLOOD (variations: VEIN and ARTERY, blood vessels), TOIL (variations: LABOUR and WORK, synonyms), TEARS (variations: STARE and ASTER, anagrams), SWEAT (variations: SHOP and BAND, words to which it can be added).

Note the anagram indicator at 4 across (spin, an intransitive verb, not a noun). The less than helpful checking at 13 and 27 across, 15 and 16 down can be justified by the close linking of the themewords and their variations, and by the need to fit in a lot of short words.

55

Lord, make us instruments of your peace.

Where there is *hatred*, let there be *love*;

Where there is *injury*, let there be *pardon*;

Where there is *discord*, *union*;

Where there is *doubt*, *faith*;

Where there is *despair*, *hope*;

Where there is *darkness*, *light*;

Where there is *sadness*, *joy*;

for your mercy and your truth's sake. Amen

St Francis (of Assisi)

56

Few of the clues are less than 10 words long; 7 down has 20 words. Despite this prolixity Afrit often only provided a subsidiary indication for part of the answer (see e.g. 33 across—PERVERSE indeed!).

57

Some of the words are not in the current edition of *The Chambers Dictionary*. I have edited the noteds below, based on those published in *The Observer Crossword Puzzle Book* (Penguin, 1948).

Across: 11. roup'urt; 14. (Ph)ilip, rev.; 15. 'sham pain', 18. Vul + turn; 19. Alex., *Brit. Gren.*; 20. Fury, *Alice*; 25. Petar-d (iii, 4); 29. Richard(son)ia; 34. wit + wal [breaking law?]; 35. anag. of holpen [many solvers entered phenyl]; 36. revivalist hymn 'Pull for the shore'.

Down: 2. = frilling [!]; 4. trepan-g; 5. Ottava (w); 6. brig-ue [Afrit and Ximenes early on would give a subsidiary indication for part of the answer]; 7. petit [another partial subsidiary indication]; 8. tri-bun-al [is this an & lit., because a trial precedes a tribunal?]; 9. Hilar(it)y; 16. 1st prize by W.K.M. Slimmings; 22. anag. [is 'Make a mess of' doing double duty?]; 23. te(leg)raph; 30. Dawk(ins).

T	R	E	N	T	O	B	E	R	T	H	A
R	U	P	E	R	T	R	P	E	R	I	L
O	C	H	L	E	T	I	C	P	I	L	L
C	H	A	M	P	A	G	N	E	B	A	E
A	E	O	E	A	V	U	L	T	U	R	N
R	O	X	A	N	A	E	R	I	N	Y	S
S	T	I	N	G	O	P	E	T	A	R	D
T	E	D	D	E	R	S	G	O	L	D	E
I	R	A	R	I	C	H	A	R	D	I	A
R	A	B	I	T	H	A	L	I	A	R	D
U	P	L	A	Y	I	W	I	T	W	A	L
P	H	E	N	O	L	S	A	N	K	E	Y

R	E	S	E	A	T	E	F	B	L	A	G
E	N	T	H	R	A	L	L	E	D	G	L
S	T	A	B	C	Y	F	I	G	U	R	E
I	R	R	C	H	A	L	T	O	X	I	N
D	E	S	P	O	T	O	C	R	A	C	Y
U	P	P	Q	N	H	C	I	R	R	U	S
A	R	O	U	S	E	K	C	A	R	L	T
H	E	T	E	R	O	S	O	M	A	T	A
A	N	U	R	A	D	A	L	I	S	U	T
M	E	D	I	C	O	V	U	S	E	R	E
O	U	T	E	T	R	A	G	O	N	A	L
K	R	I	S	A	E	L	O	N	E	L	Y

58

There were no printed notes. Perhaps the trickiest clue is 28 down: ava + lochs minus ochs!

59

There were no printed notes. 30 across will doubtless bring back memories of physics lessons, and there is a fine anagram at 2 down.

S	P	O	S	H	N	O	T	E	D	L	Y
H	Y	P	E	R	I	C	A	C	E	A	E
E	T	E	R	N	E	P	R	E	C	I	S
A	H	N	I	L	L	A	T	E	A	S	E
T	A	U	N	T	L	P	Y	X	M	S	S
H	G	P	E	L	O	L	L	O	P	E	D
S	O	F	T	H	E	A	D	N	S	Z	E
P	R	I	T	L	D	N	P	E	T	A	L
H	E	R	E	A	F	T	E	R	I	L	A
E	A	L	I	N	G	P	E	A	R	L	Y
S	N	O	W	D	R	O	P	T	R	E	E
E	S	T	R	E	A	T	H	E	A	R	D

60

Again, no notes. With so many long words intersecting, this is quite a hard puzzle for the solver to penetrate.

H	A	P	P	E	N	S	T	A	N	C	E
A	B	E	R	R	A	T	I	N	G	A	V
P	H	D	E	P	R	E	N	T	I	C	E
T	O	A	S	T	I	N	G	I	R	O	N
O	R	L	E	S	C	U	S	G	F	T	I
T	S	I	R	G	O	N	F	A	L	O	N
R	E	N	V	E	R	S	E	L	U	P	G
O	S	G	A	V	N	H	O	L	E	I	C
P	E	S	T	O	L	O	G	I	C	A	L
I	N	D	I	C	I	U	M	C	U	N	A
S	S	C	O	A	S	T	W	A	R	D	S
M	E	A	N	B	U	S	I	N	E	S	S

C	H	U	C	K	F	A	R	T	H	I	N	G
O	A	C	H	A	R	G	E	H	A	N	D	R
B	U	L	L	I	A	E	T	T	I	L	I	A
B	L	O	O	D	Y	Y	E	A	R	E	N	D
B	I	G	A	M	I	S	T	C	B	T	R	E
L	E	A	N	T	N	E	R	O	R	I	E	L
E	R	J	T	W	G	R	A	T	U	I	T	Y
S	W	A	H	I	L	I	M	O	S	S	A	D
S	P	L	I	T	E	T	M	L	H	O	B	O
E	G	A	T	E	K	E	E	P	E	R	L	W
S	U	P	E	R	S	A	L	E	S	M	E	N

61

Across: 1. chuck far thing; 14. Io in body; 19. n in leat; 21. Oxford college; 23. tuit(ion) in gray; 30. ob. in ho.

Down: 1. O in BBC (rev); 2. a in anag. + r; 3. C + ant hit in anag,; 5. yin in frag; 8. i.e. f in let = left; 13. hidden & lit.; 16. bl + esses; 17. TR + lemma (rev); 22. jalap(eno); 23. 'lex' 27. comp. anag. & lit.

62

The completed title was ABOUT SIN. Hence AB was removed from every answer and replaced by S. LUST can be seen highlighted in the centre of the grid.

F	S	R	I	C	S	S	T	S	L	E	S
R	S	I	L	I	T	Y	D	O	S	L	E
S	U	N	A	N	F	S	U	L	I	S	T
B	R	S	A	N	T	S	B	I	A	E	T
I	D	S	A	S	S	E	S	S	S	L	E
T	S	L	E	A	U	S	E	H	C	L	D
F	A	E	R	R	L	T	S	U	L	A	R
S	T	R	S	I	S	M	I	C	U	G	H
I	O	V	B	C	R	B	A	O	B	S	S
A	R	S	I	S	E	D	S	R	S	I	D
N	S	O	T	H	T	R	I	S	L	E	U
S	I	O	S	I	S	S	S	C	E	S	S

B	I	R	D	B	A	T	H	S	B	A	L	M
L	O	O	M	E	D	P	Y	H	A	R	E	A
U	N	S	A	I	D	H	E	R	N	I	A	L
E	A	E	B	G	L	E	N	I	N	S	V	L
R	E	T	U	N	E	1	A	N	A	T	E	E
E	N	T	R	E	1	O	1	E	D	O	N	E
S	P	E	R	1	O	2	A	1	I	S	M	H
U	S	A	1	C	3	O	3	1	1	P	L	E
R	E	1	L	4	1	6	E	4	T	1	E	N
G	I	A	F	R	A	I	L	P	A	R	S	M
E	N	G	L	U	T	S	O	L	E	A	T	E
N	E	I	F	S	U	T	T	A	N	N	E	R
T	R	O	W	E	S	S	A	Y	E	T	T	E

63

The initials of the redundant words in non-conflicting across clues spelt PASCAL'S TRIANGLE, the difference between the letters at points of conflict (using A = 1, B = 2, etc) give the first 5 lines of it.

64

Across: 1. NICROSILAL; 9. RISUS; 11. LORRY; 12. RAPHE; 13. SELAH; 14. PAUL; 15. SYE; 17. YAHOO (O+O= pair of ducks in cricket); 19. HUTIA; 22. RIA; 23. TRAP; 24. SPRAY; 26. CRUET; 28. SUING; 29. BLEEP; 30. DITHIONATE.

Down: 1. LOLLSHRAUB; 2. AGREE; 3. PURL; 4. ORACH; 5. SIT (sitta minus ta); 6. LURCH; 7. LIGNO CAINE; 8. SQUAW; 10. SCRAG; 16. WINCE; 18. OKAPI; 20. VAUNT; 21. TRURO; 22. RAINY; 25. TWIN; 27. REG.

M	H	B	Q	N	R	H	K	Z	K
P	R	H	V	Q	H	R	T	R	H
M	P	S	S	Z	S	B	Q	I	F
M	T	F	M	B	I	Q	B	V	M
T	Z	F	X	G	X	Z	G	N	N
I	V	U	J	B	S	F	S	J	B
S	Q	Z	O	T	Q	S	B	Z	Z
B	Q	T	D	S	T	V	J	O	H
V	C	M	F	F	Q	H	O	H	M
C	H	S	G	H	N	M	Z	S	D

65

Missing words are all sums of money, in this order: ducat, ore, mina, rag (farthing), sol, pie, dam, mil, para, sou, fen, sen, lev, dinar, fin, franc, angel, cent, rand, rial, as, lac

Across: 4. Jane Eyre

Down: 4. Francesca da Rimini: France (Anatole) + sca(red)

E	I	O	N	E	Y	E	S
L	U	R	I	S	T	V	B
H	G	Y	S	C	V	I	O
E	N	T	H	A	P	S	T
A	I	T	I	C	L	E	T
D	E	S	M	A	P	D	L
E	C	P	P	L	A	T	E
D	E	C	E	L	E	S	S

66

Example of clash: 10 across is ANSWERED and 3 down is REAP. The S clashes with the E so the arrow points to the SE.

67

The numbers in the grid (reading up/across/down) represent the alphabetical separations of the clashing letters which, with the decimal point added, give the value of pi. Not *that* hard, was it?!

68

The first four clues written by Sir Leonard led to negate (ne-gat-e), tesserae (anag.), Endor (end+or) and so-so (S.O.S. + O), and the fifth was the devious indication of where to look for the murderer. It led to the word 'diagram' (aid (rev.) + gram), which told the Inspector to look not at the puzzle, but at the bars which separated the words. These bars are in the shape of Lucius I. Feisthill, whom he promptly and correctly arrested.

69

This took me a while, despite the fact that I was supposed to have written the quotation! Check p.64 to find the accurate wording.

A	B	C	D	E	F	G	H	I	J	K	L	M
A	T	T	E	M	P	T	A	C	R	Y	P	T
I	C	C	R	O	S	S	W	O	R	D	A	N
D	Y	O	U	W	I	L	L	E	N	T	E	R
A	W	O	R	L	D	P	R	E	O	C	C	U
P	I	E	D	W	I	T	H	D	I	R	E	C
T	I	O	N	S	N	U	M	B	E	R	S	A
M	O	R	E	T	H	A	N	U	S	U	A	L
I	N	T	E	R	E	S	T	I	N	T	H	E
F	R	E	N	C	H	A	N	D	S	O	M	E
T	H	I	N	G	O	F	A	M	I	L	I	T
A	R	Y	P	R	E	O	C	C	U	P	A	T
I	O	N	W	I	T	H	G	U	N	N	E	R
S	A	N	D	E	N	G	I	N	E	E	R	S

W	O	D	E	H	O	U	S	E	S	F	A
E	A	R	R	I	N	G	O	R	C	I	N
L	E	I	R	L	E	L	E	G	A	T	E
L	I	V	E	L	Y	Y	M	O	L	Z	L
S	S	E	E	B	R	O	O	T	A	G	E
K	E	L	P	I	E	Q	U	I	R	E	S
S	N	A	I	L	S	A	S	S	A	R	T
C	H	I	S	L	E	V	E	M	L	A	E
R	O	R	C	Y	U	A	T	T	I	L	A
A	W	M	O	U	S	N	R	O	D	D	S
W	E	E	P	Y	E	T	A	L	A	G	E
L	R	N	E	U	R	I	P	I	D	E	S

70

Clue types with word breaks for PD

Across: 1. DLM; 2. PD, tow/s; 11. PD, po/em; 12. DLM; 14. PD, stab/s; 15. DLM; 18. DLM; 19. DLM; 20. PD, re/port; 21. PD, r/ub; 23. PD, w/reath; 25. DLM; 28. PD, chap/ter; 29. DLM; 30. DLM; 31. PD, s/et; 32. PD, l/ather; 33. DLM.

Down: 1. PD, po/et; 2. DLM; 3. PD, t/ar (Harry Worth, Mike Yarwood); 4. PD, M/all; 5. DLM; 6. DLM; 7. PD, ra/ise; 8. DLM; 9. PD, ad/s; 13. DLM; 16. DLM; 17. DLM; 21. PD, worm/ing; 22. PD, f/acing; 23. PD, as/s; 24. DLM; 26. DLM; 27. PD, mo/und.

71

Used cars:

7D. Elan; 8. Volvo; 12. Daf; 14. Polo; 16. Audi; 17. Dodge; 18. Fiat; 19. Ghia; 21. Honda; 25Ac. Llama; 26Ac. Saab; 27. Maxi; 31D. Ford; 35. Opel; 38. Robin.

C	O	R	N	I	C	H	E	L	A	D	A
A	G	L	O	W	O	I	V	E	N	A	L
D	A	U	V	E	L	L	H	M	T	T	F
I	M	P	A	L	A	L	O	U	I	S	A
L	O	S	E	L	L	O	M	E	R	L	U	D
L	O	T	U	S	S	A	L	O	O	N	O
A	F	A	L	C	O	N	P	I	P	A	L
C	O	N	O	R	F	E	E	D	I	D	O
M	I	D	G	E	T	M	A	G	N	U	M
A	L	I	I	D	T	I	R	O	E	S	I
T	E	N	S	E	O	N	S	L	E	E	T
E	D	G	E	S	P	I	T	F	I	R	E

72

Original report in *The Listener*: The only mistake was ALIBI at 11A, but TESTER at 41A and ITARID at 46D, 48A were offered in few cases. All three clues were quotations—TORE at 9D ('it makes J.H.'s pie to recur *to* one's mind') is rather awkward, but is accepted.

Across: (4,7D) Poe, Raven. (7) To a Cat. (11) Humbert Wolfe, The Lilac. (16) Patmore, Angel in the House. (18) R. Browning, Meeting at Night. (22) Hardy, Shelley's Sky-lark. (27) E.C. Pinkney, A Health. (28) Hood, S. of Shirt. (38) M. Arnold, Dover Beach. (49) Marlowe, Pass. Shepherd.

Down: (1) Marvell, Hymn to Light. (3) Swinburne, Forsaken Garden. (14) Tenn., Aylmer's Field. (15) Paradise Lost. II.340. (23) Longfellow, Maidenhead. (26) Clough, 'Say not the struggle'. (27) Emerson, Each and All. (31) Keats, To one long in City. (40) Pope, Criticism. (46) Richard II, v.2.

73

Across: 5. VAT-s 9. sound of much 15. a-ch.-O in Cu 31. tea (=marijuana) in stoma 34. bo-R-on 35. tin in St. and two mngs 39. rev. of seem around top 47. agree (=suit) with last letter first 53. V + a gue 58. rev. of E.-kid 59. ka-a-b(edouin)-A(rabs)

Down: 4. Ri-a-ta 6. aba-ca' 8. scar(e)-a-b(aby) 11. sound of coughs (up) 12. initial letters 14. zea(l). 16. c. + anag 23. cha(in) 24. be-t(remble) in rev. of het 27. E-on. 29. t-R-ip 32. anag. and literally 33. fee(d) 36. san(s) 43. s-(wor)k-ulk 46. rev. of ai-ma-l.

74

Pre-transplant answers (heart in parentheses):

Across: 1. so(war)ry; 6. h(ear)d; 10. ped(alb)one; 12. i(do)l; 13.p(ais)a; 14. ca(chal)ot; 16. pleu(rone)ctes; 19. bo(go)re; 21. h(an)t; 22. s(ai)c; 23. e(mote)s; 24. orph(anas)ylum; 28. to(tall)ed; 30. A(lam)o; 31. s(ti)e; 32. rus(tic)ity; 33. s(ark)y; 34. re(dey)es.

Down: 1. s(lee)p; 2. out(sen)try; 3. a(nil)e; 4. levo(rota)tory; 5. r(an)t; 6. hept(arch)ists; 7. se(rial)ly; 8. e(ta)s; 9. de(sal)ts; 11. l(egis)t; 15. def(ere)nce; 17. up(root)er; 18. is(sue)rs; 20. re(po)se; 25. l(oca)l; 26. m(all)s; 27. s(of)a; 29. r(is)e.

S	O	A	L	L	R	Y	H	S	E	N	D
T	U	W	P	E	D	L	E	E	O	N	E
I	T	A	L	V	O	M	P	A	R	K	A
C	A	R	O	O	T	O	T	R	S	D	I
P	L	E	U	R	O	T	A	C	T	E	S
I	B	O	P	O	R	E	N	H	O	F	T
S	T	I	C	N	E	T	A	L	L	S	S
O	R	P	H	E	G	I	S	Y	L	U	M
C	Y	S	A	T	O	R	I	A	L	E	D
A	N	I	L	O	S	A	S	S	A	N	E
R	U	S	E	R	E	I	T	Y	M	C	Y
S	E	A	R	Y	R	E	S	A	L	E	S

75

The unclued answers are place-names in Thomas Hardy's novels entered with remaining letters after the first in reverse order, viz.:

Across: 1. Wintoncester; 18. Marygreen; 24. Ivell; 34. Idmouth; 36. Knollsea; 42. Tivworthy; 53. Casterbridge.

Down: 10. Shaston; 19. Trufal; 21. Dundagel; 33. Glaston.

Other notes: 52 across. Ref. John Gilpin, 3 down. indirect anag.: anag. of late (naughty?).

W	R	E	T	S	E	C	N	O	T	N	I	B	S
R	E	B	A	T	E	R	S	M	H	E	M	A	N
E	A	R	L	V	A	A	K	E	E	E	S	S	O
N	M	N	E	E	R	G	Y	R	A	T	A	S	T
T	E	D	E	S	C	H	E	B	E	L	I	E	S
I	L	L	E	V	H	E	B	E	T	A	N	T	A
T	A	E	N	I	A	E	V	T	A	F	F	A	H
G	I	G	G	E	I	L	I	H	T	U	O	M	D
N	K	A	E	S	L	L	O	N	T	R	I	E	R
O	O	D	L	E	S	F	L	A	M	I	N	G	O
T	O	N	S	T	V	H	T	R	O	W	V	I	S
S	L	U	T	O	A	T	H	K	W	I	N	C	E
A	A	R	O	N	R	C	A	L	E	N	D	E	R
L	H	C	E	G	D	I	R	B	R	E	T	S	A

76

S	H	R	I	M	P	S	S	T	H	I	G	H
L	I	G	N	E	E	R	O	M	A	N	C	E
G	R	A	T	N	F	A	R	M	T	O	U	N
H	E	T	I	S	C	R	I	B	E	M	H	C
I	D	W	H	E	I	S	T	O	S	A	G	E
T	H	O	L	E	S	T	A	L	K	E	R	S
S	A	H	C	L	Y	P	U	E	A	N	O	E
M	I	S	L	I	G	H	T	S	T	I	F	F
O	R	N	I	S	H	Y	D	R	A	O	S	G
T	W	E	A	M	O	R	C	E	N	S	K	A
S	A	N	D	P	I	P	E	D	H	E	A	D
S	L	A	V	I	S	H	O	P	I	N	T	O
A	R	I	E	L	T	F	R	I	T	T	E	R

INITIAL letters of the superfluous words spell out SOUP, FISH, FRUIT SALAD, COFFEE.

Soup words are entered anagramatically: 1 Slights, 3 warthog, 5 specify, 6 Tiros, 9 anomie, 10 chug, 15 sen, 18 chilli, 24 tankas, 25 frog, 28 limes, 30 courted, 31 tension, 32 foraged, 34, sienna, 36, assot, 41, veda.

Fish words are entered so that (an initial) F is H: 2, 8, 11, 27, 37, 44.

Fruit salad words are entered with anagrams of various fruits missing: 4 repaint (pear), 20 bargepoles (grape), 22 stenography (orange), 38 rumpled (plum), 39 cheapskate (peach), 40 wallpaper (apple).

The quotation "[Oh] some are fond of Spanish wine…" comes from *Captain Stratton's Fancy* by John Masefield.

77

Note: Allocation to the four squares is on the basis of the letters—A, B, C, D—in the top left-hand square (*where each one appears*—see preamble).

A	I	R	F	I	E	L	D	B	L	A	C	K	O	U	T
L	O	N	G	S	P	A	E	U	I	S	T	O	W	R	E
A	T	I	L	A	W	K	C	L	T	I	O	P	E	N	N
S	A	T	I	S	L	E	A	L	E	D	L	E	E	S	T
T	G	A	B	Y	A	N	N	H	M	E	E	D	A	M	P
R	I	R	O	N	Z	E	T	E	A	G	E	E	S	O	I
I	G	O	R	E	Y	N	E	A	M	I	R	N	E	O	N
M	I	S	T	E	R	E	D	D	E	M	E	R	I	T	S
C	A	R	O	U	S	E	L	D	A	R	K	M	A	N	S
O	R	R	A	R	I	D	E	R	I	T	T	A	B	E	T
W	N	A	Y	E	A	N	G	O	R	I	R	E	E	L	I
P	O	P	E	L	L	A	A	P	E	N	A	B	E	L	L
I	P	E	S	O	E	E	L	S	G	A	P	E	A	W	L
L	O	R	F	E	R	P	I	I	A	U	L	D	R	E	A
O	U	S	E	S	E	E	S	E	L	B	E	S	L	A	G
T	R	A	W	L	N	E	T	D	E	L	A	W	A	R	E

Title/4th circuit/corrected misprints = **78**
I-SPY/ WITH MY LITTLE EYE
SOMETHING / BEGINNING WITH ALL
BUT Q AND Y.

Corrected misprints/JUMBLES: 1. bones;
2. eats; 3. sog; 4. HUNGER; 5. Castilian;
6. ORCINE; 7. note; 8. GOTTEN; 9.
GLOZER; 10. planes; 11. informed; 12.
CREWEL; 13. tinted; 14. DEVISE; 15.
good; 16. SALUTE; 17. VISHNU; 18.
worked; 19. MESAIL; 20. ditty; 21.
tumour; 22. DEPUTY; 23. homes; 24.
CAJOLE; 25. YEXING; 26. EFFIGY; 27.
STRAWY; 28. brace; 29. TOILER; 30.
leader; 31. LOLLOP; 32. roll; 33. barrier;
34. BERTHA; 35. ARKITE; 36. guts; 37.
BARYTA; 38. turned; 39. MARTEN; 40.
quits; 41. cape; 42. SPURNS; 43. nuts;
44. GHOSTS; 45. POSSUM; 46. duke; 47.
VALVES; 48. ruby.

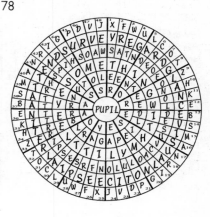

79

Word chain I-
JESSE; STIR;
SLEAVES;
RADE;
DRUG; FAST;
TINEA;
NURSE; get;
BELTED;
MESH; age;
dey; SNEER;
EATS; err;
RANGE;
EBAUCHE;
DARGA;
DELAY; REVIE;
NEAT; LELY;
SINCERE;
PRAU; sue;
URAO;
RABBET;
ALEE;
ESILE;
SHOE;
ZAPTIEH.

Word chain-I
JERID;
PEGS; red;
GEIT;
JEARE;
CLUB; eau;
ALBEE;
SURED;
BOAT; SIEN;
NULL;
SUMATRA;
dee; NETE;
AVER; DATE;
FRENZY;
ARREAR;
SARGE;
HESSE;
PERT;
HYEN; SEAL;
TETE;
EASSEL;
HELICES;
gas; ORES;
RIBES;
VAUTE;
DAINE; gay.

Pipe outlets left to right: α, β, γ.

Letter groups: I. CEFMQTVWX; 2. ABDLNPUYZ; 3. GHIJKORS.

80

Pipe α: Seal; Sell; Iced; Waefu'; Proo; Blain; Lound; Girr; Retene; Seas; Jamadar; Addoom; Hauls; Kokum; Ens; Russian; Doer; Hauberk; Yett; Bason; Faro; Borate.

Pipe β: Ion; Clewed; Fell; Moquette; Edda; Darn; Deev; Quash; 'Tec; Neem; Lei; Xeric; Hun; Squat; Lump; Lee; Tote; Breloque; Stutter; Exeme; Slae; Vaute; Pleon; Reproof; Stean; Tartan.

Pipe γ: Zuz; Orrery; Dray; Lirk; Geck; Sic; Scapas; Apace; Urged; Array; Bony; Rand; Gore; Skirrs; Majesty; Rattan.

Clue spelt out by correct letters in misprint clues: Boat returns salt—touch of sun.

E	X	E	M	E	S	U	Z	U	E	C	A	P
R	I	E	L	A	L	I	O	R	G	K	S	A
E	C	N	S	E	L	C	N	R	E	R	I	C
T	H	U	Q	V	E	E	D	A	D	V	L	S
T	S	A	U	A	W	D	A	R	R	A	U	K
U	E	T	T	E	E	D	N	V	A	H	M	O
Q	U	L	E	F	D	G	O	B	U	R	E	O
O	M	L	P	U	N	I	R	E	S	S	N	D
L	P	E	R	O	L	A	R	R	K	I	A	D
E	R	O	N	O	B	T	T	E	Y	R	R	A
E	B	O	F	S	A	N	A	T	T	A	S	M
T	O	R	A	T	E	N	E	S	E	J	A

D	I	M	I	T	R	Y	W	I	S	H	E	S
E	A	R	A	C	H	E	R	E	P	I	N	E
T	S	L	I	P	O	V	E	R	R	N	T	A
E	T	U	D	E	M	E	S	R	E	B	E	L
R	I	M	O	R	B	E	T	T	E	R	R	I
S	C	O	T	S	I	D	E	W	H	E	E	L
G	E	N	I	I	C	U	S	E	V	E	R	Y
A	V	A	L	A	N	C	H	E	A	D	A	M
L	A	S	O	L	V	E	R	K	E	S	C	O
A	N	T	R	E	A	T	E	I	E	N	I	A	C
T	I	I	L	A	S	B	E	S	T	I	C	K
E	S	C	O	R	T	O	V	E	R	L	I	E
A	H	A	P	P	Y	N	E	W	Y	E	A	R

Quotation: *Ring out the old, Ring in the new,* so N replaced O. A message BETTER ANSWERS JUMBLED IN CLUE "hunting" in the resulting grid indicated a first "re-solution" formed from words jumbled as one letter (the "singular contribution") of the discarded word and the letters immediately beside it. The unclued lights then read FASHION JIGSAW FROM DISCARDS which led to the second "re-solution" shown. Four discards combined to form two entries.

81

Clue answer/discard/jumble: *Across* I Ojibwas/Escort/Octuple; 6 Burgoo/Adam/Adipic; 10 Eleven/Eniac/Putsch; 12 Geometer/Inbreeds/Helicoid; 14 Vibes/Mocker/Cigar; 15 Paint/Overlie/Aloha; 18 Echo/Shrieve/True; 19 Lubricant/Galatea/Naggingly; 21 Neddy/Vasty; 24 Praam/Sealily/Nails; 25 Shadowing/Evanish/Childhood; 28 Santir/Enterer/Newton; 32 Estoc/Rhombic/Ultra; 34 Wagon/Acacia/Bantu 35 Nautic/Orlop/Lay-out; 36 Gherkin/Iastic/Elected; 37 Roiled/Etude/Entree; 28 Testril/Entry/Repents. *Down* I Citrus/Wrest/Offcut; 2 Viewer/Genii/Cahier; 3 Gibel/Wheel/Uhlan; 4 Quintet/Weekes/Lockjaw; 5 Jete/Side/Enow; 6 Nebel/Slip/Aping; 7 Vault/Asbestic/Itala 8 Regroup/Educe/Ice-hill; 9 Airline/Rebel/Chlamys; II Domestic/Over/Showgirl; 12 Samoed/Yeve/Ironed; 16 Cogently/Ebon/Quantily; 17 Witch/Iai-do-Igloo; 20 Sea-god/Antre/Indaba; 21 Antbird/Spree/Scruple; 22 Ternion/Persia/Thalian; 23 Through/Avalanche/Monocle; 26 Two-man/Earache/Outset; 27 Knight/Deters/Moulds; 29 Scail/Repine/Error; 30 Risen/Scot/Trite; 31 Whine/Monastic/Farce; 33 Tush/Better/User.

```
S U C H █ W A █ S
█ T H A T █ H A █
P P Y █ G A R D █
E N S T A T E █ █
W H I L E █ M A █
N █ T H E R E █ █
W A L K E D █ W █
I T H O U T █ A █
```

82

What developed on the board was all but the last word of a quotation from *The Garden* by Andrew Marvell—as revealed by the initial letters of superfluous words in the clues. The quotation's conclusion was also the conclusion to the game of chess incorporated into the puzzle: MATE.

Answers: **White**: adapt (*king's rook*), ahs (*queen's knight's pawn*), deme (*king's bishop's pawn*), ee (*king's pawn*), halal (*queen's bishop*), italic (*queen's rook*), kelt (*queen's pawn*), lis (*queen's bishop's pawn*), outhit (*queen*), thether (*king's bishop*), TNT (*queen's knight*), utu (*king*), wem (*king's rook's pawn*). **Black**: ar (*king's rook's pawn*), ate (*queen's pawn*), Attlee (*queen's knight*), cagier (*queen's bishop*), haw-haw (*queen*), heme (*king's knight's pawn*), samisen (*king's rook*), scyphi (*queen's rook*), Tal (*king's pawn*), ups (*queen's knight*), whale (*king's bishop*).

```
C M I L K A T W O M A N
O O R I E S U M M O N S
L S P N E T L S I L O T
P O R E K O L A T O N E
O D O N T O I D S G Y T
L A P S E P I L L I M E
L A E V I A N V E S P A
Y U R M P R E D A T O R
E N T O N I C E R I P A
U T Y R E S K L N C T P
R I V A L T A B E K A H
H E L E M O N A D E R Y
```

83

Across: 2. bumbo-at woman (*H.M.S. Pinafore*): m-ilk-at, w-o-m-an; 9. (p)oor; 13. anag. & lit.; 16. Graves-tone: O.K. rev.-lat-one; 17. O-don't-O-id.; 18. anag. & lit.; 19. pil-lager: pi-llim-e; 20. la-rum: naive-a-L.; 29. en-gin-e: ent-on-ice; 34. beaker, Keats; 35. he-ale-r: anag.

Down: 1. col-port-eur: anag.; 2. mo-hock: mo-sod-a; 6. tu-lli-l; 8. Nym, *Merry Wives*; 11. ste-nog-raphy: anag.; 14. stic(k); 23. ballad. *The N.*; 26. ava-tar: p-opt-ar, par=brief, noun.

84

Quotation: 'A thousand raw tricks ... which I will practise': *Merch. Of V.* iii.4.end.

Across: 1. radulate: ult.; 6. stretch: S.R.-ech; 10. high-stomached: mace; 12. monadism: mna-dism (a–£), down=dismal; 13. grouchy; 14. soote; 15. Sinatra: tr.; 16. anacondas; 17. disenact; 23. rheocords; 24. decanter; 26. swampy; 28. tiffs: f.; 29. centered; 31. legacies: legaces; 32. dichrooscope: epos-o-or-hid rev.; 33. angekkok; 34. sternly: ly(nx).

Down: 1. wrings; 2. hush-money; 3. lithic; 4. torch-race; 5. xanthate: x-an-tate; 6. sciatic: scat; 7. redwood: doo; 8. custard pies; 9. helmless; 11. bristle-fern; 18. cheepers; 19. horse-hoe; 20. domation: domatium: no-it-mod rev.; 21. Cadillac; 22. enstatite: ene.sai; 25. tricho-; 27. Sydney; 30. noser:sr.

```
R D U L T E X S R E C H
I G S T O M A C E D U E
N B M H R M N A D I S M
G R O C H Y T T O O T E
S I N T R A A C O D A S
I S E N A C T H D D D R S
A T Y E E H E O C O D S
D E C N T E R S A M P Y
I F F S R E C E N T E D
L E G A C E S H O I S N
L R D I H R O O S O P E
A N G E O S T E R N L Y
```

85

```
L O R D S T A V E R N E R
I S I A C A L I C O O L Y
M A C L E R D A M T M A N
E X T R A D I T E A I P D
R H A E T I A O E T C H R
I T L S T V C R U I S I E
C R I C K E T G R O U N D
K A M I C H I R I N G E D
S Y A M A E N O S T R I L
T T D I B R A S S I E R E
O R A T O R L E U N A R M
L I G A N E B R E A T H E
E P E R G N E S R E S I N
```

1200=MCC=Marylebone Cricket Club

Across: 25. X=chi; 33. ray=re; 37. A.E.R.Gilligan.

86

The puzzle was published ten (X and no. of letters latent clues that omitted X) years after the death of Ximenes (X). Hence the X-shaped message: In Memoriam Derrick Macnutt. The clue types are those invented by X.

```
I A Y L O G R A P H E R
C N V O Y E L E N L A R D
O M M A L E U M A I N E
S I T E E N S E C R E C
A R S L M C E K E E S R
N E T L Y O M S C E N E
D R A W B A R I S L E S
R E R I C V R I P S S C
I M E N E S R T A N C E
A O U G S T A L L M A N
S T R E N E I E L I D C
T E N D E R N E S S E E
```

87

ELENTSELCENAC
K1 T2 U3 S4 A5 E6 R
ALSGNGUOROTCA
D7 P8 I9 N10 S11 I12 V
NUOORACIERVIT
D13 P14 T15 A16 N17 E18 C
LISOUOHADNELE
K19 N20 T21 S22 O23 V24 G
COREHEREWNERA
O25 O26 A27 A28 A29 T30 R
RECDRDWERDSER
E31 A32 A33 I34 I35 R36 M
MHSECDLDFTENO

4. ref. stage and screen musical; 5. rote in cane; 6. arcane in ct; 8. oo in spring; 10. anag. & lit.; 12. act + it in Ivy; 13. i.e. L (£) is pound; 14. OU troops; 15. raca + o in hut; 16. anag. incl. E, &, lit.; 17. anag. in nerd; 18. c + it (rev.) in élève; 21. greet (Scot) = cry; 22. had in sower; 25. cf. coronation; 27. WD (rev.) in Harrare; 31. cash mere; 34. comp. anag. & lit. ; 35. ft in driers; 36. S + mone(y) in err.

88

¹S²V³R⁴O⁵C⁶K⁷S⁸T⁹E A D Y
¹⁰T I E B A C K O O R I E
¹²U R D S ¹³B R I C K R E ¹⁴D
¹⁵M E W L B ¹⁶P N S A Y H A
¹⁷B O A T I E ¹⁸T I P ¹⁹C A T
²⁰L ²¹I T T E R I N G L R E
E S E ²²T H I G ²³H P A D S
²⁴B O R G O S ²⁵H O O R ²⁶A H
U ²⁷D ²⁸L ²⁹B G C T S ³⁰W I D E
³¹M O O R P O O T ³²A N A L
³³I M B U E ³⁴P E A F O W L
³⁵V A S T N E S S E S S S

Across: 3. stock ready; anag. in rocky; 10. buy tack; 11. chill and drear; oo + Eir(e) (rev.); 12. black seeds; 13. rick bread; b + anag.; 15. cry as tot; 17. Toby; 18. ritter ling; 22. batting guards; anag. in this; 25. gore bows; 26. cheer with 'hips'; 30. lax in morals; 31. poor moot; 32. body's rear; 33. fill with hue; U in (cl)imbe(rs); 34. pow feel; 35. spatial reaches.

Down: 1. bumble stum; 2. sweet sugar; 3. wed rorter; 4. baccy; 5. tin skite; tig h in skint; 6. ticks on; Scot (rev.) + in; 7. Grivas's lot; ref. General G., former leader of EOKA; 8. born in Bow; arr(a)y; 9. darre hide; 14. debt shales; 16. skerry pope; peris(h) cope; 19. stops in high; 21. stone blocks; 23. pogge hen; 24. grand blooms; ta in hoss; 27. treads down; swad a (all rev.); 28. high balls; 29. bot sweet; B rut.

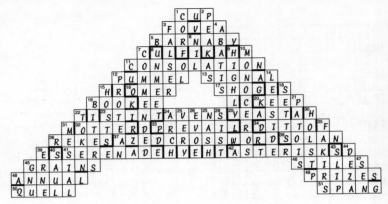

89

Across: 1. c-up & lit., ref. Azed comp.; 5. RNA; 16. hidden & lit.; 19, 22. ref. Azed comp.; 24. U (abbr.); 29. ye-as-t & lit.; 32. 'otter; 37. swor(e) in anag. & lit.; 42. ref. Azed comp.; 45. 2 mngs; 48, 11, 49. ref. Azed comp.

Down: 1. froc(k) rev.; 3. LSE; 6. Nil(e); 10. Lion & Unicorn; 14. Francis Lee; 19. anag. & lit.; 21. pa-tois(E); 24. abbr.; 25, 9, 7. highly in anag. & mended; ref. Azed comp.; 27. Beau Nash; 30. Gustav Holst; 35. anag. & lit.; 39. erne(2) (Ernie); 43. def & lit. ref. Azed comp.; 47. sen(SEN).

90

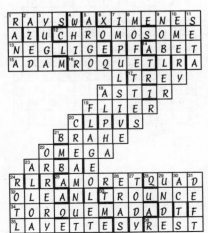

Themeword A: Torquemada
(variations: Adam, roquet; amoret, quad—anagrams)
Themeword B: Ximenes
(variations: rays, chromosome—words prefaced by X-)
Themeword C: Azed
(variations: alpha, omega—Greek equivalents of A and Z)

Across: 21. Tycho Brahe, astronomer.

Down: 3. a guy (rev.—i.e. standing on its head); 4. whi(te)r; 5. argo(n); 7. 1 + anag. of lumps + I've; 8. Fe in mottes; 9. nob(b)ler; 11. set + a; 19. flag + (lo in tee) rev.; 22. r. in ore + ry; 23. (h)alloa (near Dollar in Scotland); 26. E. ras; 27. d in toy; 31. de(l)ft.

Appendix I

Some common indicators for one, two or three letters

It is not easy to provide a definitive list because some abbreviations are not in all the three most common dictionaries (*Chambers, Collins, Concise Oxford*). While some abbreviations are universally accepted (DR = doctor, for instance) others tend to appear in some puzzles only (S = succeeded in *The Times*, for instance). Different puzzles also have different conventions about what is and what is not acceptable. The star and the asterisk give some indications of where acceptability is not universal, but even this level of demarcation is necessarily crude. This list is by no means comprehensive, and is designed for the solver to browse through rather than to refer to for specific answers. Ideally we should also provide an appendix where the solver can look up 'doctor' to find DR, BP, MP, MD, MO etc., but it is beyond the scope of this book to provide a crossword dictionary. Such dictionaries do, however, exist (see Appendix 2).

* =   used mostly in advanced cryptics

† =   unsound/not liked by all Ximeneans

Words in italics are possible alternative indicators.

A	one* [not used by all setters of everyday cryptics, more common in Azed, etc.]; acceleration*; article; adult [as once used to denote certain films]; are*; note†; key†
AB	able-bodied seaman (*sailor, tar*)
ABE	Lincoln [Abraham]
AC	alternating current; account (*bill*)
ACC	account (*bill*)
ACE	card; champion; expert; one; pilot; service (tennis)
ACT	decree; performance
AD	in the year of our Lord (*in the modern age*); advertisement (*notice, promotion,* etc.)
ADD	sum; tot
ADO	fuss
AG	silver
AGA	ruler
AGE	(long) time, mature, period
AI	first class [the letter I and the number 1 are mutually transposable in crosswords]
AID	help

AIR	appearance; display
AL	aluminium; Alan; Albert; Capone
ALE	beer
ALL	completely; everybody; everything
ALP	mountain, peak
AM	in the morning; American
AN	one* [see A above]; article
ANA	anecdotes (stories)*
ANT	worker [even though not every ant is a working insect]
APE	copy; primate
ARC	curve
ARM	limb; member
ART	contrivance; craft; cunning; painting; skill
AS	when
ATE	(goddess of) mischief
AU	gold; to the French
AY	yes
AZ	Azed* [most frequently in his puzzles]
B	billion; British; black; born; bowled; book*; breadth; note†; key†; bishop
BA	Bachelor of Arts (*bachelor, scholar, graduate, etc.*)
BAN	curse; outlaw; prohibition
BAR	inn; prevent; pub; save
BE	exist; live
BEE	worker [see ANT above]
BIT	chewed; piece
BR	British Rail (*railways*); branch; brown*
BRA	female support(er); undergarment
C	100; cape; carbon; Conservative; circa (about, around, roughly, etc.); caught; cold; speed of light; note†; key†
CA	accountant; circa (*about*)
CAN	is able to (*able to†*); vessel, etc.
CC	two hundred
CE	Church of England (church)
CH	church; child; Companion of Honour (*companion*)
CHA	tea
CHE	revolutionary; guerrilla [*Guevara*]
CHI	Greek character
CI	Channel Islands; 101
CIA	spies
CL	chlorine; 150
CO	care of; commanding officer (*commander*); company (*firm*)
COL	pass; neck
CON	study; trick
COT	bed

CR	credit
CS	Civil Service
CU	copper
D	500 (many†); (old) penny; dead; Democrat; died; note†; key†; daughter
DA	District Attorney (American lawyer); dagger*
DAM	barrier; restrain
DD	doctor of divinity (doctor, theologian)
DE	of French
DEE	river
DEN	study; retreat
DES	some French
DI	Diana (princess is becoming much less common); 501
DIS	Pluto; hell; underworld, etc
DO	act; cheat; cook; ditto (the same); note; party; work
DON	fellow; nobleman; put on; university teacher
DR	doctor [also clued by MB, MO]
DU	of the French
E	East; Eastern; Ecstasy (drug); bridge player; Spain*; energy; English; note†; key†
EA	each; river*
EAR	listener; organ; spike*
EC	London district
ED	editor (journalist); Edward
EER	always
EG	for example, for instance
EGG	bomb; cocktail; encourage
EH	what
EL	the Spanish
ELI	priest
ELL	measure; length
ELY	see
EM	printer's measure (measure); them (='em)
EN	printer's measure (measure)
EON	age
EP	extended play (disc, record); epistle (letter or short letter, short denoting abbreviation)
ER	hesitation; (the) Queen
ERA	time, age
ERE	before
ET	and French
ETA	Greek character
EX	former; one-time
EXE	river
F	female; feminine; fine; foot; forte (loud); note†; key

FA	note
FE	iron
FF	fortissimo (*very loud*)
OF	Foreign Office
FR	Father; French
FT	feet; foot
G	gramme; note†; key†; good; grand; gravity†
GA	Georgia
GAL	girl
GEL	jelly
GEN	low-down (information)
GG	gee-gee [*horse*†]
GI	American soldier (*soldier, doughboy,* etc.)
GO	bargain; energy; in good condition; ready; success; work
GR	King George
H	hard; height; Henry; heroin (*horse**); hospital; hot; husband; hydrogen
HA	laugh
HAM	(poor) actor
HAS	bears
HE	His Excellency (*ambassador*); (high) explosive; the man
HER	the woman('s)
HI	hello
HM	His or Her Majesty
HO	house
HP	hire purchase (*never-never*)
HR	hour
HT	high tension
I	electric current; one; island; isle; Italy
IC	in charge
ICE	diamonds
ID	fish; I had; I would
IDE	fish
IE	that is (that's†)
IF	provided; poem (Kipling)
II	eleven
IL	the Italian
ILL	badly; unwell, etc. [these words are also used as anagram indicators]
IM	I am
IMP	little devil (*mischievous child,* etc.)
IN	at home; batting; in fashion; not out; wearing
IO	ten
IRA	terrorists
IRE	anger (*rage,* etc.)

IS	exists; island
ISM	theory
IT	Italian; sex-appeal (*SA*); the thing
IV	four
IX	nine
J	Jack; judge
JE	In Paris, I (*I, being French, etc.*)
JO	little woman
K	constant; thousand; King
KA	double*; genius*
KM	kilometre
KO	kick off; knock out (*decisive blow*)
L	50 (*many*†); lake; Latin; Liberal; learner (*student†, inexperienced driver, novice, etc.*); left; length; line; pound (*sovereign*)
LA	the French; Los Angeles; note; look*
LAB	Labour
LAM	beat; pound
LB	pound
LE	the French
LEG	limb; member
LEI	wreath*
LES	the French
LET	allow(ed); hindrance; permit(ted)
LI	51
LIT	drunk; loaded; settled
LO	look; see
LOG	record
LOT	large amount
LP	long playing (*record*)
LT	Lieutenant
M	1000 (*many†*); married; make; male; mark(s); masculine; maiden over (*maiden*); metre(s); mile(s); minute(s); mass: Monsieur (*Frenchman†*); motorway
MA	Master of Arts (*master, scholar, graduate, etc.*); mother
MB	doctor
MC	master of ceremonies
MD	1500; doctor
MI	motorway; note
MO	doctor; short time (*second, etc.*)
MP	member of parliament (*member, politician, representative, etc.*); mounted police (*mountie(s)*); military police
MR	mister
MS	manuscript (*handwriting, writing*)
MU	Greek character
MUM	mother; quiet

MY	gracious me, etc.
N	(any) number; nitrogen; noon; North; Northern; note*; bridge player; pole; new*; knight
NB	nota bene (note)
NE	north-east
NET	capture, etc.; fabric, etc.
NI	Northern Ireland (Ulster)
NIL	love; nothing
NO	refusal; number
NT	New Testament (part of Bible, new books, etc.)
NU	Greek character
NW	north-west
NY	New York
O	zero (duck, love, nil, ring, round, etc.); old; oxygen
OC	Officer Commanding (commander)
OK	okay (all right)
ON	about; being broadcast; leg [cricket side]; on the menu, etc.
OP	opus (work); operation
OR	alternatively; before*; gold; yellow
OS	Ordinary Seaman (sailor); outsize (very large)
OT	Old Testament (part of the Bible, old books, etc.)
OX	bull
OZ	ounce, wizard place
P	page; parking; pawn; penny; piano (softly); power; pressure; president
PA	father, etc.
PAR	standard
PAS	dance; step
PC	policeman (copper)
PE	physical education, gym
PEN	author, writer; enclosure; prison
PER	by, for each, a*
PET	favourite; cherished
PHI	Greek character
PI	confusion*; Greek character; religious
PM	Prime Minister; in the afternoon
PO	Post Office; river (Italian flower)
PP	pianissimo (very softly)
PR	prince; price; public relations
PRO	for; public relations officer
PS	postscript (second thoughts, etc.)
PT	physical training (gym)
Q	Queen; question
R	King; Queen; radius; right; river; rook; run(s); take*

RA	Royal Academy; Royal Academician (*artist*); Royal Artillery (*gunner(s)*); sun (god)
RAB	Butler [R. A. Butler]
RAG	(cheap) newspaper
RAM	butter; sheep
RAT	desert(er); scab
RC	Roman Catholic
RD	road
RE	about (concerning, touching, etc.); Royal Engineer(s) (*engineer(s)*, *sapper(s)*); religious education; note, etc.
RED	bloody; cent*; communist; revolutionary
REP	agent; traveller
RET	soak
REV	vicar, etc.
RM	Royal Marine(s) (*jolly*)
RN	(Royal) Navy
ROT	corruption; decay; rubbish, etc.
RR	Right Reverend (*bishop*); Rolls Royce
RT	right
RU	rugby
RUN	manage
RY	railway (*rail, line(s)*)
S	Saint; second(s); son; South; Southern; succeeded; bridge player; pole;
SA	South Africa; South America; sex appeal (*it*)
SE	south-east
SEA	main
SET	put; group, etc.
SH	quiet [interjection]
SHE	the woman; novel [Rider Haggard]
SIN	err; evil; wrong, etc.
SO	therefore; well; note
SOL	sun
SON	boy; disciple
SP	starting price (odds)
SPA	spring
SPY	agent
SS	steamship (*ship*) [*on board* or *on board ship* denotes that something is to be placed inside the letters SS]; saints; Sunday School
ST	saint (*good man*, etc.); street (*thoroughfare*, etc.); stone
STY	filthy place;
SUB	substitute; stand-in, etc.
SUN	newspaper (*tabloid*)
SW	south-west

T	time; ton(s); temperature; model† [old Ford car]
TA	Territorial Army (*army, terriers, volunteers*); thank you; thanks
TAN	beat; brown
TAR	sailor
TE	Lawrence; note
TEC	detective
TED	Edward; (Edward) Heath
TEE	peg
THE	article
TI	note
TIC	spasm; twitching, etc.
TIN	money; cash; vessel
TIT	bird
TOM	big bell; cat
TON	hundred; weight; large amount
TOR	hill; eminence
TRY	attempt; essay, etc.
TT	teetotal; teetotaller (*abstaining, dry, on the wagon,* etc.); race [bikes on Isle of Man]
U	Universal (film certificate) (*for all to see, on view to all, suitable for children,* etc.); university; upper-class (*uppish, socially acceptable, posh, superior,*etc.)
UK	United Kingdom
UN	United Nations
UNI	university
UP	in court; excited; at university
UR	old city [from whence came Abraham]
US	America; American; you and me
USE	application; custom; employ(ment); practice; practise
V	five; verse; versus (*against, opposing,* etc.); every; see* (= vide); volt(s); volume
VI	six
VOL	volume
W	watts; West; Western; bridge player; wicket; wide; width; wife; with
WE	you and I
WI	West Indies
X	cross (*kiss, sign of love, by, times,* etc.); ten; unknown (variable)
XI	eleven (*team,* etc.)
Y	yard; year; yen; unknown (variable)
YE	you [old]
YR	year; your
ZO	cross*
ZZ	(sound of) snoring

Appendix 2:
The Crossword Library

Books on Crossword Theory and History

Chambers Crossword Manual is the successor to three significant books (all out of print except for the Ximenes book which is being reissued in 2001):

- *Armchair Crosswords* by Afrit (Warne 1949)—the preface is short and the most significant section is reproduced in this *Manual* on p.67.

- *Ximenes on the Art of the Crossword* by D S Macnutt (Methuen, 1966 due to be reissued in 2001 by Swallowtail Books, 3 Danesbrook, Claverley, Shropshire WV5 7BB).

- *Crosswords* by Alec Robins (Teach Yourself Books, Hodder and Stoughton, 1975): subsequently revised as *The ABC of Crosswords* (Corgi, 1981).

I have no hesitation in recommending one recent addition to the literature, written by the former crossword editor of *The Times*: *How to do The Times Crossword* by Brian Greer (Times Books, 2001). This covers some unusual clue types favoured by the author.

For a very good introduction to US cryptics try:

- *Random House Guide to Cryptic Crosswords* by Emily Cox and Henry Rathvon

Two out-of-print crossword history books are:

The Strange World of the Crossword by Roger Millington (Hobbs/Joseph, 1974)

A History of the Crossword Puzzle by Michelle Arnot (Random House, 1981, Macmillan Papermac, 1982)

Dictionaries

To cover all the common everyday words and phrases and some more unusual ones, every serious solver and setter needs:

The Chambers Dictionary

To access proper nouns 'you pays your money and you takes your choice' between

Collins English Dictionary and *The New Oxford Dictionary of English (NODE)*

There are many other dictionaries available, of course, including the *Concise Oxford Dictionary (COD)* (which some crossword editors have used as a sieve to disallow words *not* in it). The *NODE* is a better buy than the *COD*, however, in your author's view.

For American words and spellings I use *Webster's Third International Dictionary*. And for the ultimate English dictionary we turn to the *Oxford English Dictionary* (now available on-line for a few hundred pounds a year!).

If you are visiting a public library looking for old proper nouns keep an eye open for *The New Century Cyclopedia of Names*, a three-volume masterpiece dating from over a hundred years ago—it is wonderful!

Thesauruses and Crossword Dictionaries

Two very good thesauruses are:

The Chambers Thesaurus and *The New Oxford Thesaurus of English*

Both contain useful lists as well as synonyms and antonyms, as do

Chambers Crossword Dictionary (with introductory articles by Azed and your author) and *Bradford's Crossword Solver's Dictionary* by Anne R Bradford (published by Peter Collin).

The *CCD* includes an article by your author and a list of selected anagram indicators, and it lists synonyms by word length. Bradford's book is the result of a 40-year compilation. Both are excellent but neither is exhaustive, so buy both!

My most well-worn book of words organized by number of letters is *Chambers Phrase File*. For a general list of words by categories I also recommend *The New Hamlyn Crossword Dictionary*, a 2001 update of a book first published in 1932 by C Arthur Pearson. This was probably the first serious crossword reference book, and I bought my copy in 1964.

Other information books

There are many good books of quotations, but the one referred to by crossword setters is *The Oxford Dictionary of Quotations*.

Another book much used by setters of crossword puzzles is *Brewer's Dictionary of Phrase and Fable*.

For solvers of advanced cryptics these are both 'musts'.

For a single-volume encyclopedia, I suggest:

The Cambridge Encylopedia

You are spoilt for choice with atlases. One which will not be too expensive is

The Times Concise Atlas

After that you may want a *Cruden's Concordance* and of course the *Bible* itself. A few specialist reference books on history, literature, music, and even pop music, can be useful. And you'll want a complete Shakespeare too maybe.

Crossword Cribs

For lists of words organized in particular ways, Chambers offers a whole range:

Chambers Anagrams (alphabetically arranged anagrams of words)

Chambers Back-Words (words listed alphabetically by endings)

Chambers Crossword Completer (listings by alternate letters)

Official Scrabble® Words

Periodicals

You will, of course, have your daily and Sunday papers in your 'library' (by the way be careful lest your whole house becomes one extended cross-word library—it *can* happen!). You will know by now what papers you might buy to have a go at the cryptic puzzle. If you are a new cryptic solver, I should start with *The Daily Telegraph* and work towards the other broadsheets and Sundays. Some of the cheekiest clues may be found (not surprisingly) in *Private Eye*. Clues from that periodical have often featured as 'clue of the week' in a news magazine called *The Week*.

For a club magazine (*Crossword*) which will take you into advanced cryptics I suggest you seriously consider joining The Crossword Club (at Coombe Farm, Awbridge, Romsey, Hants, SO51 0HF). For 15 x 15 specials (many by Araucaria) try *One Across* (write to Christine Jones, The Old Chapel, Middleton Tyas, Richmond, North Yorks. DL10 6QX).

You should have enough reference books now (to be going on with). You won't be able to take them all on the train with you of course, but whatever you do don't leave home without that pencil!

Postscript

Since Colin Dexter has been so kind to me at the beginning of this book, may I be equally kind to him at the end of it. In *The Wench is Dead* he attributed a clue to me, as Quixote of *The Oxford Times*, although it was in fact his own. Here it is:

Bradman's famous duck (6)

The answer is of course DONALD, referring to Sir Donald Bradman (the cricketer) and the famous Donald Duck.

The clue is of course extremely elegant, but it is also a brilliant one because of its context. In his last test innings at The Oval in 1948 (as all cricket lovers will know) Bradman scored a duck when he only needed four runs to finish with a test match batting average of 100.

Oh that I *had* written it!

Clues such as this provide us all with magic moments and I am happy that Colin, from whom I have learnt so much, should have the last word as well as the first.

Don Manley
May 2001

Chambers publishes a range of books for crosswords of all types, providing the definitive guide to crossword success.

Chambers Crossword Dictionary

The essential reference tool for crossword lovers everywhere. Not only is it easy to use, it is also the most authoritative crossword companion around.

'I love this book…' Herald Crosswords Editor

'The Chambers Crossword Dictionary certainly is a fine book… and a safe Christmas present for any crossword fan.' *Amazon*

ISBN: 0 550 10006 7
Hardback
Price: £25

Chambers Concise Crossword Dictionary – NEW

Chambers Concise Crossword Dictionary is derived from the top-of-the-range *Chambers Crossword Dictionary*, and is a valuable aid to solving cryptic and quick crossword clues.

ISBN: 0550 12012 2
Paperback
Price: £9.99

Chambers Anagrams – NEW EDITION

This major new edition of the ever-popular *Chambers Anagrams* is an ingenious aid to solving anagrams and anagram-based puzzles. An essential handbook for all word game enthusiasts, including crossword puzzlers and Scrabble® players, it is indispensable for all wordgames based on rearranging jumbles of letters to form real words.

ISBN: 0550 12005 X
Paperback
Price: £9.99

Chambers Crossword Completer – NEW EDITION

A major new edition of *Chambers Crossword Completer*, thoroughly revised and updated from *Chambers Crossword Dictionary*. As well as being based on a more up-to-date wordlist, this new edition includes proper names, compounds and phrases. Its unique and innovative arrangement and presentation of words lets the crossword solver complete solutions from the letters already filled in on the grid.

ISBN: 0550 12013 0
Paperback
Price: £9.99